Joy to My Love

Joy to My Love

KAREN M. EDWARDS

Cover designed by Shaela Kay Odd, Blue Water Books

This book is a work of fiction. Names, characters, places, and incidents either are products of the author's imagination or are used fictitiously. Any resemblance to actual persons, living or dead, events, is entirely coincidental and not intended by the author.

Karen M. Edwards
Visit my website at https://www.karenmedwards.com

Printed in the United States of America

First Printing: January 2019

ISBN-978-0-578-41913-8

To my children and grandchildren.
And to my mother, Ruth Mitchell,
and to our ancestors who lived
in the East Neuk of Fife.

Author's Note

Scots Spelling

I spent a lot of time trying to decide how to spell the Scots dialect with words such as didn't, can't, etc. Today, most of the spelling is dinnae, cannae, etc. (dinnɪ) which reflects the common pronunciation which sounds like dinny, canny. But I chose to use the earlier and regional spelling of dinna, canna, etc. (dinnə) which is pronounced dinneh, canneh, the stress on the first syllable.

Sir Walter Scot uses the -na suffix in his *The Heart of Midlothian*; it's used in an autobiography of Belle Patrick, a woman from Fife, *Recollections of East Fife Fisher Folk;* and is noted in *The Concise Scots Dictionary* that gives historical background of Scots words as does the online *Dictionary of the Scots Language.*

See the Glossary on page 319.

If you want to know more, check out a post on my website: https://karenmedwards.com

Chapter 1

"Almost there, Granny." Effie made her voice cheerful, encouraging.

Her step-grandmother gave a baleful stare. Granny Agnes insisted on going to the kirk every Sunday though the walk took more effort each passing week. The old woman had wheezed and gasped all the way from their cottage. They were at High Street now—a level road—no longer climbing the steep lane that led from the harbor.

While Granny Agnes calmed her breathing, Effie gazed at the grey expanse of the Firth of Forth over the orange roofs of the village. The Isle of May lay slug-like on the horizon. In the harbor, the painted hulls of fishing boats punctuated the greyness of sky and sea. The familiar scene soothed her though she wished Davy Mackie were back from whaling; he'd been gone for weeks and she missed him.

"Haste ye back, Davy," she whispered.

Granny Agnes breathed more easily now and squeezed Effie's arm, signaling that she was ready to proceed. Ahead of them, the tollbooth tower dominated the squat ancient kirk. Effie thought the tower tainted the place of worship at its feet. Over a hundred years ago several witches had been imprisoned and tortured in the dungeon behind its studded door. Effie shuddered every time she passed it.

Some thought *her* a witch. She looked different from the average villager—taller and with lint-blond hair that stood out among the usual black, red, and sandy locks—and her father was unknown.

Agnes leaned more heavily on Effie by the time they reached the arched entrance of the kirk. She helped the old woman to the front pew close to the pulpit. There were fewer people at worship this Sunday. Influenza gripped the village and many had succumbed to its often-deadly grasp.

Effie looked around the kirk noting who was missing: mostly older folk and a few families with young children. She worried about her elderly employer, Isla Forbes who had come down with influenza a week ago.

Early that morning Effie had slipped out of the cottage before Granny Agnes awoke. She'd taken syrup of rosehips and made sage tea to ease Mrs. Forbes's throat, brushed her mistress's snow-white hair, and arranged a warm shawl around her shoulders. The old lady was in good spirits—sweet and grateful as usual. Though her mild blue eyes were a little glassy, she had no fever, and her cough was not too deep. Those were good signs and Effie had left the house, assured her mistress was on the mend.

But Effie couldn't stay long. If her step-grandmother knew she'd worked on Sunday, there'd be the dickens to pay. She'd arrived home flustered and out of breath minutes before Granny Agnes awoke.

Effie made sure her step-grandmother was comfortable, then turned to face the pulpit. Effie pressed her lips together at the sight of Mary McDougal sitting on the repentance stool. This practice had been abandoned years ago. Why introduce it again?

But Effie could guess who had reinstated this shaming tradition— Niall Douglas, one of the ruling elders of the parish. He sat near the altar with a smug look on his face; he must have persuaded the new minister that this was the custom in Pittenweem. Why did the other ruling elders of the Session go along with Mr. Douglas all the time? They could have voted differently.

Mary, dark hair shrouding her face, gazed at the bairn asleep in her arms. Effie squirmed in sympathy. To have the villagers stare— judging, disdaining—she knew what that was like. But Mary didn't seem bothered even though she'd have to perch on that stool, facing the congregation for two more Sundays. From time to time, Mary raised her head and smiled at her family seated on a nearby pew.

"I ken who the father is." Fiona Ballantyne's hoarse whisper came from the pew behind Effie's. "Niall Douglas told me after Mary went before the kirk sessions to name the father."

"Who?" Her daughter Moira's voice was eager.

"Andrew Stobbart." Widow Ballantyne raised her voice enough so Mary could hear. Effie's gaze flew to the lassie, but Mary gave no reaction. Maybe, like Effie, she put on a calm exterior while inside was turmoil.

"I dinna ken him," said Moira.

"A fisherman from Kingsbarns. He went whaling and left Mary carrying his burden. She hid it well."

Moira snorted. "Aye, but not after the bairn was born."

The congregation began to sing a psalm, drowning out their loud whispers. Effie glanced at Granny Agnes; she was slightly deaf and had been oblivious of the conversation. Perhaps she already knew; she and Widow Ballantyne were friends.

After the psalm, Mr. Douglas opened the large Bible on the lectern. Effie braced herself. As usual, his eyes scanned the pews—and often rested on her—as he bullied the congregation into shame. Effie couldn't fathom why he disliked her so much. It wasn't her fault she was illegitimate, but she cringed anyway when his gaze fell upon her.

This Sunday, Mary was his target.

"You see before you, this wanton lassie—Mary McDougal—and the fruits of her sin." His scrawny index finger emphasized each phrase. "This is the result of fornication—an abomination before the Lord." He went on a diatribe. He quoted scriptures and thumped the lectern, the Bible jumping at every blow of his fist. Why did he get away with standing at the pulpit so much? He wasn't a teaching elder—that was the minister's role—but as the chief ruling elder as ministers came and went, he relished to take on this responsibility.

Effie looked out the window at the clouds scudding across the sky. Over the years, she'd learned to stop listening so the elder's words were merely unintelligible sounds, but still she quailed, guilt as natural as breath, building up inside. Though why *she* should be ashamed she didn't know but habit was ingrained too deep.

Granny Agnes shifted in her seat. She elbowed Effie muttering something about shame and betrayal.

The clouds could not hold Effie's attention for long. She focused once more on the woman on the repentance stool. Her own mother, Maggie Innes, no doubt had sat on that stool eighteen years ago, holding her—the burden and shame of her family. Had she rocked and cooed at her newborn bairn like Mary, or had she hung her head in mortification?

Who had harangued Maggie those many years ago? It could have been Niall Douglas zealous to root out carnal sin and to humiliate women in general. To him it was all Eve's fault, as the enticer of Adam. It's no wonder Mr. Douglas never married. And what kind of woman would have *him*? Effie grimaced. But some women were desperate to be married; life as a single woman in her class was one of poverty and misery. Desperate indeed.

Aye. Marriage. Would any man love her? Would she ever become a wife?

If only Davy—

Granny Agnes elbowed her sharper than before. She hissed in Effie's ear, "Born in fornication. You're full o' it. Full o' original sin."

Over the years, Effie had built a shield of stoic indifference to hide the hurt. But deep down she protested: no, she wasna a sinner. She wasna perfect, but not as wicked as Granny Agnes thought. Years ago, she'd stopped trying to reason with her step-grandmother; it only brought more recriminations and accusations.

As the elder's harsh voice droned on, Effie came back to a question she'd struggled with over the years: what had an innocent newborn bairn to do with sin even if illegitimate? She rejected this notion, never voicing it to Granny Agnes, or anyone else for that matter. The clear eyes of bairns reflected not sin but innocence, a deep wisdom fresh from heaven.

Hadn't she seen that innocence in Mary's wee bairn a few days ago? She'd helped Dr. Ferguson deliver the bairn and rejoiced with Mary for his safe delivery.

She peeked again at Mary McDougal, who appeared to ignore Mr. Douglas's biting sermon.

Effie squirmed in her seat, her thoughts as uncomfortable as the wooden pew. It wasn't fair. Where was Andrew Stobbart? Fathers rarely appeared before the kirk sessions or on the repentance stool. The birth of the child was evidence of motherhood; fatherhood was not as easy to prove and was often denied. Poor Mary. Poor wee bairn. At least her family supported her.

After the elder's sermon, Mr. Mitchell, the new minister, stood at the pulpit and announced the funerals of two villagers.

How many more would perish from this disease? That marked ten deaths this month. Effie chewed a fingernail, nervous once more about Mrs. Forbes.

Then, with a lift to his voice, he announced the marriage banns of Mary McDougal and Andrew Stobbart from Kingsbarns parish. So, Andrew acknowledged his bairn and would make an honest woman of Mary? Effie was glad for her and the bairn.

Her mother had not been so fortunate; no man claimed her bairn or her hand in marriage. Maggie had escaped years of ridicule and censure by dying when Effie was a year old.

Years ago, Effie had speculated who her father might be. Maybe he was a married man who couldn't or wouldn't acknowledge mother and bairn? Or a sailor who was lost at sea? Effie had fantasized that he was an important man, but that dream had dissipated as she grew older. The knowledge that perhaps someone in Pittenweem or another village was her father lay forgotten only to surface when she learned of an unwed mother.

Maggie had never named the father; Aunt Lizzie was tightlipped when Effie asked about him. Of course, it was no good asking Granny Agnes.

The minister blessed the congregation. As though to counteract Mr. Douglas's harangue, the minister quoted from Isaiah: "I will mention the lovingkindnesses of the Lord, and the praises of the Lord, according to all that the Lord hath bestowed on us."

Lovingkindness. Effie liked that word. She wished she'd encountered more in her life.

But there were a few who had shown her lovingkindness: the Mackie family and Dr. Ferguson. She spotted Jock and Rhona Mackie and sons Jamie and Robbie at the back of the kirk. Even if Davy were home, he wouldn't be at the kirk; he didn't hold with religion.

Ah Davy. Warmth rose in her cheeks. She had loved him since she was nine, and he a teasing laddie of fourteen. She hoped one day he'd love her as much as she loved him, but Catriona Tivondeal dashed her hopes when she returned to Pittenweem and claimed him as her own. But she was a flirt. Davy wouldn't put up with that long and Effie would be there to comfort him when Catriona's affections turned to someone else.

As Effie helped Granny Agnes stand, Catriona's tinkling laugh bounced off the stone walls. That lassie had a new green bonnet and she turned her head in an exaggerated way to draw attention to the long feathers that fluttered with every toss of her head. And, unlike the womenfolk in the village who dressed in shawls and skirts, wore a fashionable pelisse and high-waisted dress like the gentry. She hung on her prosperous merchant father's arm, greeting the more successful members of the congregation.

Granny Agnes hobbled down the aisle in the Tivondeal family's wake. Effie couldn't hurry her but she craned her neck to see where the Mackies had gone; they were already disappearing through the doorway. But she was almost at the door. If Granny Agnes would just move a little faster—

Mr. Mitchell greeted parishioners as they left, his white hair ruffling in the breeze. He took Granny Agnes's hand.

"It is good to see you, Mrs. Innes. You are so faithful in coming to the kirk despite your ailments."

"And where else would I be the Sabbath?" said Granny Agnes. "I need to bring this sinful lassie to repentance."

The minister gave Effie a quick glance from benign blue eyes. She hunched her shoulders, aware her smile was ingratiating, apologetic—her usual demeanor.

Agnes wasn't finished, ignoring the group of parishioners still waiting to greet the minister.

"Mr. Douglas gave a fine sermon. I hope it knocked some sense into Mary McDougal's head. Her family was not the least bit ashamed."

The minister withdrew his hand from Granny Agnes's grip and turned to Effie.

"Mrs. Forbes was telling me what a good servant you are and how much she enjoys your reading to her. I'm sorry to hear she's poorly. I'll visit her the day and see how she fares. Will you be there? I'd like my wife to—"

Granny Agnes's face went red. "She's sick! You didna tell me!" She pinched Effie's arm hard. "You could bring the sickness home to me. Ungrateful, selfish lassie." Then she turned to the minister. "You canna expect Effie to work on Sunday, Mr. Mitchell. It's a day to read the Bible, not foolish novels."

Effie dropped her eyes, but not before she noticed the minister's wrinkled brow. What did the frown mean? He concurred that reading novels on Sundays was sinful? He'd only been assigned to Pittenweem parish a couple of months ago, so she wasn't sure of him.

"I could read the Bible." Effie lifted her eyes again to the minister, hoping for approval.

"What about me?" Granny Agnes snapped. "Leave your own kin to fend for herself? And bring home the sickness too? You see how she is, Mr. Mitchell."

Mr. Mitchell furrowed his brow even more. Effie waited for words of disapproval but his look was kind, his soft voice lost as Granny Agnes pulled Effie away from the kirk door.

She wished she could spend time with Mrs. Forbes instead of reading her Bible in the gloomy cottage and listening to Granny Agnes's constant niggling.

Two more funerals, two more deaths. If Mrs. Forbes were to die? Effie caught her breath. It didn't bear thinking about.

How glad she was to work for such a fine lady though sorrow mingled with her contentment. She'd taken over from Aunt Lizzie who had died three years ago in a diphtheria epidemic.

Could she slip away from under her grandmother's eye? She glanced at Granny Agnes's miserable face. The old woman was particularly disgruntled on dreich days which intensified her rheumatics. And it was Sunday, a day of rest. Rest from labor, but not restful for Effie's soul. Except for an afternoon nap, the old lady would berate and harangue her. Oh, to be with Mrs. Forbes instead.

As she had to keep to Granny Agnes's slow pace, the mizzle—as gentle as dew—soaked through their threadbare shawls. Effie resigned herself to spending the day drying out clothes as well as reading the Bible. With the mood Granny Agnes was in today, she doubted she'd get away. She'd have to wait until the morrow to visit Isla Forbes.

Chapter 2

Effie stood a moment on the doorstep, her tears mingling with the drizzle. The front door closed behind her with a loud click. She'd expected to see Mrs. Forbes sitting in the gold brocade wingchair waiting for breakfast, not lying pale and still beneath the blue coverlet.

Her instincts had been right. She should have visited Isla Forbes yesterday evening. But Granny Agnes had grizzled and fussed all day, forcing Effie to use extra coal on the fire to dry their clothes and warm the dank cottage.

Effie lingered on the doorstep. The bunch of snowdrops she'd picked to cheer up her mistress lay scattered at her feet. Drawing her shawl over her pale hair, she gazed with unfocused eyes at the firth and the muted Lothian terrain across the water.

She should notify Fiona Ballantyne, the midwife who also laid out the dead. "I bring them into the world and see them out," the widow often said. She was puffed up at her own importance and roles in the village.

Her feet as heavy as her heart, Effie walked toward Cove Wynd, the closest lane leading to the manse. Better to visit the minister first before Widow Ballantyne; he'd be sympathetic.

She had not gone but a few steps when she spotted Niall Douglas and Widow Ballantyne by the lane's entrance. She slowed her stride. Her pulse quickened and her mouth went dry. They'd no doubt blame her for not taking good care of Mrs. Forbes.

Perhaps she could reach Water Wynd before they saw her. Keeping her eyes on them, she sidled toward the lane. But that movement must have caught Widow Ballantyne's attention. She touched Mr. Douglas's sleeve, jerking her head toward Effie. There was no escape; Effie would have to tell the widow the news now. She lifted her chin and walked toward them.

"And how is Mrs. Forbes this day?" said Widow Ballantyne, a smirk on her round face as she wrapped her shawl closer around her ample bosom.

Effie wet her lips, tasting salt from the sea breezes.

"Speak up, lassie. Dinna stand there dumbstruck." Mr. Douglas looked her up and down.

The irony of it: she was often rendered speechless, impotent to defend herself.

"Mrs. Forbes is dead." Effie's voice trembled a little. "She died in the night and—"

"What?" Widow Ballantyne's face turned an angry red. "Did you no give her my simple of foxglove?"

Effie shook her head.

The widow grabbed Effie's arm and dug her fingernails through the thin fabric of her brown dress.

"Dr. Ferguson said not to give it to her." Effie pulled her arm away from the painful grip.

Now was not the time to tell the widow that according to Dr. Ferguson, and the little herblore she had learned from Aunt Lizzie, foxglove was too strong an herb for Mrs. Forbes's heart. Fiona Ballantyne thought herself an expert herbalist and had often been in competition with Lizzie. Now Lizzie was dead, Widow Ballantyne had more followers; few knew Effie created potions and salves for Dr. Ferguson from Lizzie's recipes.

"That Dr. Ferguson thinks he kens everything. The blame rests on you, you daft besom." The widow's voice rose higher. "Yon job should ha' gone to my Moira. She'd ha' taken better care." She turned to Mr. Douglas. "Did I no tell you how it would be? This lassie is no fit to be a servant to a well-born woman."

Effie pulled her shawl closer around her. The North Sea breeze blew cold, though it was not as biting as their reproaches. She should be used to it by now, but her stomach turned into knots. In their eyes, she could do nothing right.

Mr. Douglas's bitter mouth turned down even more in his long, thin face, and his pale blue eyes turned glacial as he glanced at the widow. "I'd no choice, Fiona. Yon Dr. Ferguson and the minister wouldna listen to me. Promoting such a lassie as this." His mouth moved as though to spit, but he held it in.

"You put coins on her eyes to keep them shut afore you left?" said Widow Ballantyne.

"No. I couldna find any." The blood rushed to Effie's face. In her shock she'd forgotten to do that. Another reason for blame.

"You glaikit lassie! You ken it's to keep off the evil eye." The widow's voice was shrill, panicked. "If there are more deaths in the parish, it will be on your head."

"It's but a superstition," Effie said before she could stop herself. "I canna think Mrs. Forbes would bring evil." She flinched at the rage in the widow's eyes.

"You are the devil's own!" Widow Ballantyne stepped away from her, a fearful expression on her face

"It's tradition and—aye—respect too," said Mr. Douglas through tight lips. "Well. We'd best hasten to Mrs. Forbes's house to remedy your neglect."

He walked away, Widow Ballantyne bustling beside him. Effie followed them, but the elder turned and motioned her away. "No. Not you. Away home. You're no wanted here."

Aye, it was true enough; not many wanted her in the village.

"I'm away to tell the minister then," she said

"No. I'll do it." Mr. Douglas narrowed his eyes.

"Away home," said Widow Ballantyne. "My Moira will clean house for the new tenant so you need no return. She'll take her rightful place as servant in the house." Her lip curled in a sneer. "What will your granny think about you losing your job?" She snickered and hurried to catch up with Mr. Douglas.

Blood drained from Effie's face. Isla Forbes's death wouldn't bother her granny as much as losing income. Finding a new job had crossed her mind, percolating up through her sadness for her mistress's death. Rumor and conjecture over the years that her mother had been a loose woman added to her badge of illegitimacy. Who'd hire a base-born lassie not accepted by the village?

She ambled toward home, putting off confronting her grandmother as long as possible. Her mind ran through the households that hired indoor servants. Who'd know of any openings? Rhona Mackie, perhaps? She was on friendly terms with a lot of the villagers. But she was sick with the grippe.

Alan Ferguson? As the local doctor he would know. He'd helped her secure the position with Mrs. Forbes after Lizzie died. Maybe he could put in a good word for her again. But he was away attending to the laird's household which had succumbed to the grippe. She could perhaps approach the minister if she could catch him when Mr. Douglas wasn't around. But as the minister was new, he was not acquainted with the households yet.

What could she do in the meantime?

She looked down at the fishing boats sailing through the narrow harbor entrance. With sickness in the village there were likely to be openings gutting fish. Granny Agnes wouldn't like it. What a come down for a family that had once owned a farm. But it was a job. Better than the poorhouse or begging for more money from the parish coffers. If Niall Douglas had his way, they'd not even have the cottage.

She flexed her shoulders and pulled her shawl tighter. She couldn't keep relying on the Mackies and Dr. Ferguson to help her. It was time she stopped hiding behind them, time to anchor her wavering mind and defy her cowardly heart. She was eighteen now, not a scared fifteen-year old grieving for the death of her beloved aunt. She had to try. Fear of Granny Agnes eclipsed her fear of the fishwives.

The scent of fish guts and the cries of gulls announced the fish mart before she could see the band of women. She stepped out from the shelter of the lane, cold gusts from the firth buffeting her.

"What's yon lassie doing here? She'll bring us bad luck!" Mrs. Baird's raucous voice rose above the shrieks of the gulls sweeping overhead. The fishwives raised their heads momentarily from the pile of writhing silver herring and looked at Effie with unfriendly eyes.

Effie hunched her shoulders, trying to shrink her tall slim figure. A tendril of pale hair escaped from her shawl and hung limply over her smoke-grey eyes. She did not push it away; it made a curtain to hide behind. She could not let them see her fear.

Isabella McIntosh, the leader of the fishwives, was at the far end of the harbor talking to a couple of fishermen. Effie braced her shoulders. She needed to show some kind of confidence despite the clutch of anxiety gnawing inside her.

"Mrs. McIntosh," she began. The woman turned, her face impassive, no welcoming smile. The fishermen gave Effie sidelong glances.

"What do you want?"

"Mrs. Forbes died last night. I'm in need of employment. I heard some lassies were sick and I wondered . . ." She raised her voice, finishing hastily, "if I could work in their place?"

Isabella raised her eyebrows.

"Only until they are well enough to return." Effie finished in a rush. There, she'd said her piece. She smiled, a mere stretching of the lips; it felt unnatural like the ingratiating baring of teeth from a groveling cur.

The fishwife frowned and narrowed her eyes.

"No. You canna work here." Isabella turned away.

Effie stood a moment hanging her head before moving toward the harbor. She'd tried. Though she swallowed resentment that Isabella hadn't given her a chance. She was tired of being a scapegoat, of meekly accepting their unwarranted treatment, of hiding her hurt.

"Wait on, Effie." A male voice stopped her. She turned, battling between hope and fear she'd receive an insult.

Iain Watson, bulky and squat in his fisherman sweater, beckoned. "Try her out Belle. You were just whinging you needed help. Jock Mackie can vouch for her."

Effie smiled timorously, her eyes darting from Iain to Isabella.

The other fishermen spoke up. "Isabella, if you canna handle a' the fish we'll be forced to leave our catch at Anstruther."

Isabella sent him an ugly glance then addressed Effie. "Come with me."

With a small smile for the fishermen who acknowledged her with quick nods, Effie followed Isabella toward the tables where the fish lay in a silver sheet. Women and lassies bundled from the cold, deftly gutted them, and threw them into barrels of brine.

"Now she'll really see what work is." Effie recognized Mrs. Baird's rough voice as they passed one of the tables. The women tittered.

"Aye. Look at her lily-white hands," said a fishwife. "No like good workers' hands!" She held up her bandaged fingers dripping red from fish guts.

Effie hoped they mistook her trembling for cold. She took the shawl off her head and wrapped it across her body and tied it in the back like the fishwives. Her light blond hair was now exposed. The fishwives murmured among themselves, but one spoke loud and clear.

"Aye, she's a selkie bairn all right with yon hair." Effie's knuckles turned white as she balled her hand in a fist. Illegitimacy was bad enough without the superstition that she was a child born of an enchanted seal.

"An' fey with it," said another woman. "Did she no predict the sinking o' the whaler in oh-seven? An' her uncle Alec on it too."

Isabella quelled their murmurs with a look. She regarded Effie thoughtfully. "You can work with us till Lizzie Gordon and Nancy Broun get better from the sickness. Here, wrap your fingers with these." She held out strips of rag smelling faintly of fish. "They'll stop you from getting cut."

Effie took them and wrapped her left hand.

"No. No like that." Isabella unwound the rags. "You must do it tight." Isabella wrapped two of Effie's fingers so tightly, she could hardly feel them; she bit back a moan.

"Now you do it." Isabella handed Effie the other strips.

It was hard to wrap the fingers of her right hand with a partially numb left hand. She glanced up. Isabella shook her head and raised her eyebrows at the other women as if to say, *Here's a dunderhead who dinna ken what to do.*

Effie vowed she'd learn quickly.

Isabella handed her a thin pointed knife. "Do you ken how to gut fish?"

"Aye."

"Good. Stand yonder." Isabella pointed to the far end of the table, at a spot exposed to the wind from the firth. "We'll see how you do—whether we'll keep you on for a bit. We'll pay you by how many fish you dress."

The rest of the day was a nightmare: the previous day's catch of rotting entrails permeated the area even though it was March; the slimy fish were hard to hold; the sharp wind stung her wet hands; the tight bandages numbed her fingers; and the knife was blunt so it took more effort to cut through the fish. She suspected Isabella had given her that knife on purpose. She'd not have much money to take home at the end of the day. She redoubled her efforts.

Dusk made the grey day more gloomy. Effie walked home at a snail's pace, taking a meandering route where the pathway to Anstruther met Kirk Wynd. The mist had soaked her threadbare shawl, but despite her chilled body, she did not want to go home to face another kind of coldness. She dawdled a short way along the path and picked sorrel and young dandelion leaves growing in the verge; they'd supplement the usual meal of kippered herring.

Too soon, she reached the cottage. She paused a moment before lifting the latch.

Granny Agnes dozed by the fire, her Bible open on her lap, her cap almost falling off her iron-grey hair. Effie tiptoed to the table and placed the dandelion and sorrel leaves into a bowl. But when she ladled water onto the greens, her grandmother's eyes snapped open. The old woman blinked a couple of times, before her ice-blue eyes took on their usual baleful glare.

"Where have you been? Why did Isla Forbes keep you longer today?" Her voice was raspy from sleeping with her mouth open. She sniffed. "Why do I smell fish? Did you get more cheap herring?"

"Granny." Effie swallowed before she chose the words she'd rehearsed on her way home. "I have sad news. Mrs. Forbes died last night but—"

Her grandmother let out a wail, head tilted back, eyes closed and mouth wide open. She clutched her hair in both hands, rocking back and forth. She stopped her keening to moan.

"What's to become of me? Who will hire the likes of you in Pittenweem? Or any other place. Your reputation is kent in these

15

parts. I dinna want to leave Fife." Her voice became a screech. "They'll put me in the poorhouse." Granny Agnes wiped her running nose and streaming eyes with the edge of her shawl then continued with her lament.

Nothing Effie could say at this moment would stop her step-grandmother's wailing. Effie had considered moving away from Pittenweem; she didn't believe her reputation was known far and wide as Granny Agnes thought. But she'd have to leave friends like the Mackies and Dr. Ferguson, and that was more daunting than remaining in the village. Effie waited until the old woman's bawling turned to sniffles.

"Dinna fash yoursel', Granny. I'm gutting fish—" She put out a tentative hand to touch her granny's shoulder. The old woman pushed it away.

"What? Such a come down in the world. To think an Innes would work as a fishwife. I'm that ashamed."

"Aye, but it's a job until I find something better." It was almost a whisper. She might have known. Her granny had no idea what an effort it had been to beg for work, any work. They couldn't afford to be fussy to put bread on the table.

"What did yon Aileen Baird think on that?" She and Agnes were old enemies though Effie didn't know their feud. Then the old woman's expression turned shrewd. "How much money did you get?"

Effie held out her hand with the few coins she'd received from Isabella.

Agnes plucked them from her hand.

"Is that all? Barely enough for two loaves of bread. We'll starve." She sniffed and wiped her nose. "The kirk gives me a pittance. They owe it to me to honor my husband's memory. No one visits." She thumped her Bible with her fist. "And they call themselves men o' the kirk. Can they no visit the poor widow as is told in the Bible?"

Effie had heard this refrain many times before.

"Mayhap the new minister will visit."

Granny Agnes snorted.

"I hope to find other work soon. I'm working at the harbor for a little while." Effie modulated her voice to keep the tone placating, swallowing the irritation that came from her fears she wasn't good enough. "I'll ask Rhona Mackie if she kens of someone who needs a house servant."

"Aye. But who will hire the likes of you? You only got yon job with Isla Forbes—God rest her soul—because Lizzie worked there. Contact Alan Ferguson when he returns; he'll ken better than Rhona."

It was true; she'd only been hired because of Lizzie and Dr. Ferguson. So much for venturing out on her own. But there had been one good outcome with the fishwives: she'd gained grudging respect from Isabella McIntosh and a few others.

She shredded the greens more vigorously than necessary, wishing she could rip up the mistrust and unfounded rumors as easily.

KAREN M. EDWARDS

Chapter 3

The work at the fish market had finished yesterday—two long weeks of hard toil. Effie hadn't had the courage to tell Granny Agnes it was over. She left the cottage at her usual time hoping the old woman would think she was still gutting fish.

It was time to visit Rhona Mackie who had recovered from the flu. At the fish market on Saturday, her husband, Jock, had said she knew of a housemaid's job.

Effie's pulse raced and her breath quickened, not only from vigorous walking but the anticipation of seeing Davy Mackie who'd returned from whaling. His warm smile and friendly nature were a light in an otherwise bleak existence. He didn't notice she was now a young woman; he treated her like a wee lassie, but that didn't deter her from seeking his company.

She'd reached the end of Water Wynd, when over the cries of seagulls, a familiar voice called her name. Effie's spirits lifted. The doctor was back from the laird's.

Alan Ferguson loped toward her, his doctor's case in one hand, the other leading his bay mare, Bessie. As usual his clothes were rumpled as though he'd slept in them. His grizzled hair stood in wispy tufts where he'd run his hand through it, but his face, lined with fatigue, broke into a smile as he approached.

"Why were you not at Mrs. Forbes's house Saturday? I sent a note to Mr. Mitchell to tell you to stay on and clean the house. You know her grandson will move in next week." His voice was stern, the smile vanished, his brow creased.

She shrank back and hung her head, pleating her shawl. "I'm sorry. I—"

"I spoke with Mr. Douglas," the doctor continued. "He told me you wished to work at the harbor and Moira Ballantyne took over from you. A likely story. What happened?"

"He . . . and Widow Ballantyne told me to leave Mrs. Forbes's house." She raised her head, her voice almost a whisper. "I should have been with Mrs. Forbes. She was rallying and in good spirits Sunday morning. And to find her dead the next day . . ." She blinked back tears.

"Dinna fash yoursel', lassie," said the doctor, patting her on the shoulder. "It happens like that sometimes. It was her heart—seventy-five years of good living. I left her in your capable hands. You know you made her last years happy with your salves—and reading to her too."

Her smile was wan. "She was a kind mistress. I miss her sore."

"Quit your job at the harbor. Monday. Go back to her house and get it spruced up. Moira Ballantyne is not the most careful housewife. I thought I was going to pay you, not her. I have the necessary to pay for one week. Mrs. Forbes bequeathed money for that purpose."

Another week's reprieve, but she wondered if Mrs. Forbes had bequeathed the money or if it were coming out of the doctor's pocket. A generosity and kindness whoever provided it.

"Thank you. I'm finished with gutting fish. Sir, I'll need—"

"That's good." They both spoke at once. The doctor smiled. "It's as well you left gutting fish. I need to talk with you about a new position."

Effie put her hand to the wall of a nearby house to steady herself—her palm dimpling from the rough harl, proving reality—as relief washed over her. Her prayers were answered.

"Effie, you're as white as chalk. Take a few deep breaths. That's right."

"Is it for someone who lives in Pittenweem? As an indoor servant?"

"It is. Do you know the professor who lives near Marygate?"

"Aye, I ken of him. He's new to the village. Does he not already have a house servant?"

20

"Aye, he does. Jonet Murdoch."

"So why does he need me? He's but one person."

"The professor wants someone to help Jonet with housework but he mostly needs a scriever to write his letters. Professor Vandemark has rheumatics—stiffness—in his hands so writing is painful for him now."

"A scriever? But isna that work for a man? Are there no students he can hire?"

"He did hire some when he lived in St. Andrews, but they didn't last long, and students are harder to find here. I thought of you. You're one of the few folk I know who can write *and* keep house."

She gave a wry smile, an iron band squeezing her lungs. She had never imagined her skill at writing would bring this kind of work.

"I'll fetch you from Mrs. Forbes's house tomorrow and introduce you to Professor Vandemark." He paused, looking her over. "Is this your best dress?"

"No. I have my Sunday dress." It was threadbare and too short for her now; she couldn't let down the hem any more. Perhaps she could use some of the saved coins to buy a strip of cloth to add to the skirt. But what to wear was the least of her worries. Could she do this job? It seemed beyond her skills and experience.

"I thank you, Dr. Ferguson." Her voice wavered. "I dinna have the skills the professor needs. Mayhap I can help Mrs. Murdoch instead? Or, mayhap there's another household that needs a housemaid . . ."

"Not that I know of. You can do this work. I have faith in you. You wrote letters for Mrs. Forbes did you not?" The doctor gathered the reins and hoisted himself on his horse.

"Aye. But for a learned man? Will I ken the words he'll need me to write?" She clutched the reins; Bessie snorted and tossed her head. "What about the scrievers? Why did they no last long?"

The doctor leaned down and pried her hands off the reins. "You'll do fine. We'll talk later. I must check on yon wee scamp Geordie Henderson. He fell from a tree and broke his arm last week." He left with a quick wave.

She watched him disappear behind the bend in Abbey Road. She gulped and drew several long breaths. Work as a scriever? Would the professor—*what was his name?*—really hire her? The breeze from the firth lifted her hair; would that her confidence lifted as easily.

But she had good news for her grandmother—a prospective job. She flexed her fingers. Could she do it? It would be good to feel a quill in her hand instead of a bloody gutting knife.

Now to find Davy. She spotted a small group past a pile of lobster pots. No mistake. It was the Mackies. She hastened toward them, the figures becoming more distinct the closer she got: Jock's and Davy's dark heads; younger brothers, Jamie's and Robbie's sandy locks; and a flash of bright red—Catriona Tivondeal. She let out a little groan. Catriona resented Effie's friendship with Davy.

Despite Catriona being there, she wished to see the Mackies to talk about this possible new job. Jock and Rhona Mackie were the closest thing to parents Effie had known, especially after Aunt Lizzie died. What would they think about her being a scriever? Should she do it? *Could* she do it?

As she neared the Mackies, she passed Tam Braid lounging on a low wall with his cronies. His loud voice penetrated Effie's thoughts.

"Ha. The selkie bairn." He spat on the cobblestones in Effie's direction. "She's bad luck. The herring drave has never been the same since she was born."

"Aye, we have to go further in the German Sea for a good day's catch," said Methven Metcalf.

"Quit your blethering, Tam and Methven," said Davy who'd walked over to meet Effie. "You ken there were good years of herring and bad too long afore Effie was born." He turned to Effie. "Take no mind of them. They have to blame someone for their misfortunes."

Effie turned her head away from the smirking men to meet Davy's smiling blue eyes. She stood a little taller, her confidence a little restored until she glanced at the lassie next to him: Catriona's face was hostile.

"I heard tell she dreamed her uncle Alec would be lost at sea. And it came true," Catriona said looking at Davy. "Tam's brother Hugh was on the whaler too so he feels the loss." She paused, eyeing Effie with a bright blue stare. "It's no wonder we—they think her a fey creature."

"But my dream didna make it come true," said Effie. "It just came to me. And others have such dreams."

The memory of that night when she'd woken sweating from the vividness of the nightmare—the churning massive waves, the ship dipping and rising, and, worst of all, the white faces of the men trying to steer the ship away from jagged rocks—still lingered though it was eleven years past.

Catriona was not listening, but stroked Davy's arm, her sun-glinted hair rivaling any sunset.

He grinned and took hold of a burnished curl. "You're a bonny lassie, Catriona." Then. in almost a whisper. "It's not only your hair's full o' fire." Davy and Catriona exchanged an intimate glance.

Effie sighed. Would a man ever look at her like that? She turned to the steely waters of the firth; its bleakness mirrored her thoughts.

"Davy, stop your dallying. You're needed at the nets." Jock's voice summoned his son and muted Tam's murmurs. "Effie, Rhona says there are no positions in the village, but Pitcorbie Farm needs an outdoor servant. You'd have to live on the farm. Too far to walk every day."

"Give her my thanks." Effie hesitated. "I'd need to find someone to look in on Granny Agnes. They wouldna want an old woman." And a fractious one who will not work, she added in her mind.

"Rhona thought of that. She and Mrs. Black can bring meals. No doubt the farm can provide a few eggs as well as your wages. Is your granny no a friend of Widow Ballantyne? Perchance she could visit? You can see your granny Sundays and take her to the kirk."

Effie supposed it could be an option. She knew how to do *that* job, not like writing for a professor.

Before she could answer, Davy said, "It's a misfortune Mrs. Forbes died. She was aye a kind mistress to you." He gave her a quick hug.

She wished she could have stayed in the comforting circle of his arm longer but Catriona pulled him back to her side, scowling until the frown changed into a lips-only smile when Davy looked at her.

"Aye, she was," said Jock. "Kindness isna the word I mind of her daughter and grandson. They rarely visited the old lady."

"I believe it's hard to visit from Perth. And Master Alasdair is busy with his studies in St. Andrews," said Effie repeating what Mrs. Forbes had said many times. But the hurt in the old lady's eyes could not be hid. Effie sometimes stayed a little longer and read one of the light romances that came with the book subscriptions from Edinburgh. But that kindness cost her dearly when she returned home to a wrathful, jealous grandmother.

"That may be. But it's no the studies keeping Alasdair Grant from visiting," said Jock, picking up a frayed piece of rope and examining it.

"More like gambling and drinking," said Davy. "I seen him at Peats Inn when I deliver lobsters."

"Will you try Pitcorbie Farm?" said Catriona with a simpering smile at Effie. "Few folk will hire you in the village." She held tight to Davy's arm, her head pressed into the hollow of his shoulder.

"That's not true," said Davy. "My ma could find something for you, Effie. We'll see little of you if you work on the farm."

The scowl on Catriona's face deepened and her eyes glittered, but Davy didn't notice. He released his arm from Catriona's grip and began coiling a rope.

Effie took a deep breath. "Dr. Ferguson told me yon professor who lives near Marygate needs a scriever and a housemaid to help his housekeeper"

"A scriever! *You!*" Catriona laughed, tossing back her head.

"Aye. It'll be a good place for you," said Davy. His cheerful voice soothed the qualms fluttering through Effie's stomach. His deep blue eyes had an impish glint. "Murdo told me there were boxes and boxes of books when he moved in."

"Why'd you need to write for a grown man? And a professor too?" The scorn in Catriona's voice was strong.

"His hands are bad." Effie kept her tone friendly. "What is he like, Catriona? Your father will have made his acquaintance."

"Aye. My da and the elders met him when he moved in three weeks back. My da said he was not very friendly. He dinna associate with us ordinary folk. He plays chess with the minister and Dr. Ferguson. The laird called on him when he lived in St. Andrews." She paused and her eyes became slits. "He's not a Scotsman. An incomer from the Low Countries. I wouldna like to work for a foreigner. I'd be afeared."

An incomer from another land? It explained his peculiar name. Was that why the student scrievers didn't stay long? His customs were so different? He was a hard taskmaster? And the laird visited him? Could she work for such an exalted person, especially with her standing in the village? Effie fought against the trembling in her lip.

"Rhona met his housekeeper, Jonet Murdoch. She says he's a good master. Been with him nigh on thirty years," said Jock. "Dinna be afeared, Effie. You'll do fine. And what a clever lassie you are to learn the writing."

A smile couldn't quite break through her depression.

"Look!" Fourteen-year old Robbie pointed out to sea. "Yonder— by the Isle of May."

Mist still shrouded the isle. Four warships, sails billowing in the wind, glided pale and wraith-like in the hazy distance.

"Do you see them? Four men-o'-war?" Excitement thrilled in his voice. "They look grand. Going to Leith, I reckon." A wistful look came over his face. "I wish—"

"Whisht ye, Robbie." Jock frowned at him. "Dinna let your mother hear such wishes."

"Do you suppose they're returning from France?" said Effie hoping to take the sulky look from Robbie's face. He balked at working on the fishing boats, and craved adventure; he and his chums were fascinated by the warships that occasionally passed through the firth.

"No." He grinned at Effie, eager to share his superior knowledge. "Neil Barclay mind the ships are here for supplies for the new war in America." He picked up a brush from the tar pot. "I wish I'd been here when yon pirate John Paul Jones came to our shores and shot cannons at Anstruther."

"Aye. And he made off with our pilot. He only went to meet the ship to be helpful," said Jamie. "And Jones was Scotland born, but didna ken these waters."

"But Jones let the pilot go in South Queensferry," said Effie. She'd heard the story many times.

"Aye, he did," said Jock. "We never hear the last of yon adventure. Robbie. Jamie. Stop your daydreaming and get back to work."

Robbie dabbed tar on the frayed rope, the pungent smell soon dissipating in the breeze, but he kept his head turned toward the firth and the progress of the warships.

"We saw a warship on the way home," said Davy. "Gave it a wide berth. Got a little close to Cape Wrath to lose it."

Effie went cold. That's where Uncle Alec had perished.

"Why would the captain do such a thing? Those are treacherous waters," said Effie.

"The navy is hungry for men," said Jock. "Press gangs are more to be feared than the sea."

She shivered; the country had been at war so long impressment was a common occurrence, especially in fishing villages.

"And they dinna just plunder by sea. They're active near Edinburgh and Glasgow," said Davy. "Near here too. Mind how they took yon men from St. Monans three months past. They're now serving in His Majesty's Navy." Davy's usual cheerful expression darkened.

"My da tells me the families are living in poverty," said Catriona. "They're a burden on the parish." Though she didn't say "like you" to Effie, she flicked an eyebrow in her direction.

Poverty. That word brought Effie back to her own predicament. If she didn't get this job with the professor or at Pitcorbie Farm, she and her grandmother would be a burden on the parish.

"Lassies, away to your homes," said Jock, picking up a length of frayed rope.

"Will you come to the kirk with me Sunday, Davy?" said Catriona. "My da and ma will be glad to see you home safe."

Jamie grimaced and whispered to Effie. "I doubt that."

She doubted it too. Jamie had told her Catriona's parents didn't approve of Davy.

Davy kissed Catriona's cheek before answering. "The kirk and I do not get along."

Catriona frowned then shrugged. It was a sure sign of courtship if they attended kirk together. Effie suspected Catriona would get her way eventually even in the face of her parents' opposition and Davy's reluctance to become a regular churchgoer.

"Aye. You should come with us, Davy," said Jock. "The new minister no longer gives Niall Douglas as much time at the pulpit. And, he stopped Mary McDougal from sitting on the repentance stool the next two Sundays. We will not see that again. He's strong under his meek and mild ways."

"Aye, but my da says they will not stop a wanton lassie from a summons to the Kirk Sessions," said Catriona smirking at Effie.

"Aye," said Jock. "The father needs to be named so the lassie and bairn are not brought up by the parish. Many a grandparent is burdened with the bairn if the man will not marry the lassie."

Heat rose in Effie's face and she hung her head.

"I wasna thinking of you, lassie," said Jock. "If anything, your granny is a burden to you. Be off with you, lassies. We have work to do."

Effie and Catriona took the winding Abbey Wall Road, silence growing large between them.

"Are your parents letting Davy court you?" Effie asked for something to say. Catriona's father though he took their money, had no love for the mariners.

"No. They still dinna want me to marry a fisherman. Davy has ambitions to own a fleet of boats. He'll do it too; he's promised a boat. His father canna last—"

Surely Catriona wasn't wishing Jock Mackie early retirement or worse? Jock's boats would be divided between his sons, not just left to Davy.

Catriona recovered herself. "Davy'll inherit, not be a common fisherman—" She shrugged. "Ma and Da dinna want me to end up like my sister living back at our home with three bairns."

"You'll find no better than Davy, fisherman or no."

"It's true. But he's a bit soft." Catriona put her hand on Effie's arm.

"What do you mean?"

"He wants me to be friends with you, but I see you making sheep's eyes at him. He belongs to me. Dinna forget it." A scowl marred Catriona's pretty face.

Effie was too much aware of Catriona's claim on Davy. Why could he not see *her* love? Why did he not see through this shallow lassie? Davy's ambitions were news to her; she wondered if they were really his. It would take years for him to earn enough money to own one boat, let alone a fleet. Catriona didn't seem like a person who could wait patiently.

Catriona looked her up and down. "Sometimes you get a look in your eyes and I wonder if you truly did come from the sea like they say—a selkie's bairn."

"They're haivering!" She dared to meet Catriona's eyes. Catriona stiffened at her candor.

"It will do me no good associating with you, but I'll do it for Davy's sake. You should be grateful." She smiled, a mere stretching of her lips. "And anyway, it may not be necessary when you work on the farm. You'll be gone most of the time. You canna do the scriever's job I'll warrant. What was Dr. Ferguson thinking?"

Catriona laughed then turned on her heel and flounced away.

Oh Davy, Davy. Effie sighed. To force friendship between two lassies who were as different as lobster and herring. How would that benefit her? Did he expect Catriona's friendship to make her more acceptable to the village? She was surprised Catriona even spoke to her let alone befriend her. She must be fonder of Davy than she showed; she still liked to flirt with other men. That lassie would lead him a merry dance once married, push him to fulfill *her* ambitions, and wear him out.

She walked a little longer on the Anstruther path, anything to put off returning to the dark cottage. A few tendrils of hair escaped from the bun at the nape of her neck whipping her face. She took out the pins holding the low knot together and shook her hair free. There was no one to see her but the seagulls veering in the wind. For a time, she lost her worries in the clean salt air swirling her hair and the sound of the waves pummeling the rocky shore. How she loved this little corner of her world.

The upcoming interview with the professor broke into her enjoyment. Could she talk the doctor out of it? Ask him to find someone else? The professor had no doubt been unlucky with his choice of students. Surely all of them weren't irresponsible.

Working at the farm would be difficult—harder physical labor, longer hours—and less money for her grandmother. It could be just a stop-gap until she found a place in the village.

Alan Ferguson was taking pains to help. He was pleased to have found this job. She didn't know which was worst: refusing to try for the job or failing to please her employer. Either way she'd be letting the doctor down. It was a big step with the possibility of humiliation.

And then there was her unwarranted reputation. What would the professor think of that? Her deepest fear was that she was never good enough. Hadn't Granny Agnes drummed into her that her bad blood tainted and overpowered everything she did?

Perversely, Catriona's last remark that she couldn't do it—though matching her own thoughts—decided her.

She took several deep breaths of the briny air and flexed her fingers. Aye, she'd write her best hand. She'd do it for the doctor's sake and to prove Catriona wrong.

Gathering her wayward hair, she screwed it back into a bun. Tonight, she'd wash and rinse it in a chamomile solution to bring out silver lights. She was no longer going to hide under dyes to fit in; she'd tried that as a child. With newly washed hair and a white collar on her Sunday dress, she'd at least look partly respectable for the interview. Would the professor see past her shabby appearance and hire her?

KAREN M. EDWARDS

Chapter 4

Stirring the grey glutinous mass of oatmeal for the breakfast porridge calmed Effie. But a sleepless night made her wits as thick and dense as the porridge. Everything hinged on the impression she'd make today.

She helped her grandmother dress, brushed her straggly grey hair, and helped her to the chair by the fire. After placing a bowl of porridge on the stone hearth, she draped a shawl over her step-grandmother's thin shoulders. She'd pinned back the tattered shawl covering the one small window, letting in enough light for Granny Agnes to read her Bible.

"I'm away now, Granny." She rested her hand on the door knob.

"Where are you going so early? To yon foreign man?"

Effie shrugged. Granny Agnes was suspicious of folk from nearby Anstruther, let alone a man from another country. He was a foreigner—another factor that added to Effie's fears he wouldn't hire her. Dr. Ferguson had told her he was Dutch but had lived in Scotland for many years and spoke good English. She'd never met a Dutchman before though they had frequented the fishing villages in years past.

"I'm going to Mrs. Forbes's house first to ready it for Alasdair Grant."

"I hope he will not be there. Alone with a young man. It isna fitting."

"He will not come for another week." Effie swallowed hard. "And then I may be working for the professor." She hadn't told her grandmother about the position at Pitcorbie Farm. That would be an option if the professor did not hire her.

"What will people think? It'll be like your mother all over again."

"Did my mother work as a servant in someone's house? Who?"

This was news to her. She thought her mother had only worked on the family farm. So, her father could be a wealthy man from the village?

"I dinna want to talk of it. Away to your work, but watch your step with Master Grant."

Aye, she'd watched her steps many years, afraid she may stumble and turn out like her mother. Sometimes she craved to run free, unfettered, but she walked through life with decorum, hesitantly, as befitting her station and the expectations of the village.

Dr. Ferguson came to fetch her in the early afternoon. She tried to match her steps to his long lope as they walked up the wynd. She laughed to herself after her gloomy thoughts about watching her step. Now she was striding out, but this fast pace was also taking her closer to meeting the professor.

She stopped for a moment and clutched the doctor's arm, forcing him to halt. "What if he turns me off like the students?"

"Well, that's his prerogative. Dinna fash yoursel'. He'll like you fine. You're not likely to spend time gaming and drinking like them." He resumed walking. She hesitated then caught him up. He smiled. "I already recommended you and he's a fair-minded man. He'll give you a chance though it will be different from taking care of Isla Forbes."

"I ken." Aye, a big change. Her pulse thundered loud in her ears, and not only from keeping pace with the doctor.

"Here we are," said the doctor.

They stopped in front of a large house with a sweeping driveway big enough for a carriage. The stables were to the left and neatly trimmed bushes and the flowers graced the entrance. She'd seen the house in the distance before, but had never ventured near. Why would she? The previous owner had been a relation of the laird's and kept herself to herself before she moved.

"Oh, it's a lot grander than Mrs. Forbes's house. No wonder he hires more servants."

"Aye. Jonet Murdock has been his housekeeper for many years and her husband, Billy, is his gardener and groom." He put his hand to the lionhead doorknocker. "I've known Vandemark these past twenty years. We met at the Edinburgh Philosophical Society."

The sharp rap of the doorknocker reverberated through Effie's head. She gulped a lungful of air causing her to cough. The doctor put his hand on her shoulder. She was glad of that support; she breathed a little more easily.

After a few minutes, the housekeeper stood at the door. Sparks of energy seemed to emit from her fierce red hair sprinkled with a few grey streaks and her green eyes were emerald bright.

"Come away in, Alan. And this is Effie Innes? I'm Jonet Murdoch." She wrinkled her brow, her gaze roaming over Effie. "I've seen you afore."

Effie waited in trepidation for her to remember. She wasn't going to remind her. She gave what she hoped was a confident smile then glanced around at her surroundings: the elegant staircase leading to the second floor, and the mahogany table with a copper bowl and three leather-bound books. The table had been recently polished as the scent of lavender beeswax permeated the air. Jonet was a careful housekeeper. Such elegance. If the doctor hadn't been behind her, Effie would have run out the door. What was she letting herself in for?

A gasp from Jonet brought Effie's attention back to the housekeeper. Jonet had a hand to her mouth, her eyes wide. "It canna be. At the fish market?" She twitched her nose as though expecting to smell fish.

Maybe there was a faint aroma though Effie had scrubbed herself almost raw. Luckily her Sunday dress had been nowhere near the fish market.

Jonet looked doubtfully at the doctor. Then her gaze dropped to Effie's ankles. She huffed.

Effie smoothed down her skirts as though that would lengthen the hem, her heart sinking. She hadn't found the money to add a strip to her skirt. Her sigh was little more than a tiny breath. She was found wanting even before she met the professor. The urge to run was growing stronger by the minute.

"You say she's experienced in writing?" Jonet sniffed.

The doctor nodded. "Aye, she is."

Jonet shrugged, then addressed Effie in a slightly friendlier tone. "The professor aye has his nose in a book. When his gout's bad you'll help him find books. The doctor tells me you're a good reader and write a good hand?" But disbelief was strong in her eyes.

Effie didn't have time to reply. Nor did Jonet want an answer.

"Himself is in the library." Jonet shepherded them into the room.

When Effie entered the library, her attention first fixed on the row upon row of bookcases lining three walls, then on the man who stood by the window, a book in hand. He was large—the largest man she'd ever seen. He was grizzle-haired and portly, and though his blue eyes were shrewd, they twinkled as he smiled. He shook hands with Alan Ferguson and motioned for him to sit. He limped over to a red leather chair and dropped into it with a little groan.

Effie remained standing, her hands clasped tight before her.

"So, this is Euphemia Innes," he said with what she assumed was a Dutch accent. "Do not be afeared. I will not eat you. I am not that kind of giant"

Effie gave a faint smile at his joke, hoping it wasn't a grimace, and bobbed a curtsey, her legs shaking. "Oh sir, I am called Effie, if you please." Then she immediately wished to take back those childish words.

"No, I do not please. In this house, you are Euphemia." The words rolled off Vandemark's tongue as though he were giving a lecture. "Do you know what your name means? It is from the Greek: *eu* meaning good and *phemi* meaning to speak, so you are well-spoken. And there is a martyr Euphemia and a Queen of Scotland with that name."

At first, she had shrunk inside afraid she'd already offended him, but then she took in what he was saying. She glanced at the doctor who was smiling, relaxed. She'd have to think more about this. Euphemia meant that? She'd never heard such a thing. There was a queen named Euphemia? Her name had been handed down from her real grandmother in accordance with the Scottish naming tradition. Euphemia Adamstone had been a good and kind woman, or so Aunt Lizzie had told her. A spurt of pride straightened her shoulders.

"Professor!" Jonet said in an exasperated voice. "You canna lecture a poor lassie who's this minute stepped in the door. You'll have her head spinning. You'll want to test her writing not fill her head with nonsense."

Initially, she believed Jonet was standing up for her, but the housekeeper's sniff and stare before leaving, deflated that little touch of confidence. The housekeeper obviously didn't think a fishwife could write for the professor. And how would Jonet be as a supervisor for the domestic work? Effie's confidence was seeping away by the minute: she had two employers to please.

Her hands were clammy. She wanted to clutch the doctor's tweed jacket; tell him to take her home. She was on her own; he couldn't write for her. She startled when Vandemark spoke.

"Go to the desk yonder, Euphemia," said the professor. "I wish to see what kind of script you have." He looked down at his gnarled hands. "It is the bane of getting old. The mind is willing, but the flesh is weak. You will find paper and ink though you need to sharpen the quill. Let me know when you are ready."

Her legs trembled so hard she stumbled once as she made her way toward the desk. She took up the knife and sharpened the quill as best she could, listening to the professor and doctor murmuring in the background.

"I'm ready, sir." The words came out thick from her dry mouth.

"Stop me if you do not understand or I speak too fast. Can you understand my accent?"

She nodded. His pronunciation was a mixture of English and Scots with a faint overtone of Dutch. She rubbed the moisture from her hands on her skirt before she picked up the quill and dipped it into the ink.

She glanced first at Dr. Ferguson who smiled in encouragement, then at the professor who with half-closed eyes gathered his thoughts. She stared so hard at the blank piece of paper it shimmered.

"Put today's date and begin the letter. *My dear Glasbeinn, I hope—*"

"Sir," she said. "How do you spell, *Glasbeinn?*" She'd interrupted the professor and she'd barely begun the letter.

"*Ja, ja.*" He gave a quick nod and didn't seem annoyed. "I suppose this is something you would not know. It is G-L-A-S-B-E-I-N-N. It is a name you will get to know well; Lord Glasbeinn and I correspond frequently.

She wrote each letter carefully keeping her hand steady. A lord would read this. She ran her tongue over dry lips.

"Now let us continue the letter." He put his fingers together to form a pyramid as he spoke.

"I hope to find you and your good wife well. It was a great pleasure to receive your letter of the 13th inst. I am honored for your invitation to a gathering of the Fifian Club in April and to stay at your new house in Edinburgh . . ."

She interrupted the professor two more times when he started to speak more rapidly and she couldn't keep up. Thankfully it was a short letter, but her hands cramped from gripping the quill in tense fingers.

Once finished, she shook sand to blot and dry the ink, blew the sand off the paper, and crossed the room, knees knocking, to hand him the letter.

He looked it over but she couldn't read the expression on his face. Was he pleased? Disappointed? Annoyed that she'd wasted his time?

Without looking at her, he handed the letter to Dr. Ferguson who read it, looked up at her and winked before handing it back to the professor. Vandemark studied the letter again, placed it on the occasional table, and with eyes still downcast, he templed his fingers and put them to his lips.

As she waited for the verdict, she gripped her hands so tight she felt every bone in her fingers. She swayed from holding her breath.

"It is a fair script, Miss Euphemia Innes," said Vandemark lifting his head. He smiled. "I trust it will become more elegant eventually. Let us see how you improve in a fortnight. I'll evaluate your employment then."

She was dizzy, torn between relief and fear. Relief she was hired and fear that the demands of the job would be more than she could handle.

"You can breathe now, Euphemia." The professor had sharp eyes. "Tell me how it came about you learned to write. It is uncommon for a lassie in a village school. I do not think writing was part of your schooling? No?"

"The dominie, Mr. Sutherland, taught me." She gulped some air. "The laddies didna like to learn the writing, but I did."

The irony! After all these years, a skill forged in loneliness and unhappiness made her eligible for a more prestigious occupation. The children had either teased her or ignored her at school, so she'd found consolation in reading while the others played. She had learned to write after Dominie Sutherland found her struggling to copy letters on her slate instead of reading the Bible or catechism, the lassies' curriculum. The schoolteacher was delighted to find an interested pupil, though a mere lassie.

"And from what her aunt Lizzie told me, Ef—Euphemia practiced on her own when Sutherland left," Dr. Ferguson added. "Do you not write letters for a few of the villagers and for your former mistress?"

Effie gave a quick nod.

"It will be a novelty having a bonny lassie as a scribe," said Vandemark, and then lowering his eyes to look at his pipe in his hand he said almost to himself. "And one who likes to learn." He raised his eyes and spoke again to Effie. "I will not need you until eleven on Thursday. But Jonet may need you earlier. Talk to her as you leave." He paused to tap out his pipe.

She gasped. "Thank you, Professor Vandemark." She gave a short curtsey before she turned to the doctor. "And thank you, Dr. Ferguson for your good word for me."

Her steps faltered as she went to the kitchen to talk to Jonet; that woman emitted disapproval. She had to prove herself to that daunting woman too. How long would it take to convince Jonet Murdock of her usefulness? How long had it taken before the professor fired the student scrievers? It wouldn't be for gaming or drinking, but for her lack of experience. She'd do her best and perhaps scrimp to buy a quill and paper to practice though not in her grandmother's presence; she'd always objected to this skill.

Chapter 5

Herbs in hand, Effie hurried from garden sunshine to the dim crimson of the library. For the past two weeks she'd enjoyed the task of bringing herbs for Jonet.

She was temporarily blinded as her eyes adjusted from bright to dark and she almost ran into a man standing by a bookcase. She stopped, startled. When her eyes became accustomed to the change of light, she saw a tall, slender young man with auburn hair pulled back into a pigtail. His olive-green morning coat and intricately-tied cravat indicated he was gentry.

He turned, book in hand, at her precipitous entrance and looked down at her with a slight smile. The man wasn't as handsome as Davy, but his tanned face was pleasant; under straight eyebrows, his hazel eyes, clear as a mountain brook, held friendliness. Her shoulders relaxed though she was still a little leery of meeting strangers, and a gentleman to boot.

"I crave your pardon. I did not mean to startle you," he said with the accent of a high-bred Scotsman. "I'm whiling away my time before dinner, waiting for Vandemark to finish his nap. Jonet told me he retired to his bedchamber."

"Aye, he left his window open. I heard his snores from the garden," she said, and when the gentleman laughed, she stammered, "Oh, that is to say, the professor needs his rest. I was disrespectful."

"You must be Miss Innes," he said.

She had made for the door to the hallway, but at his words, she paused politely.

"Vandemark told me about you. Unusual to hire a female scriever, but Vandemark never did do the conventional thing." He smiled. "Now we've met I see why he's intent on retaining you to write his letters."

Effie gripped the herbs more tightly, sending their scent into the room; blood rushed to her face. How was she supposed to answer that?

"I'm sorry," he said. "I didn't mean to discompose you. I think I've usurped your place in the library. Vandemark tells me you like to read."

The professor spoke of her? But then she was a novelty. That was gratifying but she was bewildered that this gentleman treated her with such courtesy.

"Aye, he lets me read whatever I wish." She said with a lilt in her voice. "Some of the books are too hard, but one day I'm going to read them all." She waved her hand to encompass the bookcases.

"An ambitious endeavor," said the stranger, his mouth curving in a smile. He inclined his head in almost a short bow.

"I'm Calum Moncrithe, a former pupil of Vandemark's."

She caught her breath; she'd expected an elderly gentleman when Jonet told her a university colleague would be coming to dinner.

Moncrithe was so different from Alasdair Grant, Mrs. Forbes's grandson and the only other young gentleman she'd met. Though Alasdair had rarely visited his grandmother, he'd come a few times to pay his respects to the professor, who had been his tutor at the University of St. Andrews. He had been condescending and supercilious toward Effie and barely civil to Jonet. His grandmother would have been appalled at his behavior.

Effie curtsied. "I'm pleased to meet you, sir."

"I'm here but a short time before I return to my ship."

"Your ship? I thought you were a university man?"

"No. Merely a sailor."

Jonet's muffled voice called for the herbs. Moncrithe smiled, and Effie couldn't help but smile back. "But I won't keep you from getting the herbs to Jonet."

"Aye, thank you, sir." She turned to leave and found the professor barring her way. He motioned for her to help him to his chair; Moncrithe took his other arm.

"You arrived earlier than expected, Calum," said the professor shaking hands with Moncrithe before he sat down. "I see you have been well entertained." The professor indicated the book in the sailor's hand. "What do you have there, my lad?"

The lieutenant handed him the book. The professor laughed.

"Homer. An apt choice for a warrior. The catalogue of ships perhaps?" He opened the book. "How many hours did you struggled to master enough Greek to understand these writings?"

Effie moved closer to the door. She was glad to see the professor reminiscing about his university days.

"A long time, but not as long as Summercourt," said Moncrithe.

"*Ja*, that dunderhead spent too much time playing cards."

"Your library's a little larger than the one in St. Andrews." Moncrithe looked around. "But the smell of snuff and tobacco brings back memories. I don't recall much cognac though." He inclined his head toward the decanter on the sideboard. "You must have a secret supply to risk running the French blockade."

"Professor, do you need anything? I'll take these herbs to Jonet first." She was almost at the door.

"Pour us some brandy," said the professor indicating the decanter. "But I am remiss. Miss Euphemia Innes, allow me to introduce Lieutenant Calum Moncrithe. First lieutenant now, is that not so?"

"We already met." She bobbed a curtsey; the lieutenant inclined his head. "I came from the garden and almost ran into Mr.—er Lieutenant Moncrithe."

Vandemark took up his pipe. "You must have given Euphemia quite a start."

"I did." Moncrithe grinned, a sparkle in his eyes. "It was a delightful encounter: a nereid from the firth rushing in with fragrant herbs."

Blood rushed to Effie's face. What had Moncrithe called her? She looked at Vandemark for guidance.

Vandemark merely glanced at her and winked.

"How much Homer did you read to turn so poetic?" He chuckled. "You've spent too much time in the company of rough sailors. The first pretty face you see addles your brains."

"And captures our hearts," said Moncrithe with a slight bow to her, hand on his chest and mischief in his eyes.

Effie didn't know how to reply, but her face became warmer still. After a little hesitation, she went to the sideboard and put down the herbs.

This light bantering was new to Effie. So, this was what the gentry did: engage in meaningless flirtations? It was all words; it didn't mean anything, but the lieutenant's words made her both uncomfortable and happy.

She wanted to stay and learn more about the lieutenant. She took her time unstopping the decanter and finding two brandy glasses.

"There are plenty of pretty lassies in America." Moncrithe took a seat opposite Vandemark. "At some of the receptions you'd think you were in London or Paris."

"And were there any ladies you particularly liked?" Vandemark seemed inordinately pleased.

"No. None in particular." Moncrithe adjusted his cuffs and a shadow darkened his brow, dampening his good humor. "This blasted war with the Americans is causing havoc to their social life. I met a lot of fine people in Boston and Quebec before the war. This war should never have happened."

"And it almost did not," said Vandemark. "After Percival's assassination the Orders in Council were suspended by Lord Castlereagh just days before Madison declared war."

Vandemark had told Effie a little about the Orders in Council, a directive to stop ships trading with France, though she didn't really understand what it was all about—except that it annoyed the Americans, and the Danes who, seven years ago, had joined forces with France because of trade embargoes.

Effie poured out the brandy as slowly as she could.

"Aye, it affects our industries too," said the lieutenant.

"Concessions were already written that would have appeased the Americans. We could have worked something out." Vandemark heaved a sigh. "If only our documents had got there in time. If only Madison had not given in to those hot heads who pushed for war."

"Aye. It's always about money, trade," Moncrithe said, disgust in his voice.

Effie handed Moncrithe and the professor glasses of brandy. Moncrithe acknowledged her with a smile.

She'd asked the professor about this war that was different from the war on the Continent. The lieutenant could give a new perspective.

"Some in the American government are ambitious to take British North America and add to the Union. That's why they invaded Canada." Vandemark warmed the brandy, cradling the glass and gently swirling the honey-colored liquid. "I still think they could have started peace negotiations even then."

"But you can hardly blame them for the fiasco of impressing their citizens into the navy." Moncrithe sipped a little brandy. "But it's hard to tell who's a citizen and who's not. They give citizenship to anyone who asks. But to force American sailors and merchant men into the navy to fight against their own country . . ." He grimaced. "We had a few aboard the *Falcon*. Old Baxter is a fair man and endeavored to get them back on American merchant ships when he could."

Effie had retrieved the herbs; her fingers clutched them tight sending their scent wafting through the air. This was the second time she'd heard about press gangs within a fortnight.

"We are fighting on two fronts now, so we need the extra men," said Vandemark. "*Ja*, I see why Madison took this stand. But press gangs are a necessary evil for the war effort. Everyone does it. It has been going on for years." He took a sip of his brandy. "That wretch Napoleon still swaggers about Europe. When will we cut down the little rooster to size?"

"Egad, he's already a head shorter than you, Vandemark," Moncrithe said with a laugh. "How short do you want him to be?"

They'd forgotten her, so Effie slipped out the door; the herbs were beginning to wilt. It was good for the professor to have someone to talk to about the war.

She was glad she'd worn her new forget-me-not-blue dress. She doubted Lieutenant Moncrithe would be so courteous and flirtatious if she'd been wearing her old Sunday dress. Was she becoming as vain as Catriona? But what a pleasure it was to have pretty things to wear, not hand-me-downs.

When Vandemark confirmed that Effie would continue as his scriever after only eight days, Jonet had told him it wasn't fitting for his scriever to be in rags. He'd given Effie a generous dress allowance, from which she'd bought fabric for two dresses and a warm shawl for her grandmother.

Gratitude filled her, not merely for the new dresses. She'd not only won the professor's trust but Jonet's and Billy's too. Despite their initial reluctance, Jonet and Billy had warmed to her after she'd helped with extra chores even watering the horses unasked a few times. But they seem most impressed with the change in the professor.

"He's been moping for some time," Jonet had observed. "He needs a scriever for all that correspondence. And he needed a pupil. He treats you like one of his university students—even though you're a lassie. I hear him talking your ear off about history and the like. Giving you books too. I didna have time to listen to all that talk. He'd follow me around, book in hand, while I polished the furniture. He'd look so hurt when I told him I couldna be bothered." She'd smiled. "Aye. You'll do fine."

Jonet was using a spirtle to keep a sauce from clumping at the edges of the pot, her face red and glowing to match the fire.

"The professor is happy for his visitor. I was expecting an old gentleman," said Effie, tying the herbs with string to make a *bouquet garni*.

"Mr. Moncrithe visits when he has shore leave and hasna been to visit the professor for over a year. He's from these parts over Kemback way, but he dinna visit his folk anymore." Jonet wiped tears away with her sleeve. "Had a falling out with them. Over a woman I mind. It's a shame. He's a nice laddie and the professor fair dotes on him—like he was his own son."

"I saw four warships two weeks ago," Effie said. "Perhaps Mr. Moncrithe was on one of them."

"More than likely," said Jonet. "Take the scones to the professor and Mr. Moncrithe. I canna leave the hare *ragout*."

Effie picked up the tray. "Ragoo?"

Jonet laughed. "It's a fancy French name for stew. The professor thinks he's getting a finer dish, but it's just stew."

"Jonet, do you speak French?" said Effie laughing.

"No. I learnt the names of French dishes from Lord Glasbeinn's cook." She paused for a moment. "Will you help me serve the dinner? You ken Billy is ailing. Hurt his back lifting a bale of hay. Silly man."

"Aye." Effie had noticed Jonet's worry that Billy was getting too old to do heavy lifting. He'd certainly not want to be an indoor servant if he couldn't do gardening and work with the horses. "The morrow I'll bring a salve I made. Dr. Ferguson swears by it."

When she brought the tea tray, Vandemark and Moncrithe were deep in conversation. She puzzled over the strange language they spoke.

Moncrithe moved papers away to a chair so she could set down the tray on a side table.

"Be careful, laddie, those are important papers," said Vandemark.

"I can see that. They look like bills to me—your tailor, your vintner. Crivens, you spend a lot on the wine."

"Give those to me," said Vandemark, snatching them from his hand and stuffing them in his waistcoat pockets, but the smile in his eyes moderated the stern tone. "Thank you, Euphemia. You will enjoy these scones, Moncrithe."

"You spoil me, Miss Innes. How can I go back to eating hardtack after this?" He smiled and Effie smiled back, wondering what hardtack was. Why did he address her as Miss Innes and not Euphemia? Perhaps it had something to do with the way the professor had introduced her, a scriever rather than a house servant.

The men repaired to the dining room and Effie helped Jonet serve dinner. Though Jonet claimed her cooking was plain, the food was plentiful: fresh mushroom soup, the hare ragout with red turnips, a boiled lobster with parsley sauce, a pigeon pie, and a blancmange with plum preserves for dessert. She had gone the extra mile to please Moncrithe.

The lieutenant thanked Jonet, complimenting her on the hare ragout. Jonet placed the blancmange on the table and arranged the serving dishes.

As Effie balanced the dishes in one hand, the lieutenant stood and opened the door for her, a warm smile in his eyes which shone like polished agates.

That was unexpected. The gentry were not so courteous to servants. Maybe it was because he was a navy man and they had different standards. Or, more likely, as the professor suggested, he was starved for female company. Either way, she appreciated the kind gesture.

"What a grand meal. What a pleasure to be served by a nereid."

The dishes rattled as she flinched.

"It's a compliment, Miss Innes." Calum grinned, his hand still on the handle. "Nereids are sea-nymphs who succor sailors from the ravages of the oceans. I'm glad to know one dwells here with Vandemark."

Jonet, now at the door with her tray of dishes, rolled her eyes, and Vandemark called out, "Moncrithe, leave the poor lassie alone and bring the brandy and glasses from the sideboard."

Once in the kitchen, Effie shook her head in wonder. "Jonet, I've been called a selkie's bairn but now I'm a sea maiden, a neer-ee-id." One was an insult, the other a compliment. And they both tied her to myths of the sea.

"The dear I ken what those men think with their learning and strange words. But Mr. Moncrithe's a fine gentleman. It's good to see him having a bit of fun—he's usually so solemn. No doubt it was a compliment."

"Oh, Jonet, look at the pile o' dishes." Effie surveyed the mess in the kitchen. "I'll stay late the night and help you." Her grandmother would be angry, but so be it.

She lifted the kettle to pour hot water into the basin and as she plunged her hands into the warm soapy water, she went over her encounters and conversations with Calum Moncrithe. A naval officer, a gentleman, a scholar, a kind heart—but underneath, she sensed a deep sadness.

Joy to My Love

Chapter 6

The weather was bonny, especially for April, and the air fragrant with spring flowers. Effie was glad that dawn came earlier giving a better view from the bend halfway up School Wynd. By habit, she paused for a moment looking down at the harbor wreathed in mist, watching for the Mackies' boat. She could barely make out the fishing vessels as they headed out to sea but for the gulls circling in their wake above the mist.

When she reached High Street, more people were about: a few men loaded a cart with empty beer barrels at Melville's Inn and a servant lassie hurried to her place of work. In the distance, she noticed the tall figure of Calum Moncrithe. He strolled toward her. Her heart gave a little flutter of pleasure.

"Good morning, Miss Innes." He doffed his chapeau bras and tucked it under his arm. "I know you keep early hours and thought you'd pass this way."

"And you keep early hours, sir." Had he been waiting for her? She met his gaze instead of ducking her head. She liked the way his eyes crinkled when he smiled. A glow crept into her cheeks, and an unexpected warmth in her heart. She smiled back. He took a quick intake of breath.

"I'm in the habit of waking early when on ship and it's hard to change my ways when on land." He paused and stared at the firth, his face becoming sober. "I will be leaving in a few days and wish to relish peaceful surroundings while I can." He turned to smile at her. "May I accompany you? I'm returning to Vandemark's home. He was still abed when I left." He didn't wait for an answer but matched his stride with hers. "Have you always lived in Pittenweem, Miss Innes?'

"Not always—in the last eleven years after my grandfather and Uncle Alec died," she said, not looking at him and quickening her pace.

"And before that?"

"My grandfather had a farm between Pittenweem and Kilrenny."

"So, your grandfather was a farmer?"

"Aye." She was reluctant to talk about herself and her past, especially to this sophisticated man. What if he asked about her father? "Please tell me about America. What is it like?"

"The maps tell me it's a big country. Scotland could fit into it many times. Before this war, I've only been on the eastern seaboard and a little inland to Washington. That's the capital." He seemed to sense her reluctance to talk about herself and spent the five-minute walk telling her about the places he'd visited in America and Canada.

At the front door she thanked Moncrithe for an interesting conversation. She went to the kitchen, to get coals for the library fire so it would be ablaze before the professor came down; Billy was still sick and she wanted to help Jonet.

The lieutenant was in the library by the French doors gazing out at the small lawn and bright spring flowers in the herbaceous border. Though he'd been light hearted as he told her about America, in repose he was somber and sad.

She cleared her throat. "Pardon me, Mr.—er Lieutenant Moncrithe; I must build up the fire afore the professor comes down. Would you like to sit in the drawing room?"

"No, Miss Innes. I'll stay and watch how you do it."

Her eyebrows raised a little.

He added, "If that does not discompose you?"

She shook her head.

"Jonet is nearby as a chaperone."

Effie hid a smile: as if the likes of her had chaperones.

When she glanced up at the lieutenant, he smiled. "I shall enjoy watching you keep the embers of the fires alight on the hearth. We rough sailors miss the normal domestic life on shore, and it's especially hard in times of war." He sighed. "And I've been at war a long time. I wish to keep this memory of you and know the professor is well taken care of." He looked around the room, before returning his attention to her. "Vandemark's house in St. Andrews was a home to me when I came ashore. I hope this house in Pittenweem will become a home too."

People in every station in life had sorrows and difficulties, not only the poor. That had been a revelation to Effie. Mrs. Forbes had been lonely and neglected by her family; the professor had his illnesses and still mourned for his dead wife and daughter though it had been many years. Her heart softened toward the lieutenant. Was it loneliness or unhappiness over the estrangement with his family that made the lieutenant so grave? He looked away and made a movement to leave.

"Aye, this is a comfortable home and Jonet makes it so." Though she thought it odd he wanted to watch her build a fire, she sensed his need to talk. She didn't wish to chase him away and besides, she enjoyed his company. "Tell me about the war and what it is like to be a lieutenant in the navy."

He sat in a nearby chair and settled more comfortably, crossing a booted leg.

She wanted to ask the lieutenant about his family, but she was too shy, and anyway it wasn't her place. Moncrithe described what life was like on a ship of the line in the best navy in the world. She sat back on her heels and listened. Though he made light of his experiences, she was aware he left a lot out. He made it sound delightful to visit new and exotic places and meet interesting people though he spoke little of the perils at sea. But she knew all about that: fishermen encountered dangers day by day. But the lieutenant and his crews were also in danger when they encountered enemy ships. They put their lives on the line to protect insignificant people like her who lived in unimportant backwaters.

When Vandemark came into the room, his brows drew together for a second, his glance taking in the sight of her sitting at the lieutenant's feet. Moncrithe broke off his stories and rose at the professor's entrance and helped him to his chair.

Effie went to the door, not looking at the professor. Had she been too brazen to enjoy the lieutenant's company? She thanked Moncrithe for telling her about the navy and wished she could thank him for his courage and protection of his country—of her—but it would have embarrassed them both.

She doubted she'd see much more of Lieutenant Moncrithe since he'd be leaving for Edinburgh soon. She suffered a small pang.

The lieutenant met Effie every morning for the next four days, even when it rained. It became his habit to sit with her as she made up the fire in the library. When she moved to the desk to prepare paper, pen, and ink for the professor's dictation, the conversation came around to one of Moncrithe's duties as a naval physician: to collect and record plants in the various places he'd visit.

"Why do you do that?" she said as she chose a couple of sheets from the quire of writing paper. "It seems an unnatural occupation for a man—I mean, sailor." She shifted in her chair, not meeting his eyes. Had she been insolent?

He laughed. "Aye. You think it strange to take up a pastime that ladies of leisure are known for. When I was at university, we studied subjects such as chemistry and botany as well as anatomy and physiology."

She nodded but she didn't know what those words meant; she'd ask Dr. Ferguson. She didn't want Moncrithe to know how ignorant she was.

"Botany, the study of plants, is part of a physician's education. It's so we can prepare our own remedies. And—" There was a commotion in the hallway.

Alan Ferguson appeared at the library door taking off his wet cloak which Jonet whisked away. Effie grinned; that canny housekeeper wasn't going to allow him to drip all over the library floor.

"It's a dreich day," he said blowing on his hands and warming them by the fire. "I'm glad there's a good blaze!" He shook hands with the lieutenant and winked at Effie. "How are you laddie? Are you ready to leave the navy and join me in doctoring in the villages of Fife?"

Moncrithe grimaced. "I wish I could. It would be impossible to relinquish my commission at a time of war."

Effie dropped the quill she was sharpening. War. She'd pushed it out of her mind that he'd join his ship soon. She wished he didn't have to leave. Though she'd only known him a short time, she liked him as much for his sake as for the professor's.

"I know. I want to remind you that you have a place here when the time comes." Alan made himself comfortable in a chair by the fire. "Where will they send you this time? Spain? Canada?"

"Probably to Canada," said Calum. His tone was diffident, then a playful note crept into his voice. "Alan, you need to be my witness. Miss Innes doesn't believe the drawing and collecting of plants a suitable occupation for a sailor." He grinned at Effie

Her face burned.

"Did you not tell her how our training included botany?" said the doctor.

Calum quirked an eyebrow at Effie as if to say, "I told you so."

The doctor stoked the fire as he addressed Effie. "I spent many hours in the botanical gardens, especially the physic garden, in Edinburgh. It was new at the time and had few specimens." He rubbed his hands. "Thanks to the naval physicians, we have a great many new species from the far ends of the world. There's an even larger garden near London. I was lucky enough to meet James Smith on my way back from India. I was physician for the East India Company for two years. Couldn't stand the heat so I returned home."

"Who is James Smith?" said Effie. How strange for men to think about plants, especially flowers. In the village, that was the women's domain except for the heavy digging. Of course, local farmers tended to their crops—but flowers?

"He's the naturalist who bought Linnaeus's collection in the 1780s." Vandemark's voice broke in before the doctor could answer. Moncrithe and Ferguson rose to greet him. "You probably studied Linnaeus's works, Calum. I have a copy of his *Systema Naturae* somewhere." He scanned the rows of books on his bookshelf, hobbling forward to get a better look.

Effie jumped off her chair. "Allow me to get it for you, sir. Sit down and rest your leg. Can you point it out for me?"

"*Ja. Ja.* It's second from the top in the glass case. Brown leather, gold lettering." The professor pointed with his walking stick.

Effie stood on her toes but it was out of her reach.

Calum came beside her and plucked the book off the shelf. Their hands met for a second, sending an unexpected shiver down her spine.

The professor was now settled in his favorite chair and Effie handed him the book.

"As you have visitors, Professor, I'll see if Jonet needs anything," said Effie.

"No. I need you to rub that excellent salve on my hands; they are stiffer this morning from the rainy weather. Here Calum, refresh your memory on cataloging plants." He handed the book to Calum.

"Euphemia's Aunt Lizzie had an ancient tome with remedies and simples," said Dr. Ferguson. "I saw it once. Good drawings in it too. It disappeared after Lizzie died. I'll warrant this salve is one of her receipts."

"Aye. It is," said Effie moving toward the door. "Lizzie taught me how to prepare it. I dinna recall a book."

When Effie returned with the salve, Calum and Dr. Ferguson were pouring over Linnaeus's book while the professor tried to fill his pipe, a grimace on his face. Effie took the pipe away, pulled a chair close to his, and applied the salve, massaging first one hand and then the other. The professor groaned in pain, then after a bit, relaxed and closed his eyes.

"It's a sweet-smelling salve," said Calum, reaching over and picking up the alabaster box. He sniffed the contents. "What do you put in it? I think lavender predominates."

"Aye. Lavender, lemon balm, thyme, peppermint and ginger in beeswax and almond oil." Effie continued massaging the professor's hands glancing at Calum. She couldn't quite read the expression in his eyes. Was he humoring her? Surely, he could work out those scents himself?

"An interesting mixture." He put a dab on his hand and rubbed it in. "Ah. Ginger gives warmth for rheumatics. Will you make some for me to take on my journey?"

"Do you have the rheumatics too, Lieutenant Moncrithe?"

"No." Calum smiled. "It will—" A slight flush rose in his cheeks. "Hands get so rough onboard ship."

Why that pause? What he was going to say? She was glad to do this small service for him, glad to give him ease.

"Aye. I could have it ready by the morrow, but I have no box to put it in."

"Use that gilt snuff box on the sideboard," said Vandemark, rousing himself from his rest. "I no longer use it."

"It's a pity Lizzie's book is lost," said Dr. Ferguson, putting down Linnaeus's book. "I think it would be as valuable as Linnaeus's. It's not only learned men but wise women who know the way with herbs. Most of their recipes are not written but handed down in families." He stood up. "I must away and see if there are any messages for me at home."

Jonet brought in a tray with tea, scones, bannocks, butter and a pot of jam. "You could do with a warm drink before you leave, Alan."

"That's a kindness," said the doctor breaking off a piece of bannock and taking a cup though he did not sit again.

"I need to dictate a letter," said Vandemark. "Return soon, Euphemia."

Effie and Jonet had hardly put down the trays in the kitchen when the bang of the door announced that the doctor had left.

"Dr. Ferguson must have gobbled down the scones and tea," said Effie. "He hardly rests for long."

"Aye. A doctor's life is like that. He'll return this evening for dinner," said Jonet. "He's a good companion for the master though a good ten years younger. He's a widower too with no children—like the professor now. What a heart-rending time that was when Rozamond and Betje died."

"I'd better get back to take dictation. Sorry I have to leave you with dinner preparations, Jonet."

"Dinna fash yoursel'. I'm used to it. And you're hired to help to the professor with his correspondence. He's unco pleased with your writing."

"He is? He dinna tell me." She strode to the library with a spring in her step.

Moncrithe looked up from his book with a smile as she took her place at her desk. She hardly had time to smile back, be seated, and dip her quill in the ink before the professor began dictation. Effie became engrossed in writing though from time to time when Vandemark paused to gather his thoughts, she peeked at the lieutenant who'd abandoned reading and was now sketching something. She wondered if he was practicing drawing flowers, perhaps the bunch of daffodils on the sideboard.

After the professor stopped dictation, Effie read over the letter to check for errors. Soon the professor's snores vied with the crackling fire—companionable noises. She looked up; Moncrithe gazed intently at her. She gave him a tentative smile wondering why he was looking at her so earnestly. She concentrated on sprinkling sand over the still-wet ink and only raised her eyes when he stood before her holding out his drawing.

He'd drawn her hand clutching the quill, an ink stain on one finger.

"We didn't merely draw plants, Miss Innes," he said in a low voice so as not to wake the professor. "For our anatomy classes we drew different parts of the human form. I wish I were an artist to draw this scene so I could remember it." He glanced over at the professor who was now in a deep sleep. "It's dreich outside, but I will for aye remember this day, this warm haven, a safe harbor."

Effie looked around the room. "Aye. This room gives comfort more than any other in the house." She studied the drawing. "I wish you hadn't drawn the ink stain. It's no bonny."

"But it's what gives your hand character—the hand of a scriever." He took the paper and rolled it into a scroll and tucked it into the breast of his jacket.

How peculiar to draw hands with ink stains—but the gentry were different in their ways. She shrugged, a glimmer of a smile stretching her lips.

"Let me show you Linnaeus's book," said Calum. "You'll enjoy the drawings. You can see the different parts of the plants: stamens, and calyces—"

"I dinna ken those words," said Effie. She knew him well enough now that he wouldn't scorn her ignorance. "But I can tell a plant by the shape of its leaves."

They spent quite a time looking over the book, talking in whispers. When Jonet came to pick up the cups and saucers, the professor stirred. Effie jumped up and helped Jonet balance the china on the tray. Jonet was doing all the work and she was sitting reading a book with the lieutenant, but she didn't want to leave despite a twinge of guilt.

"Will you come back soon?" the lieutenant said.

"No. I must help Jonet with the dinner," said Effie, a hint of regret in her voice. She'd much rather learn about plants, especially under his tutelage. But she should remember her place. "Dr. Ferguson will eat here tonight and Jonet wants to make a special meal for him and . . . for you."

As she helped Jonet with dinner, she pondered on her position in this household. It was extraordinary: she was not merely a housemaid, but a scribe which was a post usually held by a university student, and a male to boot. It was as though she were living a double life: the domestic chats with Jonet and Billy and the educated conversations with Professor Vandemark and Dr. Ferguson. Those conversations stimulated her mind; she mused over new information even when she helped Jonet with domestic chores. And now she'd made the acquaintance of a handsome naval officer who enjoyed learning as much as she did.

It wasn't just their love of learning that drew her to him. Being with him was more than a comfortable camaraderie. A warmth surrounded her just thinking about him, and more so in his presence. She memorized his features: his auburn hair, his brown-flecked hazel eyes, his kind smile, his mannerisms—almost a diffidence. Each day that she walked to the professor's house, her heart beat a little faster at the sight of him. She was growing fonder of him day by day. She couldn't help but compare him to Davy who was more swashbuckling, outgoing, and quick-tempered. She liked the lieutenant's quiet strength, quick mind, and courtesy which sprang from kindness. But both men were not for her.

"Where's Lieutenant Moncrithe?" said Effie to Jonet who was up to her elbows in suds. "He wasna on the High Street this morning. Did he sleep in like the professor?"

"No. He's gone. He was called away early this morning. He must return to Edinburgh." Jonet's voice became sharp. "Dinna stand there, lassie, take the tea to the professor."

Effie stood still a moment holding the snuff box with the salve she'd made for the lieutenant. A shadow passed over her as she put out the china and teapot: He hadn't said goodbye. Would she ever see him again?

The professor sat in his favorite chair staring at the large gold-framed portrait of his wife and daughter. Jonet had told her that when he was particularly upset, he'd gaze at the picture and sometimes talk to his wife in Dutch. His eyes were moist, but he blinked and took up his glasses ready to read the newspaper that had arrived this morning.

Effie put the tea tray on the table next to the fire and turned to leave when Vandemark addressed her.

"I hoped Moncrithe had finished his tour of duty," he said, putting down the newspaper. "He's a fine physician and could make a good living here or in Edinburgh. My heart misgives me each time he goes away."

"He left so quickly. I didna get a chance to give him the salve I made for him."

The professor took a scone hot from the griddle and buttered it, and motioned for her to sit down and pour herself a cup of tea. Effie hoped he was going to talk about Lieutenant Calum Moncrithe rather than give her a lecture on Hume.

Vandemark took a bite out of the scone, melted butter dripping down his chin. He wiped it away with the serviette and looked at the portrait again.

"Yes, he had urgent business in Edinburgh. No doubt he'll find out what his commission is. At least he'll have a better venue than when he first started out in the service."

"Oh? Was he not in Spain and Portugal? I mind he was too young to serve with Lord Nelson."

"He ended up in Spain after a while, but after Nelson died. He entered the service in eighteen-oh-eight. He first served with the West African Squadron patrolling the Atlantic to blockade slaving ships—you know the slave trade was abolished in oh-seven. I'm glad that commission did not last long; he was sick with a fever for a while. He stayed with me while he recuperated. What a depressing and discouraging experience."

Vandemark took a sip of tea.

"The navy discovered his skills as a physician and he was reassigned to the Mediterranean fleet for a while. He will probably now serve in British North America. He has a friend—Gérard Bertrand—serving in that arena."

"Perhaps they will be on the same ship."

"Perhaps. You say you have salve for him? Hmm." He took another scone. "I think I'll take a trip to Edinburgh in a few days. I can take him the salve."

Effie wished she could go too, but it would not be likely that he'd need her services there.

Vandemark picked up the newspaper, and looked at her over his spectacles. "How are you doing with transcribing Hume's treatise on morals? I would like to see a copy by tomorrow morning."

"I think I do well." Effie rose to leave. "Sir, can I get you anything afore I leave? A book?"

"Bring me the decanter of cognac and a glass." He motioned his head toward the wine cabinet. "I have need of Dutch courage." He gave a weak smile at his own joke.

Before she left the room, Effie looked back at Vandemark who sat hunched in his chair swirling the cognac in his glass. A wave of pity swept over her. Her thoughts turned to the lieutenant. Now she'd become acquainted with him, she was as anxious as the professor about his welfare.

Chapter 7

On the Sunday after Moncrithe left, Effie escorted Granny Agnes to the manse. Mrs. Mitchell had invited her and several other elderly women to tea. As she rarely went out in company, Granny Agnes would no doubt prolong her stay for several hours basking in any kind of attention. Effie hoped the old lady would curb her acerbic tongue. Poor Mrs. Mitchell. As the minister's wife she often had to entertain difficult characters in the village.

It was too beautiful a spring day to spend indoors reading the Bible. Like many fine Sundays, when her grandmother was asleep, Effie took the path to Anstruther. Today she'd have more time for herself.

She mused on what the professor had told her how he learned Latin and Greek so he could read what he called "the classics"— works of people called Plato, Aristotle, and Quintilian. She felt a slight twinge of guilt to be thinking of pagan writers instead of the minister's sermon.

Since working for Vandemark—was it only three weeks?—new ideas jostled into her eager mind. Though a professor of languages and linguistics at the University of St. Andrews, he was also interested in politics, history, and literature. He received letters from friends and colleagues in Edinburgh and London, and sometimes from the Netherlands. She was fortunate to write replies to many of those letters.

She'd been the only servant in Mrs. Forbes's house, but now that she worked with Jonet and Billy, she missed them on Sundays. She preferred to be in their company—better than her morose, bitter grandmother.

"Effie!" Catriona's voice, a little breathless, stopped her. Effie slowly turned to see Catriona running toward her. She instinctively drew back a little, waiting for the customary barb.

"Come to May Isle with us, Effie." Catriona's voice was bright and friendly. "Tam Braid is taking Barbara Cunningham and me. We thought you'd like to go too."

"Granny wouldna like me to go on Sunday," said Effie.

"Dinna fash yoursel'. I ken your granny's at the minister's house. We'll be back afore dinner time. Hurry, they're waiting."

Effie hesitated. She was leery of the invitation. Davy, though misguided, was still trying to promote the friendship.

"Davy would like you to join us."

"So, he's going too?"

"No. He'll meet us on the isle."

Davy often took supplies to the beacon keeper. Her fears calmed. Davy would be there.

Catriona led her to one of Jock Mackie's fishing boats. Jamie Mackie was looping a rope. He was not as bonny as Davy—with a thin face and long nose, and small bright grey eyes—but when he smiled, his kind nature shone through. Barbara, and Methven, were not as friendly. Effie smiled at them anyway, though it was thin-lipped and forced.

Tam had his back to the group, checking the oars, but when Methven nudged him, he turned and smiled at Catriona. He didn't smile at Effie but looked her over without comment. He had a peculiar glint in his eye that Effie couldn't fathom.

Was this a good idea? Deep misgivings squirmed in Effie's mind. But Catriona had assured her they'd meet Davy on the island. And Jamie was here; that was at least comforting.

Barbara's gaze traveled over Effie's jonquil dress which was now her Sunday best. Effie wasn't sure if she read admiration or envy in that lassie's face.

Once everyone was in the boat, Jamie cast off the moorings while Methven and Tam rowed away from the dock. As soon as they passed the narrow harbor exit, Methven and Jamie raised the sail while Tam took the tiller. The wind caught the sails with a loud thud and the little boat bucked and jumped over the waves. Screeching seagulls wheeled above them.

The rocking movement of the boat was soporific, though the freshness of the salty air revived and energized her. The kirk service had been long and dreary only enlivened by Mr. Douglas's caustic sermon on dishonesty.

Her grandmother had swiveled to face her, a scowl on her face. Effie could not think why her grandmother would think her dishonest. It was as if being illegitimate meant she was prone to all seven deadly sins. She pushed those thoughts away and enjoyed the view from the boat.

The tiny Isle of May was only a few miles from Pittenweem, but it was the first time Effie had visited. Apart from the birds and seals, only a few people lived on the island, the keeper of the beacon and his family and two helpers. Effie had met Mrs. Laing and her daughter Susan many years ago when Mrs. Laing was at the market in Anstruther. She doubted they'd have time to go to the beacon so she could renew her acquaintance.

As the boat skimmed across the waves, Pittenweem Harbor and the orange roofs of the village were lost to view. They passed the nearby villages—a new view for Effie—the spire of Kilrenny Kirk stood out among the trees above the houses of Cellardyke and Anstruther, then came the red roofs of Crail. The villages shrank in size as the boat carried them farther into the mouth of the Firth of Forth toward the North Sea.

Davy had told her that on the island were puffins: a comical bird with a big orange beak, white chest like a bib, and little black wings. Effie hoped to see them.

"I look forward to Davy showing me the puffins," said Effie to Jamie.

"He isna on the island but away to Crail. But I'll find them for you."

"Oh. I thought Catriona—" A sudden qualm overcame Effie. Apart from Jamie, she was among adversaries. Catriona had deliberately misled her. Effie doubted the invitation was to firm their friendship like Davy wanted. Why was she here?

As they drew near the island, little black dots wheeled around the craggy rocks. It was home to hundreds of seabirds and as the boat drew closer the chatter and shrieking of the birds that made their nests on the cliffs filled the air.

"There are fewer birds at this time of the year," said Jamie. "Not all have come back for the summer."

Jamie named different birds—many so different from the herring gulls that frequented Pittenweem harbor—as they drew closer to the escarpments which rose in sheer towers from the water. Effie became dizzy craning her neck watching the constant movement of flight overhead.

"Look, Effie! There's a puffin floating on the sea yonder." Jamie pointed to a small bird, but it was too far away for Effie to see its characteristics. "We'll see more when we get on the island."

Tam and Methven were busy keeping the boat away from hidden rocks as they skirted round the island. They moored at the landing called Altarstanes.

Jamie helped Effie negotiate slippery rocks until they came to a winding track with mossy, sandy soil which led to the promontory where they could see the seal colony. The bass grunting and barking of the seals joined with the soprano cries of seabirds. The seals lay like shiny elongated rocks on the shingle of the beach. A few slid effortlessly into the water and disappeared beneath the waves before their round heads bobbed up again. Most were content to lie on the beach, occasionally waving their flippers.

"Tell us the story of the selkie, Effie," said Catriona.

Effie turned from looking at the seals, apprehension surging within her. Catriona and Barbara were perched on a large flat rock; Tam and Methven were sprawled on the green fronds of newly-unfurled bracken; and Jamie sat on a rock rising from a tangle of sea thrift and motioned for Effie to sit next to him.

"I dinna ken it well. It's a story Granny Effie told Aunt Lizzie," said Effie.

"We ken she was from Orkney and fey," said Tam. "Ma says she picked the herbs and made magic potions. A white witch they called her. And your Aunt Lizzie too."

"The potions aren't magic. They help sick people and they were grateful, not afeared. Dinna Widow Ballantyne use herbs?"

Tam scowled.

"I dinna ken the story of the selkies. Tell us," said Jamie. "Sit here, Effie, and tell us the tale."

"I dinna care to. It's just a fairy story," said Effie. "How did you hear of it, Catriona?"

"Your aunt Lizzie told it at Jeannie McIntosh's hen night. There were many tales and songs that night, and the first time Ma had heard the Orkney tale."

Aye, Effie remembered that celebration four years ago. The women had not invited her to pluck the hens for the wedding feast, though Lizzie had urged her to go. She didn't want to face the nasty comments that she'd bring bad luck to the marriage. What had possessed Lizzie to tell that tale? It gave the villagers a new slur for her.

Catriona's voice broke through her reverie.

"Will you tell it us?"

Effie shook her head.

"If you will not tell it, I will." Catriona settled her skirts around her.

Effie remained standing. She turned her back and concentrated on the constantly whirling and spinning birds in the sky. This was not a story she felt comfortable telling to a mixed group and it was too much a reminder of the insults concerning her illegitimacy.

Catriona's voice changed to almost a sing-song cadence as she started the story. "Orkney is a wild and lonely place with more seabirds and seals than people. No much different from the May. Forby your granny Effie visit this place. It would have felt like home. The birds, the seals—"

Effie's knuckles were white. This story was for her benefit—or rather for her harm.

"Orkney is a wild and lonely place with only the cry of the seabirds and the calling of the seals on the beaches. Isna that how the story starts, Effie?"

Effie clenched her teeth. It would be no good telling Catriona to stop. How like Catriona to make the story more dramatic by coming to this island, an elaborate trick to humiliate her yet again.

Catriona laughed then continued.

"In Orkney is it any wonder a lassie feels so alone in the wideness of the sky and the beating of the waves?"

Effie was even more bothered that Catriona had used Lizzie's very wording—though Lizzie's voice had been warm, lilting, not shrill like Catriona's.

"The farms are distant places and the only company for a young lassie is her parents and maybe people she might meet at a k—k— what's the Gaelic word for a dance, Effie?"

Effie ignored her.

"Aye, what is it, Effie?" Jamie had no idea that this story was an embarrassment for her. She answered him.

"Ceilidh."

"Aye, that's it: a *kaylee*. Lassies in Orkney dream of meeting a man who will sweep her off her feet and be true to only her."

"It's also a Fife lassie's dream," Barbara said with a giggle.

"Do you want me to tell the story or no?" said Catriona. She took up the story, her voice rising and falling, sometimes tender, sometimes dramatic.

"There was a maid called Mairi who lived with her ma and da on a sheep farm on the tip of the island. She was a bonny lassie with long black hair and eyes as blue as a summer's sky. One day she was a little late in gathering seaweed for the evening supper. She was sad she could not attend the *ceilidh* the morrow because her mother was sick and needed tending. She loved to dance to the fiddle and sing the old songs. As she bent over to pick the seaweed, seven tear drops fell into the sea.

"She turned away to go to her house when in the gloaming walking towards her over the sand was the bonniest man she had ever seen. He was tall and lithe and braw with dark hair and dark brown eyes gazing with longing on her.

"'You be a stranger in these islands. I havena seen you afore,' she said.

64

"'Nay, Mairi, I'm no a stranger to these islands. You are no a stranger to me. I have seen you many an e'en collecting the seaweed and digging up the peat.'

"His voice was deep and low and when he said her name, 'Mairi,' it was as though she'd heard her name for the first time. It was like soft sweet music and her heart beat fast to the rhythm of the incoming tide. When he put his arms around her and kissed her, she forgot all about gathering seaweed, and kissed him back. His lips were so sweet she almost swooned. The stranger took a strand of seaweed from Mairi's basket and tied their hands together, saying, 'Now we are joined together for aye.'"

"Aye, handfasting," said Barbara. "They're husband and wife."

Effie went over to sit with Jamie; standing in the wind had chilled her. He smiled, but Effie returned it with a grimace.

"Barbara, stop your interrupting," snapped Catriona. "Mairi and her bonny husband spent the night together on yon lonely beach and though the winds blew cold and chill, they were warmed by their love. When she awoke the next day, he was gone."

Catriona paused. Barbara giggled. Tam winked at Catriona. Effie looked away, her cheeks flushing. When Aunt Lizzie had told the story, it was in the family, and only the lassies listened; the men were too busy drinking whisky, discussing the price of neeps and the state of herring fishing. Effie hung her head. To tell such a tale on a Sunday.

"And then what happened?" said Barbara, her arms clasped around her knees.

Catriona continued, "Mairi went home but her mother and father hadna missed her. It was as though they were in thrall to the selkie's spell too. Time had fallen still. And that's who the braw stranger was, a selkie. He turned himself into a man to seduce lonely lassies but then returns to the sea. Mairi didna ken she'd called him from the deep when she wept those seven tears."

"Is that what your mother did, Effie?" said Barbara. Effie shook her head and pressed her hands to her face. Only a foolish lassie would believe such nonsense, but the story was too close to home, too close to her own mysterious illegitimacy.

"There are no such things as selkies," Effie said, but they ignored her.

Catriona glared at Barbara for the interruption; a rumble of laughter came from Tam. Jamie put a hand on Effie's tightly clasped hands, concern in his gaze.

"I didna ken they brought you here to tease you," he said.

Effie shook her head. It was more than just teasing; they meant to hurt.

Catriona's voice droned on like a gnat buzzing annoyingly in Effie's ear.

"Though Mairi watched the beach every evening, he didna come again. Nine months later she bore a bairn, a son who had webbed feet and dark brown eyes. Mairi lived with her parents and they grew to love her little son who she called Morgan. The bairn loved to play by the sea, especially on the beach where Mairi met the selkie.

"Early one evening when the bairn was seven years old, a knock came to the door, and the selkie stood there looking as bonny and braw as the first time Mairi saw him.

"'I've come for my son,' he said.

"Mairi held tight to Morgan, saying, 'No. No. You canna take my bairn.' But the child wriggled free from his mother's arms, slippery as a fresh-caught eel, and taking the selkie's hand, ran with his father to the beach.

"Mairi chased after them. But when she got to the beach there were only two seals, a large one and a small one. Their heads turned towards her and their bonny brown eyes gazed at her in love. But the call of the deep was stronger, and they disappeared into the waters. Mairi never saw the selkie or Morgan again. From time to time she'd see seals frolicking in the surf. And two called out to her in douce haunting voices before they disappeared into the waves.

"Isna it a good story?" said Catriona coming out of her storytelling mode and looking at Effie under her lashes. "Effie, didna your uncle Alec say you were a special bairn because your father was a selkie?"

"He was only teasing me. He didna believe it." How could Catriona besmirch fond memories of Uncle Alec?

Tam came up to Effie, pushed Jamie off the rock and grabbed her by the waist. "Let's see those webbed feet then. Take off her shoes, Methven."

Catriona and Barbara laughed as Effie struggled to be free from Tam's hold. She tried to move her feet away from Methven's hands, but he caught one of them and wrenched off her shoe. The blood drained from Effie's face.

"Leave her be." Jamie tried to push Methven away.

"Aww, look at that now. No webbing," said Tam. He sounded disappointed.

"Certain sure I dinna have webbed feet. I'm not a selkie's bairn." Effie tried to push away his arms. Surely he'd let her go now. "It's only a myth."

"A myth, is it?" Tam held her against him with a vice-like grip. Effie strained against his arm. "A big word for a lassie like you. Why do you look so different from us folks? I never kent about selkies until Mrs. Tivondeal told the story to my ma. Look at you: hair so pale, the color of seal pups."

Effie, twisted round in his grip; he only tightened it and pushed Jamie away with his other hand.

"I've heard tell of people with hair like mine." Effie struggled some more. So this was the source of the villagers calling her a selkie. Catriona's family had spread the word, sharing the tale she thought only the Inneses knew; it wasn't a common Fifian legend. Aunt Lizzie had no idea she'd added to her niece's troubles once she'd told the story at the hen party.

Tam's lip curled. "Even if you dinna have webbed feet, it's the cunning of witchcraft. You're a selkie's bairn all right."

Tam still held Effie's waist, the smell of sweat and whisky strong on him.

"Whisht your blethering, Tam. Let her be," said Jamie as he pried Tam's hands away from Effie's waist. Effie dug her elbow into Tam's ribs. He grunted, cursed, and released her so abruptly she fell hard. Pain shot through her hip bone. By the look on Tam's face, she would pay for that jab.

Tam stood and took a swing at Jamie who stepped back and closed his fist ready to fight back.

Methven took hold of Jamie's arm and said, "Leave it, Jamie. You canna fight him. He's bigger 'n you."

Effie smoothed down her skirts with trembling hands and with effort managed to stand.

"Aye. You have the truth of it," said Jamie, shaking himself loose from Methven. "It's no right to tease Effie like this. Wait till Davy hears of it."

Methven shrugged and turned away, muttering, "It's just a bit o' fun. Davy would understand."

Would he? Would he? Effie hoped not. She hobbled around from the pain in her hip and the sharp stones on her bare feet. Where had Methven thrown her shoes? Jamie came to help her and found them in fronds of bracken.

Tam looked at the sky and sea. "Let's away home, afore it gets too late."

Catriona came to Effie's side and squeezed her arm. "'Twas only a bit of fun like Methven said. Dinna fash yoursel'."

Effie flinched away and looked down at the pebble-strewn mossy grass. That's all she was to them: a figure of fun, a scapegoat. She swallowed a morass of hurt.

"Leave me in peace, Catriona," said Effie. She could not meet that lassie's eyes, hiding her hurt with her lashes.

All of them, except Jamie, were in on the joke. Effie was grateful to him, that though outnumbered, he'd stood up for her. His thin face showed concern, and the limp he'd had from childhood seemed more pronounced. Perhaps he'd had his share of teasing.

The group walked toward Altarstanes. Effie dawdled behind them, rubbing her hip. Tears threatened to fall. She clenched her shawl more tightly and kept her eyes on her feet so she wouldn't stumble. How unfair to use one of her family's special stories to humiliate her.

"Effie! Hurry!" Jamie's voice pierced her thoughts. She looked up. The others were on board waiting for her. She picked up her pace and limped toward them. As she got closer, Tam cast off the rope, a smirk on his face. Before Jamie could stop him, Methven pushed the boat away from the rocks with one of the oars.

Effie gasped. "Jamie! Catriona! Dinna leave me!"

It was dangerous to jump the short distance from the rocks to the boat. What if she fell and the sea sucked her down into a watery grave?

Jamie threw a rope toward her, but it fell short. Methven pulled it away. Jamie struggled to get it back, but the older man overpowered him. Jamie's eyes were wide, sorrowful. Tam laughed. Catriona and Barbara looked dismayed but didn't help Jamie.

The boat moved farther and farther away from the shore so the faces of the occupants become more indistinct. Over the clamor of the birds, Jamie yelled, "You canna leave her, Tam."

Effie couldn't hear Tam's reply.

Then Jamie's voice came small and faint. "We'll come for you the morrow. The tide is against us now."

Effie stood rigid. Disbelief numbed every thought. She was stranded and night was coming on.

Chapter 8

The boat disappeared into the gathering dusk, and was now a mere speck on the horizon. Effie shivered. Her legs gave way and she plumped down on the mossy grass, tears now flowing. She buried her head in her arms.

It wasn't so much that she was alone on the island—she had faith she'd survive the night and be rescued the next day. Hadn't Jamie promised her? But the betrayal was too much.

"It's no fair to treat me so!" Her words came strong through clenched teeth, but only seabirds heard her.

Most of the time she'd accepted the scorns and spite of those who disliked and feared her, thinking herself at fault. After all, her grandmother had hammered that into her. Confidence in herself had soared since working for Vandemark; confidence she'd had as a bairn when Lizzie and Alec were alive.

Limp and exhausted, she raised her head. The sky was now dusky, the sea steel grey. To the east, at the mouth of the firth, a pale full moon crept over the horizon, creating a faint moonglade, a shiny path across the water. Toward Pittenweem, the setting sun tinged the grey clouds pink. The boat was too far away to be visible.

Effie could barely see the path now. If she walked too far in the dark she might stumble into rabbit holes, or worse, a deep crevasse. When would the beacon's light come on?

The noise from the seagulls, guillemots, and terns had dimmed to faint twitters and crooning as they settled for the night. Moans from the seal colony carried across the rocks, a sad siren song.

Do selkies change their skins in the pitch of the night? Effie shook her head, as though to knock that silly thought out of her mind. Pale and phantom-like in the darkening sky, a lone seagull headed toward the mainland. The sinister tale Lizzie had told—that gulls were souls of dead fishermen—surfaced to Effie's mind. Why did the dark bring out eerie thoughts? She pushed that away too. No. No. It was all fantasy, tall tales.

Effie put her shawl over her head to stop the wind on her neck. She peered at the faint moonlit trail which she guessed led to the beacon.

She'd seek shelter there. It couldn't be too far away on this small island. Effie had met Mrs. Laing and the oldest daughter, Susan, several years ago on market day in Anstruther. She hoped they'd remember her.

The moon still hung pale on the horizon but was getting brighter as the sky darkened. As though in rivalry, the beacon flared up red and gold, illuminating the churning sea and the path between rough rocks. She could now see the path with its low tussocks of grass and occasional sharp stones.

Soft chirping came from the ground and in beacon-light and moonlight, she caught a glimpse of a striped orange beak and a round bright eye staring out of one of the holes. A puffin. She picked her way through the puffin nests, careful not to stand on a brooding bird, and climbed a grassy knoll where the tall white beacon with its crown of fire came into view.

It seemed a long time before she reached the building, but it wasn't only the blaze helped her know she was near: the acrid smell of burning coal and coke was stronger.

Effie, stumbling from cold and fatigue, found the main door— above which was a date, 1636. The beacon had warned ships of danger longer than she ever knew. She rapped on the door with ice-cold knuckles. Muted voices came louder and the door opened slowly. A man with a cudgel in one hand and a lantern in the other stood in its glow. He stepped back, a trace of fear in his face, stepping on the toes of a lassie who was peering around him. She let out a screech.

"Jeannie, dinna stand so close." Though stern, his voice quavered.

He lifted the lantern, momentarily blinding Effie. "Och, I thought for a minute you were a sprite come to haunt us. What are you doing here, lassie?"

"I came with friends. They left me. Couldna come back for me," said Effie through chattering teeth. "I'm Effie Innes from Pittenweem. Lizzie Innes's niece. Your wife may recall me."

"Aye, I mind that day in Anstruther," said Allyson Laing, who had come to the door, a wee laddie on her hip. "Fine friends they be to leave you stranded." She motioned Effie to come inside. "Close the door. The wind's unco sharp. We were just sitting down to dinner. The soup will warm you." She called out into the warm darkness of the room. "Susan set out another bowl. We have a guest."

Effie stepped inside. The room was a kitchen, living room and bedroom altogether. Warmth from a crackling fire and fragrance from cock-a-leekie soup mingled with the stench of coal that permeated everything.

Susan, who'd been setting the table, ran over and hugged Effie. "I mind how we met in Anster. Oh, how chill you are. Come sit by the hob," she said, leading Effie to a chair with a woolen shawl draped over it. "Put this around you, hen." She wrapped Effie in the fire-warmed shawl.

Effie had not expected such a kind welcome from the family she'd only met once. After the treatment she'd received from Catriona, Tam, and his friends, relief and gratitude brought a lump to her throat.

Jeannie, the youngest daughter, made room for Effie on the bench. Mrs. Laing plopped the youngest bairn, a curly-headed lad, down on the bench next to Effie.

Allyson Laing ladled the soup into their bowls. With each spoonful, Effie became comforted in body and spirit. The family chatter—the sounds of family life—embraced her. It warmed her soul as much as the fire and the soup warmed her body. A little pain pierced her mind: Would she one day have a family of her own?

Fergus was fascinated with her and kept peering around his mother.

"Why is your hair so white like a granny's?" Fergus said through a mouthful of soup.

"Fergus, you're full o' cheek," said Susan. "It's no so much white as it's very fair."

"I dinna ken why my hair's so fair," said Effie. "Or why your hair's so curly and black as coal." She gently pulled a curl of his hair, which bounced back to its curlicue shape as soon as she released it.

Fergus was indignant. "Black as coal. Black as coal," he repeated. "But Ma." he said, turning to his mother, "I wasna in the coal chute."

"It's only a saying, Fergie," said Susan. "She dinna think you were in the coal chute, just a way to tell how your hair looks."

"She's like the fairy princess in yon story you tell us, Ma," said Jeannie. "You ken, the princess with the lang hair like moonbeams. Do you ken the story, Effie?" When Effie shook her head, Jeannie turned back to her mother, a plea in her voice, "Ma, can you tell us the story now?"

"Finish your soup and wash the dishes, then I'll tell it," said their mother.

The children all started talking at once.

"What a clamor! Whisht to your mother," said Peter Laing, getting up from the table and pulling on a grey-green woolen coat and black boots. He smiled at Effie. "I must away to help Philip and Ross with keeping the beacon alight. We take turns in the dark of the night."

The smell of coal wafted more strongly after he climbed up steep stairs in the corner of the room and opened the hatch to the beacon above.

Effie helped Susan wash the dishes while Jeannie undressed Fergus.

"Effie," said Mrs. Laing, "you'll sleep with Jeannie and Susan. Fergus will sleep with me and my man."

Allyson left one lantern alight on the kitchen table so her husband would be able to see when he returned from checking on the beacon.

The beds were in a far corner of the room with a curtain dividing the parents' bed from the children's. The room was dark but for the flickering of the oil lamp and the ruby glow of embers. In the seclusion of the makeshift bedroom, Effie took off her dress and, in her shift, knelt beside the bed with Susan and Jeannie. She whispered a spontaneous prayer of thanks instead of a set prayer from the catechism.

Fergus climbed into his parents' bed. "It's braw to coorie doon with Ma," said Fergus pulling the blanket over himself and snuggling up to his mother who sat, fully clothed, on the bed.

"Aye, and we lassies will coorie doon together," said Susan as she settled herself beside Jeannie. Effie climbed in next to Susan and though at first Effie's feet were cold, they soon grew warm and she relaxed. It reminded her of the time she had shared a bed with her Aunt Lizzie, cramped though it had been. Now she slept on a pallet on the floor while Granny Agnes had the bed.

Allyson Laing didn't pull the curtain to divide the two beds but sat with Fergus curled up next to her. She began the story. "Once in a land far, far away over mountains and seas lived a lassie in a grand castle . . . ." Soon Fergus's soft snores blended with his mother's words and Effie slept. She never did hear the end of the story.

Effie awoke gradually, drowsiness and unaccustomed warmth making her snuggle further under the covers. Her pallet had never been this comfortable. It wasn't until Susan stretched and turned that she remembered where she was. Her first wide-awake thought was how angry her grandmother would be she was not there to give her breakfast. Her second thought: Professor Vandemark and Jonet would think she'd deserted them. Perhaps she'd lose her job after all, if she couldn't be relied upon. She knew Vandemark and Jonet liked her, but she had only been on the job a little while. What would they think of her? If only she hadn't lagged behind feeling sorry for herself.

She needed to get back to Pittenweem as soon as possible and wondered when she'd be rescued. She didn't want to ask Peter Laing to take her home; he'd been up most of the night tending the beacon. Jamie had yelled out they would come for her today. Tam and Davy had their fishing duties. Perhaps they'd not have time to rescue her until later in the day or even the next day. But she couldn't stay in bed fretting; she'd keep a vigil outside, away of the pungent air inside the beacon.

Carefully lifting the covers, Effie swung her feet out onto the floor, found her shoes, and stepped into damp early-morning greyness. The pony that helped carry the coal whinnied a greeting, and Effie went over to stroke its soft velvet nose. Its bucket of water was low, so Effie filled it from the pump. The slag heap of coal dust reached halfway up the building, and among the black, a plant with small white flowers thrived in the grime. She'd explore those later; she needed to get a better view of the firth. She walked down a little path until she could see the leaden-colored water lapping on a rocky edge of the island.

Though she could not see them for the mist, a few birds screamed overhead. In a break in the low-lying cloud, she glimpsed an outcrop of rocks with a row of black, sharp-beaked shags ready to pitch into the sea.

The fog lifted in spots and toward the mainland, ashen and hazy in the distance, she could just make out the fleet of fishing boats from the villages heading to the North Sea. One broke away from the rest and came toward the island. Effie's spirits lifted. Someone was coming.

Susan joined her watching the boat come closer and closer. "It's heading for Kirkhaven," said Susan. "Look. Yonder. Near the old monastery. See yon pile of rocks. There's no hurry to meet it; it'll take about an hour afore she reaches the landing spot. Come eat breakfast."

Effie shook her head. "I dinna feel like eating. I'm afeared what will happen when I return to Pittenweem. I started a new job and I'm not sure what my new employer will say. I may lose that job."

Susan put a hand on Effie's arm. "It wasna your fault you were left on the May. They'll understand. Could you no eat a piece o' bannock?"

"Thank you. You and your family have been so kind to me."

"Well, it's not often we get visitors so it made for a grand time for us."

Effie was reluctant to go back into the lighthouse. The stench from coal and ashes infused everything. Though it was frigid and damp outside, the air was fresh, invigorating.

Susan returned with a couple of bannocks smeared with crowdie and two mugs of hot chamomile tea. Effie was hungrier than she thought and ate the bread and cheese quickly. The tea was fragrant and sweet with honey, and she warmed her hands as she clasped the mug.

The boat came closer. She could make out the blue-and-red bow of Jock Mackie's boat.

She turned to Susan. "It's Davy Mackie come to fetch me." She couldn't hide the emotion in her voice.

"Aye. I ken him. A braw laddie. Is he your man, Effie?" said Susan.

"No. Just a friend." Could Susan hear regret in her voice? She'd tried to sound neutral.

"I hope we can meet again, Effie," said Susan. "I am to start work in Crail in June. My aunt Betsy will find a place for me. Ma says it's time for me to earn a living now I'm fourteen. It will be good to get off the island, but I'm afeared. What's it like to work for an unknown family, learn their ways?"

"I was fortunate to have a good mistress in Mrs. Forbes and now Professor Vandemark," said Effie, turning to give Susan a hug. "You'll do fine." She hoped Susan would find a kind employer; not everyone was so lucky.

Jeannie's voice called to Fergus as she ran after him. Mrs. Laing followed more sedately.

"Can Effie no stay with us?" said Fergus, putting a grimy arm around Effie's neck. Effie kissed his cheek.

"I must away to my home, Fergus. Perchance you can visit me or I can come back one day to see you. You can tell me about the birds and rabbits."

"Aye. And we can look for flower and plants for your potions," said Jeannie. "It will be strange that Susan will not be here." Susan put an arm around her sister.

Though isolated, the family loved and cared about each other. Effie wondered how often they were able to get to the mainland. What a lonely life for the family of a lighthouse keeper.

"I see a braw boatie coming," said Fergus, waving to the three men on the boat. "Can I go doon to the quay with Effie and Susan?"

"We'll all go," said his mother taking his hand and walking toward Kirkhaven. When they arrived at the landing place with its narrow channel between rugged rocks, they could see the men more clearly.

Effie was glad to see the Mackies, but through her pleasure shot a pang of guilt. "They'll no get their share of fishing today."

"It's a sacrifice and kindness to fetch you," said Mrs. Laing.

Fergus jumped up and down as the boat drew nearer. His mother restrained him from running over to the men the minute they tied up the boat.

Jock stepped out of the boat while Davy trimmed the sail and Jamie hung onto a pole to keep the boat from lurching into the rocks from the lapping waves.

"And who is this braw laddie?" said Jock, with a nod and a wink to Mrs. Laing. He bent down to shake Fergus's hand.

"You ken who I am, Mr. Mackie," said Fergus.

"Och. You're right. It's Fergus Laing." He tousled the bairn's hair. "You've grown so big since I last saw you!"

"And that was only two weeks ago," whispered Susan to Effie.

Jock turned to Effie, "We must away now. The tide is right."

Effie gave the Laing family quick hugs and, with Jock's help, clambered into the boat. Davy took her hand to help her. His knuckles were raw and bruised, his left eye and lips swollen; a reddish-purple bruise graced his cheek bone.

"What happened, Davy?" Effie said, putting a tentative hand to his face.

"He had a fight with Tam," said Jamie. "Tam looks worse than him."

"I was so angry he'd left you, Effie. I didna mean to get into a brawl, but he took a swing at me and I saw red." His blue eyes were hard.

"Aye, it was a braw fight with many a brattle on the cobblestones," said Jamie.

"Davy. Jamie. The lassie wouldna like to hear the details of a brawl the whole harbor witnessed," said Jock.

The whole harbor? Her grandmother was going to be furious. And what would the professor think of this vulgar display? Jonet would be sure to hear about it and tell him. Bad enough that she had been stranded on the island, but now it was common knowledge.

When the boat was safely out of the narrow inlet and away from the jagged rocks, Effie turned to Jock Mackie.

"Mr. Mackie, I'm thankful you came to fetch me, but sorry you missed the fishing. I'll save some money and pay you for the loss of income."

"There's no need, lassie. The professor gave me a good sum of money to bring you back to compensate for not fishing today."

"So he kens too?" Her good mood sank into worry, but if he paid for Jock's catch, maybe he wasn't upset with her.

"Aye. Jonet was by the harbor when the fight broke out and Catriona told her all about you being left on the island," said Jock.

Effie wondered what tale Catriona had told. It would not be to her credit, and no doubt Catriona would come out looking good.

"I'm glad you had the sense to go to the beacon. It eases my mind you weren't perched on a rock in the cold and damp all night long," said Davy as he held tight to the rudder.

Jamie kept a commentary on the different birds that followed the boat. A flock of white gannets from Bass Rock flew over in a tight formation. Their huge black-tipped wings beat in unison until one plummeted into the water, a sleek projectile plunging down into the choppy sea. The other gannets followed in turn, bobbing to the surface with wriggling fish in their sharp black beaks for a moment before the writhing meal disappeared into their gullets.

"Did you see that, Effie?" Jamie turned to her with bright eyes. "Yon birds can fish from muckle great heights. They're canny fishers."

"Aye. It's a sight to see. I thought they'd drown, they fell so swift." Effie found Jamie's excitement and observation about birds endearing. He could be a scientist on birds as much as Linnaeus on plants.

Pittenweem Harbor loomed closer and closer until all too soon the men were tying up the boat.

A few of the fishwives stopped their preparations to stare at their arrival. Isabella McIntosh raised a hand in greeting to Effie. That small gesture cheered Effie.

Catriona was there and hailed her as though she were a long-lost friend.

"Effie, I am right sorry Tam left you behind on the May," she said in a loud voice, putting a hand on Effie's arm. But Effie noticed how she was quick to glance under her lashes at Davy to see his reaction. He was pleased at Catriona's words and actions, giving her a quick hug and smile.

"I'm to come with you to talk with your granny," Catriona continued.

Catriona chatted with Davy but Effie was silent, not listening to the conversation. She was too intent on wondering how her grandmother would greet her—and the professor too.

They arrived at the cottage and Davy pushed open the door, letting the daylight penetrate the dark warmth of the room.

"Widow Innes, here's Effie safe and sound."

Her grandmother sat by the stoked-up fire, a scarlet glow in the dimness. Effie crept toward her grandmother and gave her a timid kiss on the cheek. Her grandmother looked at her but didn't say a word.

The old woman smiled at Davy and Catriona. "It's good of you to take the trouble over my granddaughter. What a silly besom she is." Her words were mild, but she threw Effie a sharp look. "What a to do when I came home to find the place cold and empty. But folk helped me. Jonet Murdoch brought fresh bannocks an' cheese the morn and made up the fire."

"Effie had too much a care for her bonny dress to hurry," said Catriona. "The tide was against us. We couldna wait for her."

Then turning to Effie, she said with a playful smile, "I mind Effie was bemused by the call of the seals. It halted her feet."

Effie threw a swift glance at Catriona who seemed to be daring her to contradict her explanation. Davy and her grandmother waited for a response from her.

"The path was stony and—" said Effie.

"The others managed fine." Granny Agnes said sharply. "Well, lassie, let this be a lesson to you not to dawdle. It was good of Tam to take you to see the May. I mind going there with my school chums mony a year ago. I didna care for the birds. What a noise, what a stink. Where did you bed the night? On the beach?"

"I stayed in the beacon with the Laing family. They were so kind to me," said Effie.

Agnes Innes merely grunted.

"I must away to the harbor, Widow Innes," said Davy, making his way to the door.

"I must away too. Walk me home." Catriona took his arm.

Once the door was closed behind them, Granny Agnes's hostess smile left her face and she turned cold blue eyes on Effie.

"I've never been so ashamed. It's like history repeating itself with fighting over—" Her grandmother shook her head. "Aye. It's bad blood from your mother and who kens from your father. Well, be off to work. I hope you dinna lose your job over your daft behavior."

"What do you mean history repeating itself?" said Effie. She was tired of these half-spoken threats and innuendoes. Had her mother been fought over? Why? She'd ask Rhona next time she saw her.

"Never you mind, lassie," said her grandmother. A malicious glint came into her eyes as she looked Effie up and down. "Your yellow dress is crumpled, and your hem is clarty. What will the foreigner think on you now?"

Chapter 9

"Euphemia stop what you're doing. We must leave for Edinburgh within the hour." The professor stood at the library door, leaning heavily on his cane.

Startled, Effie paused from rewriting the letter he'd dictated yesterday.

"I'm going with you?" She knew he'd been planning on going to Edinburgh but it was news she was to accompany him. "What about my granny? How many days will we be gone? She needs someone to take care of her."

She'd never heard the last about leaving the old woman alone the one night she'd been stranded on the Isle of May. But, unlike Granny Agnes, the professor and Jonet had been understanding of her plight and Jonet had even been indignant that Effie had been left behind.

"Dinna fear, Effie," said Jonet, who jostled the professor at the door so she'd room to bring in scones and hot tea. "I'll take care o' your granny. It's all arranged. Did she no tell you? I told her two days since."

Effie clamped her mouth shut though she seethed within. How like Granny Agnes not to tell her. And why no hints from Jonet or Vandemark?

The professor lumbered into the room and seated himself in his favorite chair. His arthritis had been giving him stiffness and pain in his legs the last few days. He joked that it was the wind from the Low Countries, his old home, bringing past misdeeds of his youth. She'd better bring the liniment she had recently made.

What would her granny think of her going alone with the professor to Edinburgh?

"And you are no going alone," continued Jonet. "I told the professor he canna go alone with a young lassie. I canna go, so your friend Catriona is going with you. I spoke with her yesterday. She jumped at the chance to visit Edinburgh. Your granny recommended her."

Even Catriona had known before she did. Catriona was not exactly her friend. Effie wished Susan Laing could have come instead.

"You'd best go home and get your night clothes," said Jonet. "And bring your best dresses."

Effie kept her amusement to herself—she didn't have night clothes but slept in her shift.

"We're going in the laird's coach," said the professor, wincing a little as he picked up a scone. "We will go to North Queensferry and take the ferry across the firth. I have no liking for traveling in small fishing vessels in a choppy sea. Moncrithe will meet us in South Queensferry with Lord Glasbeinn's coach." He contemplated another scone. "Be quick now. I do not want the laird's horses to wait long."

Effie threw on the new blue shawl she had bought with her improved wages and ran home, her heart beating a little faster knowing she'd see Lieutenant Moncrithe again.

Granny Agnes grumbled about Effie's leaving, but her remarks were mild as she was pleased she was getting attention from Jonet and Rhona. Effie didn't say anything about not knowing about the trip, but caught a malicious gleam in her grandmother's eye. She'd not told her on purpose. It was almost as if she wanted Effie to lose this job or at least get her into trouble with the professor.

On the way to Vandemark's house, Effie glanced at the harbor. Catriona was talking animatedly with Davy and Jamie. If she was going to come with Effie and the professor, she needed to stop that conversation. Effie walked toward them.

Davy and Jamie's voices were raised. Effie caught a few words. "Tam . . . skelp him . . . worry our mother . . . wait till I get my hands on him."

"What's the matter, Davy? Catriona?" Effie said. Perhaps Davy was displeased Catriona was going to Edinburgh.

"It's Robbie," said Davy who looked thunderous. "He—"

"He's gone off with Tam Braid to South Queensferry," broke in Jamie, a scowl on his usually pleasant face. "And he's taken Davy's savings from the whaling, and my father's best boat."

"And with yon Alasdair Grant," said Catriona. "He hired Mr. Mackie's boat." She put a hand on Davy's arm. "Tam's a good sailor. Robbie will be safe."

"Aye. But it's not his skill with the boat I fear. He's taking Grant to a new gaming hell there," said Davy, his fists clenched. "And I warrant he talked Robbie into taking my money. He did this to spite me."

Jamie's voice trembled with anger. "He couldna get the best of Davy in a fair fight so he's using Robbie to get back at him."

"What are you going to do?" said Effie, addressing Davy.

"Go after them, of course." His voice was bitter. "We'd have left by now but Tam cut the ropes to the sails on my da's old boat. More malice." He ground his teeth. "We only now have it ready."

"We're going to South Queensferry too," said Effie. "We can keep a watch out for Robbie."

"It's a lot bigger than Pittenweem," said Davy. "But if you do see him, keep him with you if you can."

"Aye, we'll do that," said Catriona, hugging Davy's arm.

Davy gave Catriona a quick kiss. He hesitated, frowning at Effie.

"Effie. I'm glad I let Catriona go with you. She can protect you from yon fancy man."

Effie stared at him. Let her go to Edinburgh? He was as high-handed and possessive as Catriona. This was a side of Davy she hadn't seen before.

"What fancy man?" said Effie. "Oh. You mean Lieutenant Moncrithe?"

"Aye. Him. You've been meeting him each morning and entering the house alone," said Davy putting a hand on her shoulder. "You have to be especially careful because—"

"Because of my reputation." Effie shrugged his hand off her shoulder. "You ken I work for the professor so there was no wrong in it and the lieutenant was staying at the house."

Effie glanced at Catriona who was looking smug. She must have been the one who'd spread the rumor, making it out to be worse than it was. They'd sullied the lieutenant's reputation as well as hers, but her glare was lost on Catriona, who smirked.

Davy ducked his head a little, looking ashamed. "Aye, it was as I thought but . . . We must away." He gave Catriona another kiss and raised a hand to Effie; he and Jamie made for the boat.

Catriona chatted about all the things she hoped to see in Edinburgh. Effie's responses were monosyllabic; she didn't want to upset Catriona as she needed her as a chaperone. Without a chaperone, Effie couldn't go to Edinburgh. And she wouldn't be able to see the lieutenant again. Effie's heart jolted. Contrary to Catriona's insinuations, there had been nothing wrong between them, only the forming of an uneven friendship while thrown together at the professor's house.

The coach with four chestnut horses stood in the carriage way. Billy held the bridle of the lead horse, with the laird's coachman perched on his seat. The professor was already lounging inside. The carriage door was open, and the professor ostentatiously pulled out a pocket watch. Effie's spirits sank—not a good start to the journey.

Once in the coach, Effie ran her hand over the softly cushioned red velvet seats. Billy draped a wool blanket over her and Catriona's knees before shutting the door and standing by Jonet, who mouthed farewell. The coachman's son clambered up to sit next to his father and the horses leaned into their collars making the coach lurch forward. Effie and Catriona almost fell on the floor. Catriona let out a shout of laughter.

"Hold onto the straps, lassies," said Vandemark. "It is a bumpy road and we will be jostled about though the coach has sprung wheels." He sniffed and held a handkerchief to his nose. "Euphemia, I'm sure you had a good reason for keeping me waiting." His voice was sharp.

Catriona explained about Davy, Robbie and Tam, but the professor signaled for her to stop. "I am not the least bit interested in these people." He looked her up and down. "I wonder if you are a suitable companion for Euphemia."

Effie bit her lip to stop herself from laughing. The incongruity of the situation that Catriona was unsuitable for her, the pariah of the village—was comical. Catriona's indignant and shocked face added to her amusement. The professor had unwittingly put Catriona in her place.

Effie brought up a neutral topic before Catriona could reply. "How long will it take to get to Queensferry by road, Professor? I ken it's three hours by boat."

"It's about twenty-five leagues and the roads are not muddy so we should make good time. Six hours by my reckoning," he replied.

When the professor closed his eyes and fell asleep, Catriona whispered to Effie. "He's such a rude man. Why does he call you Euphemia?"

"He thinks Effie is too common. It's strange, but when I'm called Euphemia I feel different."

"Aye, but you're not," said Catriona, a slight hiss in her voice. "You're still the base-born bairn with no father."

Effie looked Catriona full in the eye. "Aye. But the professor and Jonet do not dwell on it. Now I dinna think on it either." *At least not much*, she amended in her mind.

"I'm only coming because Davy asked me to," said Catriona. "How he thought we could be friends I dinna ken. Be friends with the likes of you. Huh!" Catriona tossed her head.

Neither lassie had been farther west than St. Monans by road. Effie enjoyed seeing new places: the glimpse of the ancient Pictish standing stones by Lundin Links, the inn at Kirkcaldy where they stopped for refreshments, and the ruined Ravenscraig Castle. The professor had woken up long enough to give them histories of the various places. Catriona could barely hide her yawns.

The trip on the ferry to South Queensferry was short but rough. Professor Vandemark spent the time with his eyes closed and a bottle of sal volatile to his nose. Once they disembarked at the quay, the professor made for Hawes Inn where they would take refreshments until Lord Glasbeinn's coach arrived.

Catriona's spirits rose now there were men she could flirt with. Her charms had not captured the professor though she'd tried hard to insinuate herself into his good graces.

"If you like yon prosy, old professor, you can have him," Catriona said as she made eyes at a fashionable young man who was eating his meal two tables away.

Professor Vandemark settled in the dining room, drinking brandy after the ordeal of the ferry crossing. The lassies peered out the door of the inn while they waited for the carriage, mindful of keeping an eye out for Robbie. Effie was glad to be inside; the harbor teemed with sailors who'd come to shore from the frigates moored by the harbor. Catriona, on the other hand, wanted to be out among them.

Catriona grabbed Effie's arm. "Look, yonder. Davy and Jamie. I'm going to tell them we're here."

"No, best stay inside," said Effie. "There's a lot of rough men about. The professor told us to stay here."

"I dinna take orders from him. I want to see Davy to tell him we havena seen Robbie." She stepped outside the door, taking Effie with her.

"Wait. By that house yonder. It's Tam and Robbie," said Effie. "And Alasdair Grant too."

Davy saw them too, striding over to Robbie, pushing aside a couple of men in his way. His body was stiff and straight, anger in every fiber. He took hold of Robbie's arm. Robbie pried Davy's hand off his arm and stood by Tam. Davy and Tam started to argue, gesticulating and shouting, though their words were unintelligible to Effie; they were too far away. Tam took a swing at Davy.

Catriona rushed toward them yelling, "Tam. Davy. Dinna fight."

Effie followed, apprehensive for that lassie's safety and not thinking of her own. A few sailors stopped to watch Davy and Tam, who now fought in earnest. Catriona push past the sailors and hung onto Davy's arm. Startled, Davy turned to look at her, and Tam punched him on the side of his face. Catriona yelled at Tam but he put up his fists ready to do battle. Effie made her way through the gathering crowd. Davy pushed Catriona toward her.

"Take care of her, Effie," he said, panting, then fielded a punch from Tam.

"Catriona, you canna stop them brawling. You'll get hurt." Effie put her arms around Catriona to help her back to the inn, but Catriona stood her ground, trembling in fury. Onlookers pressed around them, and Effie couldn't drag Catriona through the wall of men who shouted encouragement to the two fighters.

Without warning, the crowd dispersed. But Davy and Tam were oblivious, punching and jabbing at each other. Davy managed to get in an uppercut on Tam's face. Tam staggered a little but put his head down and rushed toward Davy. They grappled together.

Effie, still clutching Catriona, spotted a group of men bearing cudgels and knives coming toward them. A little way off, a naval officer sat on a mooring bollard. Catriona screamed and struggled to get out of Effie's grip. Jamie and Alasdair appeared beside the two lassies and dragged them back to the inn.

KAREN M. EDWARDS

Chapter 10

"What's happening? Who are yon men?" Effie managed to say between gasping for breath. Alasdair brushed past her into the doorway and looked out at the mob. Effie was aghast to see them descend on Davy, Tam, Robbie and a few other men.

"A press gang." He turned to Catriona who was crying noisily. "Dinna greet so, lassie."

Jamie started to leave the inn to go back to the quay where Davy and Robbie were now fighting the gang. Effie caught his arm. "No. Jamie. No. They'll take you too."

"You think I canna fight cos of my leg." Jamie's response was almost a snarl. He pushed her away. She grasped him tight, and he dragged her out the door, cursing her.

Ahead of them, Effie could hardly see Davy and the others. There was a confusion of men with flailing arms. The shouts and the screams of seagulls added to the turmoil.

Then, through a break in the crowd, she saw a man pick up Robbie who writhed and tried to punch him. Davy appeared next to them and fought to free his brother, but a man cudgeled Davy hard and he fell, holding his head with his one free hand, the other in the firm grip of a burly man.

After a while, Robbie stopped fighting his captor and walked away with him, chatting vivaciously. He hadn't noticed Davy's fall.

"No. Robbie. No." Jamie shouted, then with a mutter to Effie. "He wants to see the ships. It's all he ever talks of."

"Let me get him, Jamie."

"No!" Jamie loosened himself from Effie's grip and limped rapidly toward the mêlée.

She glanced back at Catriona, who was weeping with abandon, clutching Alasdair's coat; she was in good hands. Effie sprinted after Jamie.

Several women dashed out from nearby cottages bearing brooms and iron frying pans—any weapon to protect their men. Some were able to get at least a couple of men away from the gang, the sailors getting the worst of the beatings from the furious women.

Effie reached Jamie, yelling, "What are you thinking? Go inside. They canna get you too." She pushed him toward a group of the women who had formed a ferocious protective barrier around the men vulnerable to attack.

Effie was dry-eyed, dry-mouthed, tears too deep to surface. She joined the women attacking the press gang though she had no weapon. If only she could get Davy free, he could help find Robbie.

She grabbed onto the man dragging Davy away, but the man's vicious shove sent her flying. She hit the ground hard. Effie picked herself up and grasped Davy, who seemed semiconscious, barely aware of his surroundings. The burly man momentarily loosened his hold on Davy and elbowed her in the face. If she hadn't turned away at the last minute, he'd have caught her full in the eye.

Blood spurted out of her nose and the pain was so bad she stumbled to her knees, tears flowing free from her tightly closed eyes. She couldn't get up for several minutes. The shouting had stopped and all she could hear were angry sobs which she guessed were Jamie's and the murmur of women's voices.

Firm hands helped Effie up.

"Are you alright, hen?" said a red-headed woman who looked tough enough to tackle a whole press gang on her own. "There'll be a few sore heads among those scunners." She held an iron frying pan loose in her hand.

"Here's a kerchief for your nose," said another woman. "Let me look at it." She touched Effie's nose with a gentle hand. Effie winced and let out a little moan.

"Well, it dinna seem broke, but you will have a nice shiner on your cheek," said the woman. "It's lucky he missed your eye. The scunner!" Then she yelled, "Mitchell!"

A young lad, who looked about twelve years old, appeared at Effie's side. "Here, Mitchell, take this lassie to the inn." Between them, they helped Effie stand on her feet, but she was dizzy, swaying and tilting to find her balance. Mitchell took a strong hold on her left elbow. When the world no longer whirled about her, Effie tried to focus blurry eyes to find Davy and the press gang. They were gone.

Where was Jamie? Was *he* at least safe? She could hear his wrathful voice, then her eyes cleared. Two burly fishwives dragged Jamie toward her, though he struggled and yelled and swore, tears running down his face. They let him go when they reached Effie and Mitchell, nodded to Effie, and ambled back to their cottages, laughing and chatting. They seemed to have enjoyed the battle.

"You should ha' let me help Davy and Robbie. They wouldna take a cripple like me." Jamie raged, spittle at the edges of his mouth.

"You dinna ken that," said Effie, her voice tart, though speaking hurt her face. In trying to protect him, she'd insulted his manhood. But she didn't care about that. All she could think about was that Davy was taken.

Effie and Jamie were almost at the inn when a clatter of hooves and a familiar voice telling someone to hold his horse's reins covered Jamie's angry breathing. An arm in dark blue wool with a white stripe and gold buttons at the cuff went around Effie, holding her up more firmly. She momentarily leaned into his chest comforted by the steady beating of his heart then, though it was painful to turn her head, she looked up at Calum Moncrithe's anxious face.

"Lieutenant Moncrithe—sir—go after them," said Effie, clutching his lapel. "You can stop them. They've taken Davy. Robbie and . . . Tam."

"Brownwell, go after the gang. See where they went," said the lieutenant. "I'll take care of this lady."

Lady? Her? She had blood on her face and her skirts were dirty from her fall. She'd been brawling with fishwives. If she could, she would have laughed.

"Sir, you know we cannot interfere with the press gang," the man replied in a deep English voice. "The navy needs new blood. Though why they tried at this quay I don't know. The women here have a reputation—tougher than Spanish bandidos to defend their men."

Moncrithe let out an oath under his breath then, his voice sharp, "Was this your detail, Brownwell?"

"No. Boyd's." Calum drew in his breath.

"Please, sir, go after them," said Effie turning her head and trying to focus her eyes on Brownwell.

"Yes. Go." Moncrithe rasped out the command.

"You're but the physician, you can't order me about."

"Aye. A physician, but a first lieutenant. I outrank you, Brownwell. This is an order: Go! Now!" The man muttered an expletive before the clatter of hooves signaled his departure.

Effie stumbled toward the inn, the lieutenant's arm secure around her. Winter touched her very core; it was as if her heart were carved in ice.

When they entered the dining room, Catriona was the center of attention. Alasdair was trying to soothe her. Professor Vandemark stood to the side holding a glass of whisky and looking aghast.

"I told you to stay in the inn." His voice grated in anger as he addressed Effie. He inclined his head to Moncrithe, then offered the whisky to Effie. "I would never have thought of you behaving this way. So little decorum. Here. Drink this."

She motioned it away. Aye. This wasn't like her at all. She'd always tried to keep out of trouble. But she *had* to try to save Davy, *had* to save Jamie. Though dizzy she turned to Jamie. "I'm sorry, Jamie. I couldna let you be taken too. Your mother—"

"That scunner Tam," said Jamie through gritted teeth. "It's all his fault. The glaikit—" He continued calling Tam several bad names, many Effie had never heard before. The angry voices and commotion were giving her a headache. She closed her eyes. It also helped not to see the professor's disapproving face. Would she be dismissed?

Jamie harangued Alasdair. "His lairdship is a sniveling coward hiding behind the lassies. The press gang should have taken him. Yellow-livered—"

Effie squinted at Alasdair who pulled at his neckcloth. "It wasna my fault. I didna want Tam to bring Robbie. And anyway, they wouldna take someone from the gentry." His upper-class accent slipped in his agitation.

Vandemark broke in. "That's true enough." He turned to Effie holding out the glass of whisky again. "My dear Euphemia, take this wee dram. It will make you feel better. Sit here. Careful now, Moncrithe."

Effie, lightheaded and disoriented, was grateful to sit, and thankful that the professor was being solicitous in spite of his anger at her behavior. She took a gulp of whisky, coughed, when the fiery drink went down her throat, and handed the glass back to Vandemark.

"Perhaps Catriona needs a wee dram too," said Effie.

"Huh, what she needs is a dousing," said Vandemark frowning at Catriona. He turned back to the lieutenant. "Moncrithe, you are used to wounds; what do you think on Euphemia's?"

Moncrithe knelt by Effie's chair and touched her nose and cheek, his fingers gentle and tentative. Effie could not meet his eyes for shame.

"She's going to have a bonny black eye for a few days. Thank God the blow missed her eye. Her nose isn't broken. How did this happen, Euphemia?"

"It was the press gang. They took away Davy and Robbie . . . and Tam." She gulped. "I tried to help Davy but the man hit me with his elbow." Moisture welled in her eyes.

"There now, have a good cry," said Vandemark. "But not like that lassie." Catriona's hysterics had risen in volume.

"Can you help Catriona, Lieutenant Moncrithe?" Effie put a hand on his arm. "She had such a shock. Davy is her man."

"I'll take care of her," said Vandemark. He picked up his cane and limped over to Catriona who was writhing in her chair, banging her fists on the table and her heels on the floor. People had come from the taproom to see what all the noise was about. Vandemark went up to Catriona, took a glass of water, and threw the contents into her face. She gasped and caught her breath, but stopped shrieking and merely sniveled.

Alasdair took a step forward. "I say, Professor, that was uncalled for."

"Och, 'twas a good thing. She stopped shrieking like a banshee," said Jamie who was white as a sheet. Vandemark, handed him a tot of whisky. He drained it in one swift gulp and turned to Catriona.

"Catriona, quit your greetin'. It'll no bring Davy back."

Alasdair had put a cautious hand on Catriona's shoulder, and as she recovered from her tantrum, recognized a sympathetic friend. She rose and threw her arms around his neck, sobbing into his stylish jacket. Alasdair taken aback, tried to pry her hands from his neck but she hung on tight. His eyes glazed over and his face looming over Catriona's red curly hair contorted between embarrassment and revulsion.

Effie, recovering from her faintness, started to giggle at the sight of his horrified face. Alasdair glared at her.

"Och, now we have one lassie greetin' and the other laughin'," said Jamie. "Effie, quit it. It's no funny."

"I ken," said Effie in a muffled voice. "I'm sorry. I canna help it." She put her hands to her face, being careful not to touch her wounded cheekbone, her shoulders shaking, trying to stop the laughter that kept trying to escape.

"It's the shock. She'll be fine in a few moments," said Moncrithe. "Miss Innes, drink this water." He held a glass to Effie's lips then looked up at Vandemark. "Perhaps the whisky made her a little inebriated."

"But she only had a little sip," said Vandemark. "Euphemia, drink the water like a good lassie."

"Mayhap you'd better throw it over me," gasped Effie between peals of laughter. "It worked for Catriona."

"Euphemia," said Vandemark in a stern, commanding voice. "Drink the water."

Effie couldn't hold the glass as her hands trembled so Moncrithe held it for her. After a couple of sips, the bubble of laughter died down and her shoulders stopped shaking. She drooped exhausted and embarrassed in her chair. Whatever had made her laugh like that? Perchance it was the whisky. More like it was the shock of seeing Davy and Robbie taken away. She stifled a moan.

"Our party has made enough of a spectacle," said Vandemark. "We will leave for Edinburgh now."

The lieutenant helped Effie from the chair. He dismissed the throng of men by the door to the tap room. "Be on your way, men. Grant, be so good as to escort Miss, er . . . that . . . young lady to the coach."

"I want to go home," wailed Catriona, clutching Alasdair's arm.

"I do too," said Effie. She wished to comfort Rhona Mackie. "We could go with Jamie."

"No, I think spending a few days in the city will take your mind off this calamity," said Vandemark.

Effie couldn't hide her doubt as she looked at him.

He added, "Mayhap we will be able to find out where they took your friends while we are in Edinburgh."

"Brownwell should have returned by now," said Moncrithe as he helped Effie into the coach. "Ah, there he is." He went over to talk to him. Their conversation was sharp, terse.

"Likely yon sailor stayed outside since he didna want to be part of the commotion," said Jamie. Catriona glowered at him.

"How will I get home?" said Alasdair. "I came with Tam and Robbie." He looked at the professor, now ensconced in the coach. "Mayhap I could escort you to Edinburgh, sir?"

"I have no need of another escort," said Vandemark, pursing his lips.

"Come with me," said Jamie, though he gave Alasdair a hard look. "I'll need a second hand with the boat."

Effie put a hand out the coach. Jamie took it. "Jamie, I grieve for your family. Lieutenant Moncrithe will do all he can to find out where Davy and Robbie are."

"To lose two brothers like this. How will Ma take the news?" He wiped his nose with the back of his sleeve. "I must away afore the wind changes. Grant, are you ready? Catriona, let go of his coat."

By the look on his face, Alasdair was relieved to hand Catriona into the coach. Without a goodbye to Effie or the professor, he strode after Jamie.

"Brownwell was not able to make contact with the press gang." Anger vibrated in Moncrithe's voice as he gripped the window of the coach. "I don't think he tried very hard. I'll see what I can find out myself." And then, under his breath: "I trust he will not be on my ship. Insubordinate Sassenach."

In the coach, Effie, Catriona, and Vandemark sat in silence. In his corner, Vandemark closed his eyes and fell asleep. Catriona, sitting next to Effie, was already dozing, no doubt worn out by her hysterics. Effie looked out the window as the coach wound its way through the narrow cobble streets of South Queensferry. She caught a glimpse of Lieutenant Moncrithe and Lieutenant Brownwell riding a little ahead. By the time they reached the last house of the village, although her cheek throbbed, she became drowsy from the swaying of the coach. But an image seared in her mind: those vicious men dragging Davy and others away to an unknown fate.

Chapter 11

Effie couldn't recall much except the beginning of the coach ride out of South Queensferry. Her arrival at the Lord Glasbeinn's house was hazy.

Two days had passed since Davy and the others had been impressed. Effie stayed in her room, nursing her sore bruised cheek; she didn't want people to see her in this condition. It still hurt, and when she put her hand there, she remembered the feel of the man's elbow crunching into her bone. Thank goodness instinct had made her flinch away at the last second.

Although the bedchamber she shared with Catriona was comfortable and lovely with a green-curtained four poster bed and a paler green brocade coverlet with lavender-scented white sheets, Effie fretted at being confined. She had occupied herself with copying out Vandemark's much crossed-out letter, but she worried that there was yet no news of Davy. Professor Vandemark sent short notes, urging her to leave her bedchamber and join him in the library

Lieutenant Moncrithe visited Effie a few times outside her bedchamber to check on her bruise. Catriona was a reluctant chaperone and tried to flirt with him. But he ignored her, concentrating on Effie, asking if she were in pain though he didn't think she needed laudanum. Effie didn't think it necessary for him to attend her so frequently, but she looked forward to his visits and every time he stood close, she became a little breathless.

Catriona was not good company. She was either in high spirits with tales of her meeting of the staff or weepy over losing Davy.

This morning Effie was determined to go outside. She drew back the curtains and opened a window, poking her head out to look along the street at the length of greyish-brown town houses joined to Lord Glasbeinn's house. Each house had an entrance with a few shallow steps to the front door and black wrought-iron fences guarding the entrance to a basement where the staff entered the houses. Across the street was a square of green grass with a sprinkling of daisies beginning to open their white petals to show their yellow centers in the morning sun. Dew trapped in the flowers' centers sparkled and glinted in the brightness. Young trees in their fresh green spring leaves, lined the square. Through them, Effie glimpsed a street with its newly-built row of terraced houses similar to the street where Lord Glasbeinn's house stood. Above the plume of smoke from hundreds of chimneys, the castle on its high crag stood stark and grey against the blue sky.

Effie closed the window. The air was not as fresh as in Pittenweem but it was too nice a day to be stuck inside. If she went out early, perhaps she'd miss seeing the gentry and even servants. She should probably have Catriona accompany her.

She shook Catriona, who grunted and turned over, but didn't wake up. Effie resolved to go out on her own even if she merely went across the street and picked daisies.

As servants milled about downstairs between the kitchen and the dining room, Effie used the front door to avoid them. She crept downstairs in her new leather ankle boots hoping the sound of their squeaking wasn't too loud. Tiptoeing over the intricately patterned parquet floor in the hallway, she reached the tall front door and pulled open the bolts. The hinges were well oiled and the door swung open with hardly a sound. Effie looked back to see if anyone was around and stepped out onto the doorstep, closing the door behind her.

Though it was sunny, a stiff breeze blew chill, and Effie was glad she'd brought her bonnet and shawl. Across the square was an unfinished building with several men hefting large greyish-brown stones and placing them on top of each other; they were building the wall of another row of townhouses.

She walked a few paces along the street until she came to the corner where another house-lined street met the square. Down that street, two men holding tight to their top hats and leaning into the wind, walked with the unsteady gait of the drunk. Several steps behind them a lone man walked in a more measured manner. Effie didn't wish to meet them.

She turned to head back to the house, but a sudden gust of wind caught her red paisley shawl, blowing it over her face. As she struggled, the ties on her bonnet came loose. Now in control of her shawl, she lost hold of her bonnet, which swooped and bowled along the cobblestones toward the three men. The tall buildings lining the street acted like a conduit for the wind; she galloped after her hat.

The bonnet went past the two gentlemen and came to a stop when the lone gentleman skewered the hat with his cane. Effie rushed past the two drunks. She was so focused on the bonnet she didn't pay attention to the gentleman except to notice his highly-polished black boots. As she bent to retrieve her bonnet, the man bent down too. Their heads bumped a little and their hands met as they grabbed onto the bonnet. Both Effie and the gentleman straightened up, their hands clutching the bonnet.

"Madam," said the gentleman, "I believe this is yours." He relinquished his hold.

"Well . . . aye," said Effie though she'd have liked to retort: Well, whose else do you think it is?

He was a handsome man with a small scar on his left cheek. His dark eyes looked down at her; he lifted a well-formed eyebrow in a supercilious manner as he studied her.

"Thank you for rescuing my bonnet," she said as she turned to leave.

"A pleasure, my dear. Would you like me to help you tie it on? I have much practice," he said with a sardonic smile.

"No thank you, sir. I can manage." She crammed the bonnet on her head and tied the ribbons in a firm bow. She didn't look at the gentleman. She was uncomfortable in his presence but felt compelled to be courteous to him. He was gentry, after all.

"Thank you again, sir," Effie said, bobbing a curtsy, and raising her eyes to his face. She gave a small smile.

He gazed down at her for a moment, his expression inscrutable, then, with his hand in its tan-leather glove, swept aside a lock of her hair hanging across her cheek, and tucked it into her bonnet. It revealed the bruise on her cheek, and she quickly put her hand up to cover it.

"May I escort you to your home, madam?" he said, offering her his arm. "A beautiful lassie should not be out by herself."

"No, sir, I can find my way," said Effie backing away from him. She wondered why a gentleman should be so courteous to someone like her. It was obvious she was not a lady. She turned to go back to the house but he caught her arm and pulled her close to him. He smelled of brandy, snuff, and a flowery cologne.

"Please, sir, let me go," said Effie, her voice muffled as she was pressed against his gold brocade waistcoat. She turned her head up to look at him and he smiled, but it wasn't a pleasant smile. His eyes shone like black onyx. A frisson of fear ran through her. She tried to push herself away, but he held her tighter. Effie let out a sob.

"Miss Innes." With relief, Effie recognized Calum Moncrithe's voice. As he came closer, he said in measured tones, "Unhand her, Thorburn. It's a bit early for dalliance, even for you."

Thorburn did not immediately let Effie go but spoke in a drawling voice. "Ah, Moncrithe. Is this your paramour?"

He let go of Effie so abruptly she stumbled. Moncrithe's hand steadied her; he kept it on her elbow. Effie shivered with fright but was calmer now the lieutenant was there. She glanced up at him. His face was impassive and stiff, his stare menacing as he looked at Thorburn. Though he had on his olive coat, his cravat was loosely tied as though he'd been in a hurry.

"Well, as you say, it's too early for dalliance," said Thorburn, looking down and brushing his waistcoat. Putting on his top hat, he continued. "And it's certainly too early and exhausting to brangle with you over a passingly pretty wench." He glanced at Effie, who flushed. She moved a fraction closer to Moncrithe.

As Thorburn moved away, he said over his shoulder. "But Moncrithe, a word of advice: if you must beat your woman at least don't do it on the face for all to see."

Effie gasped.

Moncrithe stiffened, his face taut, his eyes unfathomable pools. A reflex tightened his grip on Effie's elbow. His other hand formed a fist, and he breathed heavily. Effie admired his control as they watched Thorburn saunter away, swinging his cane.

"What a wicked insult. I ken you'd never beat your—any woman," Effie said in a shaking voice.

Moncrithe looked down at her, a slight smile on his still-pinched, white face. "That was kindly said, Miss Innes. Let me return you to Lord Glasbeinn's house."

He offered his arm to Effie; heat built up in her cheeks. She cast down her eyes, and with a little hesitation, tucked her cold hand into the crook of his elbow. She could not look him in the face; it was her fault he'd been insulted.

Calum pointed out landmarks of the town up above them: The North Bridge linking the old town to the new over Nor Loch; and the crown-like steeple of St. Giles Cathedral. He related the tale of Jenny Geddes who had hurled her stool at the minister for trying to introduce the English-style prayer book. Effie imagined hurling a chair at Niall Douglas; she wished she had the gumption. The neutral conversation about the town helped Effie be more composed.

Effie said shyly, "I ken now it was wrong of me to leave the house alone. I needed to get outside. But the air's no fresh like in Pittenweem."

"Hmm, no. There's quite a stench from the Nor Loch when the wind's in the right direction. They're draining it so the air will become fresher but for the smoke from the chimneys. It's no wonder Edinburgh is called Auld Reekie."

"I didna ken that," said Effie with a little laugh, her shyness dissipating. "You'd think with the strong breezes in this city, it wouldna stink so much. The wind took my bonnet just when I was turning to the house. I'm so ashamed to run after it like a . . . like a common scullion. How did you find me so quickly?"

"My bedchamber looks over the street. I saw you dart off after your bonnet."

He'd seen that? Her flush could have warmed them both.

"A lassie shouldn't walk alone in a strange city. What misfortune to run into Lord Thorburn of all people."

"He's a lord? He dinna act like one. What a hateful man to insult you like that." She put a hand out to touch the bruise. "I shouldna be out looking like this."

"Does it still pain you?" said Calum. "It's looking better—all the colors of the rainbow now—a sign of healing."

"It hurts a little. I just wanted to see a little of Edinburgh afore we return to Pittenweem," said Effie.

"You have the makings of a fine explorer," said Calum, looking down at her with a smile. "Vandemark needs to visit Baron de Grâce today. I'd be honored to take you to see something of the town with your chaperone, of course."

Chaperone? Catriona had not taken kindly to her new role, but spending more time with the lieutenant was tempting.

Effie lowered her eyes. What she saw in Calum's eyes confused her. She didn't know how to flirt, but being with him . . .

"I'd like to see the cathedral and the castle. How braw and strong it looks," said Effie, squinting at the stone edifice wreathed in hazy smoke.

"It's quite a walk. I do not have access to a carriage."

"Catriona and I are used to walking up and down the wynds of Pittenweem," said Effie.

"Yes, you'll probably walk to the castle better than I. But we can't go too close. There are French and American prisoners of war in the vaults."

"Oh. Do they ever escape? Mayhap I'll meet a French prisoner. What would I say if I met one?" said Effie, her voice nervous.

"Late morning, prisoners are allowed to sell the crafts they make to supplement their rations. But it would be too sorry a sight for a lassie. I'd not take you there," said Calum. "The poor wretches." Then almost to himself: "I don't know which is worse, being in the middle of the war with the chance of being blown to pieces or lingering in prison."

Blown to pieces? *No! Not Davy! Not Lieutenant Moncrithe!*

Bands of fear tightened around her chest and she stumbled.

"I beg your pardon, Miss Innes. That was not meant for your ears." He rubbed her frigid hand. "Take a deep breath. Ah, that's better. Color is coming back into your face."

"Are you not afeared?" Effie's hand spasmed, tightening her grip on the lieutenant's arm.

"I'm too busy taking care of the wounded. I rarely think on it."

"War is cruel. Men come home so hurt and scarred. I mind it would be better to be in prison than be killed or maimed. It must be a comfort to their families to ken they're safe."

He and Davy were targets for a cannon ball, bullet, or sword. What if they had to climb up those tall masts and fell off? What if they were swept overboard? What if—Effie couldn't catalogue any more disasters.

"That may be so, but prison life is miserable," said Moncrithe, his voice going quiet. "At least onboard ship there's something to keep you occupied." He paused for a moment, a faraway look in his eyes. "I received orders I am to report for duty to British North America— Canada— and will join my ship in a few days."

"Oh. I . . . I hadna thought." Dismay, chagrin rushed in. "I will— the professor will miss you."

Perhaps he was accustomed to spending a little time on shore and then off to adventures on a ship. He'd been with the navy for the past five years and had seen combat in Spain. Now she'd made his acquaintance, even though it was only a few days, he held a place in her heart.

The lieutenant gazed at the craggy heights of Arthur's Seat so she could not read the expression in his face, but his arm made a slight pressure on her hand still tucked into the crook of his elbow.

"If you did meet a Frenchman—you'd say '*bonjour.*' It means good day." The change of subject was sudden, but Effie understood he wished to keep to neutral topics far from the talk of war. She went along with his wishes.

"*Bon jooer. Bon jooer.* Did I say it right? What other French words do you ken?" asked Effie.

By the time they reached the house, Effie had learned five French words. But her linguistic triumph was short lived. Vandemark scolded her for going out on her own in a strange city. Later that day, Catriona badgered Effie to know more about the bold stranger; she'd learned from kitchen gossip. Effie shook her head. She didn't want to talk about her disgraceful behavior, however innocent it was, and even less about that sinister rake.

Chapter 12

Effie and the lieutenant, accompanied by Catriona as chaperone, visited the castle and St. Giles Cathedral. But the highlight for Effie was wandering around the Physic Garden which was east of the newly built North Bridge. If she and Moncrithe had been alone, they could have discussed the various plants on display, but Catriona hampered them. She was by turns bored and flirtatious, complaining loudly or hanging on the lieutenant's arm and batting her eyelashes at him. He was courteous and managed to escape from her clutches, talking mainly about the plants to Effie and ignoring Catriona's flattering speech.

Effie couldn't meet his eye; she was so embarrassed by Catriona's behavior. She concentrated on the plants. When Moncrithe's eyes did meet hers, Effie imagined they were alone together for those brief seconds, sharing bonds of friendship. He seemed mostly tolerant of Catriona's antics; he was such a gentleman. No doubt he was used to women admiring and pursuing him. Catriona—and Effie—had no chance, compared with the beautiful and accomplished women from his class. A little depression clouded Effie's enjoyment of the outing. She had to stop thinking of him in that way.

When they returned from their wanderings, they found the house in commotion. Lady Glasbeinn was giving a dinner party for a large gathering that evening.

After Moncrithe went to his room to change, Effie offered to help, but the housekeeper, Mrs. McLeod, told her she'd be in the way and to go to her bedchamber or perhaps find the professor in the library.

"You can come down for supper with the rest of the staff after dinner is served," she said. "Catriona has met the staff, but they look forward to meeting you, Miss Innes."

"She's called Effie," said Catriona.

"She's Miss Innes to us." Mrs. McLeod frowned at Catriona. "The same as Miss Craig, the governess. You ken her well and can call her Effie, but in this household, she'll be Miss Innes."

Catriona flounced up the stairs. Effie followed more slowly, pondering how the tables were turned on Catriona; the staff treated her as a kitchen servant while regarding Effie in a more elevated sphere.

"Well, that outing wasna so good. I wished to see the shops, not traipse around a lot of old buildings and weedy gardens," said Catriona as she changed her dress. "That Lieutenant Moncrithe is a braw man but unco stiff and proper. Yon gentleman could do with a bit o' fun."

Effie had not found him so. She wondered if she'd see him this evening, but doubted he'd come downstairs to the realm of the household staff. And she certainly couldn't go above stairs unless the professor invited her. No doubt the lieutenant would spend the time dancing with the young ladies at the party. She shook her head as though to shake that idea out of her head.

Catriona sat on the boudoir chair next to Effie. Side by side, Catriona's bright hair glowed in the light from the window, eclipsing her lint-white locks. Effie tidied the bun at her neck while Catriona twirled ringlets around her fingers and poked small flowers into her coiffure.

"What will you do when your grandma is no more?" said Catriona. "You could work at Pitcorbie farm or another farm. There'd be no need to stay in Pittenweem."

Effie stared at her reflection. Her first uncharitable thought: living alone in the cottage would be a relief. The second, Catriona was daft. Why would working on a farm after working for the professor be better? But the professor was getting on in years and that scared her. If she studied hard like the professor wanted, she could become a governess, or—it seemed to be the professor's ambition—set up as a school teacher. That would mean leaving Pittenweem, leaving Dr.

Ferguson and the Mackies and Davy when he came home. That would please Catriona no end. Perhaps it would be a good thing to make a fresh start in a new place that didn't know her background. Her pulse fluttered. It would also mean she'd no longer see Moncrithe. He only came to Pittenweem to visit Vandemark.

"Keep working for the professor, of course," said Effie, proud her voice was even, not revealing her worry.

"It's time to go. I ken a quick way to the kitchen," said Catriona.

She led the way across a landing that overlooked the foyer below. A footman greeted a man in a dark green coat, a woman in a blue embroidered dress with a white gauze overdress, and a man still in his cloak. As the man passed his cloak to the footman, he looked up. Effie drew back into the shadows but Catriona was in her way, gazing down in admiration at the guests. The new arrival was Thorburn. He recognized Effie and blew her a kiss. Effie pushed past Catriona and took her arm to drag her away from the staircase.

"Was that him? The bold stranger?" said Catriona. "He's a bonny man and full of cheek to blow you a kiss."

"I dinna want to talk about him. Is the kitchen this way?" Effie walked away from the landing so fast she stumbled, arriving at the kitchen breathless and flustered.

The household staff were mostly friendly and welcoming. Mrs. McLeod invited Effie to sit next to Duncan Niven and Miss Craig. Effie supposed she was on par with the tutor and governess. Miss Craig gave her a frosty smile. Duncan, a sandy-haired chiseled-faced man, smiled and winked at her. Catriona joined a group of servants and was soon chatting and laughing with them.

Duncan plied Effie with questions about the professor and his connections to the elite in Edinburgh. He was interested in politics and talked disparagingly about his duties as a tutor. He expressed surprise Effie was a scriever and boasted about *his* handwriting hinting that his would be superior to hers, a mere lassie. Effie gathered he envied her and thought he'd be a person of some importance in a village instead of a nonentity in Edinburgh.

When there was a lull in the upstairs service, Grizel and Ailsa served the staff at a long table. Effie fought down the urge to help. It didn't seem to bother Catriona who ordered Ailsa around. Effie was particularly interested in meeting Mairi who was from the Highlands. She was tall and blond and no one made jokes or thought her height and coloring unusual. Only in Pittenweem and the small villages did Effie's appearance stand out and add to her disreputable status.

The staff ate a portion of the same food as the guests upstairs. Effie marveled at the more elaborate food: raised pies of pigeon and pork, molded creams, sweetmeats of honeyed apricots and pears, tablet, marzipan, and dark bonbons made of an essence called chocolate.

When the meal was over, the staff sat down to listen to a few songs sung by the second footman, George, who had a pleasant tenor voice. He sang four old ballads and a few from the poet, Robert Burns. Effie especially liked, "My Love is Like a Red, Red Rose."

In one of the pauses between the singing, Ailsa asked Effie about the bruise on her cheek. Effie told her about trying to get Davy away from the press gang. The rest of the staff stopped chatting to listen too.

"You're so brave," said Ailsa. "I couldna ha' done it."

Unaccustomed to admiration and attention, Effie squirmed and tried to protest.

"Davy is *my* man." Catriona's voice was sharp, brittle with anger. "I'd have helped him too. Alasdair and Jamie kept me by the inn. Effie ran past them before they could stop her. There were a lot of other women too. She wasna so brave."

Fat tear drops rolled down Catriona's face. "I miss Davy so." Catriona's voice came out in a wail. "We were to be handfasted next week."

This was news to Effie. Did Catriona's parents approve of that? If it were a handfasting and not a church wedding she doubted they knew.

"I ken a lament I'd like to sing for Davy," said Catriona. In a trembling voice, she began to sing, "Black is the color of my true love's hair," but she faltered before she reached the end of the first line.

"Effie, you sing it with me," said Catriona.

Effie flushed.

Joy to My Love

"He canna mean as much to you as to me so you can sing it through. We should pay homage to him, us lassies from Pittenweem." Catriona's eyes glittered with unshed tears.

Everyone looked at Effie, who tried to school her dismay. How could she sing this lament when she too was fearful for Davy? Effie guessed part of Catriona's behavior was histrionics, but she pitied her. It was best to pacify her and show that backward villagers could sing as well as these townsfolk. Catriona was capable of making an ugly scene if she didn't sing with her. Effie rose and stood by Catriona.

Catriona held tight to Effie's hand. Was it for Catriona's comfort or so she couldn't escape? Their voices broke into song. Effie sang softly in her clear soprano though Catriona's contralto somewhat drowned her voice.

But black is the color of my true love's hair.
 His face is like some rosy fair,
The bonniest face and the neatest hands,
I love the ground whereon he stands.

As Effie sang, she envisioned Davy: the sun shining on his curly black hair with the one rebellious curl that caressed his forehead, his bright blue eyes which always held laughter, and his strong capable brown hands pulling tight the rope to fasten the boat. Her voice got louder.

I love my love and well he knows,
I love the ground whereon he goes . . .

Effie's voice wavered. Catriona stopped singing but the grip on her hand and the quiet hiss in Effie's ear, "Keep going," bound her to continue. But after a while she was singing for herself and for Davy.

If you no more on earth I see,
My life will quickly fade away.

111

She'd gladly accept his being with Catriona if he'd only return unharmed.

I go to the Clyde for to mourn and weep,
But satisfied I never could sleep.
I'll write to you a few short lines,
I'll suffer death ten thousand times.

Davy could be on a ship at Greenock on the River Clyde even now. Tears welled, but she felt compelled to finish. The words of the song expressed the years of loneliness and unrequited love.

Effie kept her eyes closed as she sang and her voice did not weaken until she sang the last line, her voice falling to a whisper. The room was quiet except for a few sobs from Catriona and one of the maids.

By the end of the song, Effie was parched and it was as if the lump in her throat threatened to stop her breath. She picked up her cup from the table and took a sip of water. As she drank, she looked toward the doorway. Moncrithe stood there, and behind him, Thorburn.

Both men stared at her for a minute until Thorburn's loud drawling voice broke the silence.

"It's too bad you're a redhead, Moncrithe. She prefers a black-headed rogue like me."

The lieutenant's mouth tightened and his eyes hardened. Effie's whole body burned in embarrassment. She turned her head away.

The staff stood up with much shuffling and scraping of chairs now they were in the presence of gentry. Effie glanced at Catriona, who'd stopped the hard grip on her arm and simpered at the two gentlemen.

Mrs. McLeod went over to them. "My Lord." A small recline of her head. "Lieutenant. What can we do for you? The butler can see to your needs. There was no need to descend to the kitchen." Her tone was frosty.

Thorburn stepped past the lieutenant and picked up a bottle of brandy from the sideboard. "Moncrithe, let us repair to the library and sample this bottle."

He took Moncrithe's arm, but the lieutenant shook it off. With a shrug, Thorburn left the kitchen, but not before his eyes met Effie's. His smile was cruel.

Mrs. McLeod asked again, "Sir. What can we do for you?"

The lieutenant inclined his head. "I'm sorry to disturb you. I came with a message for Miss Innes and to check on her welfare."

He addressed Effie who was ready to sink into the floor.

"I came to tell you the professor will not need your services this evening." He was about to leave but glanced back at Effie, his brow furrowed. "I trust, Miss Innes, you do not overexert yourself. Good evening."

Effie put a hand to her bruise. Moncrithe was a blur through her tear-filled eyes. She wondered why he had delivered the message himself and not through a servant. Perhaps he was indeed checking on her as a patient. It would be a good excuse for her to leave the party. Fatigue, heavy as a wet wool blanket, fell over her. She wished Moncrithe and Thorburn had not been witnesses to her song for Davy.

Mrs. McLeod came over to Effie. "That was grand, Miss Innes. You have a fine singing voice. I'm grieved your man was taken away." Effie tried to interrupt and say Davy was not her man, but the housekeeper continued, "Aisla's brother was taken a year ago, though she has letters from him from Spain so we ken what is going on. We're all fearful for our men in time of war. When will we beat yon Frenchie?"

The housekeeper looked around at the company. "I think we need cheering up. George, get out your fiddle and we'll have dancing. Push back the table, Angus. Hamish. You too Mr. Niven."

Effie made her way to the door, trying to slip away, but Mairi pulled her back. "Let's see if you can dance as well as you sing, Miss Innes."

Effie glanced at her wondering if she was being ironic, but her tone was friendly and so was her guileless smile. Effie allowed herself to be led to a chair next to Catriona.

George played a few notes of "The Duke of Gordon's Rant," the lively tune lifting the mood of the room.

Catriona sniffed into her kerchief, but her eyes were hard with anger. She whispered in Effie's ear, "You sang *my* song as though Davy was your man, not mine. I wouldna have asked you to sing if I kent you were going to make a fool of yourself."

Effie was tired of this silly rivalry and embarrassed by the admiration she was receiving from the staff. Before Effie could reply, Duncan was at her side.

"Would you care to dance, Miss Innes?" he said holding out his hand.

Effie didn't take the proffered hand. "I dinna ken how to dance, Mr. Niven, but Catriona is a fine dancer," said Effie smiling. Out the corner of her eye she caught fury on Catriona's face and a stony glare from Miss Craig. Catriona's face turned to smiles when Hamish, a footman, asked her to make up the set for the reel. When they joined the other three couples, Catriona glowed, sending a saucy and triumphant look at Effie. Though accustomed to Catriona's quicksilver moods Effie was dismayed to see how quickly she'd recovered from her sadness for Davy.

"The set is now complete and no room for another so I'll sit here with you. We can dance the next reel," said Duncan. Effie didn't like the way he sat so close. "You say you dinna ken how to dance I canna believe the lads in Pittenweem were not fighting for your hand to dance a reel or a jig."

Blood rose to Effie's face and she looked down for a second, shaking her head. "I'll watch for now."

Effie was glad to see that Catriona was over her sulks. Her expression showed how much she liked twirling around and weaving in and out of the dance formations. Miss Craig had not been so lucky to find a partner and she stared balefully at Effie and Duncan who clapped their hands and tapped toes with the rest of the onlookers.

People here did not know her background; they were taking her at face value and appeared to like her. It was strange to have an admirer in Duncan, who treated her as an equal to Miss Craig. Effie sighed. This was another complication: she'd offended Miss Craig, who seemed to claim Duncan as her property.

Effie had not had a chance to dance in the village but she'd watched the dancers and practiced the pas de Basque steps. When the reel was over, Duncan pulled Effie to her feet and held her hand as they waited for the kitchen staff to make up a set.

"Mr. Niven."

"Call me Duncan. May I call you Effie?"

"Mr. . . . er . . . Duncan, you'll need to tell me which way to turn," whispered Effie.

Ailsa leaned over and whispered, "I'll help you too."

The reel began; Duncan and Ailsa pushed and pulled Effie through the dance formations. One time, Effie turned the wrong way and came face to face with Hamish instead of Duncan, but he turned her around to face the right way. Though she became flustered and embarrassed and everyone laughed at her confusion, she did not feel inferior or stupid. It was friendly laughter. Effie made her way to Catriona whose face was sullen. She sat by Miss Craig. Effie thought they made a fine pair, matching scowl for scowl.

"Will you come for another dance, Effie?" said Duncan, taking her hand. The fiddler played the first few bars of a slow strathspey, "Hey Tutti Tattie."

"No, the strathspey is such a grand dance, I dinna want to spoil the formation by going the wrong way. Besides my face is beginning to ache." She'd ignored Moncrithe's admonition not to exert herself. Effie pulled her hand away from his grip."

Duncan tried to persuade her, but Effie shook her head and walked over to Catriona, Miss Craig, and Mrs. McLeod. Duncan accompanied her and after teasing Mrs. McLeod about not dancing, he asked Catriona to dance. Miss Craig looked daggers at Effie as though it were her fault. Catriona's eyes sparkled and she chatted in a vivacious manner to Mairi and Hamish who made up the longways set. Effie attempted to make conversation with Miss Craig and was met with flinty silence. Miss Craig didn't even deign to turn toward Effie but kept her face turned sideways.

The dance had hardly finished when the first footman, Angus, appeared at the kitchen door.

"I've been ringing the bell these past ten minutes. You couldna hear with all the racket," he said with a glower. "Mr. Brown isna pleased you're down here enjoying yourselves while we've been on duty. Hamish and George, get upstairs now. The guests will be wanting more refreshments in the card room. It's almost eleven."

The footmen put on their dark-green livery jackets, slicked down their hair with a bit of water, and hurried up the stairs. The female servants moved back the kitchen table and chairs.

When Effie went to help, Mrs. McLeod said, "Be off to your room, Miss Innes. It'll be naught be washing dishes for us. You can stay and help, Catriona."

"I need to show Effie the way and help her with her sore face," said Catriona, taking Effie's elbow.

Mrs. McLeod compressed her lips then turned to the scullery maids who were already elbow-deep in suds.

As Effie climbed the stairs, she went over the events of the day: taking that foolhardy early morning walk, meeting Lord Thorburn, being rescued by Calum Moncrithe, visiting the castle and the cathedral, and learning how to dance.

But the most vivid memory was the lieutenant's unreadable expression after she'd sung the lament for Davy.

Chapter 13

Effie stood at the doorway of the kitchen to let the footmen by who carried breakfast dishes to the dining room. Smiling, she greeted the kitchen staff who bustled about cooking various dishes.

"Sit you here, Miss Innes." Mrs. Gilchrist, the cook, indicated the seat next to Miss Craig, who turned slightly away from Effie and gave her no greeting. Ailsa served Effie a bowl of steaming oatmeal. Effie smiled her thanks and began to eat.

Angus entered the kitchen with extra knives and forks from setting the upstairs dining room table. He addressed Effie. "The professor asks that you attend him in the library after breakfast."

Duncan wandered in and sidled over to Effie, but Mairi wouldn't move from Effie's side. Catriona arrived and sat next to Duncan who commenced to tease her.

"Why did you no wake me, Effie?" Catriona's gaze swept over the table with its bowls of porridge, a flagon of milk, and eggs and ham. "I mind to help with the breakfast."

"Well now," said Mrs. Gilchrist, a glint in her eye. "It's a good day when the . . ." She was obviously trying to give Effie a title but gave up. "When Miss Innes comes along afore her maid."

"I'm not her maid." said Catriona in a loud, penetrating voice. "If you kent who she really is, you wouldna be so friendly with her."

The staff stopped what they were doing and turned to look at Effie. She caught a glimpse of Duncan narrowing his eyes before she lowered her gaze. She tried to eat a mouthful of porridge though her throat constricted and her hand trembled.

"Miss Innes, are you the professor's paramour?" Ailsa blurted out.

"Ailsa!" the staff said in unison.

"No! The very idea!" said Effie, looking up quickly.

Catriona smirked. Effie suspected this artless remark would give Catriona another weapon to belittle her when she got back to Pittenweem.

"Ha. No but she's—"

"We dinna want to hear it, Catriona." Mrs. McLeod's gimlet eye turned on Catriona who shrugged.

"I'm his secretary, his scriever," said Effie. "I read books to him and write his letters. His hands hurt—"

"You dinna have to explain yourself to us, Miss Innes," said Mrs. McLeod. "I've known the professor many a long year and Jonet, his housekeeper, too. If she's accepted you then, it's fine with me. I'm used to the professor's quirks and foibles. If he wishes to hire a female secretary, so be it. Ailsa, your tongue is quicker than your wits. Apologize to Miss Innes."

Effie had to lower her eyes, which had become misty with gratitude from this unexpected support.

Ailsa put a timid hand onto Effie's arm. "I'm sorry Miss Innes. That came out wrong. I think you a braw lassie."

Effie avoided Duncan's eye, though she was aware he was concentrating on her while listening to Catriona whispering in his ear. He and Miss Craig eventually left to teach their charges.

"Catriona, come help with the dishes," said Mrs. Gilchrist. "Ailsa give her a towel."

"And get one for Effie too," said Catriona.

Effie was quite willing to help, but Mrs. Gilchrist frowned; the strict hierarchy of below-stairs had to be kept.

"Miss Innes is a scriever, and her duty is to the professor." She looked at Effie. "Here's Angus to show you the way to the library."

Angus led Effie through the foyer and along a hallway lined with portraits and small ornate occasional tables with urns of white flowers making a striking contrast against the butter yellow walls. A couple of round medallion paintings surrounded by golden scrolls adorned the pale-yellow ceiling. Effie walked slowly along the hallway, craning her neck to look at the ceiling when Angus touched her arm to get her attention. Dragging her gaze away from the marvels of rococo design, she stopped and looked at his pale freckled face and steady brown eyes.

"Miss Innes, if it's not too forward," said Angus, then he paused for a moment. "I want to say Mairi and I think you grand. Just be careful of Duncan."

So her instincts about Duncan were right; he was not to be trusted. Even more reason to avoid him.

Angus turned the handle of a tall paneled door before Effie could reply. He stepped aside to let her enter the room. It was like the professor's room in Pittenweem only more spacious with a second storey of bookshelves reached by an elaborately-carved wooden staircase.

"Oh," said Effie, gazing around the room, vaguely aware of Professor Vandemark sitting in a red brocade chair, but with a heightened awareness of Calum Moncrithe standing by the white marble fireplace. Her eyes traveled over the rows and rows of books in their leather bindings. Some looked worn and shabby. They must be much loved. She longed to go over and read a few titles, perhaps with the lieutenant explaining things to her. She sent him a swift glance.

"Euphemia!"

She turned her attention to the professor.

"I think you are drunk with book gazing. Come. Sit here, my dear." He pointed to a gold-painted chair with a crimson velvet on the seat, back and arms. As she went across the room to sit beside the professor, she glanced at Moncrithe who was staring at the logs in the unlit fireplace. It was the first time she'd seen him since the previous evening when he'd witnessed her singing for Davy.

As though he sensed her gaze, he looked up and gave her a small smile.

"What's the matter?" Effie reached the chair, her gaze going back and forth between the two men. "You look so gloomy." She caught her breath, "It's bad news!"

"You tell her," said Vandemark, not meeting her eyes but tamping down tobacco into his pipe and taking out a spill to light it.

"Miss Innes, I'm afraid it is bad news," said the lieutenant as he walked towards her. "Davy and the others were taken on board ship in Greenock. The ship sailed last night for British North America. They are now in the employ of His Majesty's Navy. We can't get them back now."

Effie fixed her eyes on Moncrithe's face, but she wasn't really seeing him. She was only conscious of the pungent smell of burning tobacco as Vandemark lit his pipe and her hands gripping the velvet arms of the chair. She let out a gasp and took a deep breath. She released her grip on the chair's arms and turned her attention to smoothing out the fabric where her grip had made dark imprints on the soft nap of the velvet.

Effie looked up at Vandemark briefly. Through parched lips, she said, "Shall I fetch Catriona? She needs to learn of this news. Davy is her man."

"No," said Vandemark. "We thought it best to tell you first and you would know the best way to . . . to convey the news."

Isna that like a man! He cannot confront a woman and her tears. But she couldn't blame him; Catriona would go into hysterics. She blenched at the thought. It would it be better to confront her in their room and not bring her to the library or in front of the staff. Effie sighed. They'd set her a hard task.

"Miss Innes." Moncrithe took a couple of steps closer. "May I check to see how the bruise is faring?"

Effie turned her head so he could see the bruise, but her hands still smoothed the nap on the velvet.

His touch was gentle. Was it her imagination that it felt more like a caress than a clinical examination and that she was comforted? His hand dropped to his side. Effie studied his face; his eyes held compassion, kindness. What a fine doctor he was; the navy was lucky to have him.

"It's progressing well. Swelling has gone down." He cleared his throat. "I will do my best to find your friends. I too am called to board ship this evening."

He's leaving too? She had known that, but a pulse leapt in her throat. What was he saying? His voice came from a distance.

120

"I don't know how much authority I have, but perhaps I can arrange for them to join my ship when I get to Halifax."

"You're unco kind, sir," she said with a tremulous voice. That was all she could say, however inadequate it sounded.

His clear hazel eyes held concern and a frown furrowed his brow.

"I must go to Catriona the now," she said rising from the chair.

The lieutenant helped her to her feet.

She swayed a little, light-headed from holding her breath.

He put an arm around her to support her.

This had not been the first time he'd succored her in the past two days. He must think her a weak and frail woman. But there was more than comfort in his touch, more than safety in his arms—a response she dared not name.

"Do you have to leave so soon?" The anguished whisper could not be stopped. She glanced swiftly to his face. A flare of light shone in his eyes.

Had she said—revealed—too much for decorum?

"I'm fine, sir," she said in a louder voice. Effie pulled away from his support. *Hold me. Hold me. Dinna go!* ran through her mind. She must be daft to think such things. And it didn't help that Vandemark watched the interchange with a frown.

"Miss Innes, I have something to ask before you leave," said the lieutenant gazing intently into her face, still holding her hand. "Will you write to me? Vandemark has my direction." He lowered his voice and glanced at Vandemark. "I'd like to know how he fares. He's not getting any younger, and that cough worries me." He paused. "I may be able to tell you what befalls your friends."

Effie glanced past his shoulder to the professor whose frown deepened. She didn't want to cross Vandemark, but the idea of writing to Moncrithe was enticing. She longed to continue a friendship that was beginning to mean so much to her.

"You know it is unseemly for a single man to write to an unmarried woman." Vandemark's voice was severe. "And to hold hands with her so long."

Moncrithe turned his head slightly toward the professor and gave Effie's hand a little squeeze. "That may be so, sir, but it's not like you to be so stern about conventions. I imagine you raised a few eyebrows when you hired Miss Innes as your scriever."

The professor made a derisive sound.

"I can enlarge her knowledge of botany and report what I find about her friends." His tone was jocular, but there was an anxious gleam in his eyes.

Effie gave him a small smile.

"Hoist by my own petard," said the professor in an exasperated voice. "It is your decision, Euphemia, but know it will be frowned upon if knowledge comes of it. It does not have my blessing."

"But you do not forbid it?" She wanted to be clear on this, to follow her heart in spite of what she owed the professor.

Vandemark's mouth turned down and he shook his head. Moncrithe's stance was stiff, his eyes downcast. She wished so much to write to him—and not just to find out about Davy. The thought of receiving his letters, reading his words directed to her alone made her heart trip, sending a blush up her neck.

"Aye, I'd be honored to write to you, Lieutenant Moncrithe," said Effie, smiling to hide her dejection at the professor's disapproval and even more disturbing, the lieutenant's departure. "Even if you canna find Davy, I wish to ken how you are doing . . . that you're safe."

Moncrithe pressed Effie's hand, and a smile lifted his countenance.

Her pulse pounding, she turned to Vandemark, her voice dull. "Professor when do we return to Pittenweem? Catriona needs to be home with her own folk, and I need to tell the Mackies."

"We'll leave after lunch today. My business is finished here," said Vandemark, and he took a deep draw from his pipe before continuing. "Away to face Catriona, my dear. Tell her Moncrithe will do his best to find Davy."

The lieutenant's grip on her hand tightened briefly before their fingers—lingering for a last touch—drew apart.

Effie could not meet his eyes as her own pricked with tears.

At the door, Effie paused, swallowed the lump in her throat, and turned back to address Moncrithe. "I'll pray for your safety and good health, Lieutenant Moncrithe. I wish you well. God speed."

Joy to My Love

The lieutenant's wan face broke into a smile and his eyes were warm, even ardent. Though she'd only known him for a short time, she was going to miss him. Her heart skipped a beat with a sudden realization—more than she'd miss Davy.

She turned away, closing the door behind her. Now she hardly noticed the elegant golden hallway as she rehearsed in her mind what she'd say to Catriona. It would be best to be direct and to say it quickly. She reached their room, and paused with her hand on the door handle before entering.

Catriona sat at the dressing table brushing her burnished hair. Effie took a deep breath and walked toward her.

Chapter 14

A rosemary bush straggled over the neighbor's stone wall, its blossoms matching the blue of the summer sky. The grey-green foliage made a subdued contrast to the white walls and orange pantiled roof of the cottage. A song thrush flew up from the herb garden and perched on one of the crow-step gables while the hum of bees in the monarda plants created a soporific serenade. Peace reigned in the garden, but not in Effie's heart. Two months had passed since the press gang captured Davy, Robbie, and Tam. Two months since Calum Moncrithe had left.

During that time, Professor Vandemark kept her busy; it helped keep her mind off speculation about what was happening with the men. But today she stayed home while the professor, Jonet, and Billy went to St. Andrews for a few days. Granny Agnes was sick and needed the doctor's attention.

As Effie stood outside her grandmother's cottage waiting for the doctor, she went over the recent conversation she'd had with Rhona Mackie whom she'd met at the fish market.

Struggling with strong emotions, Rhona had burst out. "It's that Catriona!" Her eyes blazed. "She lost no time in forgetting Davy and marrying yon Alasdair Grant. Less than a month. She cuts me when we meet on the street. Not even a nod, let alone a smile."

"Mayhap she's embarrassed to see you." Effie had said.

"Catriona? She's never been embarrassed in her life. She'll always say what she thinks to your face. You ken that. It's unco strange." Rhona snorted. "And now Lorna Tivondeal goes about like Lady

Muck telling us her daughter has made such a great match—better than a fisherman anyway. Better than Davy."

Effie squeezed Rhona's arm. She also found it incomprehensible.

"Did you write to Davy? Tell him like she asked?" said Rhona.

Effie had been stunned when Catriona had approached her and told her she was marrying Alasdair. She'd seen them together occasionally after that disastrous incident at South Queensferry, but she never thought they'd wed.

"I canna write to Davy," Catriona had said. "You must do it. He needs to ken I'm married." Catriona's face had flushed pink. "I canna wait for someone who may not return from war." Her tone was firm, even harsh.

Before she turned away, Effie had caught a glimpse of her quivering lips and the sheen of a tear on her cheek. If she still cared for Davy, why was she marrying Alasdair? And so soon?

When she'd reported the conversation with Rhona, she'd said, "Och. She's a cruel lassie making you write to Davy and knowing how you feel about him."

Warmth had spread through Effie; aye, she'd been so obvious of her infatuation with him. But now she had conflicted feelings about Davy.

Rhona had said, "Mayhap he'll turn to you now. I like you better than Catriona anyway even if—" She blinked. "But that dinna matter to me—or to Davy."

Effie had become rigid; her face felt like wood. Even the Mackies had doubts about her because of her parentage. They hid it well all these years.

Rhona had hugged Effie. "You're a braw lassie, Effie. I'd be proud to have you as my daughter-in-law. And you'd be a good mother to your bairns." Her eyes were contrite.

"Well, Davy should have a say in the matter." Effie tried for a light tone, though heaviness crept through her.

Rhona smiled at the little joke,

The pleasantry didn't relieve Effie's tightly sprung nerves. It had been her dream for ages, but now—her affections had turned toward Calum Moncrithe though he was even more unattainable. Could she

126

marry Davy when her heart no longer hankered after him? Her second thought: poor Davy—deserted by both lassies.

Effie took a deep breath of the fragrant air and plunged into the dismal cottage, a more fitting milieu for her gloomy thoughts. Though warm and sunny outside and a fire blazed on the hearth, coldness permeated the walls. Effie pinned back the tartan curtain to let in warmth and light before she put the pot on the fire to make tea. Her grandmother's raspy breathing mingled with the faint melodious song of the thrush. She sounded worse today.

"Granny I've sent for Dr. Ferguson. I'm worrit about you."

"You worrit? That's no how I ken it," said her grandmother plucking at the new wool blanket Effie had bought her. "Fiona Ballantyne was saying just the other day how you neglect me. And look what happened when you went off to Edinburgh? Getting yourself into trouble. Comin' home with a bruised face. The shame of it!" She hacked and coughed and spat in her kerchief. There was a little blood in the sputum. That was not a good sign.

What could Effie say when her grandmother's cronies supported her in her delusions. Effie was doing the best she could, but it had always been this way. Whatever she attempted to do to help and appease her grandmother, it wasn't good enough. Effie pitied rather than resented this bitter old woman. But pity was a counterfeit love. Effie herself shied away from those who offered her pity rather than liking.

Effie put the warm mug of tea with the sprig of rosemary into her grandmother's hands. The old woman took the mug without comment, content to sip the warm drink. Effie was grateful even if her grandmother wasn't. The professor had given a packet of tea leaves together with her wages. Drinking tea was for the upper class and her grandmother was at first suspicious of the new drink and eventually began to enjoy it. It perked her up, especially since it was something she could brag about to her acquaintances. How many of them got to drink tea like the gentry!

By the time Dr. Ferguson arrived, her grandmother was in a fitful sleep. Her forehead felt hot. Effie had tried to cool her down with cool compresses steeped in a comfrey and peppermint infusion.

"Widow Innes, I need to listen to your lungs," said the doctor rousing her from her sleep. "Effie, help me sit her up. That's right. Now when I tell you, cough a good hard cough to bring up the phlegm."

"And what else have I been doing? Call yourself a doctor?" said Agnes Innes, her voice hoarse. She turned arctic-blue eyes on Effie. "You dinna need to pinch me and hold me so hard."

Dr. Ferguson merely raised his eyebrows.

Effie kept her arm around her granny's shoulders; she'd have fallen otherwise, but the stench of her unwashed body gagged Effie. The old woman had refused to bathe for the past several days.

"I'd rather have syrup from Widow Ballantyne to stop the cough," continued her grandmother trying to push Effie away.

Dr. Ferguson tapped on her grandmother's back when she coughed. He looked up at Effie and shook his head as he and Effie helped the old woman lie down again. He picked up the bloody handkerchief by a corner and threw it into the fire.

"What is it, doctor? What's wrong with my granny? Is it . . ." Effie lowered her voice. "Consumption?"

"No. I think not. She has a congested chest, which has turned to pneumonia. You can't do more than keep her comfortable. At her age, I think she can't fight this disease."

Effie was unprepared for this news. Most elderly people died in the winter time, but it was high summer. Granny Agnes though beleaguered with arthritis, had been healthy until two weeks ago.

Dr. Ferguson put away the instruments into his bag. He proceeded to tell her to wash her hands and not breathe too closely to her grandmother, especially when she coughed. He'd trained with James Lind, the navy physician, at the Royal College of Physicians, and Dr. Ferguson often bragged how the British navy had fewer incidents of typhus than the French because of Lind's methods. Ferguson's belief in the system caused him to stress cleanliness in his medical practice in the villages though the people did not always go along with this newfangled practice.

Effie couldn't believe Granny Agnes was so ill. She'd thought it only a cold and hadn't recognized the signs of pneumonia. Her mind had been elsewhere: worried about Davy and Moncrithe. She should have noticed. Her granny had the right of it: she was neglectful.

"All you can do is make her comfortable."

"Aye. I'll warm some stones and wrap them for her feet."

"Get some rest for yourself, my dear. I must away and see Gordon Drummond. I fear he may have rheumatic fever. It's a pity you don't have the receipt for all the potions your aunt Lizzie made." He stared out the open door. "I miss her."

That was quite an admission from him. Effie now understood how much the doctor admired—perhaps even loved—her Aunt Lizzie. She remembered how he sat by Lizzie's bed after she'd died: defeated, face grey with fatigue, and though he'd quickly hidden his face, she'd glimpsed the well of tears in his eyes. She'd never seen a grown man cry before. He was still married then. But he was an honorable man and Lizzie the most upright person she knew. Effie often wondered what would have happened if Mrs. Ferguson had died before Lizzie.

The doctor shook himself out of his reverie. "I wish you could come with me. You're good with the bairns. Will Vandemark give you leave to help me with a lying-in? Ann Imrie asked for you instead of Widow Ballantyne. The bairn's due any day now."

"Aye. I'm glad to help if he allows it." Women in the farms outwith Pittenweem were more accepting of her. They liked her potions and salves too. It was as though her new position with the professor had opened up more acceptance than she'd ever had before.

The doctor made for the door, then stopped. "Don't think you are at fault in any way."

Effie cocked her head to one side, puzzled.

"I know you, lassie. You take on yourself the weights your granny has put upon you. And she's burdened you with guilt these many years." With a nod, he walked into the brightness of the summer day.

Effie swallowed the lump in her throat. It was always the way when people were kind and thoughtful to her. She fought daily to deal with recriminations and nasty remarks, but kind words were rare and broke down the barriers she raised to keep herself from hurt. Effie wrapped a shawl around her shoulders and moved one of the chairs by the table close to her grandmother's bed so she could keep vigil.

Her granny was restless, so Effie reached for her Bible opened at Isaiah 56. Agnes read her Bible every day. Perhaps the words would be a comfort to her. She raised her voice over the noisy sound of the sick woman's breathing.

'Thus saith the Lord, Keep you judgment, and do justice: for my salvation is near to come, and my righteousness to be revealed. Blessed is the man that doeth this, and the son of man that layeth hold on it; that keepeth the sabbath from polluting it, and keepeth his hand from doing any evil'

The words seemed to calm Granny Agnes, as her breathing became quieter. The old woman kept the Sabbath day strictly and attempted to instill fear of sin and retribution in Effie. It was for her own good, she had said many times. To Effie it didn't feel like love, but a punishment and a prison.

Effie read on for quite a while, with no change in her grandmother's breathing. She stood, stretched, and peered outside. It was so bright after the gloom of the cottage. Dust motes danced in shafts of sunlight. She caught a whiff of rotting fish from the harbor mingled with the scent of the banksia rose which sprawled over the wall of the Grahams' garden next door. She lingered outside; she didn't relish going back to the tomb-like room.

Her grandmother's breath now sounded shallower and intermittent.

Granny Agnes stirred, making wild gestures with her hands. She tried to say something.

"Where's Belle?" she managed to say.

Effie was alarmed; Belle was Granny Agnes's sister, long dead.

"Effie, I did the best by you. Keeping you safe from harm and sin. I couldna let you . . ." She took a ragged breath. "Not let you follow your ma and bring shame again on the house."

"Dinna speak, Granny. I ken you looked out for me." Effie took the thin, wrinkled hand in hers. It was cold and clammy. Her grandmother closed her eyes and fell asleep again.

The day dragged on. Effie read or ground herbs in her mortar and pestle with her grandmother's stertorous breathing in the background. She left the door open to get some fresh air, and a cool

130

breeze beckoned her from the oppression of the dark room. She stepped outside and stretched her back and arms. Lengthening shadows told her it was early evening though it was hard to tell the time during the long summer nights.

When she went back inside, something was different. Silence. With dread, Effie walked to the bed. Granny Agnes's chest no longer rose and fell with every breath.

Effie closed her grandmother's eyes which would no longer spark venomous looks at her. She placed a ha'penny on each eyelid, using the reverse side that showed the figure of Britannia seated by the sea with a tiny warship at her feet. Her thoughts turned to Calum and Davy on board such a ship so far away, but she had things to do. Dry-eyed, she left the cottage to fetch the minister and Widow Ballantyne.

Chapter 15

Effie was glad she had sixpence to pay for the mortcloth. Her grandmother would have liked that, and the kind words spoken by Mr. Mitchell over the draped casket. He expressed chagrin that he'd been unable to visit Granny Agnes before she died, as he had been with a sick family in a farm on the outskirts of the parish.

The professor, Jonet and Billy were still in St. Andrews not yet knowing her step-grandmother had died. Dr. Ferguson was away on business in Edinburgh. Widow Ballantyne and the Mackies attended the funeral and had now left.

The sexton and his sons shoveled earth over the casket before Effie turned for home. She'd have to save her pennies to add Agnes's name to the tombstone on the family plot where Euphemia Adamstone, Andrew Innes and Lizzie were buried; Uncle Alec's name was on the tombstone though his bones lay in the deep near Cape Wrath.

Effie stood on the threshold of the cottage peering into the gloom. She couldn't face it right now and needed the comfort of sea and open air.

Walking aimlessly, mindlessly, she reached Billow Ness with its small sandy beach. She found a place on the springy grass verge and sat for several moments, her head in her hands listening to the water draw back like an indrawn breath then rush forward with a murmured susurrus. She matched her breathing to the lapping waves, calmness filling her.

She lifted her head. A small flock of ringed plovers foraged for crabs in the rock pools. She raised her eyes higher to where the greyish-green mass of the Isle of May lay on the horizon. It was too far to see the white beacon; her thoughts turned to Susan Laing and her family and how the Mackies came to rescue her. It seemed eons ago, but that trip to the island had triggered events she would not have imagined—Davy and Robbie seized and taken far away to a place of war. But she'd also spent more time with Calum Moncrithe, the only light in the tragic episode.

Her fears for the men surfaced. Her grandmother was in a better place, but they were in a worse place, full of danger and hardship. Her throat constricted. She gripped her Bible so hard she made dents in the worn leather.

By habit, she'd carried it with her when attending the kirk. She opened it; perhaps she'd find comfort there. A dry mottled leaf fell out. Effie let out a little moan as she bent to pick up the fragile leaf. Here was a relic that reminded her of Davy and her beginning adulation of him. It was one her happiest childhood memories. The scene came vivid as if only yesterday.

Autumn, ten years ago, Effie had stopped on her way home from school to catch a leaf. It promised good luck—she needed it. Alec and her grandfather had died, the farm sold, and Effie was newly-moved to Pittenweem.

The skittish leaves eluded her. Then Davy Mackie, already a strapping and handsome laddie of fourteen, joined her.

"'Tis a rare thing to hear you laugh, Effie Innes. Is it a wish you're after or the chance to dance with the leaves?" His smile was infectious. "That's no the way to do it. Stand still. Let them come to you." A gust blew several leaves towards them. "Look at that one, twirling like Hugh Braid on a Saturday night at the tavern. It's coming for you."

Effie caught it as it drifted toward her, holding it close to her chest. She closed her eyes and made her wish.

"So what did you wish for?" Davy's bright blue eyes shone.

"It will not come true if I tell you. You ken that. Look how braw it is. It's richer than gold an' it has red splotches like rubies."

"Aye, it's braw." Davy laughed. "Gold and rubies? You fanciful wee bairn."

"Catch a wish too."

Two leaves twirled towards him; he caught the larger one.

"Let me see. Oh, it's ripped."

"Ah well, it looks as though my wish has holes in it." Davy's smile was teasing.

"No. You deserve good luck. Take mine. I wouldna ha' caught it but for you."

"No, keep your bonny leaf." Davy had flicked her gently on the cheek. "Now I must away to the harbor."

She had pressed the leaf into her Bible, in the first Epistle of John, the verses beginning with "Beloved."

Davy had been her beloved ever since. And what had she wished for all those years? A good friend. Davy had been patient with that wee lassie who'd dogged his footsteps; he'd stood up for her many times. The leaf had lost its autumn glow and as she placed it back in the Bible, it crumbled into shreds leaving only the skeleton of its veins. But her memories of his friendship were still green though now her heart was turning toward another. Effie rose, took one more glance at the Isle of May, and took her path home.

How quiet it was without Granny Agnes needling her. Now she could have the bed instead of the pallet which never kept out the chill from the stone floor. Life was going to be a lot easier without that sour old woman. Effie washed sheets, spreading them over the garden wall to dry and was cleaning under the bed when the broom hit something in the far corner. She maneuvered the broom so the object gradually moved toward the edge of the bed and into sight.

It was an intricately carved wooden box she had never seen before. That was strange. Why would her grandmother hide such a thing? She put it aside and picked up the pail of dirty water she'd used to clean the floor and opened the door. She was on the point of pouring out the water when she heard footsteps coming toward the cottage.

She looked up. Niall Douglas stood there with his customary scowl rather than sadness for her loss.

"Effie, you canna stay here," he said. "It's for the deserving poor. The parish willna support the likes of you."

"Does the minister have a new place for me?" She wished she could add *for the likes of me*, but it wouldn't do to be cheeky to this man.

"No. It's my job to watch over tenants who are beholden to the parish."

She thought it was the deacon's job, not a ruling elder. Did the minister agree with this action? Why did this elder have so much power? The other elders and Watson Smith, the deacon, though not particularly friendly toward Effie, were fair in their parish duties.

Douglas smirked. "Mayhap you could find a room in one of the taverns hereabouts."

"But that's where—"

"Aye. Where your mother no doubt would have gone if she hadna left. Did you not entertain a navy man some months back? Like mother, like daughter."

Effie gasped and stepped back at the glitter in his eyes and his appalling suggestion. Then heat surged through her so strong it was as if lightning ran through her veins. She glared at the elder whose gaze roamed over her, an unpleasant gleam in his eyes.

She stretched to her full height so they were eye to eye. "How dare you insult Lieutenant Moncrithe. Why do you persist in slandering me and my mother?"

"If it hadna been for you, your aunt Lizzie would ha' married me."

Was there a hint of an angry sob in his voice?

"Lizzie marry *you*?" She couldn't help the sharp laugh that burst through her incredulity but immediately put a hand to her mouth. The water in the pail slopped about as she took a step backward.

The elder's face contorted in rage and he step closer, his knuckles white as he gripped his walking cane.

"Laugh at me, would you?" Spittle foamed at the edge of his lips. "I could ha' been your stepfather. I was willing to accept you to win Lizzie's hand. But I would have chastening you betimes. Lizzie and your granny were too soft on you." He took another step toward her. "But it's not too late. I'll teach you a lesson you'll never forget." He raised the stick.

"No!"

Terrified, Effie swung the pail at his cane. The pail glanced off the cane but the elder had stepped forward and the pail hit him on the temple, splashing dirty water over both of them. She dropped the pail, covering her mouth in horror at what she'd done. The elder slipped on the wet cobblestones and landed on a knee, bellowing with hurt and wrath. Effie's first instinct was to help him up but she backed into the open door of the cottage. She slammed the door shut and turned the key, trembling as though with the ague.

Effie took up the poker that leaned against the door though her grip was soft as her hands were wet from sweat.

The elder beat on the door with his walking stick, his voice thundering. Then his face appeared at the open window. A streak of blood ran from his temple and his face was distorted beyond recognition.

"Dinna come in. I have a poker and I'll use it," Effie yelled though she could hardly get the words out. He backed away and she closed the window, small sobs escaping as her fingers fumbled with the latch.

"I'll run you out o' the village." Mr. Douglas's voice was now a little muffled but the anger pulsed in it. "What will the minister and your employer think of your behavior—striking a kirkman? You've shown your true nature—bad blood will out—though you hide it well. I'll see you lose your job. Then you'll stoop to the level of your mother. Follow in her depravity if you havena already."

She leaned on a wall which held her up, though her legs almost buckled. She dropped the poker and wiped her sweaty palms on her skirt.

Effie wondered how long he'd stay outside. She was trapped until he left. Then she heard faint footsteps and the voices of a man and woman. She strained to hear their conversation.

"Ah good day to you, Peter, and you too, Mrs. Black," said Mr. Douglas. "You are my witnesses that Effie Innes attacked me. I was just asking her to clean the cottage for new tenants. First she lured me in to seduce me to let her stay. But when I repelled her, she attacked me. Like mother, like daughter." He raised his voice for Effie's benefit. "Be out o' this place by sunset."

Effie couldn't hear the murmured voices of Peter and Iona Black, though she heard the elder accepting their help back to his home. The sound of their footsteps and voices faded away.

He'd courted Aunt Lizzie? Unbelievable to think she'd lower herself to marry *him*.

Effie put a trembling hand to her mouth. She shouldn't have laughed. Who knew he was capable of love. What a stepfather he'd have made! But she couldn't think of that right now. She had to leave immediately in case he returned.

Her future would be dire if Mr. Douglas's slanderous words were believed. It was her word against his, a kirkman and she a pariah though since she'd been working for the professor, her reputation had improved. But not now. If the Blacks backed him up? She shuddered. The Mackies would support her, but would the professor when he learned how she'd behaved like an ill-bred besom from the gutter—the very thing the elder accused her of? Perhaps underneath it all, she really did have bad blood, couldn't help the inherited depravity? Mr. Douglas's suggestion that she belonged in places of ill-repute had repulsed and sickened her. No! She'd didn't belong there!

Surely the professor wouldn't believe that she's hit him for no good reason? Douglas had insulted the lieutenant, but he'd no doubt lie about that. If she lost her job she'd be at the elder's mercy if she stayed in the village—the Mackies couldn't protect her all the time and if she were dismissed, the professor not at all. She'd have to leave Pittenweem, fend for herself, not get a reference for a new job. She'd be friendless and vulnerable to any indignity of the destitute. Her stomach roiled and she retched, bile burning her throat.

She feverishly tied her belongings in the damp sheets, including the box she'd found, and set the iron griddle and cooking pot on top.

As she lugged the bundle out the door, her mind raced through possible places to stay, at least for the night. She couldn't stay with the Mackies who had rented out Davy and Robbie's old room. And anyway, Rhona was in Anstruther with her sister; she couldn't stay with just men in the cottage. That would set tongues wagging even more. Who else had room for a lodger? Dr. Ferguson was away and his servant, Andrewina, was antagonistic toward her. Her budding friendship with Isabella McIntosh was too tenuous. She could sleep in the ruined doocot by the path to Anstruther; there was still a partial roof. But tramps and tinkers often used it.

If Jonet in her absentmindedness hadn't pocketed the key, she could have stayed at Vandemark's house. She needed somewhere to hide until the professor and the Murdochs returned. She rubbed her forehead. Somewhere close by. She dared not risk meeting Mr. Douglas in the street on her way to work. A surge of nausea made her dizzy.

The stables. The horses were gone and a straw bed would be as comfortable as her thin pallet. It would just be for one night.

Streaks of apricot and gold burnished the high clouds. Time to leave before the elder returned. She'd taken him by surprise, but that wasn't likely to happen again. How he'd enjoy explaining that bruise on his temple and the hurt knee. And that embellishment that she'd tried to seduce him. She gritted her teeth. He'd unnerved and humiliated her in the past, but she'd never feared him. Until now. She'd suspected that under his pious exterior lurked an ill-tempered and dour personality, but she'd never dreamt it hid such viciousness.

Effie looked around in case the elder should be lurking about then stood for a moment with her hand on the door knob. She peered into the dark, sparse room with only the mattress, the small table, and two chairs left to furnish it. She'd hoped to make it into a cozy home for herself even with the bad memories it held, but it was not to be.

A twinge of guilt overcame her. She couldn't seem to mourn Granny Agnes. She closed the door sharply shutting out a grim chapter in her life. But would it get grimmer?

She trudged toward the professor's home, looking over her shoulder and approaching each wynd with caution in case the elder lurked in one. As she walked, she rehearsed in her mind how she'd tell the professor about the loss of her home and, worse yet, how she'd struck Mr. Douglas. There was no room in his house for her; he already had Jonet and Billy in the one servant's room; the spare rooms were for visitors . . . visitors like Calum Moncrithe.

Her pulse skittered and she had to stop a moment to catch her breath. If the professor sent her away, she'd never hear from the lieutenant again, never read his interesting and friendly letters, or, when he returned from Canada, see the teasing light in his eyes and warm smile that lit a warm glow inside her. She thought she loved Davy, but it had been a childish infatuation. Now Lieutenant Calum Moncrithe was her beloved, and though she loved in vain she longed for at least his friendship and approval. If he heard of this latest escapade, he'd turn from her in disgust. That little flicker of hope that he liked and admired her dimmed, and shadows descended over her hopes and dreams.

Chapter 16

"Here, let me pick that straw off your back," said Jonet. "You'd think you'd been sleeping in the stables." She laughed at her own joke.

The blood rushed to Effie's face. Since their return two days ago, she'd not found the time or the courage to let the professor and Jonet know she was homeless. She'd visited Rhona Mackie who was making enquiries about a suitable place for her to stay—she'd even offered to tell her lodger to leave so Effie could take his place. Rhona had urged her to tell the professor and suggested talking to the minister, but Effie was too afraid Douglas would be at the manse. So far, she'd managed to avoid him and had even stayed away from going to kirk last Sunday. Granny Agnes would be turning over in her grave.

Swallowing hard, Effie turned to Jonet. "I have been."

"What? You're joking me!" Her smile was unsure.

"No. I was told to leave the cottage, and I've no found another place to stay."

"Why did you no tell me?" Jonet put her arms around Effie. "It's a sin they told you to leave. What is the minister thinking?"

Effie shook her head. Aye, what was he thinking? Did he even know? More like it was Douglas's doing. He'd not yet come to see the professor. Every time there was a knock at the door, Effie had opened it with trepidation, expecting to see the elder's dour face or the minister's disappointed one.

"I'm away to tell the professor," said Jonet briskly taking off her apron. "Chop the turnips for the stew."

Effie was washing and cleaning carrots by the time Jonet returned. The woman was red in the face and her bosom heaved. Effie braced herself to hear she'd been turned off.

"Take off your apron, Effie. The professor needs to talk with you. He's received a letter." Jonet's voice trembled with wrath. "An' such a letter!"

Effie untied her apron with shaking hands. She hung her head, not wanting to look Jonet in the eye. That letter must have been from Mr. Douglas or the minister. It was all over. The professor would dismiss her. It was her word against the elder's. Each step closer to the professor brought more fear racing through her veins.

At the library door, Jonet put a hand on Effie's arm. Effie still couldn't meet her eyes. "I dinna believe it though it came from the minister."

Effie swayed, feeling faint. Jonet had been angry about the letter, not about her. Would the professor support her? How could she tell this learned person what Mr. Douglas had said to warrant her violent action? She hadn't even told Rhona. Shame stopped her tongue.

Vandemark looked up at Effie with a piercing gaze. She quailed inside but managed to walk toward him with some semblance of grace, though her head was bowed and her lip quivered. She gave him a slight curtsy but didn't raise her head.

"Jonet, you may leave."

"No. I'm staying." Jonet put an arm around Effie. The professor hmphed.

"I received a most disturbing letter from Mr. Mitchell." He cleared his throat. "You need to explain yourself."

She wet her lips. "I dinna ken what's in the letter, so I canna explain." Her voice came out in a croak; she dared one peek to Vandemark's forbidding face.

The professor let out a dry laugh. "Sit down, lassie. Sit down." He handed her the letter.

Effie sank into the nearest chair, the letter rustling in her trembling hands.

Mr. Mitchell had written that Niall Douglas had gone to Effie's cottage to offer his condolences for her grandmother's death. The elder had found Effie packing her belongings with the purpose of moving into a room at the tavern where she'd supplement her income with lewd behavior. She no longer had her grandmother to keep her in check. When he tried to dissuade Effie from taking this drastic measure, Effie had tried to seduce him and when that didn't work had attacked him. Mr. Mitchell himself had seen the cut and bruise on the elder's forehead and how the elder hobbled on his wounded knee. And that the attack had been witnessed by Mr. and Mrs. Black.

Effie took a sharp intake of breath. The Blacks hadn't seen that Douglas had tried to beat her first. It was his word against hers. Mr. Mitchell wrote that he would meet with the professor on the morrow, but he strongly urged him to reconsider keeping Effie in his employ.

Effie struggled for breath. Lies. Twisted truth. She looked up at the professor whose face was impassive. She smoothed out the letter over and over again as her mind endlessly repeated the refrain: it was her word against that man's.

"It's true I hit him with a pail." Bile stung in her gorge and she put a shaking hand to her mouth.

"It must have taken some provocation," said the professor. His voice was gentle.

Effie looked up, hope fluttering in her breast. His face swam before her then she knew no more until a sharp pungent smell brought her around. Jonet took the smelling salts away from her nose, allowing her to breathe normally.

"Now, take your time, and tell us your side of the story." The professor tamped down tobacco in his pipe and proceeded to light it.

Jonet had an arm around Effie's shoulders. Effie looked up at her worried face, took a deep breath and proceeded to tell them what happened. She hung her head so she didn't have to look into their faces.

Silence. Effie raised her head gradually. Jonet was red-faced, fuming, and the professor's eyes were like flint. Effie's pulse raced.

"Are you about to turn me off, sir? Are you angry with me?" Effie managed to say that much. "Granny Agnes was right I'm a—"

"The wickedness of that man!" Jonet spluttered, her words shooting out of her mouth.

"No. You will remain in my employ." The professor leaned back in his chair. "I am not angry with you, but with that—" He muttered something in Dutch under his breath.

"But it's my word against his," said Effie, wringing her hands. "He's a respected kirkman."

"Why he's respected I dinna ken," said Jonet. "We believe you, hinny. Have you told the Mackies?"

Effie shook her head. "Only that I need to find a place to live." She looked up at the professor. "Can you forby ask the minister if he kens a place?"

"We talked of this while you were in the kitchen," said Vandemark.

So he'd believed her even before he'd spoken to her? He trusted her more than she had ever believed possible.

"We'll make a place for you in the attic, though it needs work," Jonet interrupted. "You'll stay in the guest bedroom until it's done. Why didna you tell us afore now, you silly lassie?"

"I thought you'd no believe me. Most people in Pittenweem dinna." It was almost a whisper.

"This village!" Jonet snorted. "If they ken you like we do, they'd change their tune."

"This is what comes from superstitions and ignorance on the one hand and religious bigotry on the other," said the professor in his lecture voice. "You have been much maligned, my dear."

Tears threatened to spill over; Effie rubbed her eyes vigorously. With a couple of sniffs, she managed to keep her composure.

"Michty me! The stew!" Jonet walked briskly toward the door, stopping to say. "I'll talk with my Billy about the attic. Dinna fash yoursel', Effie. The professor will get this sorted."

"I do not need you as a scribe today, Euphemia," said the professor. "Go fetch your things from the stables." He drew on his pipe and blew out a cloud. He had a satisfied smile on his face. "I look forward to meeting the minister the morrow."

"Do I have to be here when he comes?" It would be an excruciating experience, but she would do it now she knew she had the professor's support.

"No. Not unless you wish it. I will represent you as locus parentis—in place of a parent—be your advocate though he may wish to meet you later." And then almost to himself. "I hope he brings Douglas. I wish to see him squirm."

Effie wished she could see the elder squirm too though she didn't want to be anywhere near him. She rose and walked to the door. "Thank you, sir. Thank you for believing me." Relief made her lightheaded and she clung to the door handle.

"I believe you because I believe in you, Euphemia." His voice was serious and his eyes were soft. "And others do too. I have taken your measure these past months. Now you just need to believe in yourself."

Chapter 17

Effie drew back the curtains from the windows in her attic bedroom, letting in the morning light. She'd moved into the attic a week ago and was still amazed at the difference in her life. Instead of the cramped, dark cottage with her grandmother niggling at her as soon as she woke, she opened sleep-refreshed eyes to a large room, bigger than two rooms in a cottage. And it had two dormer windows. The extravagance of it. Granny Agnes had grumbled about how much the burgh charged per window which was why many cottages of the poor had only one window. Now she was living in a house with many windows—two in the attic alone.

The house was set at the top of the village and Effie was at the uppermost story. She had a bird's-eye view of the roofs of cottages, the green of their little walled gardens, the harbor with bobbing multicolored boats, a view of the firth with its many moods, and, on a clear day, the distant Lothian terrain across the firth.

Though she helped Jonet and wrote and read to Professor Vandemark, her evenings were her own: to keep the professor and sometimes Dr. Ferguson company, or retire early to her room. It was a novelty to have a room of her own.

She looked around the room with pleasure. The brass bed had a cream blanket and pink quilt to match the curtains at the window. A mahogany kist held her clothes—her serviceable old grey dress and the jonquil and blue muslin, the first dresses she'd made from her allowance. Now she owned two new dresses: one a deep pink, and a sprig muslin with tiny pink roses on a cream background. That would be her Sunday best now. She'd never owned such finery before, even when her grandfather's farm had flourished.

The professor had insisted she get new clothes when he discovered she only had two dresses; he hadn't noticed before. She and Jonet enjoyed their outing to St. Andrews to choose fabric and discuss dress patterns with Katy Bonthrone the mantua-maker and modiste whose seamstresses had sewn the dresses.

A chair by a small desk under the window and a dresser by the closet made up the rest of the furniture. Even though she'd been in this room for a few days, Effie had established a routine to make comfort in her own room. Though she wrote letters or studied books in the library sometimes she'd bring them to her bedroom. The library was the professor's domain. When she read Plato's writings or Cicero's speeches, she believed it was more fitting to be sitting straight up in a chair. She could concentrate more on the dense language and complicated ideas if her back was restricted by the tall, hard back of the chair to read those works.

But when she read a novel, she read in the comfort of her bed, being sure not to let the candle burn down too quickly. She had two novels by Fanny Burney that Mrs. Forbes had bequeathed to her, though Alasdair Grant begrudged handing them over.

Vandemark told her they'd give her recreation. He'd fanciful ideas. How many lassies of her station had time for recreation? He seemed to forget who she was sometimes. But she had found time, reading after her chores were done. Effie smiled and shook her head at the professor's whims. She was growing fonder of him as the days passed; he was more of a father than an employer. An all-too-corporeal father to replace that unknown shadowy figure of Effie's imaginings.

She had escaped to her room when the minister visited the professor, but Jonet had listened at the keyhole and reported what happened. The professor had stood up for Effie and confounded the minister, who had left flustered and embarrassed. He must have believed Vandemark, for he and his wife had visited Effie a few days later, encouraging her to continue to attend kirk. Mr. Mitchell had assured her that Niall Douglas would not harm her. He shook her hand and smiled at her when she and Jonet left the kirk. Effie noticed

Mr. and Mrs. Black's puzzled expressions as they stood next to Mr. Douglas who gave her poisonous glares. From that time on, Effie crossed the road when she saw the elder. She didn't want to go anywhere near him.

Two evenings ago, she'd written a letter to the lieutenant in Halifax, Nova Scotia. Vandemark told her it meant New Scotland. She'd forgotten to ask the lieutenant if it really was like Scotland.

"I suppose I should study French," she said to the tabby cat sprawled on her bed. Jonet didn't like that the cat came indoors, but it was the same cat that had kept Effie company in her straw bed in the stables. It deserved a little comfort too. "I'm sick of conjugating verbs."

She glanced out the window at the grey clouds tinged with pink from the rising sun. The small wooden box she'd found hidden under her grandmother's bed sat on the window sill. Effie had put off opening it as though Granny Agnes's disapproval hovered over it. With the move to the professor's house, it had lain hidden in a kist where she kept shawls and her pelisse. The box had surfaced as she arranged and tidied her new bedchamber. Better to look through it than study French verbs.

Effie opened the box and found what looked like a piece of white bone intricately carved with a bird with a curved beak, white head, dark body, and white tail feathers. Turning it over in her hand, she remembered Uncle Alec's strong brown fingers running over the grooved picture. He'd told her it was a bald eagle, and she'd said in perfect six-year-old logic, it couldna be bald because those were feathers on its head. He had laughed and rumpled her hair, calling her his bonny wee lassie. He'd returned from a year-long trip on a whaling ship, hoping to make extra money for the family. He had brought back this carved whale tooth for Effie, a trade with a sailor from the Americas. What had he called it? *Scrim . . . scrimshaw.* What an odd name. Effie thought she'd lost it.

And here was Lizzie's brooch which Alec had brought back from Orkney. Effie ran her fingers over the pattern of silver scrolls. All she had left were mementos of those she loved and who had loved her.

Two years later, Alec was lost at sea and laughter in the home had died with him. Aunt Lizzie, Granny Agnes, and she had moved from the farm, bought by an incomer from Aberdeen. The new owners did not want to keep on Lizzie if it included a decrepit old woman, and a young lassie. Lizzie had said it was for the best to make a clean break.

With a lump in her throat, Effie placed the whale tooth in pride of place on the window sill—after all, an eagle needed to see the sky.

She took out the leather-bound book tied with linen ribbons. This had no memories for her. The ribbons looked newer than the binding, and Effie carefully undid the knots pulled tight as though daring anyone to open the book. When she loosened the last knot, the book fell open to a painting of a flower on yellowed parchment paper; she didn't recognize the flower. Next to the flower were words written in a strange hand: black, round, bold. This must be the mysterious book of herbs belonging to her real grandmother, Effie Adamstone, and the book Dr. Ferguson had mentioned when they were discussing Linnaeus's book. Lizzie must have studied it in secret; Effie had never seen her reading it. Effie had overheard Widow Ballantyne asking Granny Agnes about it after Lizzie died.

Effie put down the book. She'd study it later and perhaps ask the professor's advice about the writing. In the bottom of the box, hidden by the book, was a stack of letters on brittle beige paper. She undid the ribbon tied around them. She opened the first letter. It was addressed to Granny Agnes. Should she read it? Curiosity overcame her qualms. Her grandmother couldn't yell at her now, but Effie couldn't help looking over her shoulder before she smoothed out the creases of the letter. The letter was dated 7th July 1810, three years ago.

Dear Ma. Dear Ma? Effie stopped reading. Her eyes widened. She turned over the letter several times. What was this? Was it a letter from Aunt Lizzie to Granny Agnes? Impossible! Lizzie had died by then. Effie turned over the page this time to look closer at the signature. The name, *Maggie* was scrawled at the end. Maggie? The only Maggie she knew who was related to her grandmother was her mother.

Effie let the letter drop in her lap as her mind whirled. Was it possible her mother had not died when Effie was a year old, but was alive and living in Edinburgh only three years ago? A pulse hammered in Effie's temple. Was Maggie still alive now?

Effie sat in a daze for several minutes. She turned over the letter and read the ink-blotted, scrawled writing.

> *7th July 1810, Edinburgh*
>
> *Dear Ma, A scriever is writing this for me. You ken how I canna write. You told me Lizzie died. She was a good sister e'en though she never wrote back to me in all these years. I canna think you want to keep my bairn, Effie with you now. I have another bairn, Alec. He isna baseborn, but son of my wedded husband, Archie Wallace. Effie can come live with us. She must be of age to take up service. It may as well be in Edinburgh to help me. The parish will see you right. You dinna need her. Mayhap Jock Mackie can bring her and we'll meet her by the hostelry Shepherd's Ha in Portobello. We live in Canongate so it isna a long walk from Portobello. Let me ken when to expect her. Your daughter,*
>
> *Maggie.*

Effie turned it over and read it again. And then a third time. Her mind finally grasped that her mother was still alive—at least three years ago. She had a stepfather and a stepbrother. It also meant her mother had abandoned her when she was a baby. Why did no one tell her? Perhaps not earlier, but now when she was grown up? Effie stared into space, the letter loose in her hand. So, she had other kinfolk. What else would the other letters reveal? She picked them up and put them in order of earliest to latest.

> *26 July 1795, Edinburgh*
>
> *Dear Lizzie: I'm married. He's Archie Wallace, not the man I ran away with, so you can tell Ma Agnes I'm respektible. Archie is having a hard time finding work so I'm working in a sewing place. I make hats for rich ladies. That's unco comical. You ken how I canna sew but a straight seam. You tried so hard to teach me. I like life here. It's no so dull as in Pittenweem but I miss the sea and the sound of the gulls and the air so fresh. I dinna miss going to the kirk ony Sunday and reading the Bible. Does Ma still do that? Write to me, Lizzie. Come visit me one day. Luv, Maggie.*

PS: How is the bairn, Effie? I'm glad I left her with you. Archie wouldna like a by-blow of mine to bring up and anyway I dinna have the time.

Effie would have been two years old at the time and, with a shock, she realized that Maggie would have been just a little older than she was now—nineteen. How fortunate she'd stayed in Pittenweem with Lizzie instead of living with parents who didn't want her. But the thought she'd been unwanted, even as a bairn, brought the darkness that ever lurked deep inside her. Now she understood those shadows. She licked her lips that had become dry and unfolded another letter.

2 December 1795, Edinburgh
Dear Lizzie, Why have you no replied? Have you cut me off like that auld carline? I left the sewing job and now work as a maid in a tavern. Archie still canna find a job to suit him. What I would give for a fresh piece of Pittenweem herring covered in oats and fried crisp and tasty. And I'd even eat neeps and tatties. It's unco cold in the tenement. Can you send us money? Three guineas would be guid.

Three guineas! That was a lot of money. Effie shook her head at her mother's audacity.

I ken there's plenty o' food at the farm. Think o' it as my heritance. Write to me soon.
Luv, Maggie.

The letters to Lizzie were the same year after year: occasionally asking how Effie was doing., and telling Lizzie she liked life in Edinburgh. Her husband seemed to be in and out of jobs, and Maggie often asked for money. In all the letters, Maggie asked why Lizzie had not answered.

Jonet's voice penetrated Effie's dazed thoughts. Time had passed by so rapidly, she'd not yet brought the library fire to a blaze before the professor woke up. Effie put the letters in the box and put on her apron. While tidying and brushing her hair in front of the oval mirror, she studied her face for a while as though she was trying to find herself in those letters from her past. Her face was merely more pallid than usual with a faint crease of worry on her brow. Why did Lizzie not answer her sister? And why did Maggie not visit Pittenweem? Perhaps Rhona Mackie held the key to these questions.

KAREN M. EDWARDS

Chapter 18

Jonet in the mornings was a small dynamo, whirling through the kitchen to reach for eggs and milk. Her husband, Bill, stood at the kitchen door, taciturn and stolid, chewing on his pipe. He liked to watch his wife bustling around the kitchen for a few moments before he went about his duties. This morning he nodded at Effie before turning away to see to the garden. But in that nod his glance was shrewd.

Once Jonet had the kitchen in order and food bubbling on the fire, she finally looked at Effie.

"Michty me. Are you ailing for something, dearie? You look so peelie-wally. I must stir the sauce. Talk to me. I'm listening."

"I found out something that's made me tapsalteerie."

Jonet reached up and touched Effie's lightly on the cheek. "I warrant it was more than your granny dying. You were so calm and accepting of her death these past weeks. We'll get the professor his breakfast and then we'll talk."

Though Effie tried to hide her face from the professor when serving his breakfast, his glance was questioning. Jonet shook her head at him. When all the dishes were served, Jonet took Effie by the arm and led her to the garden.

"Now sit here, hinny," said Jonet, pushing Effie down on the bench, which faced the herb garden. "The sunshine's better than a messy kitchen. Effie, what ails you?"

Effie told her about the box and letters, giving her the gist of what they said. Jonet sat staring and frowning at a clump of sage.

"You have the right of it; you need to talk with Rhona Mackie. It's a puzzle all right. Why Lizzie didna write back. And you need to talk with the professor. He can find out if your mother is still alive."

"I'll visit the Mackies after I write the treatise for the professor."

"Did you forget? The professor's going to St. Andrews and will not be back until the morrow."

In a quick movement, Jonet stood up, smoothed down her apron, and said looking down at Effie, who still sat passively on the bench.

"That's settled then. You'll visit Rhona the day and tell the professor about the letters when he returns."

Effie got up and threw her arms around Jonet. "Thank you, Jonet. You are a good friend to me." Jonet patted Effie's arm and kissed her cheek.

"I've grown unco fond of you, Effie. You're a good lassie and deserve to find out what has been going on. Now, let's get back to the kitchen." She looked around for a while then raised her voice. "It does me good now and again to see the sunshine and to see what yon husband of mine is doing all day among the roses." A muffled thud came from behind the garden shed and a puff of smoke drifted toward them. Jonet winked at Effie who tried to smile.

It took a while for the professor to leave. He kept adding to his luggage: more books, his favorite snuff, his preferred slippers, a pillow he could not do without, and a bottle of French brandy. While Billy was putting his bags onto the coach, Professor Vandemark appeared at the library door where Effie was dusting and polishing the furniture, the smell of beeswax and lavender permeating the room.

"Jonet told me you have something troubling you and you will tell me when I return. In the meantime, do not worry, my dear." He tapped her lightly on the shoulder. "By the by, should any letters arrive from Moncrithe, you have my permission to read them. I know you are anxious to hear if he has found your friends and how they are faring. I do not want you to fret and wait until I return." Looking around the room he said, "Now where did I put my walking stick? You know, the one with the carved fox head."

Effie retrieved it from beside the red brocade wing chair where he'd sat the other night. The professor reached to pick up Aristotle's

Poetics lying on the small mahogany table, when Jonet's voice made him start.

"Are you after taking all your library with you, professor?" asked Jonet. "You have six books in the carriage already and the horses are getting restive." She ushered him out of the door, but Vandemark turned and winked at Effie, who was trying hard not to laugh. That Jonet. She had a lot of nerve to talk to her employer that way.

The carriage had hardly turned the corner when the carter, Joe Bonnyman, brought a packet of letters.

"Are those letters from the navy?" Effie peered over Jonet's shoulder. Aye, that was a navy frank. The pulse in her throat thumped harder.

"Whisht you. Gie me time to open it," said Jonet, taking a kitchen knife and cutting the string.

Four letters fell out: two for the professor and one addressed to her in what she guessed was the lieutenant's disciplined hand; another with Davy's sprawling writing was addressed to Catriona. Effie's was glad. It meant Davy was alive. But she swallowed annoyance that the letter wasn't addressed to his mother. What a shock Davy had in store for him.

"What should I do, Jonet? Catriona's a married woman. I doubt she'd like to receive a letter from Davy."

"More like her husband wouldna like it." Jonet waved the envelope as she pondered the question. "Hmm. It has her name on it. Best to take it to her. Forby she'll share its contents with his mother." She nudged Effie with a smile. "And what about your own letter? I can guess who it is from. Lieutenant Moncrithe? Unless you have another admirer."

"Aye, it's from him. Though he's not my admirer," said Effie. "I'll read it later." In the privacy of her room, away from prying eyes. Jonet patted her cheek and grinned. "I must get this to Catriona so we can hear how Davy's faring."

It was strange to knock on Mrs. Forbes's door after letting herself into the house the past three years. It was no longer Isla Forbes's house, but Alasdair Grant's and, stranger still, Catriona was now mistress.

Catriona answered the door. Her maid, Moira Ballantyne must be busy in the kitchen. The smile faded from Catriona's face when she saw Effie.

"What do you want?"

Effie thrust the letter into Catriona's hand. "It's a letter from Davy. Perhaps I should give it to his mother instead."

Catriona snatched the letter out of Effie's hand. "How did you get this?"

"It came in a packet of letters for the professor. But this has your direction. I ken Davy's writing. It was aye like a spider dipped his legs in the ink and crawled o'er the page."

"Davy dinna ken yet you are wed. My letter will not have reached him." Catriona began to close the door; Effie put a hand out to stop it. "Will you share the news with his mother? She'd like to ken how he fares."

"This letter is addressed to me. Does she no have her own letter?" Catriona's face peered through a crack in the door.

Effie put more pressure on the door to stop it closing completely. "No. Mrs. Mackie is anxious to ken how her sons be."

Catriona pushed the door against Effie's hand. "Mayhap I will, mayhap I will not. What a romance, to receive a love letter." With one last push, she closed the door leaving Effie fuming on the doorstep.

Catriona was still jealous and possessive about Davy even though she was married to another. Would she share it with Rhona Mackie? She had been avoiding Davy's parents after she married Alasdair Grant.

Perhaps the lieutenant had news of Davy and Robbie. Effie returned to Vandemark's house and took Moncrithe's letter to the garden in the little nook sheltered from the winds by the stone wall. Lavender and dark-purpled buddleia bordered the teak bench weathered to a silver grey. In the warmth of the sun, the scents of the plants were strong and the hum of the bees a tranquil melody.

The letter was dated two months ago, not long after Calum had arrived in Halifax. It had got here quite quickly probably on a packet boats built for speed to bring letters and documents from outposts to the British Isles.

Joy to My Love

14 May 1813, Fort Erie
Dear Miss Innes, or may I call you, Euphemia?

I have good news. At least I think it good news. Davy, Robbie, and Tam are assigned to my ship, HMS Bristol. *I found them when I arrived in Halifax and they traveled with me to the West. Robbie seems to be enjoying the Adventure. I remember how I was at 14 years old. Davy is well-accepted by the officers and crew; he does a full day's work and gets on well with people. But Tam seems to defy all authority and has befriended some of the* [a word was scratched out—it looked something like scum] *more low-bred sailors and soldiers. We traveled to Lake Erie. I wondered how can we use a Frigate or a Battle ship in a Lake, but when we arrived at the Lake 'tis as big as an Ocean. You asked me once what the Americas were like. I had been to coastal Towns that in many respects are similar to those in England and Scotland, but I have never been so far Inland or so far North. It's a deep wilderness all around. On the way to the Lake we passed through the St Lawrence River and then to a river called the Niagara and a waterfall so huge you could hear it roar from miles away. And when I saw it, it was immense, magnificent. I wish you could see it.*

Something was crossed out. Effie raised the paper to the light but it was too thick to see. It looked like he'd written *I wish you were here.* Her sigh was a mere soft breath and a smile curved her mouth.

I hope Vandemark is faring well and your "black eye" is healing and you are returned to full Beauty. Though the Scenery here is spectacular and overpowering, it is grand to think of a pleasant Garden in a small fishing Village in Scotland, and of the Friends there. I trust I will hear from you soon. It is refreshing to think about and hear from a fair Nereid while living amid the disagreeable conditions of War.
Your obedient servant and friend, Calum Moncrithe.

PS: I often open the snuff box with your sweet-smelling salve. The scent brings me back to Vandemark's library and [two crossed out words] *happy memories.*

PPS: If I have permission to call you Euphemia, I would be pleased if you called me Calum. Do not tell Vandemark; he will not like it. Underneath his radicalism, he's still conventional.

Call him Calum? What could he mean by it? It brought their letters to an intimacy she had never expected.

"Calum. Calum." Saying his name out loud made her heart beat faster. She held his letter to her breast for a moment.

Effie endeavored to decipher the crossed-out words in the postscript; she held the sheet to the light. Those words could have been *to you.* Effie traced her fingers over the hidden words. She blew out her breath with force. Perhaps it was only a blot.

Effie read the letter twice. She knew they would find Davy worthy and reliable and Tam's character would be soon revealed. She could imagine Robbie's enthusiasm for action and new venues. She'd never thought of herself as beautiful, so those fair words brought a smile to her face and tenderness to her heart. She was glad she'd defied the professor and agreed to write to the lieutenant. But what was his motive? Loneliness? To help her learn about Canada? She had asked him a lot of questions. In a secret corner of her heart she hoped it was because he liked her even if she wasn't of his class. And perhaps asking her to call him Calum was evidence of that.

Chapter 19

The afternoon sun warmed Effie's back as she walked to the Mackies' cottage.

Effie stepped through the door after Rhona's greeting; the scent of her special salve drifted through the warm air.

"Jamie's fingers are sore from mending the nets. I'm using your salve. It seems to help," said Rhona.

Jamie's smile was welcoming. Rhona scooped a small portion of the salve and massaged Jamie's hands and fingers. Effie sat down at the kitchen table and unfolded Calum's letter.

"This isna from Davy but from Lieutenant Moncrithe. He talks of Davy and Robbie. And Tam too. You may get a visit from Catriona. Davy wrote to her."

"What?" Jamie jerked his hands away. "Davy wrote to her and not Ma?" Effie had never heard Jamie so indignant.

"Well, perhaps the next letter will be to me. I doubt he'll write to her again," said Rhona, soothing not only Jamie's hands, but his feelings too. "You have many letters, Effie. Are they all from Mr. Moncrithe?"

"Only one's from him," said Effie. "The other letters are from . . . from another. I need to talk to you about them. I'll read Calum's letter first."

"Calum, is it?" said Rhona with a smile and a wink at Jamie. "You're mighty friendly with the navy." The blood rushed to Effie's face. That familiarity had slipped out.

Effie read Moncrithe's letter. Occasionally she stumbled over unknown words.

"I dinna ken how to say this word here," she said pointing to Erie. "Mayhap it's *Erry*. And look at this. Is it *Neeagra*? What strange names they have."

When she heard what the lieutenant had said about Effie's beauty, Rhona's smile was broad.

Jamie nodded and said, "Aye, it's true what he says. You are a bonny lassie."

Effie blushed again. She was astonished to be described as beautiful twice within a couple of hours. She'd always believed her unusual coloring a detriment.

"Robbie and Davy are getting to be world travelers to see another land," said Jamie. "I wish—"

"Dinna finish those words, Jamie," said his mother, her eyes filling with tears. "It's enough to have two sons in far off places." Though she finished rubbing salve on his hands, she kept a hold of them, as though to keep him from running away that minute.

Shame-faced, Jamie squeezed his mother's hand and put an arm around her. She hugged him—not quite clinging, but a more lingering embrace—before he left for the harbor.

Rhona put away the salve and returned to the kitchen table. "I can tell you have more news than the letter from Mr. Moncrithe. What is the matter, dearie?"

Effie took up her mother's letters. "I'll read these to you first," said Effie. "But I have questions. It's about my mother, Maggie." A hint of a frown marred Rhona's forehead.

Effie read the letters quickly. Rhona let out a gasp at the first letter but was quiet after that. When finished, Effie stared out the window at a flock of seagulls peppering the blue sky; she couldn't yet meet Rhona's gaze.

Several minutes passed. Rhona cleared her throat. "That wicked auld besom," she said. "Hiding those letters from Lizzie. She'd ha' told me if she'd heard from Maggie. What would life have been like if you'd lived in Edinburgh?"

"Probably more difficult than in Pittenweem by the sound of things. Granny Agnes did me a favor hiding those letters. On her deathbed, she said she had done the best for me." Effie smoothed out and refolded the letters.

Rhona shook her head, voicing Effie's thoughts. "Poor Maggie, she kept writing and no one wrote back, even Lizzie. She thought everyone was still angry with her for shaming the family."

Effie exhaled. She'd kept the shame raw and alive for her grandmother, but Effie was a necessary help to keep them both from being destitute.

"Agnes Gillespie was aye so jealous of her step-bairns. It was a bad day when your grandfather married her. But what could he do with three young bairns after your granny Effie died? He needed a wife to raise them. Maggie was but a year old."

Effie hadn't figured that out. So Maggie was mostly raised by her stepmother. Perhaps it explained a lot about Maggie's character; Agnes wasn't exactly the motherly type.

"Did Lizzie speak of your granny, not Agnes, but your real granny Effie who you were named after?"

"Not a lot. She did say she was a douce and bonny woman. I mind Granny Effie died from a fever."

"Aye. That confinement was hard and the birthing of Maggie harder. Mayhap because it was nine years after Lizzie. She ailed from that time but hung on until Maggie began to walk. Yon Agnes Gillespie had been after Andrew Innes afore he went to Orkney and brought back his bonny Euphemia Adamstone."

Rhona folded Maggie's letters and handed them to her. She exhaled a gusty sigh. "In the end Agnes got her man."

"Poor Granny Agnes," said Effie. "Grandpa would aye remember Granny Effie as a young woman, and here Granny Agnes was getting old and bitter with disappointment, especially when I came along."

"After all her treatment of you, you canna still feel for her?" said Rhona, putting her hand over Effie's clasped hands.

"Aye, but I do. She turned people against her all the time with her sharp tongue. And she lost her only son. She was aye talking about Murray, comparing him to me."

"You may have the right of it. She turned more bitter after Murray died, saying Lizzie brought the sickness home from helping Dr. Ferguson."

"I hated it when she talked ill of Lizzie. She was almost glad when Lizzie became sick, saying it was retribution." Effie walked to the sink and rinsed off her cup.

"Murray was aye sickly—that's what comes from having a bairn late in life. He was a bad-tempered wee laddie, like his mother." Rhona tutted. "What a terrible day it was when he died. Agnes was crazed with sorrow. She stopped working and took to her bed. Lizzie and Maggie had to take on her chores. Your granddad too. Alec was away at sea; he didna want to be a farmer. I think her stubbornness helped ruin the farm. It wore your granddad out living with that besom."

"And I was the only one left—a reminder of the family disgrace." Effie sighed.

"You have a look of your granny Effie too," said Rhona. "Not your hair—she had hair the color of a new copper penny, like Lizzie—but your eyes, and bonny mouth and the shape of your face."

"No wonder Granny Agnes hated me. The more I hear about Granny Aggie's early life, the more I pity her."

Rhona, folded the letters and grimaced. "Not me. Her nature was aye fractious even as a lassie. Others have a hard life and dinna become so difficult. Look at you. You've had a lot of people against you but you are a douce and loving lassie all the same."

"I have Aunt Lizzie to thank for that. I ken she loved me and took the brunt of Granny Agnes's bad humor."

Rhona grunted, and said softly, "You have no idea how much you have to thank her."

Effie wrinkled her forehead. "What do you mean?"

Rhona gave Effie a long considering look. The silence grew between them. She finally said, "Do you hope to visit your mother?"

"I think so. I'm her daughter. She did ask for me to stay with her."

"I must tell you, Effie, finding Maggie may not be the best for you. She was not a good mother. I dinna think Maggie's changed much. You need to ken what Lizzie sacrificed for you." Rhona's face was grim, somber.

"Sacrificed?" It came out sharper than Effie wanted.

Rhona went on, ignoring Effie's outburst. "But Lizzie didna feel you were a burden. She loved you. All the goodness in you is because

164

of her. What kind of life would you have led with your mother? She was a dreamer and aye took the easy way out. No like Lizzie. No like you."

"What do you mean, Lizzie sacrificed for me? I ken she never married and had a bairn of her own."

"It was more than that, Effie. Lizzie took the scandal of your birth upon herself."

"Why has no one talked of this afore?" Frowning, Effie looked down at the stack of letters from her mother.

Rhona wrinkled her brow then sighed. "It's about time you ken— now Granny Agnes is gone," she said. "I dinna want to turn you against your own mother but she dinna come out as a braw person. I'll make peppermint tea; it's a long story."

Effie fingered the letters; it was better she knew the worst. Rhona, a close friend of Lizzie, knew the story long since. Why had she not told her? What difference did it make now Granny Agnes was gone? The chill of a sudden breeze from the open window stirred her hair. She shivered. Rhona brought hot tea and draped a shawl over Effie's shoulders.

Chapter 20

Rhona seemed reluctant to start and stared into her tea for a while. She lifted her head and looked at Effie, her bright blue eyes tender and sad.

"Lizzie told me all about it and I witnessed part of it too. I was Lizzie's best friend. No one kent your mother was with bairn except Lizzie; she didna tell me. Maggie was frantic with fear and she confided in Lizzie she'd fallen pregnant, but didna ken how." Rhona shook her head. "In many ways Maggie was such an innocent. She couldna name the father and that worried Lizzie. Had she been forced? Surely she'd have told her. Lizzie said she'd help her when the time came. She'd think of a plan." Rhona took a sip of tea. Effie grasped her mug more tightly.

"Lizzie persuaded your granny to let her and Maggie visit Carnbee for the spring planting. It's but a five-mile walk. She had to get Maggie away from your grandfather's farm, away from your granny. On the way, the birthing pains came strong. They took shelter in a doocot and that's where you were born with the cooing of doves and the trill of a blackbird as a lullaby Lizzie said.

"Maggie suckled you that night and was to stay at the doocot for a day or two until Lizzie finished helping with the spring planting and then they'd go back to the farm. Lizzie said they were going to say they'd found you and wanted to take care of you. It was a daft idea, but Lizzie couldna think of another solution then for Maggie to avoid facing a kirk session."

Effie could appreciate that after seeing Mary McDougal's humiliation.

"When Lizzie came back the third day, you and Maggie were gone. Lizzie was frantic. She searched all over, wondering if Maggie had abandoned you."

Effie let out a small gasp, her stomach churning. She had felt abandoned when Alec and Lizzie died, but the real abandonment had happened when she was just days old.

"Then Lizzie remembered that Maggie had wanted to leave you with the minister at Pittenweem."

Rhona stopped and took another gulp of tea. Effie slopped the hot tea over her fingers. Rhona reached over and took the cup out of Effie's hands and put it on the table. She held on to Effie's hands for a minute.

"When Lizzie got to Pittenweem, the village was in a commotion because a newborn bairn was left on the steps of the manse. Nobody guessed whose it was. Lizzie rushed home to see Maggie and they argued something fierce. I was there. Lizzie told Maggie they'd put you in an orphanage if you were not claimed. You'd be a foundling."

Effie tightened her grip on the letters. At least that fate had escaped her, but her lip trembled. Rhona gazed out the window as though she couldn't meet Effie's eyes.

"Maggie said she'd brought you to Pittenweem so the bairn couldna be traced to her or Lizzie. She kent the minister was a kindly man. It's true he was. I've never seen Lizzie so angry. She said she'd ask to raise the foundling and if they said no, she'd claim the bairn as hers despite the scandal."

Effie clenched her hands together. Aunt Lizzie would do that? She knew she had been courageous, but to expose herself to shame? A warmth swelled in Effie's breast. How she wished she'd known this. How she missed her.

Rhona blurted out, "Maggie said she could do as she wished. She didna want any more to do with the bairn—Oh!" Rhona stopped, her hand to her mouth.

Effie's throat constricted. *She* was that unwanted bairn!

Rhona reached across the table and rubbed Effie's hands. Though her hands were cold, Effie was colder still inside. The only thing she could think about was that her mother didn't want anything to do with her.

"I'm sorry, Effie. I didna mean to say that."

"So how is it everyone kens Maggie was my mother if Lizzie claimed to have born me?"

"I'm getting to that," said Rhona. She got up and poured more hot water into Effie's cup. "Drink this. You're shivering." Effie could hardly hold the mug steady, but she finally took a sip which warmed her, and motioned for Rhona to continue the story.

"Lizzie went to the manse and asked if she could raise the foundling—you—but the minister and the kirk committee said they would seek for the mother and any road, it would be better she was a foundling than to burden Lizzie." Rhoda snorted. "That's when Lizzie told them she was the mother of the bairn."

Effie had a hard time believing Rhona was talking about Lizzie who was usually so quiet, dignified.

"No one could believe it. First, they couldna believe Lizzie would leave her newborn bairn at the kirk—I dinna ken how she explained that. Or that she'd had relations out of wedlock. She was known to be a good and moral woman. Hugh Braid and Niall Douglas were beside themselves with rage. Both wanted to marry Lizzie. They'd pursued her for aye and now she claimed to have had relations with another man."

So what Niall Douglas had said was true. Effie even now couldn't believe it. She was still surprised that he'd blurted that out when he'd evicted her from the cottage.

"Hugh Braid? Tam's older brother? No wonder Tam is so against me," Effie said shaking her head. "I thought it was fear I had the evil eye, but his family holds a personal grudge."

"Aye, his whole family. Lizzie was well out of it. Hugh's true colors came out in the end." Rhona frowned into her cup.

"And Mr. Douglas? What would she see in that dour old man?"

"Well he wasna old then, just over thirty. And he wasna sour and bitter. A little zealous with his preaching, forby. He was mad for Lizzie. She went about doing good—a perfect wife for an elder. And, she was a bonny lassie."

Effie had a hard time picturing Niall Douglas as a young and infatuated man. She shook her head in disbelief.

"Lizzie brought you home from the minister's manse. Your granny was so angry all the village could hear her screaming. Your grandpa looked as though he'd aged ten year. The look in his eyes . . ." Rhona sighed, her eyes downcast.

Effie sat as though turned to stone.

"Lizzie forced Maggie to feed you in secret so they could keep up the pretense you were Lizzie's bairn," said Rhona. "In a week or so Lizzie would claim her milk had dried up and give you goat's milk."

Rhona squeezed her hands.

"Effie, shall I go on? You're as white as a ghost."

Effie nodded, her mouth and throat too dry to speak. She took a sip of tea, but still no words could come.

Rhona continued, "But, Hugh Braid and Niall Douglas wouldna let it be. Niall demanded Lizzie be brought to a kirk session again and tell who the father was. Lizzie faced those dour men to tell your parentage. And among the witnesses in the session was the minister, the laird, and your grandfather.

"Lizzie said she was more ashamed having to face her father than any other. I can believe it," said Rhona. "Isla Forbes told me more. Mr. Forbes was appointed to the Session afore he died."

"So Mrs. Forbes also kent my true history?" said Effie. "She was even more kindly to hire me."

Her thoughts sped as she took in what she was hearing. Everyone seemed to know except her. Effie wondered if Catriona or Tam knew. No, probably not. They'd have said something or hinted at it. And why didn't someone tell her? She tried concentrating on Rhona's words.

"Effie," Rhona said, her voice warm and compassionate. "This is a sorry tale but I want you to ken we love you dearly. I loved Lizzie and pitied Maggie. She was so young."

"Go on." Effie's voice came out quiet, raspy.

"Lizzie insisted you were her bairn and she didna ken who was the father. Hugh Braid and Niall Douglas became more enraged; they imagined she had relations with lots of men. The minister, the laird, and your grandpa thought perhaps she had been forced and shame

170

had stopped her tongue. Niall and one of the deacons talked and ranted for a long time asking her to name the father. Then Niall had an idea."

"Aye, he would."

Rhona quirked an eyebrow. "He said he wanted proof, and if not, the bairn—you—would go to the orphanage." Rhona grimaced. "He'd bring Fiona Ballantyne—she was not a widow at the time—to search the paps like they did in the old days. Do you ken what that is, Effie?"

Effie nodded. She'd heard of the barbaric practice, but it was observed many years ago, long before Effie was born, and usually when a dead bairn had been found. If the mother was found guilty she'd be hanged or, if the verdict was not proven, sent to America and sold into servitude, almost a slave.

"And that's what happened. Widow Ballantyne came. Granny Agnes and I were witnesses. Lizzie asked me to stay. We took Lizzie to a side room. She took off her chemise. We could see her breasts were not milk-swollen, but that didna stop Widow Ballantyne. Though tears came to Lizzie's eyes, no milk came from her paps. Fiona Ballantyne is an awful cruel woman." Rhona tsked. "Lizzie was defiant and said her milk hadna come yet and maybe never would. It happens with some women. Your granny slapped her hard and asked her to tell the truth."

Gratitude, pride, and sadness for Lizzie mingled in Effie's thoughts—and anger at those men and Widow Ballantyne. Lizzie had loved her more deeply than she had ever known. What courage to stand up to everyone for her sake.

"Widow Ballantyne and Granny Agnes went to tell that Lizzie wasna your mother. I stayed to help Lizzie put on her clothes and comfort her."

Effie rubbed her hands over her face as though it would clear her mind.

"Niall said he kent it. He was cock-a-hoop, smiling so broad I thought his face would crack. Your grandfather sat ashamed and confused. The Session thought Lizzie was protecting someone. Lizzie wouldna tell but they guessed it could only be Maggie. Niall Douglas and Colin Braid were eager to get Maggie but your grandfather said he'd do it. He took Lizzie home. I stayed with you." Rhona swallowed with effort. "Granny Agnes wouldna hold you."

Effie's heart was granite, as though it had stopped beating, her face stiff and cold. She pulled the shawl more closely around her.

"I was happy for Lizzie's sake she was not branded a loose woman, but I also feared for Maggie. And I feared for you. Would Maggie send you to the foundling home?"

A foundling home! Many babies died there. Effie took a deep breath. Living with a mean old woman for the past few years was better than that.

"When your grandfather dragged Maggie shrieking and crying into the room, you started greetin'. Maggie's milk let down and the front of her dress was droockit. I mind Mrs. Ballantyne was disappointed she couldna search Maggie's paps."

"I betrayed my mother." Effie's knuckles were white as she clasped the shawl.

"You were but a bairn. None of this is your fault," said Rhona prying loose Effie's hands and vigorously rubbing them. "When the committee bullied Maggie to name the father, she kept telling them he was a selkie. She'd found him by the beach near Boarhills. Lizzie remembered the man Maggie claimed she'd rescued. She thought Maggie had made him up."

"What man?"

"A shipwrecked man. Lizzie and I thought he was a Swedish sailor—not a selkie. Your uncle Alec made enquiries when he sailed to northern ports. Ships come and go from there on their way to the Low Countries. And at one time they came with their families to fish with the villages of Fife. Some had hair like yours. But the war put a stop to that. No one kent anything—or they werena telling."

"So you do ken something of my father?"

Rhona shrugged. "Maggie told us it was a man she rescued from the sea during a storm near Boarhills. Many a ship founders in that spot. Aye, I mind there was a storm that night and two ships from the north countries got into trouble. Jock was there and said the lifeboat pulled out many men from the shipwreck; they stayed a few days afore they left on the one ship that was seaworthy. The Gillespies said Maggie was nowhere near Boarhills though she was good at disappearing when chores were necessary. Against all reason she stuck to her story she'd rescued a sailor." Rhona ran her finger around the rim of her cup and looked thoughtful.

"Your middle name tells me it is true. You must take after your father being so fair and tall. I've seen sailors from the north lands when they stop at the harbors in stormy weather."

"My middle name? I didna ken I had one." Effie took a sip of the now-cold tea. This was why she looked so different from the shorter, darker villagers.

"Maggie was firm you should carry the name Inga." Rhona grimaced. "Inga. What kind of name is that? Not a good Fifer name, not even a good Scots name."

"I ken I'm named Euphemia after my real granny, but Inga—it's an unco strange name."

"It's on the kirk records and was spoken by the minister when he baptized you. Oh, how you cried when the minister held you over the font. 'It's the devil coming out of her. She's cleansed from Adam's original sin,' he said. It's more like you were scared to be held by a doddery old man." Effie tried to smile at Rhona's joke.

"Maggie said she wanted you to have this name as it was a magical name spoken by the selkie," said Rhona. "She thought he'd come back for her and you like in the stories. But he'd vanished. Aye, she began to believe he was a bewitched seal-man."

Effie fiddled with her shawl, her mind blank.

"Though she was seventeen years, Maggie was such an innocent. She just wanted to believe it." Rhona gave a short mirthless laugh. "Alec didna help. He kept saying you were fey, the daughter of a selkie. He loved you. Thought you special. I've never seen a grown man play with a bairn like he did you. 'Tis a pity he didna have bairns of his own."

Effie rubbed her temples. So that's why they call her a selkie? It was once a term of endearment, but now an expletive.

Memories came flooding in of Uncle Alec: days of laughter, riding piggy-back, dancing jigs, singing silly songs, and, later, when she was older, the little gifts from faraway places. Lizzie and Alec—the two people who loved her most—dead. And with their deaths, poverty of both body and soul.

173

Rhona's voice broke into her reverie. "Lizzie thought the man had his way with Maggie and told her he was a selkie. What a wicked way to get out of responsibilities.

"Your grandfather resigned from being an officer of the kirk sessions. Ian Bruce took his place. Granny Agnes had been proud to be the wife of a man of the kirk. She'd put on airs, turned her back on old friends too poor for her new station." Rhona shook her head. "Then Maggie humiliated her in front of all the important folk."

Effie sat stunned, trying to take it all in. A lot made sense now. All the people who looked askance at her had been caught up in the scandal of her birth: Niall Douglas, Widow Ballantyne, Colin Braid, and the most bitter: her step-grandmother, Agnes Gillespie Innes.

"Hugh Braid and Niall Douglas was happy Lizzie was innocent," said Rhona. "They kept asking her to wed. But she'd have nothing to do with them. She told them she'd help raise you—she couldna trust Maggie. Hugh was aye resentful and angry toward her after. Niall was more angry with Maggie and you."

Aye, Effie kent all about his hatred. Hadn't she felt it all her growing years?

"I think Hugh loved Lizzie in his own way, but his father is unco swift with the switch. I mind Hugh would have followed in his father's footsteps. Lizzie was well out of it. Hugh never married and perished on the same whaler as your uncle Alec"—she swallowed—"and my son, Jock."

"That's why I often see Tam with bruises on his face and arms. His father beats him," said Effie. She'd made sense of that detail, though she was still reeling from the story of her birth.

"Aye. And I've a mind Colin Braid beats his wife too." Rhona picked up Effie's mug and poured more tea leaves and hot water in it. It smelled like chamomile, an herb to soothe troubled nerves. "That's the story how Lizzie sacrificed for you: her reputation and the chance to be married."

"Wasna there other suitors besides Hugh Braid and Niall Douglas?"

Rhona sighed. "Aye. There was a man who worked for the laird, but she kept their friendship secret. She sent him away, but there were times she regretted it. I caught her crying once in a while. But, she never regretted raising you."

"He didna want me." She should be used to being unwanted by now after all she'd heard.

"No. Lizzie said he'd raise you as his own, but she said he needed to make his way in the world and a wife and bairn would hinder him. I believe he went abroad and may have died. Anyway, he never returned.

"And then, Maggie ran away when you were about a year old, but Agnes said she'd died. Lizzie went along with that story and when she didna hear from Maggie she thought she *had* died."

Effie crossed her arms in a protective gesture, her heart as well as her mind throbbing.

"Some think Granny Effie passed on her witches' wisdom to you," said Rhona. "It's why many think you and Lizzie kin to a witch. She was skilled in brewing healing herbs and taught Lizzie how to make potions and salves. Lizzie had her book of remedies. Mayhap your Granny Agnes threw it out after Lizzie died. She wouldna want a witch's book in her house."

"She didna throw it out," said Effie. "I found it. In the box with these letters. It's an old book, but I canna understand some of the writing." Effie stood and rearranged her shawl and gathered the letters off the table.

"I'd like to see the remedy book," said Rhona. She took Effie by the shoulders. "Dinna go to Edinburgh to find your mother. Let it be."

"I *want* to meet her. It was three years past, and who kens where she is now." Maybe she had changed after all these years, regretted abandoning her. She had to find out.

"You have a lot to think on," said Rhona. "We didna tell you about Maggie because we thought she'd died, hoped you'd have a good memory of her. Lizzie thought it best to no bring up the past. You already had those against you and we wished this story forgotten."

"I'm surprised Mr. Douglas or Widow Ballantyne dinna share it," said Effie.

175

"I think the laird and the minister asked them to keep quiet. They both respected your grandfather and Lizzie. And Niall Douglas still wanted to marry Lizzie, in spite of you. That certainly showed his devotion; men don't usually accept a wife's bastard. The men of the parish dinna show up well in the story either so they wanted to keep a good image.

"As for Widow Ballantyne, no one would trust her to nurse them if that story became known. She's not as respected as she makes out. Jealousy made her treat Lizzie so ill." Rhona looked off into the distance. "So Maggie has been alive all these years in Edinburgh? Michty me."

"I want to find her. Mayhap she's changed after all these years," said Effie. "But this is something I need to do. There have been too many secrets. She needs to ken I'm still alive."

Rhona had painted a picture of a naïve, frightened, and selfish seventeen-year old. And maybe luck had changed for Maggie since she wrote the last letter.

"Dinna do anything hasty." Rhona looked doubtful "I told you the whole story so you can see what kind of person your mother was." She touched Effie's arm. "Talk things over with the professor. I dinna think you should be beholden to Maggie—mother or no."

As Effie walked home, she had a daunting thought: when she walked along the crowded streets of Edinburgh, she could have passed her mother unawares.

Chapter 21

When Effie entered the library the next day, the professor's face was grave and his blue eyes sharp and searching.

"Euphemia. You have no kin left, and after this incident with that man Douglas, I have a proposition for you." He motioned for her to sit down across from him, not at the desk. He pulled out a piece of tobacco, tamped it down in his pipe, and lit it, his ritual preceding any kind of deep discussion.

Effie sat rigid, gripping the arms of the chair. Was he going to send her to a school? Help her become a governess after all? He spoke of that often. But she did have kin. She hadn't yet told him that her mother may still be alive. But she'd do him the courtesy of listening to him first.

"As you know it's been twenty years since my dear Rozamond and Betje died," he said with a quick glance at the portrait of his wife and daughter. He concentrated on lighting the tobacco and drawing in air to get it to light. "It has been a lonely life. Books are not enough."

Effie smiled. "Well, that's quite an admission coming from you."

He gave a slight smile. "How well you know me. I've missed having a family, burying myself in studies all these years."

"You have Cal— Lieutenant Moncrithe. I ken you look upon him as a son."

"It's true. But he's away most of the time. Since you've come to work for me, I've grown fond of you. I want the best for your happiness and that includes your education and your future well-being." He drew on his pipe, blowing out a cloud of smoke.

"Do you mean to send me away to a teacher's seminary?" said Effie in a frightened voice.

"No! I wish you to stay here with me as my ward and heir. You will be under my protection should anything happen to me in the future. I am an old man." He glanced at his bandaged foot swollen with gout. "That last bout of flu made me feel my age, and I considered what it would mean to you should I die."

Aye, it had scared her too.

"Perchance I could live with Jonet and Billy."

"A possible solution. And they will be provided for. That is not a future I have in mind for you."

Effie stared at the professor. First, she didn't like the idea of the professor dying, and, second, what would it mean to become his ward. She could guess that what he had in mind was more education.

"I thought you'd want to leave an inheritance for Lieutenant Moncrithe."

"He will inherit from an aunt on his mother's side, and he will have his pension from the navy. But, you, my dear, are alone in the world. Any relatives you have seem to have deserted you."

Effie drew in a breath. That was closer to the truth than he knew.

"We must think of your future. I will have papers drawn up with my lawyer in Edinburgh if you agree." His expression changed. "Euphemia? What's amiss? Is this such a bad shock? You're alone in the world and so am I. It would make me happy to have you as my ward. It will give you a better life."

Effie swallowed several times before she could speak. Her voice came out in a croak. "Sir, I'm not as alone in the world as I thought. My mother may be still alive and living in Edinburgh. I found out when you were gone to St. Andrews. Here are her letters. Granny Agnes hid them all these years." She drew out the letters and passed them into his hand.

Vandemark looked at the letters for a moment then looked back at Effie. His eyes were troubled and his brow furrowed. He muttered under his breath. It sounded like Dutch and the way it exploded from his mouth, it was probably an oath.

"I wanted to consult you about them," said Effie. "Dinna look so sad. I am honored you want to make me your ward but now . . ." Her lip trembled. "Now I dinna ken."

"I will read them," said Vandemark, an undercurrent of anger in his voice. "Stay here. I may need to ask you questions."

Long minutes passed in silence except for the rustling of papers as the professor read the letters. Once in a while, he looked up at Effie, frowning, and a couple of times let out a Dutch expletive.

Effie slouched as though all energy had drained out of her. She gazed around the familiar and crowded library noting the hodge-podge of objects representing the professor's interests: the shelves where books on classical studies were jumbled in their tooled leather covers next to larger tomes on law and politics; an old bronze Venetian astrolabe with its intricate wheels within wheels was propped up on the Queen Anne chest, no longer an instrument of navigation but a novelty like the nearby pocket globe the professor had told her was all the rage in high society; and behind glass doors, was the precious copy of the tenth edition of Carolus Linnaeus's *Systema Naturae.*

She smiled to herself; it would always remind her of Calum and their discussion on botany. Tension returned. She couldn't tell him about her mother or that she was possibly a bairn of a Norseman. Finding her mother could change their relationship. Perhaps her mother now prospered and was respectable or was that wishful thinking and she was still deep in poverty? She wanted to prove Niall Douglas wrong.

Effie's gaze eventually came to the portrait of Rozamond and Betje Vandemark who had died within two days of each other a few weeks after the professor returned from a trip lecturing in Leiden, his old alma mater. The portrait showed a large fair-haired woman and a pudgy blond lassie with rosy cheeks. The artist had captured the placid comfortable presence of the mother and the vivacious daughter, her impish smile forever pinned on her face. Their eyes seemed to acknowledge Effie, and she promised—though she could never take Betje's place—she'd honor and love the professor as a grateful daughter.

Effie dragged her eyes away from the portrait and glanced at the professor. He was taking a long time reading those letters. It made her nervous. What must he think of her now he knew the kind of mother she had?

Sorrow swelled up inside as she thought of the lost opportunity to better herself. How wonderful to be the ward of this kind man. By law did she have to live with her natural mother even though she was no longer a bairn? What hold could her mother still have on her after all these years? *Honor thy father and mother*: the fifth commandment sprang to her mind. Perhaps it was her Christian duty to live with Maggie. Granny Agnes had drummed duty into her mind all these years.

Vandemark finally looked up. It was a long, thoughtful look. Effie met his eyes but she pressed her lips together, a darkness within. She found her voice, though it shook.

"I warrant you wouldn't want me as a ward now. Must I live with my . . . my mother as my nearest kin? Isna it my Christian duty?"

"No!"

The explosive retort startled Effie, and she gripped her hands in her lap more tightly.

"No," he said more quietly. "She has no hold on you by law or by duty. She abandoned you years ago, and from these letters only thought of you the last few years. And as for not wanting you as my ward"—he swallowed—"my offer still stands despite what your mother . . . er . . . may be like now. As my ward, you will have my protection from her and anyone else. But you must make up your own mind about my proposal."

"If I do not agree, will I still be able to stay as your scriever?" said Effie, her voice tremulous. What if she let the professor down? Be an embarrassment to him? Not be good enough?

"*Ja*, of course," said Vandemark. "Think on it, my dear. Do not try to be noble and self-sacrificing." He put up a hand to stop Effie from speaking. "I know your nature, your upbringing by your grandmother. Piety is good, but not her kind."

"You are a devious man, sir," said Effie with a slight smile. "You wish me to make up my own mind, but you undermine any good Christian intentions I may have."

"Hmph." The professor concentrated on relighting his pipe. Effie noticed his hands shook a little. He really was concerned about her. A surge of affection ran through her.

"I'll give you my response tomorrow. People will talk, you know," she said, a fond smile on her lips.

"They always do." He hesitated. "Are you not used to that? If it is any consolation, I spoke with Alan Ferguson about making you my ward, and he thinks it is a good idea. He has your interests at heart too. We are both worried about your future. He admired your aunt Lizzie and told me how well she took care of you. Her influence has made you the way you are, not your mother's or your grandmother's."

"Professor Vandemark," said Effie, with a subdued laugh. "As I said, you are a devious man!" Then she sobered, and sat down on the chair opposite him, leaning forward the more to emphasize her earnestness. "Dr. Ferguson dinna ken how much Aunt Lizzie did for me. He was not here when I was born. After I found my mother's letters, I spoke with Rhona Mackie who kent Lizzie well and the whole story of my birth. I will tell it to you and Dr. Ferguson. It is a sorry tale and perhaps you may change your mind after all to make me your ward."

"My dear, I have witnessed unhappy and unscrupulous deeds in high and low society for many years. I am not easily shocked," he said, leaning back and serenely puffing on his pipe.

"I do want to find my mother," said Effie.

The professor wrinkled his brow. "I strongly advise against it. It is not a good idea or necessary. She could risk your future." His frown deepened. "But I may be able to find her if it means so much to you."

"Why do you think I'll need protection from her?" said Effie. But she could guess: he thought it unlikely she has come up in the world, and Rhona did too.

He shifted in his chair, not meeting her eye. "And now I need a little nap," he said, ignoring her question. "I'm not used to emotional upheavals so early in the day."

Effie stood, hesitated a moment, then leaned down and kissed his cheek. The professor let out a contented sigh.

Chapter 22

Effie had agreed to becoming the professor's ward. She'd tossed all night. It had been a difficult decision; she'd have financial security even if she never married, but it would mean associating with people on a different level of society. She didn't want to lose her friendships with the Mackies and Jonet. What would Davy make of it? Would Calum be pleased?

A few days later, Effie, Vandemark and Jonet left for Edinburgh. With Effie's new status as the professor's prospective ward, the Glasbeinn household gave her a guest bedchamber, but Jonet would stay in one of the staff bedrooms which was on the upper floor of the mansion.

Though Jonet hadn't changed toward her, the staff's demeanor had subtly changed. As the professor's scriever she had been stationed in the upper tier of the staff like Duncan Niven and Miss Craig, but now she had passed even their level. The staff would no longer welcome her in the kitchen. All the camaraderie of her previous visit was gone and she was bereft of friends in this household.

When Effie asked Jonet to stay with her in her room, Mrs. McLeod looked affronted and insisted Jonet stay in the servants' quarters, that she shouldn't get preferential treatment. Jonet told Effie not to be daft and she'd prefer to be in the servants' quarters. Jonet did grumble about having to climb up two flights of stairs. Effie insisted on accompanying her.

It was a small room, sparely decorated, but Jonet was content. Effie put her bundle of clothes on one of the two beds. Jonet poured water from the ewer into the basin on the chest of drawers to wash off the dust from her travels.

Mairi was outside Jonet's door. "I'll be your personal attendant, Miss Innes," she said. "Let me show you to your room."

Effie stared at Mairi, not knowing what to say.

"It will be an honor to serve you," said Mairi, a timid smile on her face. "I volunteered. I hope to become a lady's maid."

Effie had forgotten the strict hierarchy of below stairs. This would be a step up for Mairi.

Jonet gave Effie a little push. "She has the right of it. Go with Mairi."

Mairi led her down several hallways. Duncan strolled toward them. He stood in their way, smirking.

"Well, Effie. You've come up in the world if the rumors are true. That besotted old man should never have hired a lassie over an educated man."

"She's Miss Innes to you, Duncan," said Mairi before Effie could reply.

"Aye. It's true," said Effie. "He could have hired a man to do this job, but he hired me, and there's naught you can do about it. Please let us pass." If Mairi hadn't been there she would never have dared talk to Duncan this way. The professor had told her that Duncan had tried to insinuate himself and usurp Effie's place. Being a scriever was an easier job than being a tutor to young gentlemen.

Duncan moved out of the way, but the expression on his face was ugly.

Mairi tutted under her breath. "Och. That Duncan. How bold to speak with you that way. I'll have a word with Angus who'll talk with the butler and housekeeper. It's about time upstairs kens how he really is. He hasna been here long. The only person who likes him is Miss Craig. Poor soul."

"I wouldna like to think he'd lose his position because of me."

"It isna just you. He pesters the maids, especially Ailsa." She opened the door to Effie's bedchamber.

The room was beautiful. Its soft blue curtains and large bed were quite a contrast to Jonet's attic room. Someone—probably Mairi—had unpacked Effie's valise and hung her clothes in the armoire. Effie anticipated some awkwardness as she interacted with the staff and wasn't sure how to act. Though she had gained much, she had lost much. Effie rubbed her brow. It was so simple when in Pittenweem.

Mairi didn't seem to be the least bit uneasy. "I'll bring you a hip bath so you can refresh yourself."

Effie went to the window and pulled back the drapes. Her room overlooked the garden. As both house and garden were new, the trees were small and she had a clear view of the neighbors' gardens and the backs of their houses. Effie wished she were back in the professor's house.

After a short knock, the door opened and Ailsa and Grizel walked in with pitchers of hot water. Behind them were two male servants carrying a hip bath; they and Grizel left as soon as they'd put down the bath. Effie avoided their gaze. Hadn't she danced with them in the kitchen so many months ago?

What was she to do if Mairi offered to dress her? She supposed it would give Mairi experience, but it would be embarrassing, especially as she was no lady.

Ailsa's gaze kept darting toward her even as she poured the hot water into the tub. She'd better say something.

"I thank you for your service." Effie licked her lips, her mouth dry. "I need your help. I dinna ken how to behave with my changed circumstances. I wish I could be down in the kitchen with you all because I felt so welcome the last time I was here."

"Aye, it must be strange," said Ailsa. "You're neither fish nor fowl. That's what Mrs. McLeod said." Effie had to agree with her, and wasn't it just like Ailsa to spurt out truths?

Mairi rolled her eyes. "Miss Innes, it's out of the ordinary for us too. But I wish you well."

Ailsa thawed a little and gave a genuine smile. "Can I watch Mairi dress you after your bath? I want to learn what a lady's maid does too."

Effie glanced at Mairi. "Er . . . No. . . . Thank you," said Effie. "I'll dress myself this evening. I've done so for many a year." At their fallen looks, she amended. "Perhaps tomorrow when I go to the dinner party. I'll need a fancy hair style. Tonight I dine alone with the professor." She smiled. "He's used to my simple dress." And *his* household was a lot more casual and comfortable.

"Miss Innes dinna have dresses with many buttons or any jewelry so you dinna need to come, Ailsa," said Mairi.

"I'll pick some flowers from the garden for your hair," said Ailsa. She was determined to be a part of Effie's transformation. They were being kind and helpful. Effie nodded but stifled a sigh. She wanted to be left alone.

"The water is getting cold so you'd best take your bath now," said Mairi taking Ailsa's arm and leading her to the door. Effie laughed a little after they closed the door. Mairi would be a perfect lady's maid and gently lead her mistress to do the proper thing. Hadn't she, instead of Effie, taken charge?

The bath refreshed Effie. After putting on her blue dress which Mairi had laid out on her bed, she pinned her hair in a soft chignon with no embellishments. Anyway, she didn't have any.

Angus waited on Vandemark and Effie, so she was unable to talk openly about her fears with him. They discussed poetry and the music of Mozart whom Effie had never heard of. With the dishes taken away, the professor took residence in a comfortable chair, a glass of brandy in his hand. Effie was content with a cup of tea; she didn't like drinking wine or spirits, though the professor told her she'd need to learn how to drink wine at a formal dinner.

"Angus will escort you to your mother's home the morrow," said the professor.

Effie glanced quickly at Angus under her eyelashes before answering. "So you have already found her?"

"Yes, I sent a courier from Pittenweem two days ago to the constabulary." The professor paused to sip more brandy. "The place where your mother lives is not in a good part of the town, and it's important Angus escort you. Glasbeinn cannot spare his carriage so you will walk. Do not stay long. Angus will wait for you and escort you back. Return and report to me directly."

"That's unco kind, professor, but I dinna wish to disturb Lord Glasbeinn's household. Angus need not wait. I can get a map—" She didn't want Angus to learn about her mother and pass on that news to the household.

"Did you not understand me, Euphemia? You cannot go out by yourself in the city. It is a different matter than wandering around Pittenweem. There are dangers you are unaware of. Remember what happened when you went for a stroll last time you were here?"

Effie hung her head and whispered, "Aye, Professor. I mind it well. I'm sorry to be the cause of problems. And you're being so kind as to help me find my mother." How could she forget running into a man like Lord Thorburn or how Calum had rescued her?

Calum. The last time she'd seen him was in this room; the light in his face as she wished him God speed was imprinted for aye in her mind. But not just her mind. Her heart leapt at memory of the comfort of his arms around her as he steadied her. It was more than comfort—fondness, affection.

Professor Vandemark cleared his throat, dragging her thoughts away from Calum.

"I hear you have made a conquest in Glasbeinn's tutor. Niven, is it? It won't do you any harm to have an admirer, but you will not encourage him, no? I declined his petition to court you." He took a longer sip of his drink.

"I do not encourage him," she said in indignation. And he'd petitioned to court her? The gall of the man. Should she tell the professor about Duncan's behavior toward the maids? She had not made a conquest but was just another target for his unwanted attentions.

"Good. Good," said the professor. "How are your accommodations? I hear Lady Glasbeinn has been kind enough to provide a maid for you."

"Aye, but it's strange to have Mairi as my maid when only a few months ago I was enjoying her company in the kitchen. And the others too . . ."

"*O je*," said the professor. "You will find all kinds of social conundrums now you are my ward."

Aye, and she didn't know what was ahead of her. How was she going to navigate through her new status without tripping over an unexpected solecism? Vandemark would help her as best he could, but he may not recognize potential stumbling blocks. Her best teachers would be Jonet and Mairi. Effie appreciated the irony. They knew more about social mores than the gentry, who took things so much for granted.

Later that evening, curled up in bed after drinking the posset Mairi had brought her, Effie had more time to reflect on another aspect of her situation. If the professor was not happy Duncan was pursuing her, what must he think of her attachment to Davy, a mere fisherman? He hadn't mentioned him, and he was far below Duncan. Rhona's remark that the professor was taking her away from her own folk, still rang in her ears.

What had she done? Her life was going off in a direction she had never anticipated. And yet, she couldn't go back. She was still fond of Davy, but there would not be a meeting of the minds, conversations about books and ideas. He wouldn't be interested. But those times with Calum . . . She sighed.

Aye, those times with Calum. She could see him now: frowning over a book from the doctor's library, his auburn hair aglow in the firelight, and his quick smile which brought light into his face. Effie fought hard to push him away from her mind. It was no good thinking about him. Though she was now the professor's ward, she was still the servant lassie whose once respectable family had come down into poverty. And even when she had been the granddaughter of a prosperous farmer, Calum and she would never have met let alone have a conversation, let alone become friends, let alone become—

If Jonet and the professor believed she was still hankering after Davy, it could be a foil against their knowing of her growing attachment to Calum.

She'd made a choice from the moment she walked into the professor's library and was drawn to learning, drawn to knowledge. It had served her well in the past to assuage her loneliness, but now she was off-kilter as circumstances plunged her into a different kind of insecurity.

Her thoughts turned again to Calum. She knew all the arguments: he was gentry, his father a knight. A romantic relationship with him would be out of the question. He was destined to marry someone from the gentry class. He was even further out of her reach than Davy had ever been. With Davy she had reached for a bright star. But Calum—he was a distant galaxy.

He was not only kind but courageous; after all he was an officer and naval physician who had survived being in the navy for several years. Effie was sure the vulnerability underneath his confidence she had glimpsed that day had something to do with the old scandal.

Effie pummeled her pillows. She dragged her mind away from Calum to a disturbing thought: tomorrow she would meet her mother.

Chapter 23

In the morning, the professor dictated letters. The hours dragged. He had to repeat sentences several times and after the third time he became a little irritable. Effie forced herself to concentrate on the task at hand. She kept peeking at the ormolu clock when the professor paused to gather his thoughts. She and the professor ate a noonday meal. When he was settled in his favorite chair, Effie ran upstairs and grabbed her blue plaid shawl. Taking a deep breath, she walked down the stairs where Angus was waiting.

Angus loped along at a rapid pace, but Effie was able to keep up with him. The elegant new houses around Charlotte Square thinned out as they walked toward the grimy buildings of the old town huddled high on the ridge above the drained Nor Loch.

They climbed the steep steps of a narrow vennel, which led to High Street. The buildings on either side made the street a conduit for noisy traffic and howling winds. People were everywhere, both the high-bred in their fine clothes and linens, and the low in coarse and sometimes tattered clothing. To the right stood the massive structure of St. Giles Cathedral and past that the esplanade of the castle.

But Angus turned to the left and Effie had a view of High Street plunging down through escarpments of tenements toward Netherbow and Canongate.

"Take my arm, Miss Innes," said Angus. "I dinna want you to get separated from me by this rabble."

"Please call me Effie. I canna get used to being Miss Innes."

191

"You'll need to get used to it . . . Effie," said Angus. "Now take my arm."

Effie was happy to comply. People brushed past her and bumped into her. Effie wondered why they were in such a hurry. Angus sometimes had to push through a crowd which dispersed and came together again, a kaleidoscope of movement and color. People disappeared into and appeared out of the closes and wynds that branched off High Street.

As they walked, Angus told her about the Tron Riots a couple of years ago when a gang of boys had attacked people and killed a policeman. Though they had increased the police force, Effie was glad Angus was with her and they were not here at night.

The crowds became less dense the closer they got to the Canongate, and fewer and fewer gentry further down the hill.

"We're leaving Edinburgh town now, Effie, and entering the Canongate," said Angus. "I mind there used to be a gate to pass through but they tore it down to let the traffic through."

A carriage rattled down the street and Effie and Angus stood aside to let it pass.

"It was safer then. Carriages had to slow down to pass through the gate; now they go at break-neck speed." Angus glowered at the now disappearing carriage. Effie shared his sentiments. How fast-paced everything was compared to the slow meanderings in Pittenweem.

Angus slowed down. Effie peered into the narrow wynds ducking beneath the tenements to a close or courtyard with a few showing patches of green and the lacey branches of small trees.

They stopped at a rust-colored tenement, where a young lad in a tattered sweater and pair of threadbare trousers lounged on steps leading to a door with peeling green paint.

"This is it, Effie. The place where your mother lives," said Angus. "I mind she will live on the bottom or the top floor unless her husband is a merchant or a lawyer's clerk. What is your mother's name? We'll ask this laddie here if he can direct us."

"Maggie Wallace."

The lad looked up. "What do you want with Maggie Wallace? She didna do it." He leapt up, his tone belligerent.

"We're no from the authorities, laddie. This lassie is her daughter, Effie Innes, and she wishes to meet her," said Angus.

"That canna be. Her daughter is dead," said the lad. "I ken it cos I'm Maggie's son. Granny Agnes wrote an' told us."

Effie marveled again at her grandmother's duplicity. So that's why there had been no more letters from Maggie.

So, this was her half-brother. He looked about eleven years old. Effie took a closer look checking to see if there was a resemblance to Uncle Alec or to herself. His eyes were blue like Alec's, but Effie had never seen an expression of hard suspicion in Alec's eyes. The lad's shaggy and unkempt hair was a sandy color instead of dark. His face was almost gaunt with a long thin nose with flaring nostrils and his skin had a greyish tinge. He came to just below her shoulder. He had been studying her too.

"I truly am your sister, at least your half-sister," said Effie, and she put out a hand toward him. He shrank away.

"Dinna touch me. I ken your sort. You've come to take me away to the poorhoose." His voice was shrill, fear in his eyes. She turned to look at Angus in dismay.

"We're no from the poorhoose," said Angus. "If you dinna fetch your mother, we'll get the constable to you."

"She isna here. But my father is an' he's asleep. I will no wake him and get a skelping," said the lad.

Angus said to Effie, "We canna stand here on the doorstep for aye. Who kens when she will return."

Effie hadn't foreseen this. "Can we no bide a wee and see if she comes or her husband wakes?"

Angus looked the lad up and down, a stern expression on his face, but when he turned his eyes to Effie, his expression softened. She had a good protector.

The scent of pie and bread wafted through the air as Angus opened the packet of mutton pie and bannock he'd brought. He'd said it would be a good introduction. He was right; the lad looked half-starved and his eyes lit up at the sight of the food.

Angus broke off a piece of the pie and handed it to the lad who first looked at it suspiciously then snatched it from his hand. He stuffed it in his mouth not taking the time to chew it. When it was gone, he stared at the package, then scanned Angus's face, his expression less harsh.

"Will you tell me your name?" said Effie. The lad's expression turned suspicious again. She added, "But only if you want to."

He hesitated for a moment, then mumbled, "I'm Alec Wallace."

"Do you ken you had an uncle called Alec? He perished at sea many years ago."

"Aye, Ma told me of Uncle Alec. Are you truly my sister?" said Alec. "Is this your man?"

"No, he's no my husband," said Effie glancing at Angus. "He's a friend who kens Edinburgh, so he brought me to see my mother."

"Shall we return the morrow, Effie? We canna wait too long here," said Angus. He motioned his head for Effie to look across the street. A couple of older boys loitered in the pend, leaning against the archway leading to a nearby close. They stared boldly at Effie and Angus. Effie didn't like the look of them, especially after hearing about the Tron Riots.

"Perhaps it's for the best," said Effie. She turned to Alec, "Will you tell your mother that Effie came to see her, and I'll come the morrow?"

Alex still gazed at the parcel of food still in Angus's hand. "Can I have that? And will you bring more pie?"

Effie laughed and said, "Surely." She wanted to hug him. Underneath that surliness she glimpsed a little lad who was starved of both food and affection.

Before Alec could hand over the food, a woman shouted, "Alec, what are you doing? And what's in that parcel? Are they bribing you?"

A woman came up the steep incline leading from Holyrood House. Effie turned. Could this be her mother? She looked a little older than she had expected. Her face had the same grey complexion as Alec's; a deep crease of discontentment ran down both sides of her red painted lips; white strands streaked her straggly red hair peeking out of the shawl covering her head. She looked at Effie and Angus with grey eyes, just like Effie's, though poverty seemed to have dulled the silver sheen.

"What are you about with my son?" she said. "Are you from the poorhoose? What is this?" She took the parcel of food from Angus's

194

outstretched hand, sniffed it, and opened it. She turned to Alec and cuffed him on the ear. "It's as well I came along when I did or you'd have scarfed a'."

She turned to Effie and Angus, her tones conciliatory, almost whining. "Much obliged for the food."

At least she seemed grateful. Effie wished she'd brought more.

The woman took a bite of bannock, then spoke while chewing. "Are you with a charity hoose? My husband lost his work. We canna keep food on the table. This lazy laddie must work cleaning the clarty streets. Here he is spending the time sitting doon." She glared at Alec, then noticed the two boys by the close. She raised her voice which was harsh, menacing. "What are you looking at, Geordie and Sandy? Get on with your work, you scunners." The boys disappeared into the archway after making a rude gesture.

Alec was undaunted by his mother's bad temper. Tugging on her sleeve, he said, "Ma. Ma. They isna from the charity. It's my sister, Effie. Who you thought died."

The woman turned and looked Effie up and down. "That canna be. My mother writ me she died along with my sister Lizzie three years since. What trick is this?"

Effie took a step toward Maggie, not knowing what to do. Hug her, kiss her cheek, or merely shake hands? The woman moved backward, leaving more space between them.

From that little gesture Effie was in two minds about leaving, but she'd come this far and talked with Alec. It would be another lie if she walked away. She took out the letters from her reticule and thrust them toward her mother.

"Here are the letters you wrote to Aunt Lizzie and Granny."

The woman looked at the papers clutched in Effie's hand but didn't take them, holding fast to the packet of food.

"It truly is you? Michty me, what a bonny lassie you are. And so tall." She moved forward to hug Effie.

This time it was Effie who recoiled. Her mother smelled of whisky and the sour smell of an unwashed body. Her mother stood away from her and put up one dirty hand and stroked Effie's face.

"I canna believe it. After all these years. How old are you now?" She didn't wait for an answer. "We must talk, but my Archie is asleep the now, and we best not disturb him. We can talk at the tavern where I work."

As Maggie looked around, Alec grabbed a piece of bannock and stuffed it in his mouth. His mother tried to cuff his ear but he ducked away from her, a practiced move.

Effie looked away from her mother and Alec, who were cramming pie and bannock into their mouths. She'd never been that hungry, even in those lean years when it was only her and her grandmother. Angus stared at the ground. He seemed to sense Effie looking at him and met her eyes. He gave her a wan smile, his eyes compassionate.

"I dinna like the idea of going to a tavern," said Effie in a quiet voice. "Can we no talk here?"

"Aye." He looked around for a less exposed place than the doorstep with the noise of carriages and loud-talking pedestrians. "Mayhap we can go to the kirkyard yonder. It will be quiet and better than the tavern. I must take you back when the kirk bell strikes three of the clock."

That long? Why did she come? What good would it do? Maggie and Alec would have been none the wiser. Was she now exposing the professor to her uncouth kin? Making more complications for her too, now that her life was turning around? Vandemark had only met Granny Agnes once, and that hadn't gone well.

Maggie and Alec were reluctant to go to the kirkyard. They said they were afraid of ghosts. But Maggie agreed to sit on the low wall that skirted a wynd. Angus persuaded Alec to go with him to White Horse Close to watch the stagecoaches bound for London.

Chapter 24

Now she was alone with her mother, Effie wasn't sure how to address her. Maggie? Ma? She was a stranger to her, so she waited for her mother to start the conversation.

Maggie sat on the wall and concentrated on eating the remains of the mutton pie.

"That was tasty. I'm surprised that old carline allowed you to come seek me," said Maggie, wiping crumbs from her bodice. "In her last letter telling me you have died, she said not to write again. Not come near Pittenweem."

"Granny died four weeks past," said Effie sitting next to her mother, but not too close. "I just found these letters she hid. I didna ken if you were still alive."

"She kept bitter and cross and unforgiving till the end," said Maggie, looking as though she was going to cry. "I couldna do anything right for her. I couldna stand her evil eye on me all the time. And you were such a fractious bairn. I didna have time for pleasure but to take care of you. It was all Lizzie's fault. I wanted to leave you—"

Aye, Effie knew where her mother wished to leave her: the steps of the minister's house and a foundling home.

Maggie glanced sideways at Effie. "Where to begin—"

"Rhona Mackie told me about the kirk session and what Lizzie did."

"It's aye Lizzie this and Lizzie that. So, she raised you as her own? Did she no have bairns of her own with Hugh Braid or did she choose Niall Douglas? He always hated me."

"Lizzie didna marry. She chose me over them. Hugh was lost at sea with Uncle Alec and Jock Mackie the younger."

"Alec. No!" Tears trickled down the lines in Maggie's face. "My brother, my sister! No one telt me."

"No one kent where you were. Granny hid your letters. She told us you were dead. After Alec died, we had to move from the farm. It was Granny, Lizzie and me for a while—"

"Why did her kin at Boarhills no take you in?"

Effie looked down at her clasped hands.

Maggie snorted. "Ah. I ken how it was. They didna want you. That Gillespie family was full o' themselves. And with no reason."

"They lost the farm twelve years back and moved to Dundee. We stayed in Pittenweem." It was no good telling Maggie how the Gillespies had ignored Granny Agnes, another slight. The Gillespies struggled with poverty themselves and couldn't add two more mouths to feed, especially an old woman who refused to work.

Effie told Maggie about working for Mrs. Forbes and her new job with the professor and how she now lived in his house.

"So you are being taken care of by a rich old man." Maggie let out a crack of laughter. "Who'd have thought it with the Bible-loving stepmother. She didna keep you out of trouble. The village would expect no better of you as my daughter. And who's that fancy man with you?"

Effie could hardly keep her voice pleasant, "It's no like that. The professor is an honorable man and old enough to be my father, maybe even my grandfather. He is kind and generous and he has other servants." How to wipe that sneer and skeptical look off Maggie's face? People always thought the worst. "It's true. I'm here with Jonet, his housekeeper. He helped find you. Angus is no my fancy man but a servant at—a friend's house." Better not to tell Maggie Lord Glasbeinn's direction. She might pester that household. "The professor said I'd need protection in the city."

"Aye, a bonny lassie like you'd have been set about by the men," said Maggie looking her over. "I last wrote to ask for you to live with me. Now that you are here what think you? You could find work as a maid or with your looks ... something that pays better in Edinburgh. Mayhap yon Angus could help you. Edinburgh is a grand place to be."

Effie was silent for a few moments, clasping and unclasping her hands. What could be better than working for Professor Vandemark? Her mother didn't understand how this job had lifted her up.

Maggie was not what she had expected. Her life away from her family and small village life had changed her for the worst. How could she say Edinburgh was a grand place when her husband couldn't find a job, and she and her son were working at menial jobs? Maggie and Alec had eaten the pie and bannock as though they were on the verge of starvation.

"I dinna want to leave Pittenweem," said Effie. "I'm comfortable there. I have friends, and it's different after Granny died. I canna find a kinder employer than Professor Vandemark."

Effie was reluctant to tell her mother the professor was going to make her his ward. At least not yet. She'd vowed not to lie, though faced with the reality of her mother, there was less of a connection that had been nebulous before—a romantic notion. She had wanted to disprove the talk about her mother, but it had been too true.

She should have listened to the professor's hints; he knew the realities of city life. She should have listened to Rhona. But this woman before her was her flesh and blood. What else had she inherited from her mother besides her grey eyes? She wasn't sure she wanted to know.

"Living in Pittenweem and living in his hoose you canna need a lot of money." Maggie dug her elbow into Effie's side. "You can spare a few guineas for us until you move here."

Maggie had obviously not accepted that she had said no. She'd have to be more direct. She wished to help her mother and Alec, but she could never live with them. How different Maggie was from Lizzie. Perhaps this was how people became when they scraped by on meager earnings. Effie stopped those thoughts; she was being as judgmental as Mr. Douglas. And if that man knew how Maggie had ended up, how much more he would discredit her; he'd been partially right.

"Did Ma give you hell?" Maggie's voice broke into Effie's reverie. "She was aye an auld carline. The dear I ken why Da would marry Agnes Gillespie. I was sorry to leave Da and Alec even Lizzie, but I couldna put up with it any more. I couldna stand the long looks from folk. How talk stopped when I walked by."

She could have been describing Effie's life.

Maggie spat on the pavement.

Effie was familiar with the villagers' spite all too well; her life had been miserable too—because of Maggie.

Her mother sniffed and wiped her nose. "I lost friends. I was alone except some of the men; they'd pull me behind the wall for a quick kiss an' cuddle . . ." Maggie sniffed. "They thought I was easy."

Effie wanted to stop her ears, not hear any details. She fixed her attention on the many-windowed tenements across the street.

Maggie was in full spate and didn't seem to care that she was talking to her own daughter, exposing her wretched past which Effie had only recently guessed at. Effie only heard the last part of Maggie's tale.

"I was scared all the time."

"Could you have not told Lizzie?" Effie put her hand on Maggie's restless hands to show her sympathy. At least Effie hadn't experienced unwanted advances; the men seemed more suspicious of her mysterious selkie background. Her mother went on and did not acknowledge Effie's sympathy.

"Ha! Lizzie? She'd have blamed me. Said I was wayward and didna ken how to work. Didna ken how to be a mother." Maggie scowled. "Folk thought I was a bad and loose lassie, so I behaved like one." She didn't look at Effie but stared across the street at the tall tenement houses. "I flirted with the men and kissed many behind the hedges and walls, but I didna let them do more than that.

"One day I met Archie Wallace. He was tinkering in Fife on his way back to Edinburgh. He was a braw-looking man and I was unco smitten with him. He didna want you. A bawling bairn was not good for the tinkering business." She stopped for a moment, a frown on her face as she gazed across the street.

"I telt him I'd only go wi' him if we were handfasted. When Alec came along, we married in the kirk. But he got in wi' a bad lot. It isna his fault he keeps losing work and drinks for comfort." She touched the faint bruise on her wrist in an unconscious gesture. "I'm bound to him the now."

Unable to make a sound; Effie could only stare at the raddled face of her mother. Maggie wiped her nose on her sleeve then smiled and winked. Effie recoiled. Though she didn't physically move, inside she shrank away from this stranger.

"I ken Lizzie would take care of you," said Maggie. "I was only there to gie you milk. You were a greedy wee thing. I felt like a milch coo. I wanted to wean you, but Lizzie said no and stood o'er me all the time I gave you suck. I think she was jealous she couldna do that too. Lizzie would pick you up and cuddle you and you'd smile at her; with me you bawled when I picked you up."

Effie knew what it was like to be shunned and gossiped over, but the logic to deliberately choose to behave the way folks perceived her was hard to understand. She had taken the opposite way, tried so hard to be good and virtuous. Now she understood better why some tarred her with the same brush because of her mother's reputation. Why couldn't upbringing be more powerful than blood? Bad blood from this pathetic creature next to her. Lizzie had been so loving and caring and she was a virtuous and kindly woman. Why did they not think she was more like Lizzie?

Effie became aware Maggie's voice had stopped.

"Hey, daydreamer. Do you wish to hear about your father? It was him who got me into trouble. It's no fair how mistakes changed my life forever. But at the time it didna feel wrong." Maggie again stared off into space as though she were looking back through time.

The tall grey buildings seem to crowd in on Effie, and the noise of the street jangled her nerves. She wasn't sure she wanted to know more.

Chapter 25

"It's still green in my mind," said Maggie. "Lizzie and I were at Boarhills visiting the Gillespies when word came of a ship foundering by Babbet Ness. I ran after Colin and Graeme, the hired hands. I didna want to do the chores while the men had all the fun." She sighed. "That was my first mistake."

Effie hands laced the cords of her reticule in between her fingers. This was what she had come to hear.

"I'm usually afeared of storms but the wind was no so fierce. Close by the pier I heard women's voices wailing and keening. The lifeboat was out to sea to reach the ships. One had a broken mast and the sails ripped. I hadna seen a shipwreck afore.

"Lightning flashed then thunder so loud it was like the sky cracked. I turned for home, but on the beach, I saw a pile of clothes washed up in a tide pool. They were mine. Shipwreck spoils. I went to get them; lightning flashed and it wasna clothes but a drowned man. I shrieked so hard. Then he moaned. He was still alive. I didna ken what to do. Help him or go for help. He could have drowned with the incoming tide so I dragged him further on the beach. Och he was unco heavy." She paused for a moment and turned to Effie, her voice bitter. "That was my second mistake."

"Surely it was a good thing to save a man's life." Effie was relieved Maggie had shown kindness and compassion.

"His life was saved, and mine ruined." Maggie, once more stared into space. "But I didna think so at the time."

"He had a gash on his head and when I got hold of his arm, he tried to sit up. He puked up and started a-shivering. I helped him stand. Just then one of the Norsemen came and helped the man to a cottage at the edge of the village. I followed them. There were many Norsemen saved from the wreck and they were unco glad to see the man I was with, like he was an important person. They called him Beyawn. I still mind his name. Before he went inside the cottages, he turned to me. I think he said thank you in his tongue."

Effie squirmed on the stone wall to get more comfortable, but hearing this story was harder than any stone. But it all seemed innocent so far.

"The next day, I stole out of the farm and went to the cottage to see Beyawn. His friends were away looking at the wreck. Och, but he was bonny. Tall, with hair lint-white like yorn—" She took a strand of Effie's hair between her fingers for a moment. "And his eyes were like the blue of summer skies." A happy lilt crept into Maggie's voice, and though she was staring at the tenements across the street, she seemed to be seeing the past, a half-smile on her lips. That smile transformed her face so she looked ten years younger, almost beautiful. Effie could imagine now what she must have looked like as a young lassie—vibrant, playful, and willful.

"Beyawn kent a little English. We walked to the ruined doocot and the beach. We met for three days. No one kent that, not even Aunt Fiona or Lizzie, though they scolded me for leaving my chores. I learnt the name of his mother and father. Inga and Eye-nar." Maggie shook her head. "Aye, after a' these years I mind their names."

"Rhona told me my middle name is Inga," said Effie.

"Aye, you're named after both your grandmas. I thought when Beyawn came for me, he'd ken you were his bairn. He kent my name too. I told him it." She shook her head, compressing her lips, before she turned back to her reminiscences.

"On the last day—but I didna ken it was the last day—we walked by the seashore and he took my hand to help me over some rocks like we were old friends. And of a sudden, I didna want to be parted from him. I longed to get away from that old carline who didna want me and Lizzie who made me work. I asked him to take me with him. I didna care where that was.

"I thought he kent what I said though he shook his head at first. I begged him and kissed him. I embraced him long and held him tight. Well, he kissed me back. I took the ribbon from my hair and tied our hands together. I telt him we were handfasted. He laughed and kissed me again. I took him to the doocot and we became man and wife."

Maggie took Effie's hand, her eyes asking for understanding.

"I had to bind him to me so he'd take me with him. He couldna take me to the cottage wi' the other men that night, so he said to meet at the doocot the next day. I gave him my Innes tartan shawl and the hair ribbon as tokens of our marriage."

Maggie stifled a sob.

"But he wasna there. To this day, I canna abide the voices of doos and pigeons that bring to mind how I waited and waited." She put a hand to her breast. "I ran to the pier. They told me the ship had left as the sun rose. He left me. He left me. My bonny Beyawn. My bonny husband." Tears now flowed down Maggie's cheeks.

Effie didn't know what to say. That's not how handfasting worked; there had to be two adult witnesses. In Maggie's mind, she'd made a marriage compact with this man, Beyawn—that man who was her father. Maggie still mourned his abandonment after all these years. And what of him? What did he know of handfasting in his culture? All he'd know was a young lassie who was eager and willing to lie with him.

Maggie had been young, foolish, and naive. Effie could partially understand how loneliness and Granny Agnes's bitter tongue had driven Maggie to such a rash decision. But to have a relationship out of wedlock and be willing to go away with a complete stranger— especially a foreigner—was hard for Effie to comprehend. Impulsive, reckless indeed. How easy it was to have a life changed with one impetuous decision. She squeezed her mother's hand.

"I dreamed every night of Beyawn. I'd wake up to the same work, the same scoldings . . . the same sad feeling inside. It was as if he was a selkie, that I dreamed him. But no, it wasna a dream. I became sick every morning and the monthly bleeding stopped." Maggie scowled and chewed an already short nail before continuing. "One morning, Lizzie found me puking. She supposed I'd eaten something bad. I told her I was increasing. I begged her to take me to Heggie Brown in Anstruther who kent how to get rid of bairns with the herbs. I didna want to face the men in the kirk sessions without Beyawn there. It was weeks and he hadna come for me. Lizzie—she was aye so religious and thought she kent what was best—said she'd help me to hide my growing belly and she'd help with the bairn too. She'd think of something to tell the family when the time came."

Maggie's eyes focused back to the present. "And that's how you came to be. I aye wondered what happened to Beyawn. When they asked about him, I told them I was handfasted to a selkie. Wasna that clever of me?" She giggled, then sobered. "I didna want them to think I was a—" She frowned then focused her eyes once more on the buildings across the street. "Och, but he was braw and tender too, no like—I'd ha' gone anywhere wi' him."

Effie cleared her parched throat, scanning the wrinkle-riddled face of her mother who had been fated to carry her. Maggie still loved Beyawn after all these years even though he'd deserted her, and yet she had run off with Archie who had dragged her down to a level of poverty and degradation that Effie hadn't imagined.

"Perhaps he perished at sea and couldna come back for you?" That could have happened, but Effie didn't say it was more likely he'd never planned on taking her with him, or returning for her. Poor Maggie.

She squeezed Maggie's hand again. "It must have been unco hard for you. But I'm glad I was born."

"Aye. Lizzie was glad too, but she didna have to sit on the repentance stool for all the world to see. Beyawn, and you, and Lizzie ruined me. Never trust a sailor." Maggie snatched her hand away.

Never trust a sailor. That warning rang loud in Effie's ears. It was too late for that: she trusted Calum. Like Beyawn, in his travels, he'd meet many women, but she was certain he'd behave like a gentleman. He'd be more likely to court someone from his own class whether in Canada or in Scotland when he returned. And, now that she'd met her mother, her dream of him was receding further away, even if she was Vandemark's ward. She thrust those miserable thoughts from her mind and turned to what her mother was saying.

"Perchance you can make it up to me. Come and live with your own ma. You could help keep me from . . . I dinna want to . . ." Maggie shook her head and pursed her lips. "Think on it—it's your duty."

The professor said it wasn't her duty to live with her mother or a breaking of the fifth commandment. Effie wrung her hands. Surely she could honor her mother in another way than living with her? If she saved her earnings, she could send some to her mother and stop her from taking a direction she only hinted at.

"I could send money—"

"Ma. Ma." Alec ran toward them, Angus following more slowly. "I earned a penny when I helped put bags in a stagecoach. I'll go there the morrow. Bettern cleaning the clarty streets."

Angus looked harassed; Alec had probably been a handful.

"We must be getting back," said Angus. Effie stood and brushed down her skirt. Her legs were weak and numb so she stamped her feet a few times to get the blood flowing. And her mind was numb too. She needed time to digest it all.

"I'll see you again, Effie? When you come live with us," said Maggie with a wink. She gave Effie a hug. Effie strove not to draw away too quickly. To hide her quick withdrawal, Effie leaned down and gave Alec a kiss on the least grimy part of his cheek. He looked up startled, a sudden smile lighting his face. He took her hand.

"I'm unco glad to have a sister."

Effie looked Maggie in the eye. "We return to Pittenweem tomorrow." She blew out her breath. "I canna live with you . . . Ma." How odd to use that word she'd never used before. "But I can send a little money to help with . . . food."

Maggie scowled and spat on the cobblestones, narrowly missing Effie's shoes. "Lizzie taught you well. Too high and mighty by far. Too proud to be with your natural mother."

Aye, mayhap that was true, but she couldn't do it however sorry she felt for Maggie and Alec.

"Goodbye, . . . Ma. Goodbye, Alec."

Effie turned her back on the pitiful figures of her mother and half-brother and walked away. She and Angus did not speak until he handed her a handkerchief; she wiped her wet cheeks.

"It's hard to find your mother in such a state," said Angus. "I grew up in a part of Edinburgh no much different. I swept the streets, like your brother. A school teacher helped me find a position with a corn merchant. Then I trained as a servant at Lord Glasbeinn's house."

He was proud to be a first footman, especially when his father had been a sluggard, and most of his family had gone to the poorhouse where all but Angus and a sister died.

Alec's wan face haunted Effie. Perhaps he could get help like Angus. Would Maggie and her husband allow it? How much money would it take to persuade them?

When Effie and Angus arrived at Lord Glasbeinn's house, Effie put a hand on his arm and said, "Angus, I beg you not talk about my mother to anyone yet. Wait until I leave. I dinna want to see pity or disgust on their faces." She was such a coward. It was true: she had become high and mighty.

"I ken. I will tell only Mairi; we are handfasted and hope to be married soon."

"Thank you. I wish you and Mairi well,"

Effie went straight to her room. She wanted to bathe and change her clothes. She felt dirty both inside and out. Dirty from the hugs and kisses from Maggie and Alec, and dirty inside because of the things her mother had told her.

She put back the letters in the box. Her step-grandmother had done her good service even though the way she did it was often cruel.

Effie was reluctant to meet with the professor. He'd hinted that she'd find her mother in straitened circumstances. He didn't know the half. Did she deserve to be his ward?

But she had to get ready for the wretched dinner tonight with gentry, sit through it all as though nothing had changed. Hope that she had a mother worthy to give her confidence in her heritage had been torn and shredded.

Effie lay on the bed with an eyebright-infused strip of cotton on her eyes. Though her body relaxed, her mind was in a turmoil. How would this knowledge of her mother, of her base lineage, affect her relationship with the professor? And even worse, with Calum?

Presently, she, the daughter of a naïve lassie—now fallen woman— and a foreign seducer, would be dining with highly respectable people. She must learn to put on a brave face though quaking inside. Now she had to make an impression—even a false impression—for the sake of the professor who was doing so much for her.

She had a fine new sarcenet dress that made her look elegant, able to fit in with high society, but it was all a façade to hide her insecurities, and shameful background.

Chapter 26

Effie managed to keep up with the conversations around the dinner table. She sat next to Professor Vandemark's friend, a professor of literature at Edinburgh University. He expounded on Alexander Pope's poetry, and all Effie had to do was ask a few questions and listen, though her mind was not always on his lecture. The dinner went better than expected. She discovered she could indeed hide her insecurities under a mask of politeness.

The next day, Effie found the professor in the library with his foot propped up on a stool, his bare toes showing red and puffy—an attack of gout.

"Well, Euphemia," he said, taking off his spectacles. "How do you find your mother?"

"I would never have known she was related to Aunt Lizzie." said Effie. "You did warn me she would have changed." She proceeded to tell him a spare version of what her mother had recounted. He listened in silence, twirling his spectacles around by their handles and occasionally letting out a small incomprehensible murmur.

"Beyawn is your father's name?" He put his spectacles to his lips. "Hmm. I think it might be Bjorn. B-J-O-R-N. It would sound a little like Beyawn."

"Aye, I thought it a strange name. I dinna ken Norse names."

"Knowing his name will not help you."

"But it makes him more real now." And definitely *not* a selkie.

Vandemark raised his eyebrows and hmphed. "When I discovered the place where your mother lives, I surmised what you would find.

There are some fine people who live there but also those who are close to leading a criminal life they are so poor."

"But sir, if a person is poor it doesna mean they turn criminal. I am from a family which was poor and—"

"What you described is not the case, is it? People do desperate things when they think they have no other recourse but to steal or engage in—" He paused to push tobacco into his clay pipe.

"Euphemia. Listen to me," Vandemark said, his voice gentle. "Sometimes women in such straits become . . . well . . . . It's quite common in the cities, especially London."

"Surely not . . ." Effie had guessed what her mother had hinted about, but it have it confirmed by the professor lowered her spirits. She'd have to send a lot of money to help her mother avoid taking that drastic step.

"You have never been that desperate, Euphemia. Village life has sheltered you." Effie hung her head pleating and unpleating the handkerchief in her hands. There was so much she did not know.

"Do you still want me for your ward now you ken what bad blood I have? What the village said was true." And yet, she had rejected that idea until she'd met her mother.

The professor snorted. "Bad blood indeed. Nonsense! Yes, I do still wish you to be my ward. The papers are now ready for my signature." He leaned forward and took her hands. "Euphemia, remember, she abandoned you many years ago."

"Aye, but she did ask if I could live with her in her last letter, so she did think of me."

"Only for her own ends. You would have ended up like her if your grandmother had allowed you to go. She did you more of a kindness than you realized when she hid those letters."

"It's true. I thought she was doing it for spite." Her grandmother could have let her go to her mother. Was it to protect her from her mother's life in Edinburgh or to have someone take care of her in her old age? She had feared the poorhouse as much as Alec. Effie would never know for sure, but she gave her grandmother the benefit of the doubt: it was not *all* for spite.

"Well, that may be. Decisions and actions, even small ones, from the past will sometimes come back to haunt us and sometimes change the direction of our lives forever. Sometimes for the bad, sometimes for the good."

Maggie had made a desperate choice, but Effie was free now to make her own choices, not hampered by what was best for Granny Agnes. Others' choices—Maggie's, Lizzie's, Granny Agnes's—had been thrust upon her.

The professor cleared his throat and drew Effie away from her reflections. She noted the anxious expression in his blue eyes. She smiled. Her heart went out to this learned but lonely man. He leaned back in his chair, relaxed.

"Your thoughts were far away, Euphemia. We will return tomorrow to Pittenweem. We cannot go today." He pointed to his gouty foot. "I will miss going to Lord Devize's dinner tonight. I was hoping to hear more about what is happening in America."

"I meant to ask you, sir, if you'd send my letters to Davy and Lieutenant Moncrithe."

"Ach! I too have a letter for Calum I need to finish. It's on the desk; sharpen your quill and I'll finish it so they can go out today. And you can finish your letter here too."

It was peaceful in the library sitting at the desk writing to the professor's dictation. After Effie had finished the professor's letter, he took a draught of medication and took a nap—she wondered if it was laudanum. She turned to her half-finished letter.

> Dear ~~Lieutenant~~ Calum, she'd written, *I am unco glad to hear of Davy, Robbie and Tam. It is comforting for me and their mothers they are on the same ship as you. We are to go to Edinburgh the morn. The professor wants to hear more about the war in America and news is slow to get to Pittenweem. I think he'd like to go to London and get the news earlier, but he couldn't take the journey. He's sending these letters through a friend, Captain Bertrand who will be leaving for Halifax on June 20th so you will get our news soon.*

That was as far as Effie had written. She sat for a while fingering the quill, wondering what to say next. What news did she have to tell him? What right did she have to write to someone from his station, especially now she knew what her mother had become and that her father was a seducer? Was it true the sins of the fathers were upon the heads of the children? How could an innocent new born babe sin? How Granny Agnes had harped on about that. She had tried to live a good life, be a good person. It had been her choice to overcome the unfair prejudices. Her mother had chosen a different path.

Effie sighed. Should she finish this letter or sever the relationship? What harm would it do to keep up the correspondence? She'd promised she'd write to him. He wasn't likely to think of her as more than a friend, a correspondent who shared an interest in botany and healing herbs. Loving thoughts were probably all on her side anyway.

She decided to tell him about her French lessons and the latest argument between the professor and Jonet. She dipped the quill into the elegant brass inkwell and wrote.

I am finishing this letter in Lord and Lady Glasbeinn's library where we last met before you left for Canada.

She remembered that parting all too well. She gripped the quill more tightly and let out a sigh.

Professor Vandemark didn't tell you in his letter but he has the gout again. I wish I could find a remedy to help him.

I have some sad news but also good news. My grandmother died. But I have a new home. I now live in the professor's house. It is braw to look out of my bedroom window and see the village and the harbor and the firth. And when I see the warships sailing towards Edinburgh, I think of you and your comrades defending our country.

Professor Vandemark is teaching me French. Perhaps I can talk with a French prisoner of war in Edinburgh Castle. All I can do is conjugate verbs in the present tense. I can see myself trying to talk with a Frenchman and going through the verb conjugations before I come to the right one. Je suis, tu es, etc. The Frenchman would think it unco strange. It's so different from Scots but it has its logic.

You know the professor and Jonet don't always see eye to eye. The professor told Billy to pull up all the flowers so we can grow cabbages and beans. Jonet talked him out of it by telling him he was supporting local farmers and there was no need to pull out the flowers. He was funning. He likes to sit in the

214

garden on warm days and enjoy the scents and beauty of the flowers. I am sending you a gillyflower, and sprigs of rosemary and lavender. The scents of the plants may remind you of Pittenweem.

She hoped they would remind him or her too.

No doubt you have found more interesting plants where you are. I hope you will send a drawing or part of a plant. Mayhap you are busy with sick soldiers and sailors so I will only expect a letter which I always look forward to.

Effie read over that last phrase wondering if he'd think it too intimate; she decided to leave it in.

Wishing you God speed and His protection,
Your humble servant and friend, Euphemia

That afternoon, between the midday meal and preparations for the evening meal, Effie took a stroll around the garden behind the house. She'd find plants to send to Calum and hoped to find some different plants there too, though they were the same as those in the gardens in Pittenweem—but it was comforting, like meeting old friends. She picked a gillyflower and breathed in its clove scent. Now to find rosemary and lavender to send to Calum.

"Is that for me?" Duncan's voice made her jump. She faced him, not liking the smirk on his face. Surely he wouldn't accost her, especially now she was the professor's ward?

He tried to take her hand, but she pulled it away, anger mounting.

"You forget yourself."

"No. You forget yourself, Effie. Even though Vandemark made you his ward, you're still from the common folk," he said an edge to his voice, taking a step toward her. "I asked the professor's permission to court you so we can get cozy."

"And he said no. And so do I." Effie took a step back into the prickles of a rosebush.

Duncan's expression was grim.

"You still have feelings for Davy."

Effie started and clenched the gillyflower. How dare he bring up Davy.

His smile was callous. "Aye, I remember the name of the man you sang about. But he's gone to the navy, gone to war. You canna shut me out because of him. Forby he may not return have you thought of that? Anyway, he's merely a fisherman. I can be a better husband, relieve you of your scriever duties, especially when the bairns come along. I mind living in a small village will suit me fine. You'll come to love me."

"Never! Get out of my way." She slid away from the rosebush, feeling a slight tug as thorns caught her clothing.

"How about a kiss?" Duncan put his arms around her and tried to kiss her mouth. She turned her head away and he kissed her cheek. She pushed him away; a shudder of anger ran through her. Thorns from the rosebush pricked her and a few petals dropped onto her shoulder. Her escape was cut off. Panic flooded through her, her heart thudding painfully as she remembered the confrontation with Mr. Douglas.

With all her strength, she pushed her hands against Duncan's chest and slipped sideways out from his embrace. She'd slap him if necessary.

He merely smiled and tried to catch her arm as she walked past him. She flinched at his touch and did not meet his eye. As she reached the door he laughed and called out, "I didna ken there was such fire in the ice lassie," before the door closed behind her.

She smoothed down her dress with trembling hands and walked toward her bedchamber. What did he mean? That he didn't believe her? That he liked the stolen embrace and her fighting back? Perhaps being private in the garden was an invitation to be intimate. She had a lot to learn about how to act with propriety. And what if Duncan found out about her mother? He'd force himself on her even more, think her an easy prey, think her akin to her mother. She should tell the professor who would no doubt report him to Glasbeinn. She was no longer squeamish if Duncan lost his job; he'd deserve it. She still needed to pick flowers for Calum; she'd bring Mairi with her.

Joy to My Love

How vulnerable women were, how easy to be overwhelmed by a strong and determined man. Duncan had merely wanted a kiss, but after hearing her mother's story, she knew what that could lead to.

Now, if it had been Calum—or even Davy—asking for a kiss, would she have resisted? Probably not. But they would not have forced themselves on her like Duncan. Even so, it was a troubling and disturbing thought that she'd welcome their embraces. Was she like her mother after all?

Chapter 27

Effie was relieved to return to the familiar sights and sounds of Pittenweem after the visit to Edinburgh. There had been much to disturb her: meeting her mother and the dashing of her dreams that her mother had grown from a selfish young lassie to a fine woman. And then there had been the confrontation with Duncan.

Rhona Mackie joined Effie and Jonet in harvesting and preparing herbs while the professor was in St. Andrews. Effie was glad of the everyday chores that kept them busy as they waited for news from Canada—interminable waiting, the lot of women whose men were away in the military or on long distance fishing trips.

She brought out her grandmother's herbal so they could make salves and potions for Dr. Ferguson to stock up for the winter months when sickness was rampant. He'd been happy to see it as it reminded him of Lizzie and he said it brought him back to the days when he studied botany. Effie wished she could share the book with Calum. How enjoyable to have him sit beside her and discover new recipes. She dragged her mind away from him.

Rhona stood far away from the book—suspicion—almost fear on her face.

"It isna a witch's book, Mrs. Mackie." Effie beckoned to her to come closer and turned over a page to show her a drawing of peppermint, one of the herbs they were drying.

"The writing is uncanny. Is it even in Scots?" Rhona peered at the page from a distance.

"Some of it is. Look there's Lizzie's hand, and I think this may be Granny Effie's." She laid her hand on the page almost in a caress. How many of her female ancestors had handled this book? How many lives had they influenced for good, curing ills and giving comfort to family and neighbors? How many of these wise women practiced in plant lore had been called witches? Had any died by fire or water or hanging?

"Professor Vandemark says it's very old, handed down for many generations. The oldest writing is Gaelic uncial writing—like the writings of monks from times past—but the language is Norn."

"Norn?" A spasm of alarm crossed Rhona's face.

"It's the language they speak in Orkney. You ken not all folk speak Scots; in the north they speak Gaelic."

"The writing's bonny as well as the drawings," said Jonet. "Rhona, you should look in some of the books in the library. Language and writing you've never seen the like."

"What does this say, Effie? I ken that flower." Rhona took a step closer.

"*Belenuntia.* Though we ken it as henbane," said Effie pointing to the painting. "See the jagged, hairy leaves and the seed pods like little sacks."

"Henbane?" said Jonet, "Isna that the flying herb witches use?"

"I dinna ken about that," said Effie, peering at the page. "It says it is good for stomach spasms but it can give fantastical thoughts and too much is poison. Hmm. I saw this plant at West Braes. It has yellow flowers but the leaves stink. It's nature warning us."

"Be careful you do not delve too deeply into this book," said Rhona Mackie, a worried frown wrinkling her forehead. "Take care you do not get the reputation of a witch. Witches do not fare well in Pittenweem."

"Killing witches was over a hundred years ago," said Effie. "We're more civilized now."

"I ken there are witches buried outwith the kirkyard," said Jonet.

"Aye, but there's one not buried by the kirk," said Effie, shaking her head. "She died a terrible death."

"I dinna ken yon history," said Jonet.

"I gars me grue to think on it," said Effie. "I had nightmares after I heard the story and I was afeared for Aunt Lizzie because she dealt with healing herbs from this book."

"Tell me," said Jonet who was bundling mint still sparkling with raindrops to hang to dry in the still room in the attic. The fresh pungent scent filled the air and masked the smell of the fish they ate at luncheon.

"It's a terrible tale. Took place over a hundred years ago. We've changed since then," said Rhona. "Folk already treat you poorly, Effie. If they ken you have this book . . . and if Widow Ballantyne hears of it, she'll spread the word to Niall Douglas. And you ken what that scunner would do. He'd bring the minister too." She wrinkled her nose. "Ugh! When I think how Niall behaved toward you—I can hardly meet him in the street!"

"He's no preaching as much as afore," Jonet said. She grinned, a glint of mischief in her eyes. "Isabella McIntosh told me—and she kens all the gossip—they sell more than fish at the market."

"What? What did she say?" said Rhona.

"Oh, that he may leave the village. Go back to Dundee; she says he wasna born here. The minister is asking for his resignation or his dismissal from the kirk committee, but that has to be put to the vote."

"Is it because of me? I wondered what the professor said to Mr. Mitchell." Effie snipped the ends of a bunch of parsley, the clean fresh scent mingling with the more pungent peppermint.

"No one kens what he did to you—we all kept it quiet—if it had been me, I'd have shouted it to the roof tops." Jonet waved a bunch of herbs around her head. "But the Blacks didna keep it quiet, tried to blame you. He shouldna have lied to them about what happened. They backed him up but then when you weren't dismissed and the minister is friendly to you, it stirred up the village wondering what was the truth."

Rhona tied another bundle of herbs. "Good riddance to the man."

"I'm not bothered if he stays or goes. I dinna care what people say of me anymore."

Effie jotted down a note. Those were brave words; she didn't quite believe them. But she felt a twinge of pity for the man whose nature had been warped because of his thwarted love.

"Whatever I do will be talked about. I want to be like Aunt Lizzie and help people. More people ken now that I make simples and salves for Dr. Ferguson. And more women in farms outwith Pittenweem ask for my help in delivering bairns. They still dinna trust Dr. Ferguson to be the midwife."

"Aye that's true. But to get back to the witch. Tell me her story," said Jonet tying string around the mint with quick impatient movements.

"As I heard tell," said Mrs. Mackie.

Jonet rolled her eyes; those words were a signal for a long, drawn out story. Effie laughed. How she loved Jonet and her straightforward manner.

Rhona grinned. "Her name was Jean Cornfut and a village laddie said she'd put a spell on him. She was heard muttering after he'd delivered nails to her house. He fell sick—so he claims—and decided she was a witch. It didna help he told the minister about his fears. The minister of the day thought himself an unco virtuous man to fight evil even if there was none to fight. They put Jean in the prison at the bottom of the kirk by School Wynd."

Jonet and Effie exchanged glances. They knew that place. Jonet had stopped bunching the herbs; Effie kept working as though by doing something she could lessen the horror.

Rhona also stopped tying the herbs, her eyes fixed on the motto hanging over the fireplace. *Clean hands and a pure heart.* She shook herself then continued the story.

"Jean escaped from that dark fearful place, but a mob caught her. What got into them I canna believe. They strung her up by a rope between two ship's masts and dipped her in the harbor. It was January so the water was freezing. Drookit and half-dead, they hauled her onto the street."

The rustle of dried herbs broke the silence in the room.

"And then," Rhona continued, her hands clenched around the herbs so hard her knuckles went white. "I canna mind what cruelty, what evil took hold of them—they put a door over her. Piled it with rocks until she died. But they did more. What maggot got inside someone's head! After they pulled off the rocks—though she was dead—they ran a carriage back and forth over the door and broke all the bones in her poor old body. They threw Jean among the rocks at West Braes."

"I canna believe it," said Jonet, her face chalk-white. "The poor woman. And all because of a dimwit laddie."

Effie shuddered. "I had nightmares for weeks. I imagined the crushing weight of the stones and the wheels of the carriage breaking my bones while the folk jeered and laughed." Her hands shook as she stripped the rosemary stalks. "People think I'm fey, and some have called me a witch. It's not witchcraft to deal in herbs but what God has provided in nature to heal our ills."

"We'd never let anything happen to you," said Rhona. "All the same, dinna give folk a weapon to use against you. Keep this book hidden from prying eyes."

"I mind Effie has no need to hide from such folk any longer," said Jonet. "She has more friends now. The professor would soon put a stop to anything bad happening to you."

Effie hugged Jonet and Mrs. Mackie in turn. "I ken I am the luckiest lassie, to have such braw friends," said Effie, a catch in her voice.

She turned the page away from the recipes for henbane with its association with witchcraft.

"Look at that now," Rhona said. "I ken that flower."

"It's meadowsweet and has a braw scent," said Effie examining the page. "It says it's good for the dropsy and it's good to strew on the floor to make it smell sweet."

"That's queen o' the meadow. I see it by the burn and the loch by Kilconquhar," said Jonet looking over their shoulders. "Sweet smelling or no, I think a good scrubbing with a brush and soap and water is better than strewed plants on the floor. Can you think what the professor would say if he came home to a layer of queen o' the meadow on the floor?"

The three women laughed.

"I think he'd give us a lecture on how the ancient Greeks or some other heathen folk use sweet smelling plants on the floor," said Jonet.

"And find a book with a picture of it," said Effie. "The professor aye likes to lecture us."

"And much of it useless and a lot of nonsense," said Jonet. "I like the modern ways better."

"I wonder how the professor is doing in Edinburgh and if he has found out anything about Davy and Cal—Lieutenant Moncrithe," said Effie before she could stop herself. The atmosphere changed.

"It's long syne we had letters," said Jonet.

"They'll be busy with the sailor's work. I dinna expect much writing from my laddies. Schooling was no something they liked," said Rhona.

"The professor will be home in a few days," said Jonet, "and then we'll ken more."

Rhona picked up her shawl. "I must away home. Jock and Jamie will be looking for their dinner."

That night, Effie read more of the herbal book. It was unfair: the law and kirk did not punish doctors for using similar potions to the ones handed down from mother to daughter for generations. How did the doctors know laudanum worked any better than meadowsweet? Of course, they didn't burn witches in 1813, but superstitions were not easily dispelled. Jonet and Rhona were right to warn her.

How easy it was to stir up contention and twist what was good into something evil. Like the mystery of her birth causing some to speculate about her. If the villagers had known about this book, they'd see it as secret and unholy writing when it was merely an old script. Rhona's reaction was proof of that. No wonder Granny Agnes had hidden it. Effie was thankful she hadn't destroyed it or handed it over to Niall Douglas.

Calum Moncrithe and Alan Ferguson had trained as doctors at Edinburgh University. Why did no women study at the medical facility? They'd already know many of the procedures the men were learning. She admired those two men who genuinely cared about people. Calum had to deal with terrible and disfiguring wounds as a navy surgeon. How had he dealt with that for all these years? It must affect him to see the mutilations of war.

She remembered how gentle he'd been when he touched her cheek to examine the bruise. No. She shouldn't think of him—but her thoughts drifted back to him anyway.

Effie went to the window. The sky was clear with only a few wispy clouds. On the dark expanse of water, a moon glade led a pathway to the burnished cliffs of the Isle of May. As a wee lassie, she'd imagined it was a path the kelpies—shape-shifting water horses—took to reach the moon, a meeting of water and fire leading to her heart's desire. Was Calum looking up at this same moon, thinking of Pittenweem? Maybe thinking of her?

"God be with you and keep you, Calum," she whispered. "And Davy and Robbie."

Chapter 28

Days passed with humdrum normal activities and still no letters from Canada. Effie remembered the men in her prayers each evening, sometimes falling asleep on her knees after a busy day.

One evening more than stiffness and cold woke her. She had an impression of turmoil and terror. *Sea. Sky. Blood. Calum!* He was in mortal danger. Davy too.

Her breath came quick, her heart pounded. She couldn't move from kneeling by the bed.

Then the nightmare changed, catching on the edge of consciousness, to a hazy view of a huge expanse of water with tall, dark trees mirrored at the edge. Dark figures in strange clothing roamed among the trees. The scene changed to a white canopy where men lay in bloody bandages. Calum lay on a cot, a threadbare blanket over him and a bandage stark against his auburn hair. In his hand, he clutched the professor's snuff box which held the salve she'd made him. Davy sat on a log nearby, his dark head bent and shoulders lowered—dejected, defeated.

As the vision faded, Effie yearned to take Calum in her arms, to comfort him as he had comforted her when she received the wound on her cheek. She put her hand there in an unconscious gesture. How long ago that was. That bruise had healed though the deep, unseen bruises to her heart since he had gone, were tender.

The dream was as vivid as the one she'd had about Uncle Alec. And if true, then Calum was not dead, but wounded. Davy too.

She climbed into bed but lay tense and stiff until exhaustion overcame her and she slept.

The next day, she hid the effects of her restless night, bathing her eyes in cold water and pinching her cheeks to bring color to them. She would not tell anyone of her dream. What good would it do? It would only worry others. And she doubted the professor would believe it.

That evening Alan Ferguson had dinner with the professor and Effie. Though Effie would rather have been in the kitchen with Jonet, the professor preferred she eat with him and his guests. It was an opportunity for her to learn proper table manners.

A lively discussion about travels brought them to stories of the Far East. Vandemark had been with the Dutch East India Company, and Ferguson with the British East India Company.

After the doctor left, Vandemark and Effie sat in the library—he with his brandy, she with her tea.

"Euphemia, when I talked with you earlier about your relationship with Calum, I did not wish to discourage you, to suggest you will never find a husband. I hope you will also make new friends and eventually an educated man to cherish you one day. You're young. Not on the shelf yet." He grinned. "If not, I hope this experiment will—"

"Experiment? What do you mean?"

"I have said too much. We'll talk on it later. Go look on the desk. I acquired a new book by a French count, Chateaubriand. It is about America and the native people who live there. It's called *Atala* and I think it will appeal to a young lady. There's an English translation so you can read it side by side and learn new French words." He held up two slim volumes. "Bring your quill and paper; we'll list words you do not know and make a glossary for the book."

Effie picked up a sheaf of paper, puzzling over his earlier words. "Sir, please explain what you meant by experiment."

Vandemark hesitated, looking at Effie over his glasses before he answered.

"I used to know a man called Hugh Blair, a brilliant scholar, rhetorician. He died several years ago. He hypothesized that through education a person could be raised above their station. I know he was speaking about middle class men, though since I met you, I took it a step further. Can a woman and a person from a lower class be raised to a higher level? She would be a novelty. Do not look offended, Euphemia. I'm merely telling you the way of the world with its class distinctions."

"I know about the gentry and us common folk. I know you miss teaching but . . . I thought you liked me and that was why you were giving me the lessons." She swallowed. "As you said, I am a novelty." Effie was proud her words came out so calmly.

An experiment? Just because she craved knowledge from those unexplored books? It had given her great pleasure to learn the words of wisdom of people who lived long ago and to learn French. She hadn't considered how unusual it was for the professor to take such an interest in her until she went to Edinburgh. Some of his friends had quizzed her, some raised their eyebrows. Perhaps they had discussed her in their intellectual meetings as he'd shown her off. It was men who went to university, not women and certainly not from her class. She was an *experiment*; it sounded so callous, objective, scientific.

"My dear, I am sorry I did not discuss this with you. With an experiment you cannot tell all, and let nature take its course. See what happens. I had some qualms. I know you may find it difficult to make friends in a different class. But I always remember your face as you looked at the books in my library the first day we met." He smiled and leaned toward her. "I could not resist the opportunity of putting Blair's theory to work. I thought it would amuse me for a while, but teaching you has been a delight and an honor. You are much more than just an apt scholar."

She wrinkled her brow. Was he only saying that to appease his guilt?

"You've gone beyond my expectations and—" He chewed on his pipe.

Effie lifted her chin. "So, you didna think I could do it. A mere lassie? Or any lassie, even from the gentry, for that matter?"

He put out his hands as though in supplication. "No. No. I did not mean it that way." He sighed. "I seem to be getting into deeper water. I planned for you to find a job working as a governess; though you'd need elocution lessons if you want to work for the gentry—"

She struggled to keep her face devoid of expression. A governess like Miss Craig? *No thank you.* And she'd have to change her speech. Though with a little twinge—and to be fair—she realized she had already done so especially when she talked with the professor and wrote to Calum.

"Sir!" Effie stumbled as she rose, breast heaving so she could hardly get the words out. "You're like that Greek person Pig—, Pigma—"

"Pygmalion." He grinned. "I am glad to know you enjoyed Ovid's stories. Mayhap you can read it in Latin one day and—"

"Professor, you—" It was enough to make her swear; an expletive. the fishwives used flashed through her head. She'd never use it, but at such a time as this, it was useful to relieve irate feelings. "Aye. That person. I'm no bonny statue brought to life. I have a history that's made me what I am today. You will take me away from my own kind. What have I done?" She put her hands to her face, repeating even softer "What have I done?" Then her voice quivered. "You'll mold me so I dinna ken myself."

"Euphemia. Sit down. I beg you. I will admit I am a foolish old man. I did not think it through. You *are* more like a daughter to me. It is why I made you my ward."

Effie's fingers dug into the book she was holding.

"And perhaps one day you would find a suitor; there are plenty of single scholars at the universities. If not, I think you could run a school, maybe for people from your class. You would be wasted as a governess. I was talking to Professor Craig of the possibility and he knows of a place in Perth and I know one in Stirling—"

"I dinna ken what I feel at this moment." The reality of Effie's position was beginning to sink in. She'd been so enamored about learning new things and becoming the professor's ward, she hadn't realized the magnitude of the sea-change in her life.

Effie put down *Atala* on the table next to the professor and walked to the door. She spun round, her hand on the door handle— at least that felt real. "Jonet and Mrs. Mackie are right: I'm neither fish nor fowl."

The professor stirred in his chair as though to rise and winced as his foot touched the ground.

Normally she'd turn back to help him, but she hardened her resolve to shun him. She'd been betrayed; the professor was usually forthright and honest toward her. Perhaps she'd deceived herself, caught up in the excitement of learning new things. Could the correspondence with Calum also be some kind of experiment? The professor had only mildly objected to it. There was too much turmoil in her heart and mind at present to sit in the same room as the professor.

"I think I will not continue the French lessons," said Effie. Her voice was firm, but not her mind; she had to be alone to think through this quagmire.

Before she closed the door, she caught a glimpse of the professor, his eyes downcast, hands hanging down—without a book in them.

When the professor dictated letters a few days later, Effie merely acknowledged his greeting and busied herself filling the inkwell. She'd spent many restless nights pondering about her position and what she'd come to mean to the professor. Surely, he wouldn't have made her his ward if he didn't like her and only thought of her as an apt student? He'd said as much. Could she believe him? Could he cancel the wardship? What then? Could she continue working for him? Find another position? Certainly not as a scriever. If she did continue her studies, she could become a governess after all, but that life was not much better than a domestic servant's. How could she go back to working as a servant or—heaven forbid—a fishwife? She'd tasted a freedom that could never happen for a domestic servant.

Effie had tried to explain how she felt to Jonet, who had told her she was a fool to think of giving up this opportunity. Hurt still burned within her, and anger muddled any logical thought. Vandemark was high-handed and imperious.

Her hand shook a little as she topped up the ink. She forced her mind to concentrate on her duties as a scribe for the day. It was no good brooding over the idea she was merely an educational experiment, but she had a hard time meeting the professor's eye and keeping disgruntled thoughts out of her mind.

Vandemark did not try to cajole her and merely began dictation. She wrote the words automatically but was monosyllabic when he tried to hold a conversation with her between the correspondence.

When she looked in his direction he smiled. She did not smile back. That appeared to make him smile all the broader.

As she smoothed out the paper for the next letter, thoughts chased through her head. What was he about? Why would he laugh at her expense? Didn't he know how much he'd hurt her? She agreed with Jonet—it was in her best interests to be his ward. She tried to convince herself that it wasn't only because she'd never see Calum again or that by being Vandemark's ward she could help her mother, that she'd never have to face poverty. She'd come to love the professor as the father she'd never known, and that made the betrayal worse.

She'd enough of their estranged relationship. It would mean subjugating her anger. Didn't she have a right to be angry? She longed to get back to the easy camaraderie they'd had before, though the professor's behavior today was making things worse. A shot of anger rushed through her.

He was dictating a particularly complicated missive in which he kept changing his mind. She had to start over with a new sheet of paper. She caught her lip between her teeth as she dipped her quill into the inkstand. Her ire grew when Vandemark chuckled.

"I dinna find wasting paper so amusing. Hmm, er . . . sir," said Effie, putting down the quill.

Vandemark laughed outright. Was he tipsy? It was too early in the morning. Effie glowered at him.

"Euphemia, I am delighted you are annoyed with me," said the professor, putting down his pipe. His smile broadened. "You should see your face—so petulant, so indignant."

"I dinna understand, Professor," said Effie frowning. "Why are you delighted? I'm being rude and ungrateful. I'm sorry I—"

"No. Do not apologize. Stand up for yourself. You have every right to be angry with me. Now you are so comfortable with me you dare to become irritated and upset with me. It brings our relationship to a different footing. More like father and daughter."

"Is this some theory of Hugh Blair's?" said Effie in a huff.

Vandemark threw back his head and laughed until he coughed. Effie poured a glass of water from the carafe and handed to him. She wished he wouldn't smoke so much; it made him wheeze. He took a couple of sips.

Now in control, he said, "No, you pert lassie." His smile was broad. "I did not think I would ever hear myself saying that of you. You were such a little mouse when you first came here." He chuckled again. "It is something I observed all on my own. Maybe I should write a treatise on it. Do not glare at me, Euphemia. I'm only funning."

Effie smiled reluctantly, the pain of betrayal easing a little. The professor reached over and took her ink-stained hand.

"Am I forgiven, Euphemia? I should have told you long since. Originally it was but a foolish notion of an inveterate scholar. I did not want to see a sharp mind wasted . . . even in a lassie."

Effie narrowed her eyes.

"No. I should not provoke you." His eyes twinkled. "I have met many intelligent women, good scholars but they came from good . . . er the gentry. I know what you are capable of. You have not let me down. Far from it." He squeezed her hand, his smile warm. "Then I got to know you better as a person rather than only a pupil."

"Did guilt about using me as an experiment make you decide to make me your ward? Or did you feel sorry for me, as I was alone in the world?" Effie was still uncertain of what had motivated him.

"No, no guilt. Nor pity. I grew fond of you. As fond as a father for a daughter. That is no lie, no subterfuge."

Effie could meet his eyes fully now. She squeezed his fingers briefly.

"Let's finish the letter to Lord Carnarvon to find out what is happening in the Americas."

Picking up her quill, she waited for the professor to begin dictation though her mind was elsewhere. Why, oh why, was there no word about Calum and Davy? Beneath her now-lightened mind, was an ocean of sadness. She'd mended her relationship with the

233

professor, but she could not repair her anguished, shattered thoughts about Calum and Davy's wellbeing. She had to stop herself from running to the door whenever she heard the rattle of Joe Bonnyman's cart as he passed by. She welcomed yet dreaded letters from the professor's navy friends that would confirm or refute her dream.

Chapter 29

At last letters from Canada! It was unsettling to see the professor smiling over Calum's letter, letting out a little chuckle every few minutes. When Calum had written those letters, he had probably enjoyed a somewhat pleasant existence: fulfilling his duties as a physician, joking with his colleagues, doing all the normal everyday things. But not now, not after that fearful battle. She couldn't tell the professor; he looked askance at fanciful ideas preferring to rely on logic and facts. Science he called it. Except science couldn't explain everything. She knew many people, especially women, who had premonitions like her.

Effie didn't open Calum's letter in front of the professor. Not yet. She might betray her feelings. She hugged the letter to herself for a minute before putting it in the pocket of her apron.

"I'm away to take Davy's letter to his mother," said Effie. She didn't wait for his permission. He looked up for a second and merely grunted.

Rhona was happy to see Davy's letter, but as she didn't feel comfortable reading handwriting—she could manage the printed word of the Bible—she asked Effie to read it. Once more, Effie had to stifle her worries that the writer was now likely sick or wounded.

She read the letter, glancing now and again at Rhona's eager face. Davy wrote about the friends he'd made among the soldiers and sailors. Robbie was making himself useful. He was in his element, Davy said, running errands, chatting with the soldiers, even learning to talk with the Indians though he mostly talked with his hands. Then

Davy expressed his disgust and anger with Catriona. Even his handwriting was thick and blotchy.

Effie stopped, not knowing if she should read aloud what he'd written. It was about her. She skimmed ahead.

> *Catriona was my all. If Effie thinks she can take her place, she is haivering. I ken how she feels about me. You ken I think of her more like the little sister I never had. An' you asked me to look out for her for her Aunt Lizzie's sake. Mayhap you could talk with her, Ma.*

Effie ran her tongue over her dry lips. It was something she had suspected though she had always hoped it was not so. But to see it written down . . . She caught her breath—surely he didn't mean to be so cruel? He'd probably forgotten she'd be the one to read the letter to his mother. Sometimes Dr. Ferguson or the minister read letters to the villagers. That was it. It must be his bad memory. The letter blurred in her vision for a moment; she blinked a few times. She got the message, though she couldn't read this to his mother. What's more, unbeknown to Davy and Rhona, Effie no longer had that old longing for Davy. But it hurt all the same.

Effie continued with the rest of the letter, which told of Davy's admiration for Calum, how vast the country was, and the uncanny customs of the Indians. It was a long letter for Davy.

Rhona had Effie read some of the letter over again, especially the news of Robbie. It was hard for Effie not to blurt out about her presentiment.

Effie took her leave and trudged up Cove Wynd. It was hard to hear a home truth even one she'd guessed. In some ways, she felt a sort of freedom to turn her heart and mind to Calum. She smiled bleakly—*to another unrequited love*. Was she doomed to fall in love with every man who paid her any attention? She remembered Duncan. No. She hadn't fallen for him, but then he was repellant, a womanizer, and who knew what else.

After Effie and the professor ate lunch, he shared news from Calum's letter; it was as usual about politics and war maneuvers.

"He's at a place called Amherstburg. He talks of the sloop-of-war *Queen Charlotte,* and Captain Barclay. He's not sure if he will be assigned to that ship. We are building another ship—how odd to build a warship on a lake. There is plenty of timber around he says. They are lacking provisions and men though and they are blockading the Americans." He looked up from the letter. "I wish I could see the landscape; Calum describes it well. I visited Quebec many, many years ago but did not venture that far west."

"You'd like to be an explorer yourself?"

"*Ja, ja.* I did some traveling and not just for business. I did not always have my face in a book." He smiled a secret smile. "One day I will tell you about it. I have three letters to dictate. Before I begin, I must say something."

The professor emptied the bowl of his pipe and tamped down new tobacco. He didn't light it but chewed on the stem of his pipe. He usually did this when he had something unpleasant to say or that needed diplomacy. Effie put down her quill.

"As you know, Calum is like a son to me. I have dreaded hearing . . . hearing bad news of him over many years." Effie lowered her gaze in case she revealed her secret knowledge of his wounds. "Your correspondence no doubt has brought him to a closer friendship more than you anticipated. It has been a novelty for him to write to a young woman, and good for his morale. Do not read too much into his letters though."

She'd been telling herself this though hearing it out loud made her spirits sink.

"Has he no found a lassie to write to him after all these years? It is unco strange he writes to me."

"But you are no ordinary lassie. You made quite an impression on him wanting to read all the books in the library. You were introduced as a scriever so he thinks of you that way."

"I understand. If he kent more of my background he'd not wish to write to me, a common servant, a former fishwife." Her tone was grating even to her own ears. "Should I not write to him anymore? Should I tell him of my humble beginnings?" She swallowed. "Of my mother?"

"No. I hope his writing to you will help him not be so reticent with women."

On her first encounter with him, Effie had found him far from reticent, but she supposed the professor knew him better. She focused once more on Vandemark's remarks.

"Moncrithe was badly let down by women and has not trusted any since," said the professor putting a taper to his pipe. "As my ward you have been brought to a new station in society. I need to be blunt. I do not know what your sentiments are toward Calum, but there can never be a union between you. His family. . ." He shrugged. "His family, even though they are estranged, will want him to marry someone from his class. And I think this may come to pass."

A sharp pain stabbed so strong Effie felt it through her whole body and her face became taut and stiff, though her lips began to tremble.

"I ken. I . . . I'm glad I wrote to him." Though it was a bitter thought she was merely a substitute for a future liaison. That knowledge added an agonizing twist to her pain. She stood up, putting her chin in the air.

"Sir, I do not have expectations above my station." Her heart shouted *liar, liar,* as her mind forced her to say those words. She had tried to steel herself from too ardent an attachment. She'd had some practice with her friendship with Davy. She was older, but certainly not wiser.

"You say there's hope of a union for him? He mentioned someone in his letter?" She was now proficient in damping down emotions and talking as though the words were commonplace and not charged with torment.

"He mentioned he was sick of war and longed for wedded bliss. He'd met someone kind and loyal, unlike other women he'd known. I heard from an acquaintance he has been much in the company of a Miss Amelia Fortescue. She's the daughter of Sir Morris Fortescue, an army colonel. It would be a suitable match . . ." The professor's voice droned on, but Effie had stopped listening. A stab in her heart—sharper than the first—stopped all thinking, stopped all feeling. She wet her lips, her eyes downcast, remembering every word, every smile from Calum.

"Euphemia?" Vandemark's voice broke into her reverie.

"Aye. The letters to the Admiralty." Her knees gave way so she sat hard in the tall-backed chair which would hold her spine rigid. Though how she was going to hold a pen was beyond her. Her hands were as frigid as the water in the firth.

After he'd dictated the letters, Vandemark took his usual afternoon nap and Effie escaped to her bedchamber. She still lived in the attic though the professor had said she could use one of the bedrooms on the second floor. She threw open a window and gazed at the foggy September morning.

A few leaves had changed color with golden highlights showing among the green. Dark clouds gathered in the south across the firth and gulls sailed along on the air currents. This was reality.

And now, she had to face another reality—she and Calum could never be together. Deep down she'd anticipated this. She let out a ragged, bitter laugh. Had he ever been attainable? His letters suggested a warmth and regard for her. Was she reading too much into it? Was he trifling with her? Was she just a person he could flirt with so he could be more comfortable now with women of his own class?

She let out a breath and with trembling hands broke open the seal to Calum's letter—but didn't unfold it. What would he have to say about Miss Amelia Fortescue? *Miss Amelia Fortescue.* Even the name suggested beauty, accomplishment, breeding. And he said she was kind and loyal. Effie had never hated anyone in her life, even Catriona, her grandmother, even Niall Douglas. A blind, irrational sensation made her throw the letter across the room and fling herself on her bed and grasp her pillow with tight fists. She buried her face to muffle her violent crying.

When no more tears came and her body was no longer wracked with convulsions, she lay spent and limp, then curled up holding onto her bent legs, a protective position she'd used as a wee lassie.

She became aware of familiar sounds—the way the wind blew shrill through a crack in the window, the muted cry of a seagull, the purring of the cat which had hidden under the bed at her anguish, and now curled warm beside her. She put out a hand and stroked its soft fur gradually straightening her legs. The sweet trilling song of a blackbird pierced her to the core.

All emotion had drained out of her leaving a chasm of desolation. Somehow the birdsong filled the void, offering hope. Hope. But that hope wouldn't include Calum or Davy. The words of the old ballad "Joy to the Person of My Love" came into her mind and she mouthed the words.

> *Joy to the person of my love*
> *Although he me disdain.*
> *Fixt are my thoughts and may not move*
> *And yet I love in vain.*
> *Shall I lose the sight of my joy and heart's delight?*

Love for Calum had stolen upon her gradually. Her quick love, almost idolization, for Davy had lasted many years. It should be easier to forget Calum, but it wasn't.

Effie sat up and rested limply on the bed for a few moments before going to the mirror. She did not look closely at her reflection—avoiding her own eyes, scared of what she'd see—and concentrated on tidying her hair which had come loose from her thrashing around on the bed. The memory of the safety and haven of Calum's arms around her—those few precious times—only grew stronger. Her body had known long before her conscious mind admitted her love for him. Now she had to put him out of her mind though he'd always remain in her heart.

But that little spark of hope was there too. She'd survived many losses before. Now she should plan for her future—a plan without Calum, without Davy. A sensible—no longer delusional—plan. She would immerse herself in her studies, no longer think of romance. She'd fulfill the professor's hopes to become a learned woman, a future teacher, a female dominie.

She picked up Calum's letter. Would she have the fortitude to read it dispassionately, especially if he wrote of Amelia? Better to find out the worst.

Three leaves fell out as well as a piece of bark and something rootlike, almost like an iris rhizome. She set them aside with a trembling hand. These would be the last specimens from America, the last letter from Calum. The sheet was smaller than usual.

Joy to My Love

Amherstburg, 3 August 1813

Dear Euphemia,

This will be a short letter as we've been unusually exercised these past few weeks. I will not bore you with the preparations for war. I wrote to Vandemark about it.

We've had stormy weather, and a few men came down with the grippe so I have been busy with medical duties. Davy and Robbie are rarely sick; they have strong constitutions so you need not worry about them. How I wish I had some of your liniments and potions, though I am learning new receipts from the savages. They tell me that in autumn, the leaves on the trees are glorious colors: reds, oranges and yellows of the brightness rarely seen in Scotland.

The piece of bark is from the aspen tree as is the small round leaf. The trees are a shimmer of green and gold when the breeze runs through them. It is a sight to see. The Indians here use the bark for fever, coughs, and pain. The larger leaf is palmate like a sycamore. It is from a sugar maple tree. They say the Indians use the sap which is as sweet as honey. I haven't tried it yet. The other leaf is from a hickory tree. I picked it from a tree in Quebec where we stopped on our trip down the St. Lawrence River. The root is of a plant called Goldenseal; its leaves are palmate. (Look that up in Linnaeus's book.) The Indians grind it and use it for fevers, pneumonia, stomach problems and even consumption. If I have time and the supplies, I will sketch a picture of an Indian savage. They are our allies but their ways are so strange and different from ours.

Every day I open the snuff box and enjoy the sweet scent of the salve you gave me. I hardly like to use it as I don't want to diminish it. It refreshes me and brings me back to the library in Pittenweem when we sat together. I often take out that drawing of your hand with the sink stain. So many good memories to keep me from black moods. I cannot write more—all that I long to say to you—but wish you well.

I remain, your—a smudge as he crossed something out—*sincere friend, Calum*

Calum hadn't mentioned Miss Amelia Fortescue. And why would he? It was none of her business. Apart from his memories of the salve and the picture that he drew of her hand, his letter was about practical matters—his interest in botanicals as a physician. What black moods

241

troubled him? No doubt being in the midst of war and treating wounds and fevers was discouraging and arduous. Effie wished she could smooth away his pain of mind and was glad that her salve gave him ease. And memories of her. But the line she kept reading again and again was how he longed to say something to her. What could that mean? What couldn't he write in a letter? If he were engaged to Miss Fortescue, surely he could write about that.

Effie couldn't bear to think he'd been courting Miss Amelia when he wrote this. Perhaps that lady was even now at his side, helping him recuperate from the battle.

She refolded the letter and tied it up with his other letters and put them in the box. Her throat constricted to suppress a sob as she rested her hand on the box that contained precious hopes and dreams. One day, perhaps when she was old—a lonely spinster dominie—she'd reread those letters. Didn't the passing of time help heal sorrows?

Chapter 30

Another week came and went and still there was no word from the Admiralty. The professor had gone to Edinburgh to talk with his cronies about the situation in America, leaving both Jonet and Effie behind. They expected his return today.

Effie peered out the door into the gloaming. Dry leaves blown by a chill gust skittered across the cobblestones, signaling the dark days of winter. Effie shut out the cold and lit lamps and candlesticks in the library. The professor would make for this room first when he returned.

A few minutes later, the carriage arrived and Effie opened the door, a smile of greeting on her lips, until she saw the professor. Billy held Vandemark's arm as they entered the house. Vandemark looked frail and older, pouches under his eyes and deep lines around his mouth. He did not meet her eyes but seemed to look through her.

Time slowed as Effie watched the professor's labored progress into the library. He knew. He knew what had happened to Calum. Only a severe shock could make him look like that.

Jonet helped Billy take him to his favorite chair in the library, taking his cape and outer clothing and bringing him slippers for his swollen feet. He let out a deep sigh. Effie poured him a glass of brandy, her hand unsteady, while Jonet went into the kitchen to bring a bowl of hot broth she'd kept simmering on the coals awaiting his arrival.

He wouldn't eat and motioned for Effie and Jonet to sit down. Jonet was unusually quiet. Effie took Jonet's hand; she could sense Jonet's anxiety as she sat rigid next to her.

"The news is not wholly bad," said Vandemark, his voice was calm as though he'd been rehearsing this speech. "There was a battle— September 10"

Effie stirred. Wasn't that the day she'd had the premonition?

"—on a lake called Erie and our ships were beaten, some destroyed, by the American navy. Unfortunately, the HMS *Bristol* was one of the ships destroyed. Captain Sharp was killed and half of the crew, most of the others were wounded." He paused and took a drink of brandy. Effie had seen the carnage in her dream. Jonet's grip on her hand tightened.

The professor handed Effie a newspaper and pointed to an article. She scanned through a long list of names and found Calum and Davy in the wounded list. She exhaled loudly. She read further looking for news of Robbie and Tam.

"Oh no!" The words were wrenched from her. She put a hand to her mouth.

"What? What happened?" Jonet's voice was shrill.

"Calum and Davy are wounded. At a field hospital." A quick breathy sob. "Robbie is dead. No mention of Tam." Effie's heart hurt so much. She dropped the paper and reached out for Jonet and buried her face into her shoulder; Jonet's tears dripped on her head.

Vandemark rose from his chair. "Now I am going to bed. It has been a trying two days. I am feeling my age. I—" He shook his head slowly, sorrow hung on his shoulders.

Effie and Jonet stood up, tears still streaming down their cheeks. Jonet was the first to speak, "I canna find the words to say how sorry I am. But if Lieutenant Moncrithe and Davy are wounded there's hope. Isna that right, Effie?"

Effie merely nodded, the lump in her throat squeezing her ability to speak. Hadn't her dream prepared her for this? She'd been mourning secretly all that time, and now it was out in the open, it was as though sadness permeated every pore. Jonet put an arm around Effie but she slipped from it and walked over to the professor, who stood swaying slightly, his hand on the back of his chair.

She put her arms around him and laid her head on his ample chest, whispering, "Calum's not badly wounded. I feel it." He merely patted her on the back.

"Leave me now, my dear." His voice was hoarse.

"Go to bed, dearie," said Jonet. "Will you take care of locking up? Billy will help the professor to his room."

The professor stood by his chair staring into space. He did not acknowledge Effie's quick kiss on his cheek.

Effie locked and bolted the front door, the click of the bolt sharp and final, shutting in the sorrows in the house. The stairs loomed tall and steep before her; it was an effort to pick a foot up each step. Even the air around her seemed solid and oppressive, the weight of grief crushing the breath from her lungs, compressing her from head to toe. The candle in her hand shook so the flickering light projected weird shadows on her way to her bedchamber.

The shadows of the night before had not dispersed in Effie's mind. She stopped stirring the porridge to rub her eyes swollen from crying and gritty from lack of sleep. The Mackies should be told and it would probably be her job.

Effie couldn't take it in: Robbie, the youngest son, mischievous and hot at hand, gone and buried in a far, far country. She could see him now, a younger version of Jamie with unruly sandy hair and bright blue eyes, a cheeky grin perpetually on his face.

What had made him go to South Queensferry that fateful day? If he hadn't gone with Tam, Davy and Jamie wouldn't have gone to find him. And, as luck would have it, none would have encountered the press gang.

Should she tell Catriona, now she was married to Alasdair Grant? And what about the Braid family? They'd like to know about Tam. She couldn't take the news to the Braids; they already believed her a harbinger of evil. Better for Rhona to tell them. The news would soon spread in the village.

The professor's tall, large figure appeared at the kitchen door startling Effie who almost dropped the milk jug. He was in his brocade dressing gown and had not shaved, the stubble on his cheeks and chin making a prickly, grey-blond shadow on his face.

"I see from your eyes you did not sleep much last night."

Effie carefully put down the milk jug, her hand unsteady. She didn't ask how he felt: his appearance told her that. "It will take more than an hour to bring you the morning repast. There's crowdie and oatcakes. Would you like some until we finish the cooking?"

"No. I do not care to eat at present. I will go to the library and . . ." he searched for words—"and read a book." He walked away, the click of the library door shutting in his grief. Effie's heart cried out for him. He'd not merely read a book but begin drinking brandy, even in these early hours.

Jonet arrived with the bread and she and Effie bustled about preparing the morning meal.

"I mind the professor will no eat much," said Effie. "He came down early and retired to the library."

By the time they brought the food, the professor had finished half a decanter. He turned bleary eyes on them and motioned for them to put down the tray and leave. Jonet, who'd normally scold and tease the professor, was silent and walked out the minute she set down the tray. Effie lingered a little longer, hoping she could say something to comfort him. He picked up the decanter and poured himself a drink; he looked at Effie, a challenge in his eyes.

"It's best you leave now, Euphemia. I need to be alone. Send Billy to me in an hour." He looked down at the glass in his hand studying it for a while before bringing it to his lips. Effie left, eyes moist. She hadn't seen him in such despair. From the gossip Alasdair Grant let fall, drink had been his undoing as well as the loss of the enrollment of students at the university.

Jonet banged pots and pans around so hard Effie thought she'd dent them.

"I think he will not eat the breakfast. I'll make lamb broth and maybe a curd pudding for his midday meal. It's best you stay out of his way the day. Your job is to talk with Davy's family. And Catriona too."

Effie plodded to the Mackie cottage. The misty morning was changing to rain and her feet slipped on the wet cobblestones on the steep incline of the wynd. She caught a view of the harbor. Only a few boats were left; the majority were already out to sea. Jock Mackie's boat, *Bonny Lassie*, was still in the harbor.

Mrs. Mackie opened the door a few minutes after Effie knocked. At first Rhona greeted her with her usual warm smile, then it faded, replaced by a wide-eyed stare of fear. Effie had tried to school her feelings, but something must have alerted Rhona she was bringing bad news. Rhona motioned her inside.

On the table were the leftovers of a hastily eaten meal and the chipped brown bowl with steam rising from hot porridge. The ordinariness of it all. She was going to shatter the comfort of the day. Effie took off the damp shawl and Mrs. Mackie put it by the fire to dry. Such little kindnesses deserved better than this news. Effie steadied herself by taking a deep breath. How do you tell a mother one of her sons was dead and the other wounded?

"I have news of Davy and . . . and Robbie." She choked on Robbie's name. She related what the professor had told her, telling it straight and without emotion, before her voice cracked and she broke down in tears. Mrs. Mackie collapsed on a chair, threw her apron over her head and keened, rocking back and forward in her sorrow.

"I dinna want to leave you." No reply. The heaviness in Effie's heart broke into sharp shards with Rhona's every sob. There were no words she could find to comfort the inconsolable mother.

"I'll away and get your man and Jamie," said Effie. What more could she do? Rhona nodded but did not look up.

Jamie and Jock Mackie sat on a low wall, laughing and joking with a couple of older fishermen who liked to oversee fishing activities though they could no longer participate. When Jock and Jamie saw Effie, they rose up, their faces sobering. Effie quickly told the news, offering condolences. They answered not a word, and strode away toward their house, Jock with a hand on Jamie's shaking shoulders.

Effie turned into High Street. Catriona sauntered along it going toward her new home. After a moment's hesitation, Effie caught up with her before Catriona opened the door.

"And what do *you* want?" Catriona turned narrowed eyes on Effie, the front door key gripped in her hand.

"It's Davy. He was in a battle and is wounded."

Catriona dropped the key and put a hand on her swollen belly in a protective gesture. Effie picked up the key and held it out to Catriona who stared at it.

"I kent how it might be. I'm glad I—" Catriona wiped her eyes. Effie unlocked the door and was about to help Catriona over the threshold, but Catriona pushed her away and closed the door. The key rasped in the lock. Effie heard faint sobbing.

With a sigh, Effie turned toward home. Who knew she would have sympathy for her old enemy? For all Catriona's bravado she still loved Davy. Effie wondered what she felt for Alasdair. She was carrying his bairn— *Surely not? Could it be Davy's?* She shook her head. No. *Catriona wouldna do that, would she?* But that would explain the hasty marriage.

Poor Catriona. Poor Alasdair. Poor Davy. Aye, Davy. It was her fault he was wounded. Guilt fought with common sense. She stopped for breath, the rain falling on her upturned face; she wiped off raindrops wishing she could wash away those self-recriminations. Her thoughts ran back to all that had happened: her abandonment on the Isle of May, Davy and Tam's fight, Tam's act of vengeance in taking Robbie to South Queensferry, and the capture by the press gang. No, she was not to blame; if anything, it was Tam who had set the stage for the events. But she was the catalyst.

When Effie peeked into the library the professor was asleep. She crept in to put more coal on the fire and to put a small quilt over him. He stirred but didn't open his eyes.

The day dragged on and on. Effie couldn't concentrate on anything, pacing for a while then stopping, dust cloth in hand and staring into space for a moment before wiping dust from furniture in a desultory way. She didn't want to be alone in her room with her thoughts so she helped Jonet. Even the idea of reading did not appeal to her, though books had become a haven. She had to keep moving. By exerting herself she could lessen the tumbling thoughts and dejection coursing through her.

How long would it be before they knew the nature of the men's wounds? Would they send them home? How long before she saw them? *How long? How long?* That refrain swirled around her mind.

Chapter 31

Rhona Mackie swung open the door seconds after Effie knocked. She did not invite Effie in even though the sky was dark with rainclouds.

"I wished to see how you are," said Effie handing her a basket. "Jonet sent you tea leaves and scones. Do you need any potions to help you sleep?"

After a little hesitation, Rhona, pale and drawn, took the basket though she still didn't invite her in. Effie was no longer welcome in her home.

"The professor has a letter. Davy and Lieutenant Moncrithe are in a field hospital. They're well taken care of. It will be months before they can return to service."

"Return to service! Return to service! Why not send them home?" Anger sharpened Rhona's voice.

"Mayhap the wounds are no so bad." She didn't voice what Alan Ferguson had said: men often didn't die from their wounds but from infections. That dark knowledge Effie would keep to herself.

"Professor Vandemark is writing to people in London and Halifax—in Canada—in the hopes of bringing them home." Effie sighed. "I wish I could be there to nurse them, give them comfort."

"No doubt, your lieutenant will get more comfort than my Davy," said Rhona bitterness in her voice. "As an officer and a gentleman, he'll get the better treatment."

Effie had no words to rebut this. It was probably true.

"I wish . . ." said Effie, struggling not to cry.

Rhona choked back a sob. "It's the way of the world. Now run along." She closed the door.

Effie trudged home, a sudden squall drenching her. So Rhona Mackie did blame her. Why treat her so coldly otherwise? Perhaps Jonet could talk with her. Rhona would not take comfort from Effie.

After dinner, the professor set up the chess board while Effie finished a letter to Angus adding coins for her mother. The fire crackled and sputtered and the room seemed even more cozy by the sound of the rain drumming on the windows. A pot of tea warmed Effie, while the professor chose a snifter of brandy, his hands clasped around the bulbous glass. She looked over the chess pieces deciding her strategy when Vandemark cleared his throat. She looked up warily.

"You have a kind heart. I know you want to help your mother and brother but you cannot associate with them without compromising your own person. I gather you send money to them from your allowance."

Did he object to that? It wasn't much. Effie wished she could send more.

"I do not disagree with your actions." He moved a pawn. "It is the best you can do in the circumstances. But I do not want them coming to Pittenweem to bother you—and me."

"I ken I canna help my mother, except to send money, but Alec . . ."

The professor looked at her quizzically, then rolled his eyes.

"Can he no find a place at a charity school? Like Angus." She moved a rook, taking out Vandemark's pawn. "You mind the footman who works at Lord Glasbeinn's house? Alec is young enough his life could turn around with some education. Like Angus. Like me."

"No one is like you, my dear," said the professor, busy spreading butter on the scone. He glanced up when she sighed. "Oh, very well. I will see what I can do to get him out from under his father's thumb and set up in a school. I think it better he not stay in Edinburgh. I know someone in Stirling who has a charity school for boys—Ian Brown."

"Thank you, sir," said Effie, touching the professor's hand for a second. "You are taking on my problems. Are you regretting making me your ward? Am I becoming a burden to you?"

"No. Never that," said the professor, his eyes merry. "I must admit I am no longer bored." He coughed. Effie was worried. Was it the beginnings of the influenza or because he was smoking more these past few weeks?

"By the by, there is someone you know at Stirling. He asked after you."

Effie scalded her mouth by taking too big a sip. Who could that be? Was it Duncan? Had he moved there? But Vandemark was smiling. It couldn't be him. Effie gulped down her tea.

"Who?"

"Michael Sutherland. You remember him? The dominie who taught you how to write? He is teaching at Brown's academy. I'd told Brown about you and Sutherland was pleased to hear that you are now working for me."

"Aye. I wondered what became of him."

"Perhaps I could arrange for you to teach at the academy. Brown is interested in adding some female children to the school."

"You want me to leave you? Leave Pittenweem?" Effie put down her cup with an unsteady hand.

"I would go too. Move the household to Stirling." The professor's eyes twinkled. "Sutherland is still a single man. You would have a lot in common as fellow teachers. And—"

"No!"

The professor startled, the smile vanishing from his face.

"Aye, he's a braw man. He'd be near twenty years older than me. But marry him? I think not." Effie envisioned Michael Sutherland: gangly and thin with a prominent Adam's apple that bobbed up and down in his throat when he talked passionately about literature. Aye, a good man, but not someone Effie wished to marry. Vandemark was determined to push her toward teaching and marrying a teacher. And it was a sensible ambition, especially now that Calum was to be married. Effie lifted her tea cup again, slopping hot tea over her fingers but scalded fingers were nothing to the pain in her heart.

251

"Ah well. It was but a thought. I want to see you settled before I die."

Effie leaned over and took the professor's hand. She smiled and squeezed his hand.

"Dinna talk like that. You have many good years left. Plenty of time for me to marry. If you want me to go to Stirling, then—" Effie took a deep breath "then we shall go. But let's visit first before we pack up the household. I think Jonet—"

"*Ja, ja.*" The professor chuckled. "I must give Jonet plenty of time to think about leaving." He looked around the room. "It will be hard to leave this house. *Mijn lieverd* Rozamond asked me to buy it so we could live here when I retired. She fell in love with Pittenweem. It reminded her of home in Volendam." He sighed. "But it was not to be." He took a long draw on his pipe. "I will write to Brown about your brother when we get to Edinburgh."

"We're going to Edinburgh?" Effie was not ready to face Duncan, but it would be better than this interminable waiting for news about Calum. She wouldn't visit her mother; it was too painful to see her in her degraded position though she wondered if the money she sent made a difference in her and Alec's life. At Pittenweem she dreaded meeting Rhona Mackie who had turned cold toward her—no comfort there—so a trip to Edinburgh would be welcome.

"Possibly within the week. I await news from Captain Bertrand. I hope he can persuade the authorities to let him bring back Calum and your friend Davy." He paused, the fire on the lighted taper getting dangerously close to his fingers. "Unless—" He put the taper to the tobacco and puffed until a wisp of smoke rose in a thin spiral. "Unless they are not fit to travel."

Effie clasped her hands so tightly her fingers dug deep into her flesh. He'd spoken her fears out loud. She closed her eyes tight. A fervent whisper, almost a prayer. *Please let Calum be well enough to travel. Please bring him home safe.* How she longed for Calum to find the peace and comfort she enjoyed in this house—the glow of bright embers, the shelter of a sturdy house in a storm, the companionship of loved ones though she wished she were the loved one, not Miss Amelia Fortescue. Would that lady return to Scotland with him?

Chapter 32

I go to the Clyde for to mourn and weep. That line from the song she'd sung for Davy so many months ago, ran through Effie's head as she gazed on the wide estuary of the River Clyde. She was not on the banks of the Clyde to mourn and weep. Calum and Davy were on their way home from war, wounded but alive. Like in the song, she'd suffered "death ten thousand times"—her imagination running wild wondering what kinds of wounds they had and how they were faring on the long voyage.

She wished they could have waited for them in Pittenweem in the comfort of the professor's home, not staying with strangers.

News had reached the professor that Calum and Davy were returning to Scotland. The voyage from Halifax in Nova Scotia took at best six weeks, but now that it was January, stormy weather could curtail their progress.

As though being nearer to the ship's port of call would speed Calum's arrival, the professor had moved westward: he'd been restless and anxious in Pittenweem; morose and grumpy the two weeks in Edinburgh; impatient and irascible in Glasgow; and now resigned and depressed in Greenock, the furthermost western port.

Vandemark had friends in many places, even in Greenock. Sir Malcolm Ballingry had invited them to stay at his mansion overlooking Cardwell Bay so there was a good view of ships entering the estuary

Effie lost count of the days she looked out the Ballingrys' drawing room window. Instead of the familiar low-lying Lothian terrain across the Firth of Forth, rose the bleak panorama of the snowy mound-like mountains of the isthmus cradling the mouth of the River Clyde. Many ships came and went, and still no sign of HMS *Raven*.

Turning from the window, Effie let out a sigh as she surveyed the artfully decorated room with its floral-patterned Aubusson carpet and blue tapestry chairs. A bowl of hot-house freesias wafted a sweet scent mingling with the pungent smell of burning logs in the fireplace. It was beautiful though not as comfortable as the professor's book-filled library. She picked up Fanny Burney's novel, riffled the pages then set it down. Nothing kept her interest.

The professor hadn't needed to write letters to the Admiralty the last few days so time crawled slower than a slug. There was no other activity for her except reading and she preferred to do that silently on her own and not in company.

Her face burned at the memory of her experience two days ago. Lady Ballingry had invited Effie to sit with her older daughters, Caroline and Sophia, and ply their crewel needlework while they took turns reading the novel, *Camilla* by Fanny Burney. Though Effie had learned to sew when a wee lassie, it was practical sewing: stitching hems and buttonholes, and darning sock. She'd not learned the art of fine embroidery like daughters of the gentry.

Lady Ballingry, in an attempt to make her feel included in this genteel activity, had suggested she read to them while they sewed. Effie had read to Mrs. Forbes and the professor so she wasn't too nervous about the task.

"Start where Sophia ended," said Lady Ballingry as she picked up a length of crimson wool and threaded the needle.

Effie commenced to read, "*she kissed her hand at the last glimpse a friendly hill afforded of her native town . . .*" Effie paused to swallow a lump in her throat. Like the heroine in the book she was missing her native town. "*and made an effort to forget the regret with which she lost sight of it.*"

Though she was self-conscious of her strong Scottish accent compared to the more refined accents of the Ballingry family, she was able to read the novel quite smoothly until she came to the word *sagacity* which she stumbled over, using a long "a" instead of a short. Carolina and Sophia snickered.

"*Sagahcity*—not *sagaycity*, Euphemia." Lady Ballingry corrected her as she frowned at her daughters. "You're doing very well, my dear." Then in an undertone to Sophia but loud enough for Effie to hear, "You shouldn't laugh at your inferiors."

Effie looked down at the page, the words slightly distorted. When she read to the professor, he'd corrected her diction, but had never been condescending. Effie's mouth was dry. She persevered until the barely concealed laughter and lessons on diction became more frequent.

She had put down the book and forced her tight jaw loose so she wasn't speaking through gritted teeth.

"I'm sorry for all the faults. I mind I spoil the enjoyment of the story," Effie said, handing the book to Sophia, before she left the room.

A brisk walk in the garden had tempered her resentment, and she was able to meet Lady Ballingry and her daughters with equanimity at the dinner table. Only Sophia had apologized.

Effie had been cooped up in the house, with an occasional walk in the gardens, for days. It was not fitting for her to go to the harbor. It bustled with warships bringing soldiers, sailors, and prisoners of war and merchant ships unloading their cargoes of sugar cane and other products from the West Indies. She had to be content watching from this high citadel.

"You're needed in the salon, Miss Innes." A footman stood at the door.

Effie's left the room in a hurry. News at last!

The whole family was assembled but Effie was unaware of them: she only had eyes for the professor who stood by the fire warming his hands. He looked up and held out a trembling hand. When she clasped it, he smiled a smile she hadn't seen in many months. A ray of sunshine pierced through the clouds and shone into the room as though celebrating Effie's elation.

"Euphemia, I have splendid news." The professor's voice quavered a little. "A ship of the line came into port this morning and reported they had seen *HMS Raven* off Ireland yesterday evening. It means Moncrithe will arrive sometime tomorrow afternoon."

Effie pressed his hand. At last! She'd see them soon. "That's good news. When will we leave for the harbor?" said Effie. "I want to be ready in plenty of time."

"Euphemia. I do not think this will be a place for a lady," said Lady Ballingry. "All those rough sailors ogling you. And who knows what wounds your friends have received. Leave it to the men and Dr. Thompson to take care of them."

Euphemia shook her head. "I'm sorry, Lady Ballingry, but I insist on going." She wanted to say she was not a lady, which was true, but she didn't wish to offend her hostess. "I shall be perfectly safe with the professor and your footmen."

Lady Ballingry frowned; Vandemark gave Effie a quick wink before turning to the lady.

"My dear Lady Ballingry, your disquiet does you credit. Nonetheless, Euphemia will accompany me. I know it is out of the ordinary, but she has experience with ministering to the sick."

Effie let out a quiet sigh. She'd been afraid the first time she'd see Calum and Davy would be under the eagle eyes of Lady Ballingry and her housekeeper, Mrs. McPherson. It was going to be difficult enough meeting them for the first time with the professor and Sir Malcolm.

It was a miracle they were coming home. The professor had written several impassioned letters—she'd been his scribe— requesting that they send Calum and Davy home rather than lingering in a field hospital in Canada. The professor had even thought of going to Canada himself, taking Effie with him if they hadn't granted his request.

Chapter 33

Effie and Vandemark took turns looking out the parlor window to catch a glimpse of the ship that was bearing Calum ever closer. She'd stared so long and in vain at the mouth of the firth, it took her a moment to realize she was seeing the tips of the masts of a ship behind the snow-covered headland.

"I see a ship. I canna see its colors from this distance," said Effie in a breathless voice. "Look. Yonder." She pointed before taking the professor's arm and hugging it tight.

Sir Malcolm raised his telescope to his eye. "I can't tell if that's the *Raven* until we see its prow. Would you like to see, Vandemark?" he said, handing the professor the telescope.

The professor's hand shook as he raised it to his eye. "*Ja. Ja.* I see it." He turned to Effie and handed her the telescope. "Euphemia, put this to your eye and close the other one."

It was as though the masts of the ship leaped toward her. Effie recoiled and put down the telescope for a second, then looked again.

The ship slowly appeared past the headland. Vandemark who now had the telescope exclaimed. "Yes. It's the *Raven*. I see the figurehead."

Effie's heart beat so fast she thought she'd faint. She had to sit down on the window seat. *Calum's here. Davy's here. They're truly here.*

Vandemark sat on the window seat too and put his head in his hands. His shoulders shook under Effie's hand before she stood up and put the telescope to her eye.

She scanned all over the ship. Aye, there was the carved black raven on the prow and three officers in their blue uniforms standing on the deck while sailors pulled ropes and scurried up the masts. Was one of the officers Calum? She couldn't see faces from that distance even with the telescope.

When would they leave to meet the ship? She wanted to be on the move, get closer to seeing Calum. Effie walked around the room, her skirts and petticoat swishing with her agitated stride.

By the time she, the professor and Sir Malcolm climbed into the landau, Effie's nerves were frayed. Mrs. McPherson had thrust a vial of sal volatile into her hand before she walked out the door. That was kind of her. She may need smelling salts for the professor.

As it was afternoon, the roads were no longer slippery with mud and ice, nevertheless progress was still maddeningly slow. Sir Malcolm kept up a quiet discourse though Effie couldn't remember what he talked about; all her attention was on the coming meeting.

The dock was teaming with people: sailors, soldiers, townsfolk. The carriage moved slowly through the throng. The *Raven* was anchored in the bay; two row boats came closer and closer to the quay.

Sir Malcolm climbed out of the carriage first and the two footmen, bundled up from the cold, jumped down from their perches.

Professor Vandemark heaved himself up to exit the carriage, but Sir Malcom dissuaded him. "It's best you stay inside, Jan. They may be able to walk or may need to be carried. I'll find out."

"May need to be carried?" The professor turned to Effie, anguish in his eyes. Effie's lips trembled. Aye, how bad were their injuries?

The boat drew closer and Effie could now see Davy sitting at the back of the boat, his dark hair blowing in the wind. But she couldn't see Calum. Perhaps he'd died on the voyage. An iron band—bitter and pitiless—squeezed the breath from her body.

The boat turned as it came closer to the pier. Calum sprawled in the middle, leaning on an officer. His face was pale and thin, his eyes closed. Effie turned to the professor who had a hand to his mouth, tears welling in his eyes.

"Stay here, sir." Effie jumped out of the carriage without waiting for a footman to help her. Her hood blew off her head and strands

258

of hair whipped over her face, but she didn't take the time to put it up to hide from the interested gazes of the sailors.

Sailors at both ends of the boat were mooring the boat to posts. The captain got out first followed by a sailor helping Davy, who was a little unsteady on his legs, to the pier. He looked around scanning the quay. Effie lifted a hand and smiled at him. He did not respond but turned away to look at the harbor. Was he deliberately shunning her?

Torn between wanting to greet him and waiting to see Calum, Effie took a few steps toward Davy, then stopped. She turned her attention to the rowboat where two sailors were carrying Calum out of the boat.

What was wrong with him? She ran over to see better as Sir Malcolm directed the men to the carriage. Calum appeared to be in a deep sleep. A wound marred his left temple at the hairline and one of his legs was heavily bandaged.

"What's the matter with him? Why is he so still?" She tried to take his hand, but Sir Malcolm held her back.

"Let them get him into the carriage, Miss Innes," he said.

"He's heavily dosed with laudanum." The deep voice with a slight French accent answered her questions. She looked up at the dark swarthy features of the man who, from his uniform, must be Captain Bertrand. "How sorry he will be not to be awake to be greeted by so bonny a lady." He gave a slight bow. Effie's smile was perfunctory.

"Of course. I expect it was for the best," she said vaguely, turning away to watch Calum being put into the carriage. Then she remembered Davy. He, at least, was on his feet, but why did he not greet her? She barely acknowledged the captain but went to Davy.

He stood by the boat looking out toward the ships in the bay. She could at least talk to him while they were making Calum comfortable in the carriage.

"Davy, it's so good to see you home in Scotland," she said holding out her hands. He turned fully to her and Effie couldn't help but catch her breath. The left side of his face had a livid scar from his eye to his chin. It made the skin by his left eye so puckered only a sliver of his blue eye shone between the folded skin. Effie read anger in his good right eye.

"Oh, Davy. Your bonny face," said Effie putting a tentative hand toward his scar. He flinched and stepped back slightly. "Oh. I'm sorry. Does it hurt much?"

"It dinna hurt the now," said Davy, looking her up and down. He spoke through gritted teeth. "I was expecting a better welcome from you. What is Moncrithe to you? He had more letters from you than me. But he's an officer and a gentleman. More to your taste now." She'd never heard such a harsh tone in his voice.

"Davy! If it were not for him and the professor you'd still be in Canada. Did he no treat you right?"

She shook from the chill breeze and suppressed nerves. Professor Vandemark called for her. She signaled they were coming, but Davy still looked mulish.

"Let's talk later. You need warmth and food. Go to that carriage," said Effie reaching out to take Davy's left arm. Once more he flinched from her touch.

"Not that one," he said. "It's still sore. I dinna want to go to yon muckle great house with the officers." He surveyed the carriage. "I can get a place at the inn. I have common sailor friends there. I can be on my way to Pittenweem in the morning."

"No." Effie stamped her foot and took his right arm. "You're coming with me. You'll bide with the groom so you dinna need to associate with the gentry." When he resisted, she said, "And no arguments."

A hint of a smile reached Davy's eyes.

"You've become quite the grand dame," he said with a small laugh. Effie's mood lifted. That was more like the Davy of old. "That little spirit suits you. Where's the timid little mouse?" Then he sighed. "I miss her. I was hoping you hadn't changed but—so have I." Effie squeezed his arm, hoping he'd understand it came from old affection. She was no longer the lovesick lassie he used to know.

Davy climbed into the second carriage where Captain Bertrand was waiting for him. As soon as Effie climbed into the landau where Calum lolled in the corner, she forgot Davy and his megrims. Professor Vandemark sat beside Calum, looking glum. Effie sat beside Sir Malcolm, her eyes only on Calum.

She longed to hold his hand and soothe his furrowed brow. Those precious few letters that had fostered a fondness that she had to hide. But there was Miss Amelia Fortescue to consider. Would that lady join Calum here in Greenock or later in Pittenweem? Right now, it didn't matter. Effie was just glad he was home in Scotland.

When they arrived at the Ballingry home, two footmen carried Calum to a bedchamber. Mrs. McPherson followed them. Effie took one step on the stairs, but Vandemark took her arm; her gaze followed Calum and his entourage.

"Euphemia, leave them to make him comfortable before we go up" said the professor.

There was a little commotion in the hallway. Captain Bertrand came in; Davy stood stiff and grim-faced on the front door steps. Vandemark turned to Davy. "Mackie, go to the kitchen for a bite of food. This footman will direct you."

Davy touched his forelock briefly. He gave Effie a darkling glance before he followed the footman. Davy was right; there was a chasm between them now.

Effie was torn between chagrin about this break from past friendships and her worry for Calum. The professor's voice broke into her thoughts.

"Euphemia, my dear. Moncrithe will be well looked after. The Ballingry's have invited Captain Bertrand and other guests for dinner, so you will need to change."

"Do I have to go to dinner?" She twisted the fringe of her shawl into knots. "I'm worried about Calum. I . . ."

"And Davy?"

"Aye, of course. Him too," said Effie, not looking at the professor but up the stairs where Calum had gone. "He has a strong constitution. I've never kent him sick."

"Calum is stronger than he looks," said the professor. She supposed he was trying to reassure her. "A naval physician encounters many hardships. They need to be strong of body and mind."

Why did he have to have laudanum? And why did he look so thin and pale? She couldn't find answers to these questions until she talked with Captain Bertrand. She waited to talk with the captain, but

Carolina and Sophia were monopolizing him and he flirted outrageously, sending them into whoops of laughter. A few times when he looked in Effie's direction, he smiled and was about to approach her. But Lady Ballingry drew his attention away, and eventually he excused himself to go to his bedchamber.

Vandemark also excused himself to dress for dinner and had planned a short visit to Calum. Effie left with him though Lady Ballingry tried to persuade Effie not to visit Calum, but to spend the time dressing. When she told her hostess the professor needed her help, he backed her up though he gave her arm a soft squeeze.

"You seem to have picked up the ways of the world, Euphemia," he said as they walked up the stairs. Effie glanced at him. Was he serious or joking? She was ready to defend herself but noticed he was smiling with a wry twist to his mouth.

She sighed. "I wasn't very truthful, but I need to see Cal— Lieutenant Moncrithe—to see if he needs anything."

Vandemark nodded, his eyes kind. "It's as well you no longer seek after Mackie. He would not do for you. But, my dear, forget any attachment to Moncrithe."

"Aye. I ken. I ken." Effie hung her head, her feet faltering a little as they reached the door to Calum's room. He kept telling her that; she kept telling herself that.

Mrs. McPherson opened the door at the professor's knock. "Lieutenant Moncrithe is bathed and dressed. Simpson, Sir Malcom's valet, has shaved him. He's sitting up the now, but he should be sleeping. Dinna stay too long. Are you going in too, lassie . . . er. Miss Innes? I dinna think it decent." She glowered at Effie.

"Thank you, Mrs. McPherson," said Effie before the professor could answer. "I am here in the capacity of a nursing attendant."

"She is well chaperoned by me and Simpson," said the professor, ushering the housekeeper out the door. "Miss Innes will be happy for your help later. But for now, we would like to spend time with the lieutenant. We will not tire him." He gently closed the door on Mrs. McPherson's disapproving face.

"I hope I was not too rude. I may need to eat humble pie because I will more than likely need her help," said Effie ruefully.

Calum sat bolstered by several pillows. His eyes were closed.

"But I do *need* to be here." Whispering so softly it was almost a quiet breathing.

When Effie and the professor approached the bed, Calum opened his eyes. At first it was as though he had a hard time focusing on them. He passed a hand over his eyes.

"Miss Innes? Euphemia?" He held out his hand. After a little hesitation, Effie took it; it was icy, clammy. Calum seemed to have a hard time focusing his eyes and clutched Effie's hand so hard she winced.

"It *is* you. I've dreamed . . . I thought I was hallucinating." His gaze consumed her face, then focused on the professor who now stood beside her. "Sir! Professor Vandemark. It can't be a dream. You are all too real." His smile was warm, but he didn't let go of Effie's hand, though she sought to pull it away to make way for the professor.

Simpson brought chairs for the professor and Effie.

"How are you feeling, my lad?" said the professor in a shaking, quiet voice.

"I've felt better. The fever is not from my leg wound; it's healing well," said Calum. "And the head wound was but a glancing blow from shattered wood. It looks worse than it is. Something else is causing this cursed fever. I was well until yesterday." He rubbed his head. "I have the devil of a headache. I hope—" He grimaced and squeezed Effie's hand more tightly. She let out a little gasp of pain. But the physical pain was secondary to the heart pain: those symptoms sounded serious.

Calum turned to her, his eyes feverish. "I'm sorry. I didn't mean to hurt you." He loosened the grip of her hand a little, but when she moved to free herself completely from his grasp, he tightened his fingers. Effie glanced at Vandemark; his face was impassive. What did he think of this hand holding? If holding her hand filled Calum's need, then so be it. Being near him, touching him, after all these months, melted any resolve to keep him at arm's length for her own sake as well as Miss Amelia Fortescue's.

Effie motioned for Simpson to bring her medicine bag which she'd put in the room earlier.

"Let me soothe your brow with lavender water. It was distilled from the professor's garden this summer." She made her voice light, cheery, though her mind wallowed in fear. He'd survived the Battle of Lake Erie and now a more lethal enemy threatened him.

His smile was tender. "Aye. Mayhap it will help," he said, releasing her hand.

She rummaged around in the bag, her fingers familiar with the bottles and sachets of salves and potions she, Jonet, and Rhona had made.

Effie drenched strips of cloth in lavender water, bathing Calum's face and the back of his neck. She left a cloth draped over his hot brow. Calum let out a sigh and relaxed a little. He closed his eyes and drifted into sleep.

"We should leave him now," said Vandemark. "You had best dress for dinner."

"I dinna want to go." Now she'd seen Calum's condition, she was loath to leave his side. She didn't care about social convention at a time like this.

Vandemark stood up and walked toward the door. "Simpson will watch over Moncrithe. Sleep's the best thing for him now." He held out his hand for Effie to follow him.

"I will take good care of the lieutenant, Miss Innes," said Simpson. "I spent time in the navy as a surgeon's mate."

"Aye, but—" Effie glanced at the professor. He tutted, frowning. She rose. "I'll leave the lavender water." She took one last look at Calum before she joined the professor at the door. "And if there's any change, please come for me."

"Dr. Thompson will visit early tomorrow. He had to see to another patient this evening," said the professor ushering her out the door. "We cannot do more at present."

Aye, but she'd be with Calum, be near him, watch over him. Why did the gentry spend so much time with trivial pursuits like dinner parties and card playing? She clamped down her frustrated thoughts and flounced into her bedroom, almost slamming the door behind her.

Chapter 34

Effie and Vandemark were late assembling for dinner. It was a larger group than she had anticipated. She smiled and curtsied as Lady Ballingry introduced her and was shocked to see a familiar face: Lord Thorburn. What was he doing here? She didn't like his sardonic smile as he bent to kiss her hand, holding it a little longer than necessary. She was glad she was wearing gloves. The thought of his lips on her hand made her skin crawl.

Captain Gérard Bertrand led Effie into the dining room and sat next to her. Lady Ballingry was on his other side and spent a good deal of time engaging him in conversation. To her dismay, Effie sat opposite Lord Thorburn, who kept trying to get her to respond to his fulsome compliments—which was bad manners. Even Effie was aware of that solecism; he should have spoken only to those women sitting next to him.

Eventually Lady Ballingry turned to the guest on her other side, and Effie now had the captain's attention, but she wasn't going to start off with pleasantries; she would only talk about Calum.

"When did you notice Cal—Lieutenant Moncrithe start to get sick? He says it was but yesterday. Are others sick like him?"

Before Bertrand could answer, a server came between them and offered Effie a charger of quail braised in red wine. She allowed him to serve her one piece, and like the other courses, she hardly took a mouthful. She moved the food around her plate but couldn't bring herself to eat.

"It is quite delicious, Mademoiselle Innes," said the captain. "You do not need to chase it around your plate."

"I'm sure it is. I'm not hungry," said Effie. She looked up and met his smile.

"To answer your questions, mademoiselle: I do not recall Calum was ailing until we passed the Isle of Arran, a half-day's sailing from Greenock." The captain paused for a moment as though gathering his thoughts. "I believe our surgeon, Gregory, thinks there are a couple of men with la grippe." He looked around the table, then lowered his voice. "This is probably not a suitable topic for the dinner table, but I can tell you a little. We are so careful to delouse ourselves so we don't catch the slow fever. The only thing a little untoward was finding a lone rat. Who knows if there were lice or fleas. Calum helped Gregory with the two sick men. I am sure with rest he will get over this sickness soon. He has before."

No, that was not a suitable topic for the dinner table, but the little she'd seen of the captain, he seemed to flaunt convention. She was not convinced of his cheery confidence that Calum would recover with rest.

"Is Dr. Gregory here at dinner?" Effie said, looking around the table.

"No. Visiting family, I believe," said the captain. "But let us not talk about Calum. I'd love to know more about you—a much more fascinating subject." He was smiling more broadly now, his chestnut eyes warm and appreciative.

"I have no time for flirting, sir," said Effie sitting stiff and tall. She'd rather be upstairs checking on Calum.

The captain gave a loud laugh and several heads turned toward them. "*Tiens!* I must have been too long at sea and lost my abilities to talk to beautiful young ladies to receive such a set down."

"I'm sorry, Captain. That was impolite," said Effie trying to smile in contrition. "Tell me, why is a Frenchman serving in the British navy?"

"Ah. So, you are going to turn the tables on me so I cannot find out more about you," said Bertrand.

Effie flushed.

"Very well, mademoiselle. My father is French. My mother is Scottish and comes from Stirlingshire though we lived in France for several years. My sister and I were born there. We fled France in ninety-one—the revolution was under way—and came to live in Scotland. It was only natural I desired to curb that upstart Napoleon, so I joined the navy. I knew Moncrithe when we were at university in St. Andrews." Effie gave him a sharp look. "*Oui*, that surprises you. It is where I also met Professor Vandemark. I never matriculated like Moncrithe, who went on to medical school. I joined the navy and did not meet up with him again until Gibraltar, with Nelson's fleet. Moncrithe's a good physician, and I wish he could have sailed with me."

"Did I hear you say Moncrithe? Lieutenant Calum Moncrithe?" Lord Thorburn's penetrating voice broke in on their conversation. "I might have known he'd be here if Vandemark was about. And his . . . er . . . ." He raised his glass at Effie. "Where is the gallant lieutenant by the by?" Thorburn had been trying to flirt with her across the table, but she'd barely glanced at him. Now he had her attention.

He raised an eyebrow and leered at her.

Bertrand bristled and sat up straighter. He nodded and said in a wary voice, "Thorburn, I trust you will be a gentleman."

Thorburn smiled, his eyes glistening obsidian. He addressed the lady next to him, but his voice was overloud. "They *were* talking of Moncrithe," said Thorburn, and he took a sip of wine. "No doubt you know the story of how he brought shame to his family?"

The hum of polite conversation ceased.

Lady Ballingry and the professor attempted to begin a new conversation, but Lady Carruthers, a middle-aged lady in a purple turban, said, "What did he do?"

"This is neither the time nor the place, Thorburn," said Bertrand, his French accent strong in his menacing tones.

"My dear Bertrand. Captain now, *n'est-ce pas*? I cannot leave a lady's curiosity hanging in the balance."

Effie looked round in dismay at the avid faces greedy for gossip. She was curious herself, but surely Thorburn would be discreet in mixed company. Yet the smug smile on his face told her otherwise.

"Oh, he was found *flagrans delictum*—you know, caught red-handed—that's for your benefit, my dear," he said, winking at Effie. "I doubt you know Latin."

Heat rose to warm Effie's face, but it wasn't the insult to her intelligence that caused it. A rising anger brought the flames to her cheeks.

Thorburn addressed Lady Carruthers, "Yes, *flagrans delictum* in his sister-in-law's arms—in her boudoir, no less. No wonder his parents banished him from the house." The lady tittered. Thorburn turned to the professor. "I don't know how you can have befriended him, Vandemark. Or you, Bertrand, son of a French marquis."

A few of the other ladies laughed, but Lady Ballingry looked embarrassed, the men wooden-faced, and the professor's face was beetroot, his eyes as hard as pebbles.

Before the professor or Bertrand could speak, Effie stood up, almost knocking over her chair. "How dare you malign Lieutenant Moncrithe. How dare you speak scandal about someone who serves his country—and you all." She looked around the table at the now-astonished faces. "I dinna believe your slanderous tale." She stormed out of the room to a babble of voices, and the scraping of chairs as men, by convention, stood up at the departure of a lady.

She was on the point of running up the stairs when Captain Bertrand's voice stopped her. "I dinna want to hear more," she said between clenched teeth.

"Mademoiselle Innes. Please listen to me."

Effie stiffened as he took her arm and escorted her to the library. "Professor Vandemark asked me to come after you. Please sit down. He will be here presently."

Effie strode toward a chair and plunked herself down while the captain waited by the door. When Professor Vandemark closed the door behind him, and sat next to Effie, the captain sat down too, though with more grace than Effie.

"It's true he was found in his sister-in-law's embrace in her boudoir." The professor held up his hand to interrupt Effie's retort.

Her spirits sank. How had she not been aware he was a womanizer? That he'd committed adultery. She had thought a woman had trifled with his affections. What she knew of him in her heart did not match this news.

"He'd been lured to her room by some pretense to help his brother, but only found Gavina there." Vandemark shook his head. "He was such an innocent. Gavina tore her dress and flung herself at him the minute Ewan entered the room. She accused him of trying to rape her. Despite his denials, Ewan and his father believed her. But I believe him. Nothing untoward happened."

Relief flooded Effie. She could breathe again.

"And I believe him, too," said Bertrand. "I know the lady well. *Oui*, you can raise your eyebrows. I am an incorrigible flirt and she is too." He gave a deprecating smile. "Do not scowl at me so, Miss Innes. But I trust I'm not the sort of flirt as she is. Gavina was annoyed Calum failed to fall under her spell. She had quite the reputation before she snared poor Ewan."

Effie shifted in her chair and flushed, but her fury had died down.

"But isna the lady punished and shunned by society?" said Effie. "Why did Calum take the blame if it was untrue?"

"She's extremely persuasive and adept at telling lies," said Bertrand. "And she brought a substantial dowry with her. The family did not wish to lose that—they had incurred large debts. And they were afraid of the scandal of divorce. Sir Finlay sought to hush it up and so did Ewan."

"How could Calum's father and brother not know him, not support him?" Effie's indignation throbbed in her voice.

Vandemark and Bertrand glanced at each other.

"Calum in those days had quite the temper, but he still honored his father and was concerned for his mother. He disappeared for several days to cool his anger," said Bertrand. "I found him drowning his sorrows in a tavern near my house in Edinburgh. Calum is too much of a gentleman to contradict Gavina and make trouble for the family."

"His mother was an invalid and believed him, but the strife in the family was making her sicker. She begged us to help him. We thought it best to get him out of the country," said the professor. "Calum had recently finished his medical examinations at Edinburgh and I was willing to buy him a commission in the navy. Unfortunately, he rashly accepted the first assignment offered to him—the West African Squadron."

"I often wonder if he had a death wish," Bertrand's mused. "It is a necessary mission, but rife with sickness for the crews and it is hard to stomach the misery of the slave trade. Calum was a changed man after serving there, more morose, more disillusioned."

"Yes. It was such a worry to Lady Ann that she died a year later," the professor broke in, giving Effie's hand a squeeze. "Calum blamed himself, though why I do not know. I was not without influence and Calum was assigned to the Mediterranean fleet. Too bad he was not assigned to your ship, Bertrand."

"I did not get my captaincy until later, but at least we were in the same squadron and I was able to keep an eye on him. He was in demand as a ship's surgeon; his physician's training made him stand out among those butchers who called themselves surgeons. He seemed content on board ship." Bertrand took a pinch of snuff. "When on land I tried to get him to attend balls and soirées, but he was standoffish with the ladies though they thronged after him. He is a fine figure of a man. Calum did not trust women since . . . er . . . that unfortunate incident. His fiancée deserted him too. He didn't even frequent . . . and I too—we were of the few not visiting the ladies at our stops in Portugal and—" The professor cleared his throat loudly. "I do beg your pardon, Miss Innes. I am fresh off the ship and I need to remember how to comport myself in good company. I do not wish to give you a distaste of us sailors." But his eyes were mischievous.

"Well, your manners are a lot better than Lady Carruthers's," said Effie. The captain laughed.

"Now I know why Calum has such regard for you. He talked of you on our way home. You are no simpering lassie."

Effie shook her head. "No, this is not like me. I should not have lost my temper." She turned to the professor. "I dinna want to apologize to Lord Thorburn, but I'm sorry I caused pain to Sir Malcolm and Lady Ballingry."

"Talk with them tomorrow, my dear. I think it best you not join the company. But I will go. I'll make your excuses for you. Bertrand, give me your arm."

The captain didn't immediately take the professor's arm but turned to Effie. He took her right hand, raised it to his lips. He held on to her hand for a minute, his dark eyes showing his admiration. Effie blushed but did not lower her eyes.

"I hope your sentiments about the navy defending these shores, includes me," he said with a quirk of an eyebrow.

"Of course," she said curtly. He grinned. "Of course," she said in a gentler voice. "I am thankful you brave the seas and wars for us." She lifted her chin a little. "*Bon soir*, Captain Bertrand. Thank you for . . . for telling me about Calum. You are a good friend to him." She pulled her hand away. "The professor is waiting for your escort."

"I will call again tomorrow. I'd like to become better acquainted." He bowed.

"*Oh je!*" said the professor. "You French cannot resist sweet-talking the lassies. Let us face the party."

"I'd rather face a barrage of cannon fire," said the captain, with a wink for Effie. "I'm shaking in my boots."

"Not you," said Vandemark, before the door closed.

Effie sat in the library for several minutes, her throat aching. Calum had had to face censure and gossip like she had. It was fortunate he had good friends in the professor and Captain Bertrand. And he was away at sea, away from the gossip. She couldn't believe Calum would have behaved in such a fashion. He was a man of honor. The captain, on the other hand—she couldn't read him; she was not familiar with society banter.

And Calum had talked of her? No doubt he'd said that she was bookish and was learning about botany, nothing more. And yet he had held her hand, found comfort in it. Forby he thought her used to ministering to the professor and helping Dr. Ferguson.

All was quiet. Effie took a taper from the credenza, lit it, and quietly ascended the stairs. She stopped by Calum's room. It was in darkness except for a pool of light from a few candles on the dressing table. Simpson rose from the chair by the window when Effie entered. He assured her that Calum was doing well.

Effie smoothed back the hair from Calum's brow. It was a little feverish. She wished to do more. If Simpson hadn't been there, she'd have risked kissing him on the cheek. Now she knew his secret shame, she yearned to comfort him more than ever. But wasn't that Miss Amelia Fortescue's role?

Chapter 35

Simpson rose bleary-eyed from his chair when Effie entered Calum's room the next day. His face was grave. She put her hand on Calum's head; he was hot and feverish, tossing and turning, and moaning a little.

"Calum. Calum. I'm here." She took the hand outside the bedcovers; the other was hidden under his pillow. "Be still" Then in a quiet undertone, "My darling dearie." The endearment came out naturally.

He stopped thrashing around and his eyes opened. "Miss Innes. Euphemia. I dreamed—" He wrinkled his brow and squeezed Effie's hand. He struggled to sit up. "Where am I? In Pittenweem?" Effie motioned for Simpson to help him sit up.

"No, you're in Greenock," said Effie. She helped Simpson plump up the pillows and as she did so, heard a crackle of papers as she moved them. She pulled them out. They were her letters to Calum. He put out his hand for them.

"Your letters are the only things that kept me sane," he said as he pushed them under his pillow. "That and the salve." The snuff box was sitting on a side table near at hand. He shut his eyes for a moment, as though in pain. When he opened them, his gaze was intense. He was about to say something, hesitated, wet his lips then said, "But now you are here my d—my nereid." He gave a small smile. "Remember when I called you that? It's my first memory of you. I knew you'd bring me good fortune."

273

"Aye. And I thought you were insulting me," said Effie trying to speak lightly though her heart was full. "But luck could not have been strong. You were injured in battle."

"Many more died and had worse wounds than I. I was lucky that spar didn't pierce my eye, do more damage."

"I've more lavender water to soothe you but I think you need stronger potions. Do you think it's la grippe? Dr. Thompson thinks so. He will come to bleed you. He'll be here about noon."

Calum grimaced. "No. Euphemia, promise me you will not let him bleed me. I think it's more than the grippe. I'm afraid—" His hand shook. "Yes, bathe my brow with lavender water. Tell the professor I wish to speak to him on an urgent matter."

Simpson was putting out Calum's clothes when Effie left the room. Calum planned on getting up for breakfast. She sent one of the servants to rouse the professor who did not like to wake early. There was a fine spread of foods for breakfast and the family was not down yet. Effie wondered where Davy was. A twinge of guilt pricked Effie; she'd all but forgotten about him in her worry about Calum. She ventured down to the kitchen. Davy was eating as though he hadn't eaten in a week by the state of the pile of food on his plate.

"I'm happy to see you have a grand appetite," said Effie smiling as she sat down at the table. She took a piece of bannock and buttered it but could hardly swallow it. She tried not to stare at his injuries, but she couldn't help remembering him as he was.

"Well you'd have too if all you'd had was hardtack and small beer for the last few days. We daren't put into harbor in Ireland for fresh supplies for the riving storm was against us. That won't give a body strength," he said, nodding at the buttered bannock on Effie's plate.

"I'm not very hungry," said Effie. There was a small silence as one of the servants poured milk for Davy. "Can you tell me about the battle, Davy? Is it too painful a story to tell? I'm grieved to hear about Robbie." Effie put out her hand and lay it on his arm.

Davy blinked and rubbed his eyes. He appeared to have a hard time swallowing.

"You dinna need to tell me now, if it's too painful."

He cleared his throat. "No. I need to talk about it. Tell you. It'll be easier to tell Ma and Da later. The ship was bombarded hard and broke up, taking on water fast. Moncrithe was on the cockpit taking care of the wounded. I was assigned to carry them to him." He stared at the kitchen range. "He couldna have done more. He kept going even after a spar shattered from a mast hit his head. The wound bled so hard he couldna see. I thought he was a goner. It was time to get him out of there. The wounded were past healing."

Davy passed his hand across his face as though trying to erase his vision. "A black man, a former slave from the United States—Jacob—carried Moncrithe to the main deck and put him in a row boat. The captain was dead. I couldna see Robbie. I looked and looked, and then a fragment of wood ripped my arm." He choked back a sob. "I was useless with only one arm." He looked down at the scarred arm. "Jacob saved me too." Effie covered his clenched fist with her hands.

"Jacob got me in a boat with Moncrithe and two other sailors and rowed us out of midst of the battle. I dinna ken how he did it. Moncrithe and I requested he come with us, but the authorities wouldna allow it." He scowled and took a bite of bread.

Talking with his mouth full, he said, "We're fortunate to be here. The navy was unwilling to let us go. Your professor kens some powerful people. They wanted Moncrithe to stay and administer to the sick and him wounded himself."

The cook poured more milk. Davy glanced at her, his lips pulled into a twisted smile from the scar. His voice came out hoarse and low. "Eh, that was a braw meal, Mrs. Fleming" He turned to Effie. "How's Moncrithe?"

Effie shook her head and sipped tea. "Not good. Still ailing. The ship's doctor thinks it is the flu."

Davy snorted. "That man only kens how to doctor the pox." Effie raised her eyebrows. He turned red. "Er. He's not a shade to Ferguson or Moncrithe. Now I've seen a bit of the world I can tell you we're fortunate to have Ferguson in Pittenweem." Davy looked out the window for a minute. "Effie, I must talk with you. But not here. Not with the gentry and servants about. Get your bonnet and wrap and meet me by the shrubbery."

"Davy, I canna stay long. Calum—."

"Aye. Calum. We'll talk of him." Davy frowned and moved toward the door. "Give me five minutes of your time." He rose from his chair. Effie collected a shawl from the foyer.

By the time Effie and Davy reached the garden, a glimmer of sunlight had pushed through the clouds. They found a place sheltered by yew trees that softened the breezes from the sea.

"What do you wish to say to me?" said Effie, impatience putting an edge to her voice.

"My, my, Miss Crabbit. How you've changed." He grinned.

"I'm sorry." Effie put out a hand to touch his arm. "I'm no crabbit, only anxious about Lieutenant Moncrithe."

Davy covered her hand with his. It was warm and strong. "Whisht you, Effie. You ken . . . you and Moncrithe canna be. Come back with me to Pittenweem. I'm leaving the day to get home. We can take a boat to Glasgow, then it's overland to Cramond, then a boat to Pittenweem. A three-day journey I reckon." He took Effie's hands.

"Effie, I ken you liked—loved—me once. We can marry and live with my parents until we get a wee cottage." She looked down and studied her shoes. He was taking a lot for granted, but it would be a solution against a lonely spinsterhood. After all, Calum had Miss Fortescue. And she did like Davy. She'd listen to what he had to say. "As my wife, you'll give up that nonsense working for the professor. What does a woman need with schooling?"

"Well, it gave me a good job," said Effie, her voice tart.

But she ground her teeth. Why would she have to give up her studies, reading and writing? If she loved Davy, as she had before, that wouldn't stop her from marrying him, even if Vandemark didn't sanction the marriage, but to force her to give up intellectual pursuits . . . Couldn't she do that *and* be a fisherman's wife? She could also supplement their income. Didn't he understand that?

He was still talking.

"You'll have plenty to do especially when the bairns come along, even if your mother—" He recovered himself. Effie stiffened. There it was again. He echoed his mother's reservations about mingling his heritage with her bad blood.

"And when the professor dies, he'll leave you something in his will. I could buy another boat. Moncrithe told me you're now his ward. You kept that quiet. What else has been going on?"

His bright blue eyes held a smile, and the wind lifted a curl of black hair off his brow. Even with the scar, he was a handsome, vigorous man. A man Effie had loved for years. But not now. Not in that way. If he'd asked her a year ago, she'd have jumped at the chance to be his wife. Effie could only stare at him as jumbled thoughts ran around her head. She'd never seen this side of him before, only the kind and jovial laddie who'd befriended and defended her over the years.

"You've changed your tune from the last letter you wrote your parents." Effie couldn't keep the bitterness out of her voice.

A faint flush on Davy's face. "You read that?"

"Who else? I think you kent."

"I was so angry about Catriona I wasna thinking straight. Forgive me?" His smile was disarming and he pulled a strand of her hair, playfully, like he used to do with Catriona.

"Aye, I will for auld lang syne."

"Effie. What ails you? You said you're not angry, but the snow couldna be whiter than your cheeks," said Davy, lifting a hand and stroking her cheek. He put his good arm around her, drew her close, and kissed her. And she felt nothing, no passion. No, not nothing—irritation.

She pushed away from him. It wouldn't be fair to marry him and yearn for someone else, even if she could dismiss his high-handed manner. He let her go, but his eyes narrowed, and she caught a flash of temper.

Effie shook her head—cold to the core—but not from the chill air. "I canna, Davy. I canna."

"Is it because of what I said in my letter? I didna really mean it. I thought of you often when I was lying in my hospital bed."

"No. It's not that. I said I'd forgiven you. I've changed though you are still a dear, dear friend."

"Yon professor has a lot to answer for," said Davy, the scar more livid with his scowl. "He's made you put yourself above your friends in Pittenweem with his learning and gentry-ways." His brow darkened further. "Is it Moncrithe? When did you set your sights on him? You canna hope to be his wife. He might take you on as mistress. He seems to like you. Asked a lot of questions about you." His frown grew more fierce. "You'd rather be a mistress than wife to an honest fisherman? You're more like your mother than I kent."

"Davy!" Effie's voice trembled. *So Calum knows the worst.* Be his mistress? Would she consent to that? And how dare Davy liken her to her mother. Whatever vestige of love she'd left for him dissipated with every heave of her chest, every gasping breath, every clenching of her fists.

"I canna be your wife, but though I canna be wife to Calum." She gulped. "Nor mistress neither—I canna love another."

She put her hand on his good arm, as though contact with him would somehow convey her pain, her true feelings. "I will never marry. I'm thinking I could teach lassies—at a school in Stirling. You mind Dominie Sutherland? He teaches there. The professor's friend will hire me too—" She was babbling. Saying out loud her new, more rational plan. Davy put his good arm around her. She sobbed so hard her body shook.

"Effie." He kissed her bent head. "What a pair we are. I felt the same way about Catriona when she married Alasdair. I thought the two of us could comfort each other. You're unco sad the now. Stay and nurse Moncrithe. When you return to Pittenweem mayhap you'll feel differently in a few months, especially when Moncrithe marries or—does not recover."

A coldness so profound crept through Effie's veins and settled like a block of ice deep within her.

Davy's voice droned on. "I was thinking we could go to Canada. Leave Pittenweem. Leave all the old sad memories. It's a grand country. Tam Braid is there though he left for a place called Kentucky in the States. I dinna think this war will last long. What do you say, Effie? It will be an adventure."

She no longer felt comforted in his arms, more like imprisoned. Imprisoned in the past. She stepped away from him and shook her head.

"You're not the meek, biddable lassie I used to ken," said Davy his mood changing, blue eyes hard as sapphires. He shrugged. Bitterness made his voice harsh. "Dry your tears and go to

Moncrithe. Tell him I bid him farewell, and hope for a speedy recovery. I will no doubt see him should he visit the professor. I'll be on my way."

Davy picked up his bag and strode down the path. Effie watched him go until the shrubbery that skirted the Ballingry estate hid him. It was as though with his disappearance his friendship and her past hopes and dreams died. She swallowed the lump in her throat.

Chapter 36

Befuddled and sad, even a little angry, Effie marched through the house to Calum's bedchamber.

He sat on the window seat looking out over the garden. He turned around slowly and gazed at Effie. She was puzzled by the relief in his face. He must have seen her and Davy. What must he be thinking?

He put his head in his hands.

Effie rushed to his side. "Does your head hurt? I think too much laudanum is not good for you. I have a tincture of willow bark and chamomile to relieves the pain. And hot lemon and honey though you're hot from the fever, it may break it."

Calum appeared to be incapable of speech, keeping his head in his hands. She wanted to put a hand on his shoulder to comfort him, but just stood close to him waiting for him to speak.

"Has Davy left for Pittenweem?" The words came out quiet, despondent.

"Aye. He's taking a boat to Glasgow and then—"

"Did he ask you to . . . to go with him? He kissed and embraced you."

"Aye, he kissed me," said Effie warmth spreading over her cheeks. A soft sound from Calum. "But I said no I wouldna go with him. Why do you ask?"

"Why did you say no?" Calum's voice was raw with emotion. He still had not lifted his head. "Did you stay for the professor?"

"Aye." She paused. "But mostly I stayed because of you." Was she revealing too much?

Calum lifted his head and looked at Effie for a minute before putting his arms around her waist and drawing her toward him so his face was buried in her midriff. She held his head, stroking his hair, tenderness welling up inside. She could feel him trembling before he pulled away. His lips moved. Effie had to bend down to hear what he said. "Don't leave."

Effie cried inside: *I dinna wish to ever leave you.* But out loud her answer was prosaic. "No. I'm here to take care of you."

Thoughts jostled thick and fast. What was going on with him? How sick was he? Normally he'd never have made that intimate gesture of holding her close. Could he hear her heart breaking as she cradled him?

Calum drew away from her and looked up more fully into her face. "Euphemia." He took her hands, looking down at them. "I lost the picture I drew of your hand. But I aspire to the real thing and more than just your hand. I want to take care of you—"

Effie backed away, releasing her hands from his grasp, her pulse hammering away her dreams and hopes. Was he asking her to be his mistress?

"No. I canna." The words burst out high, tormented.

"What?" He looked up with such shock and sadness in his eyes.

"No. I canna be your mistress."

His hazel eyes widened and darkened to brown-green pools, his face whiter than before.

"No. No. I'm not expressing myself clearly." He rubbed his head then took her hands again, perspiration moistening his brow. He cleared his throat. "Euphemia. I'm asking for your hand in marriage."

Effie's mind, heart, and body went still. She stared at Calum. Then with her pulse tripping, stuttering, she finally managed. "What did you say?"

"Euphemia. Would you do me the honor of being my wife?"

"What about Miss Amelia Fortescue?" He couldn't mean he wished to marry *her*? It was the fever talking. Perhaps his disordered mind thought her Miss Fortescue though he'd called her by name. Tears pricked her eyes.

"Who?" He wrinkled his brow. "Oh. Miss Fortescue. A mere acquaintance. Someone I danced with. No one important."

Effie's legs gave way; she almost fell on the window seat. Calum still held her hands.

"Your rank, your family— My mother is—"

"Your station doesn't matter to me. My family? Well, they can go hang! I think you like me a little? Perhaps not as much as Mackie, but he— Marry me. It's important."

"I like you more than a little," said Effie. He hadn't mentioned the word love so she was hesitant to declare her love for him. He looked at her with beseeching feverish eyes. For whatever reason, he did mean it. Two marriage proposals in one day. But this one was true, right. And yet . . . She drew a shuddering breath.

"Aye. I will marry you."

"My dear. I'm so happy." He bent to kiss her hand but drew back at the last moment. He smiled ruefully. "I cannot kiss you properly because of this sickness." The smile vanished from his face. "Euphemia. I need to tell you . . . I believe I have typhus."

"Typhus? No!" Her heart lurched. He might die. The happy haze that had enveloped her vanished as she was now fully alert to her surroundings, fully alert to the worry in his eyes.

Professor Vandemark entered the room.

"Wish me happy, my dear sir," said Calum turning to look at him. "Euphemia has accepted my proposal."

Vandemark smiled faintly but did not look glad. Did he disapprove of their engagement? He'd warned her Calum was unlikely to be more than a friend to her. Was she not worthy of Calum after all? The pressure of Calum's hand caused her to look back at him. His eyes were pleading.

"We need to be married today because I don't know how this sickness will progress."

He was afraid he might die. Why marry her so she'd become a widow? How could he be so cruel? He had no idea how much her feelings were engaged, how much she loved him. What did he feel for her? She was sure he liked her, but marriage—?

"Today? Is that possible?" Effie said with a sharp intake of breath. She looked at the professor for guidance. It was as though his tall, bulky presence gave stability to her whirling thoughts; Vandemark nodded and came over to stand by them.

"It will be an irregular but legal marriage without the reading of banns." He gave a small smile and patted Effie on the arm. "I know you would rather be married in the kirk, but . . ." He shrugged.

Aye. He knew too well how insecure she felt about her mother's irregular handfasting to that Norseman.

"It will be like those English that come to Gretna Green and other border towns to marry without banns," said the professor.

"Aye," Calum said. "There was an English crew member who married a Scottish lassie in Leith last year. I attended the ceremony. Made sure it was registered with the sheriff. We could marry in the kirk later. This is no trial marriage." He scrunched up his eyes.

He was obviously in pain. Her thoughts automatically ran through the potions and salves to treat pain but it was a mere academic exercise—nothing felt real.

"I'll send Bertrand to find a minister," Vandemark said. He leaned over and kissed Effie's cheek. "I wish you every happiness, my dear."

The words were right but below them Effie could sense a deep melancholy. Vandemark limped out the door.

Effie turned to Calum who was still holding onto her hands with a firm grip. Sweat beaded his brow."

"You've stayed up too long and need your rest. I'll call Simpson to help you to your bed."

"No. Don't call him yet. I wish to spend as much time with you as I can."

That sounded ominous. Her emotions had soared like gulls gliding on the air, but now they plummeted as swift as gannets plunging into icy water.

"As you know some people recover . . ." Calum's voice was calm and even. "But if I don't recover . . ."

A sharp pain pierced her and she gasped.

"No, my love." He squeezed her hand.

He had called her his love; she hung onto that endearment.

He reached up to stroke her hair. "You have to hear this. If I don't recover, as my widow you will be able to receive my navy pension and my inheritance from my aunt when she dies."

"As Vandemark's ward I will inherit from him. Dinna do this out of care for my future." She had to be the practical one, had to be certain this was what he desired.

His brow wrinkled. "I don't want to leave my inheritance to Ewan's progeny."

So was he only doing this for revenge against his brother and sister-in-law? A bitterness rose in Effie's throat. She had to make him see sense—that marriage to her wasn't necessary—though she wished to marry him with all her heart.

"You could leave your inheritance to the navy, could you not?"

"I don't want to. I wish to marry you." Calum coughed and said when he caught his breath, "I *need* to marry you."

Her insides tied up in knots, Effie was finally able to whisper through her swollen throat. "I dinna care about your pension or your inheritance. You must get better."

Effie swallowed hard to keep her voice from catching. She squared her shoulders to shrug off the leaden weight on them. Her eyes roamed over Calum's face as though she were remembering every dear inch of it.

"I will nurse you to health. I have new recipes from my grandmother. Now you must recover your strength, so you need rest."

"Yes, my dear," said Calum, a soft laugh in his voice. "We'll fight this together." He squeezed her hand. "Now please get Simpson; he'll help me to bed. I want a little rest so I can be fresh for our marriage."

Effie bent down and kissed Calum on the cheek in defiance of his strictures not to come too close to him. He smiled but there was a crease between his eyes. One symptom of the early stages of typhus was a bad headache.

Laudanum might help, but he'd already had a heavy dose. As Simpson helped Calum to his bed, she asked the valet to administer the willow bark tincture she'd used the previous evening. She was glad she had an ally in him to help nurse Calum.

Effie couldn't go downstairs and face the Ballingry family. Her emotions were too raw and confused. A proposal from Calum was more than her heart desired, but it came with a price. She doubted he'd have proposed to her if he'd not been sick, but she was not too proud to take those crumbs, to take him on these bitter terms. And it seemed to be his dying—*no! not dying*—wish.

She went to her room and took out the ancient book of medicines. She prayed she'd find a remedy in Granny Effie's book. Dr. Ferguson's methods and theories about cleanliness should help too. The writing blurred and her brain numbed with sorrow. She wished she had more time. She forced herself to concentrate on the words, desperate to find something that would help.

When Effie entered Calum's room, he was asleep. Simpson told her the professor wished to speak with her in the library. Reluctantly she went in search for him.

Vandemark sat on a divan smoking his pipe, the epitome of ease, but his hand clenched the pipe bowl tightly and his eyes were unusually bright.

Effie sat beside him. They stared at each other for a moment. The professor put down his pipe and held out his hand. She grasped it. Was it to find comfort for herself or to comfort him?

"Bertrand has gone to fetch a minister. I suppose Calum told you why there is the need for haste?"

"Aye." It was but a whisper.

"It is a gallant gesture," said the professor. He drew on his pipe and blew out a cloud of smoke. Effie stiffened.

"I see you do not approve, sir," said Effie, sharpness in her voice. "I ken he wouldna marry me else. I am not worthy."

"That's not true," said Vandemark. He puffed out his breath. "I had not realized when you were writing to each other his sentiments were engaged. I know yours were and I did not want to give you hope in that direction." He smiled at Effie. "In my heart of hearts, I wished you two joy in marriage but I never expected it to be to each other. His family connections . . ." He shrugged.

"Aye, and *my* family connections. He dinna ken about my mother or my father, a ravisher," said Effie. "I mind, should he recover I could always desert him," she choked on the words, "so he could get a divorce and be free to marry someone from the gentry." But as those words came out of her mouth, the rest of her body rebelled at the thought, pain ripping through her.

"My dear. I see you love him very much," The professor's expression was compassionate. "But who knows what Calum will think about that. He will commit to you. He has been estranged from his family for many years. Mayhap, should he—" He blinked for a second. Effie filled in the gap: *should he live*. "He will see how fortunate he is to have you. He could find no better among the gentry."

"Thank you, sir," said Effie much moved. "I'll meet whatever comes in the future, but now—day by day—we must do all we can to get him better. Simpson tells me he has banished you from his room." She raised her chin and compressed her lips. "He'd better not try to banish me."

The professor gave a little laugh. "I can see you are becoming wifely already."

Effie reddened.

The professor stayed in the library while Effie kept watch over Calum as he slept. The one interruption was a visit from Dr. Thompson.

"What are you doing here, lassie?" Dr. Thompson said as he opened the door. "I hear Moncrithe has the fever so I'll bleed him to give him ease. You should leave. Simpson will help me."

"No. You shall not bleed him," said Effie standing between the doctor and the bed. "Lieutenant Moncrithe told me he should not be bled."

"What nonsense is this?" said Thompson, turning puce in the face. "What do you know of physicking? Who are you to speak for him? Get out of my way." He tried to push Effie aside.

"I am to be his wife and I say you will not bleed him." Effie stood her ground, glaring at the doctor. "Simpson, you are my witness. Did he not say he should not be bled?"

Dr. Thompson turned to Simpson, who reluctantly nodded. The doctor exhaled loudly. "Am I to be overridden by a servant and a chit of a lassie? Well, be it on your heads if—no—*when* he dies." He picked up his bag then stopped and turned, scowling. "You're to be his wife? Do the Ballingrys know of this?" He marched out the door.

"Thank you, Simpson," said Effie. "I hope you are not in trouble with the Ballingry family."

"Dinna fash yoursel', Miss Innes," said Simpson. "I mind yon surgeon—" he inclined his head in Calum's direction—"kens what he is talking about; there are some fevers that dinna do well with bleeding."

Vandemark lumbered into the room followed by Morag, one of the maids, who had brought clean bedlinen.

"Bertrand should be back with the minister shortly," said the professor. There was a commotion in the hallway. "And here he is already."

Captain Bertrand, breathing heavily, strode into the room. He shut the door sharply behind him and turned the key.

"I had to run up the stairs. They'll be here soon."

"What's amiss?" Effie's voice wobbled.

"The minister is not allowed into the house. He came willingly enough, but Sir Malcolm forbade him to perform the wedding. He said Calum's father would not sanction such a marriage. You must wake Calum now."

Calum was still a little groggy from sleep and struggled to sit up. The pallor of his face worried Effie as she plumped up pillows behind him. She caught her breath: he looked more ill than earlier in the day.

"I'm awake. I heard. My father? Aye. He'd stop the marriage. But he's not here."

Effie tried not to gasp. He was defying his father. But was it only to thwart his brother?

Calum's mouth was drawn into a thin line. "Simpson, fetch my uniform jacket. I'll be married in it." Calum held out his hand to Effie who took it, though her hand shook. "My dear. This is not how I excepted our wedding to be." He put his other hand to his head, a deep crease furrowed his brow and he seemed to be having a hard time focusing his eyes. "We must make haste."

"*Ja, ja.* Bertrand will perform a marriage of consent," said the professor.

"Or a handfasting," said Bertrand grinning and fingering his intricately tied cravat. "I'll even sacrifice my neckcloth for the bands though it took ages to tie a trone d'amour knot."

No. Not a handfasting. Effie shrank from the idea, though there were witnesses unlike her mother's unorthodox handfasting. She gazed beseechingly at the professor.

The professor gave Effie a reassuring smile. "No. There's no need to use your cravat, Bertrand. I think a marriage of consent will suffice. Although I cannot legally be a witness as I'm not considered a citizen, we have three citizens here." He indicated Simpson and Morag who was hiding behind Simpson, her eyes wide and questioning.

Someone started pounding on the door. Sir Malcolm's voice demanded they open it, and Dr. Thompson bellowed to be let in to doctor Calum.

Calum squeezed Effie's fingers. She bent down to hear him over the thumping at the door.

"All I know is, I wish you to be my wife."

"That is declaration enough, Calum, as you know, but let's be more formal." Bertrand raised his voice over the din. "Do you Calum Alexander Gilchrist Moncrithe wish to marry this woman before you, Euphemia—do you have a middle name?"

"Inga."

The captain raised his eyebrows then said, "This woman, Euphemia Inga Innes?"

"Aye. And I—" The rest of Calum's words were drowned by the thundering of the door.

"And do you pledge to cleave unto her only and to love and cherish her for aye?"

"Aye." Calum's voice cracked. He was sinking fast.

"Euphemia Inga Innes do you wish to marry this man before you, Calum Alexander Gilchrist Moncrithe?"

"Aye." Effie said loud and clear, but in her mind she added *with all my heart.*

"And do you pledge to cleave unto him only and to love and obey him for aye?"

"Aye." Effie said as she gazed into Calum's eyes that were now glassy with fever.

Effie's hands were so ice-cold the warmth of Calum's burning hands couldn't thaw them.

"I now pronounce you man and wife bound together in love and respect in front of these witnesses." Bertrand nodded at Simpson and Morag who inclined their heads in agreement. Simpson took Morag's arm and spoke quietly to the maid who was visibly upset.

Bertrand helped Calum push his blue sapphire signet ring onto Effie's ring finger as Calum was shaking so much.

"I'll get you a real wedding ring later." Calum's voice was raspy and quiet.

Effie could hardly hear him for the uproar outside the door. The ring fit just right; she didn't want another; it was part of him.

Calum sprawled his signature on the piece of paper that Vandemark thrust before him, then coughed so hard his whole body shook.

Effie scribbled her signature without looking at the paper. She unstopped the bottle of syrup of rosehips. When Calum stopped coughing, she spooned a couple of doses into his mouth.

"I'll be sure to register with the sheriff soon," said Captain Bertrand folding the marriage lines after Simpson and Morag made their mark. He put the document in the breast of his jacket. Effie could not read the expression in the captain's dark eyes when he bent over to kiss her cheek and congratulate her on her marriage.

Vandemark also kissed her cheek and patted Calum's shoulder. The banging on the door had stopped and there was the scrape of something metal in the lock.

Vandemark and Bertrand went to the door. With a nod from the professor, Bertrand turned the key and opened the door; blocking whoever stood outside. He and the professor stepped outside to confront their irate host.

"You can congratulate Lieutenant Moncrithe and Mrs. Moncrithe later," said Bertrand before the door closed on his words. Simpson locked the door behind them and motioned for Morag to follow him to a corner of the room where they spoke in whispers.

Outside the room, angry voices rose and then faded as the men moved away from the door, but Effie soon forgot them as Calum coughed hard. His face was pale and he shivered.

"My dear, will you bring me another covering? It seems to have become a lot colder."

Chapter 37

Had her wedding only been two days ago? If it were not for the wink of the sapphire ring on her finger, it could have been a dream.

High fever gripped Calum a few minutes after the wedding ceremony. Simpson helped undress and bathe him and saw to his personal needs and cleaned up after his bouts of vomiting. When Calum complained of aches and joint pain, Effie smoothed salves of lavender and peppermint on his chest, back, arms, and legs. She was particularly gentle of the old scars probably from earlier skirmishes and especially those on his back that looked like the reminder of a flogging. Why would an officer receive a flogging? There were so many things she didn't know about Calum.

Though they were officially married, Effie was embarrassed at first to perform this intimate service, but after a while as she kneaded and stroked his taut muscles, she sang to bring a rhythm to the massage. She imagined she was smoothing and banishing away poisons out of his body. It was her will against the sickness.

About the fifth day, he had the telltale rash on his torso—a sign of typhus. She and Simpson were diligent in keeping Calum and themselves clean. They took turns sleeping on the camp bed in the dressing room. Day and night blended together, the only break were the meals delivered outside the door and the time she spent poring over the herbal book trying to find a cure.

She decided to use garlic with honey, lemon and hot water. She plied him with different kinds of teas and ground a little of the goldenseal into broths. She was determined to wash out this evil from his body so he'd recover.

Calum's fever came and went, but there were times when he was delirious, tossing and turning, and calling for Effie not to leave him. She wanted to cry, Dinna leave *me*.

One day, Simpson suggested Effie get some fresh air. Though reluctant, Effie agreed it would invigorate her. The January air was indeed bracingly cold and the bite of wind woke her from the living nightmare of the sick room. Sea gulls swooping over the grey sea screamed their mournful cries while the ships in the harbor bobbed about in the sea swell. Life was carrying on while Calum was in a deadly fight for his life.

She was about to turn back into the house when she caught sight of Professor Vandemark with Captain Bertrand. It was the first time she'd seen them since the wedding.

"How is Calum?" said the professor. "Is he improving?"

"The sickness is running its course," said Effie as she took his arm.

"And how are *you* feeling, Mrs. Moncrithe? Are you keeping well?" said the captain.

Effie looked at him surprised. She still wasn't used to her married name.

"I delivered the marriage lines to the sheriff so all is shipshape."

Effie smiled, a waft of hope blew away the fog of despair. "Thank you. I'm tired mostly. Simpson has been a grand help. We take it in turns to sleep," said Effie.

"Will you allow me to help? A third person will give you more rest," said the captain.

What kind of help could he give? He was a captain of a warship. She took a deep breath of frigid air. She was loath to insult him, so she deflected his question.

"How are your two men who came down with typhus?"

"One seems to be improving, but the other is not doing well," said Bertrand.

"It's good news that one is getting better." Effie's spirits lifted a little. "If he is doing well then there's hope for Calum."

"And I will warrant Calum is getting the better care," said Bertrand. He chuckled. "I heard how you stood up to Dr. Thompson. Calum is fortunate to have such a doughty champion. And a beautiful one what is more."

Effie was impatient of his pleasantries, especially at a time like this. She was about to make a retort, but when she looked at him, his mien was kind rather than mocking. She inclined her head.

The three of them ambled toward the house. Though she kept looking at the professor, he didn't seem disposed to join the conversation.

"Are you well, sir?" Effie squeezed his arm to get the professor's attention. "You look a little peaky. Are you eating well? Does the gout pain you?"

The professor smiled a little wanly. "I am well. All the better for seeing you. Sir Malcolm wrote to Calum's father to let him know his son is wed and ill. I doubt Sir Finlay will make the trip here—the weather has been snowy from Glasgow to Linlithgow they tell me."

Effie fervently wished that Sir Finlay Moncrithe would not come.

"Your marriage will not sit well with the Moncrithes," said the professor.

"I think your marriage to Calum is good news," Bertrand broke in. "At least for Calum." His mouth twitched. "I for one envy him." He held up his hand when Effie frowned. "Don't look so *indignée*. I know I'm an incorrigible flirt." He became serious. "But I mean it. You are the best thing that has happened to Calum. Better than that namby-pamby Felicity Lennox he was courting. She left him as soon as she learned of his so-called dishonor."

So that's why Calum had called out for her not to leave; he thought she was like Felicity.

"But I fear Sir Finlay will not share my sentiments," said the captain. "He is a proud man."

Effie could guess how he'd react. Sir Malcolm and Lady Ballingry had been incensed on Sir Finlay's behalf. Could Sir Finlay void the marriage so Calum could be reconciled with his family and join his place in high society? That was something she'd be willing to sacrifice if it were the best for him. But perversely, it was different if she were forced to do it on his father's whim. The professor interrupted her depressing thoughts.

"I have not yet written to Jonet and Billy about your marriage," said the professor. "I think it best we wait."

Effie looked hard at him. Was it because he was not really reconciled to the marriage?

At the terrace, Effie bid the professor and the captain goodbye, though Gérard called after her as she climbed the stairs that he'd visit Calum later that afternoon.

Bertrand surprised Effie. He followed Simpson's instructions exactly and was calm but firm in administering medication and cleaning up vomit. He quirked an eyebrow when he caught her staring at him.

"When you're in the navy or army, you learn to deal with sickness and wounds. It's not all left to the surgeons. We all take a hand in caring for our comrades. I think of Calum as a brother. How does your Shakespeare say it? *We band of brothers.*"

Effie was glad of his help though he did flirt with her, but now she knew him a little she could see it was second nature to him and not threatening. It was his way of trying to lighten up her spirits. When Calum slept more soundly, they talked about *Atala*, Chateaubriand's book that Vandemark had given her. He helped correct her French pronunciation and a couple of times he even made her laugh. She needed that lift to her spirits.

Simpson returned and it was Effie's turn to rest. She was reluctant to leave but the captain and Simpson assured her they'd come for her should there be any change. It was good to sleep in her own bed for a change, and she slept as soon as her head touched the pillow.

"Your husband is resting quietly," said Simpson when she returned to Calum's room. Her husband? Effie was still not used to the idea. But it sounded good. She rehearsed her new name: *Euphemia Moncrithe, Effie Moncrithe.*

The next day, Calum's fever was less. Effie hoped it was a good sign. But his head was hurting so she massaged his forehead and the back of his neck with verbena and peppermint salve.

"Euphemia. If I wasn't hurting so bad, I'd be enjoying this," said Calum with a hint of humor in one of his lucid moments. He put up a hand and gently touched Effie's face. There was that tender look again. Effie had to force herself not to slip into his arms.

The lump in her throat made her voice hoarse and low, "I want to give you ease from this pain. I wish I could do more. I wish—"

"I know," said Calum. "I often wonder why I decided to be a physician." He gazed out the window where rivulets of rain distorted the view of Greenock harbor. "I wanted to save everyone, but I couldn't. It was God's will, not my skill that saved many. Pray for me, Euphemia."

Aye. She'd been praying for him for months, long before he got sick. And she'd been praying every day that this sickness imprisoned him.

By the end of the fourth week, Calum's symptoms ranged from burning fever to clammy coldness. Effie was exhausted, walking about in a stupor. She tucked Calum into bed every night, making sure he was warm and comfortable, falling asleep in a chair by his bed, breathing in rhythm to his loud ragged inhalations and exhalations that had become a familiar background.

In the grey of the morning, she jolted awake.

Something was different.

She couldn't hear Calum's loud, stertorous breaths.

Her anguished cry echoed through the room.

Chapter 38

No! No! No!

Effie flung her arms around Calum, burying her face in his neck. Deep tremulous breaths shook her body.

Then he moved and gave a small sigh.

Joy caught up her heart in elation so exquisite she became faint. She took great shuddering gasps. She caressed his face.

"Calum. My heart. My darling."

His breathing was faint but regular, his pulse strong. She touched his brow. It was no longer clammy or burning hot. The fever had broken. He was alive, on the mend.

Simpson came rushing to her side from the anteroom where he'd been sleeping.

"Oh, Mrs. Moncrithe. I'm so sorry. Is he——? I'll fetch the professor." He scurried out the door before Effie could stop him.

Effie was sponging Calum's face with peppermint water by the time the professor hobbled into the room leaning on Simpson. He was in his dressing gown, his face haggard.

"No, dear sir. It's not what you think." Effie could hardly hold her joy. "The fever has broken." She swallowed the lump in her throat. "He's beaten the sickness. He will live."

The professor sat down heavily on the nearest chair and put his head in his hands. His shoulders heaved as he wept silently. Effie got up and with stiff, cramped feet walked to his side. She put her arm around him and kissed his cheek.

"I ken. I ken." She patted him on the back as though soothing a frightened bairn. "Can Simpson get you anything?" He shook his head.

"Now you need to rest, Euphemia. Leave the sick room for your bed. I'll watch over him," said the professor wiping his eyes.

Effie shook her head and said a little shyly. "No. I dinna want to leave him. I'll sleep here." She was accustomed to sleeping in a chair by now, but the professor misunderstood her.

"Rest will be good for you. Well, you are married. It is your right to lie with your husband," he said. "Simpson escort me to my room when you are finished. I wish to return to my bed."

Simpson was changing Calum's sheets, pulling the old sweat-stained sheets from under Calum's sleeping prone body. The valet looked up at his name and nodded. He too was pale and teary-eyed.

"I'm at your service, sir," he said. "Mrs. Moncrithe, you made my heart stop when you let out that unearthly cry. I jumped up so fast I didna ken if it was morning or evening."

"Dear Simpson, you are a good man. Help Professor Vandemark to his room." She drew Simpson aside and whispered. "Take care of him. Stay with him. I think this shock has not been good for his heart. Tell everyone I do not want to be disturbed. Sleep is the best for us all right now."

When they'd gone, Effie was going to take her usual place in the wingback chair, but climbed into bed wrapping her arms around Calum. She put one hand on his chest to monitor the rhythm of his breathing, which though soft and shallow, was now steady. That sound lulled her to sleep.

Calum was in a deep sleep when Effie slipped out of bed to the chill of a bleak morning. She poked around in the fireplace and added more kindling. She really ought to change her crushed dress, but fashion was far from her mind. Simpson came with tea and surprisingly, the professor followed him. He rarely woke this early.

Though they were quiet, Calum must have heard the chink of teaspoon on cup or their whispered conversation. He began to stir. Effie went over to him and took his hand. He turned his head and opened his eyes. At first, he seemed to have a hard time grasping his surroundings. He blinked and rubbed his eyes. But then he smiled, recognizing Effie at last.

"Euphemia. You're here. How long have I been sick?"

"Four and a half weeks," said Effie.

"Well, Calum. You gave everyone a fright," said Vandemark. "Thanks to Effie and Simpson you have had the best of care."

"I can see her as an administering angel. But I don't remember much," said Calum with a faint smile. He hadn't taken his eyes off Effie, nor she him. "I'm as weak as a kitten."

"You need nourishment to get back your strength, but first you must drink the tea," she said, testing the warmth of the liquid.

She was unexpectedly shy. It was good for her to concentrate on lifting the tea cup for him instead of conversing. Calum, her husband! It was hard to look him fully in the face. The marriage had been so sudden with no courtship; she wasn't sure how to behave. But she needed to be with him, to touch him, to hold him.

Simpson urged Effie to change her dress while he saw to Calum's needs. When Effie returned, Calum was shaved, and wore a fresh linen nightshirt. He held out his hand to her in greeting. She moved to take his hand but wished she had the courage to kiss him.

"Euphemia, I—" The door opened, bringing Vandemark and Gérard Bertrand.

"The devil—" Calum squeezed Effie's hand, then released it to grasp the captain's hand. "You're very *de trop,* Gérard."

Bertrand grinned and raised an eyebrow at Effie. "We'll not stay long. I wished to see you before I left. My mother has summoned me home."

The two men stayed about five minutes, but even that was too much for Calum who yawned. "I'm sorry, my love—I hoped—"

"You need your rest. I'll stay here while you sleep."

Calum smiled but couldn't keep his eyes open. He drifted off. Effie looked down at him for a moment and kissed him lightly on his lips. A thrill coursed through her body. He did not stir but slumbered deeply. That was the second time he'd called her his love. She'd count every endearment until—that small worm of doubt—he came to his senses and realize what he'd done.

She settled herself in a chair and pulled out her book wondering what he had been about to say before Vandemark and Bertrand came into the room.

Without warning, Calum began to thrash around moaning and yelling. "Tighten that tourniquet! Billy more cloths. Need to staunch blood. Midshipman, more sand for the floor. Move those limbs to make room—No. No. Not Perkins!" It was almost a scream. "I can't see. Wipe my eyes, Billy. Billy? No, Jacob, I can't leave . . . I must carry on—"

He shivered, his jaw clenched, his teeth chattering. Effie climbed into bed and put her arms around his emaciated trembling body. She held him close, stroking his back and smoothing the hair from his eyes. She sang a few ballads, which appeared to soothe him and though his sleep was restless, he did not shout out again.

She couldn't imagine the horrors he'd witnessed. How often had they come to haunt him? All her potions and simples could not heal the mind. But she'd be there for him, to help the shadows recede. How easy to get used to lying snug and warm with her husband. A tenderness filled her and she relaxed into a doze.

A rap on the door woke her and she scrambled out of the bed, smoothing down her crumpled dress. Sir Malcolm, Lady Ballingry and Mrs. McPherson bustled into the room. They stood near the bed, almost shouldering Effie out of the way and without greeting her beside side-long looks.

"Well, how is the patient this morning?" Sir Malcolm's voice was unnecessarily loud.

Calum opened bleary eyes. Effie remained by the bed but caught a grim smile from Simpson who had also been pushed aside. If Calum had not been so sick, Effie would have gladly left this house.

"Here's a special broth Mrs. McPherson made for you," said Lady Ballingry, moving aside for Mrs. McPherson to put down a bowl of steaming brown liquid. "Simpson, be so good as to help him sup."

"I'm not hungry, my lady," said Calum.

"Well, I'll leave it here so Simpson can feed you later."

They prattled away and after a few moments Calum's responses were monosyllabic and his face became paler and paler.

"Calum needs to rest now," said Effie moving closer to the bed. The Ballingrys ignored her and kept talking to Calum.

"I agree with Mrs. Moncrithe," said Simpson who moved to stand by Effie.

Sir Malcolm frowned. "We'll talk later, Simpson. I'm having doubts where your loyalties lie."

The Ballingrys left the room with Mrs. McPherson who darted a smug and malevolent glance at Effie.

Calum was already asleep.

Each day, Calum was a little better though he slept most of the time. And there was little time for intimacy, with visits from the professor, and, occasionally a member of the Ballingry family and servants. Dr. Thompson was underfoot a lot, staying with Calum longer than necessary. Simpson was unable to attend to Calum as much as Sir Malcolm monopolized his services. Effie worried that he'd lose his job as he'd gone against his master's wishes in supporting her.

On the fifth day of Calum's recovery, Vandemark stomped into the room with Simpson behind him.

"Simpson will take care of things, Euphemia," said Vandemark without a word of greeting, a frown on his face.

Effie's pulse skipped a beat. What now?

"Sir Finlay arrived last night. He desires to see Calum and to meet you."

She was slicing the pages of a new book. Her hand slipped and she almost sliced her finger. She inhaled sharply.

"I will come with you and introduce you," said the professor. "But first he wishes to see his son. It is best you leave them alone now."

What if Sir Finlay persuaded Calum to void the marriage after all? They were man and wife on paper only. But that was not sufficient grounds to void a marriage.

Effie bent to kiss Calum who was in a deep slumber. Would this be the last time she'd be able to kiss him?

"Euphemia. Come. We'll have a little luncheon. You will meet Sir Finlay this afternoon."

KAREN M. EDWARDS

Chapter 39

The man who stood by the fireplace didn't look like Calum at first glance until he turned and stared at her and the professor with green-brown hazel eyes. But unlike Calum's, Sir Finlay Moncrithe's eyes were hard, like dull mossy, pebbles devoid of any spark.

He inclined his head. "Vandemark, your servant," he said. He took up his lorgnette and looked Effie up and down. She gripped the professor's arm.

"Sir Finlay," said the professor. "Allow me to introduce your daughter-in-law and my heir, Euphemia Innes Moncrithe."

Effie gave a deep curtsy. Sir Finlay neither smiled nor inclined his head, but said, "Vandemark, I would like to be alone with Miss Innes."

"Mrs. Moncrithe," the professor corrected. Effie gripped the professor's arm even tighter. "I would like to stay with Euphemia. I'll sit there," he said, pointing at a wing chair by the window. "You two can converse quite confidentially here." He pried Effie's hand off his arm.

"No. I insist you leave," said Sir Finlay.

Sir Malcolm appeared at the door, his face haughty. He darted a sharp glance at Effie.

"Vandemark, I request your attendance. I have matters of business to discuss."

The professor looked recalcitrant, but followed Sir Malcolm out the door as courtesy required.

Sir Finlay looked up from contemplating the fire and motioned for Effie to sit on one of the chairs ranged against the wall, but she chose to stand. He stared at her measuredly for a few moments. She gathered her hands together and waited for him to speak. Though her pulse raced and skipped, she forced herself to appear calm.

"Mrs. Moncrithe—I call you that for the moment—I consider your marriage a charade, a travesty." He took a pinch of snuff but didn't inhale it, continuing to hold her gaze with a basilisk stare.

Her quick intake of breath almost made her dizzy.

"But it's legal. Captain Bertrand performed a marriage of consent before two witnesses." Her pulse beat a rapid tattoo.

"Those witnesses—a valet and a servant lassie—they can be bought off to deny the marriage took place. And, of course, the professor's presence doesn't count."

"Aye, but Captain Bertrand wouldn't deny it. He took the marriage lines to the sheriff."

Sir Finlay patted his pocket and drew out a folded document.

"Oh, you mean this?" Sir Finlay waved what looked like the marriage lines. He smiled, a mere thinning of the lips; his eyes gleamed triumphant. He tore the paper into shreds.

Effie gasped and sat down hard on the wooden chair. How did he get that from the sheriff? Coercion? Bribery?

"I'm sure Calum, in a moment of weakness—even a hallucination from his sickness—succumbed to a foolish impulse to provide for you should he die." His lip curled. "Give away an inheritance that should go to Ewan's family. You seized the opportunity to hover around him when he was sick and not in his right mind so he felt beholden to you" Sir Finlay sniffed up a pinch of snuff, sneezed and wiped his fingers on a lace handkerchief. "But now he is going to live, you will void the marriage. You have not had time or opportunity to . . . er . . . to consummate the marriage. Sir Malcolm and Dr. Thompson made sure of that.—a good dose of narcotics and visitors kept you apart."

That explained Calum's excessive sleepiness and the many visitors to his room and the times she'd been forced to receive company in the drawing room in a chilly atmosphere barely covering their disdain for her.

"I've been in his bed." If that was too forward, then so be it.

"And?" Sir Finlay raised his eyebrows.

Blood rushed to her face and she put her hands on her cheeks to calm down the heat.

"I don't want you around him as he recuperates," Sir Finlay said through gritted teeth.

She was speechless for a moment.

"But I love him and—he loves me." At least she hoped so. He'd called her his love and his eyes had been loving? But what if he had married her in a moment of weakness, in a hallucination brought on by typhus and had not expected to live? She wrung her hands in her lap.

"Love! You're delusional. What's that got to do with a mismatched marriage," said Sir Finlay. "You have to think of his position if he were to return home with a woman like you, a baseborn chit."

She started. "How do you ken that?"

"Thorburn was kind enough to delve into your background. Now Calum's mentioned in dispatches for bravery, he can hold his head high and take his place once more in society. He'll be back in the bosom of his family. There's no place for you."

She could only stare at him, her thoughts dull, frozen.

"If you truly love him, you would wish the best for him, not pull him down to your level."

Hadn't that very thought crossed her mind? Hadn't she said as much to Vandemark? Effie gripped her hands together tighter.

"He can then find a more suitable match. I already have the lady— and I stress—*lady*, in mind." He held out a small pouch to her. "I have money here." He shook the pouch so she could hear the muffled clink of coins. "This will give you safe passage to Pittenweem. But you must leave now—today. A carriage awaits you. Desertion is a perfect reason to void a marriage."

Effie could only stare at him, rooted as a storm-tossed tree.

He laughed. "My son is asleep and watched over by Thompson. He won't let you in. Don't bother talking to Vandemark; Ballingry will keep him out of your way. Leave now! I don't want you around my son to confuse him and worm your way into his affections, especially in his weakened state."

Effie fixed her eyes on the pouch as though mesmerized. She looked into his stern face, her lips pressed together to hold in her pain.

He was bent on filling the void her silence offered. His lip curled in a sneer. "If it's true you can read and write, I'm sure you'll be able to find a position as a governess or teacher. Vandemark will help set you up no doubt."

It was hard to hear the same idea she'd expressed to Davy. Was fate pushing her in that direction after all? But now to hear it spoken by Calum's father? Now she was married—it changed everything. Her mind battled with her heart, her mouth so dry her tongue stuck to the roof of her mouth. She had to get away to think, away from this arrogant and overpowering man. She'd talk to Calum first; she'd find a way to get past Dr. Thompson. *But she wasn't getting on that carriage.*

She stood, feet firm on the ground, and thrust the pouch away from her. "I dinna want your money!"

He looked at her with eyes as hard as flint. "Think about it, Miss Innes. Don't destroy him and his future prospects. Or—"

She opened the door with trembling hands, closing it quickly so she couldn't hear the rest of his cruel words.

Her legs were unsteady, her chest tight, her thoughts in turmoil. A walk in the fresh air might clear her head. She grabbed her wool shawl she'd left in the hallway and stepped outside. A voice called her name—Professor Vandemark?—but she ignored it. She rushed into the garden where recent snow hushed her steps and icy air stung her lungs.

What was the best thing for Calum? Had Calum considered the consequences while weak from sickness? Was his gratitude mistaken for love? Was the marriage only a ploy to foil his brother? No. From his actions and words, he seemed to love her.

At least for now. She gulped down a sob.

Would he resent her in the future if being married to her took him away from making his way in life in his own sphere, brought him down into poverty? Lizzie had told her family lore that an ancestor had fallen from gentry status because he had married beneath him. And her own family's bad luck with farming . . . look where she had ended up—in desperate poverty.

Her feet took her to the furthermost corner of the garden, where a rowan tree hung over the goldfish pond. She stood by a bed of snowdrops nodding their white and green heads in the breeze which carried the tang of sea. The only sound was the wind soughing in the long tendrils of a willow tree and an occasional plop when a fish rose to the surface. She vigorously rubbed her temples trying to concentrate her jangled thoughts.

Calum didn't know the full extent of the bad blood coursing through her veins. How could she have been so stupid and selfish? He wouldn't want bairns with her, taint the family lineage. Even Davy, who wasn't gentry, had reservations. She should have told Calum about her mother before she agreed to marry him. But he'd pressed her so earnestly, and everything happened so quickly. If she truly loved Calum must she desert him, give him grounds for a divorce? *Let him go. Let him go.*

She'd have a useful life as a teacher. Professor Vandemark would help her find a place to hide, wouldn't he? Hadn't Lizzie sacrificed for her? Could she make that sacrifice for Calum? But the loneliness without him . . .

Her heart's desire battled against a rip tide of rational thought that threatened to engulf her, carry her away from Calum. She wrapped her arms tightly around the trunk of the tree to control her trembling. The bark grazed her face as she pressed into the solid mass. Her mind skittered away to an inconsequential thought: a rowan tree, the witch's protection from malicious beings, a threshold to something new.

As she moved away from the tree, she trampled a few snowdrops. She picked them up. They were as delicate and ethereal as her dream of spending her life with Calum.

She could stay: fight for her right to be his wife, fight for her love. More than once he'd pleaded for her not to leave him. Why believe his father? Why did she not believe Calum? Why did she not believe her own heart?

No! She would not leave him.

Her mind lightened with a clarity that dispelled the doubts that had crept into her mind from his father's forceful reasoning and her own long-held insecurities. The decision should be between her and Calum, not by coercion from his father. She hadn't given Calum a chance to make that decision. The professor hadn't been upset about her mother's situation, telling her it was all nonsense about bad blood. It's what she had struggled to become—who she was now—that mattered.

Effie looked down at the snowdrops in her hand. Though they looked delicate, they were the first flowers to brave the cold, often pushing up through a blanket of snow. And they came back year after year—resilient, defying inhospitable winter.

She moved resolutely toward the house, her mouth set firm and determined. Calum was worth fighting for. *She* was worth fighting for. The past few days she believed she was loved, though there had been no declaration from him except he'd called her his love. And none from her. He still believed she loved Davy. Calum had to know the truth—how deeply she loved *him*, not Davy. Her legs quivered as she moved toward the house; it was all she could do to stay upright.

Chapter 40

Muted male voices grew more distinct as Effie neared the terrace. The loudest was Sir Finlay's almost drowning the other voice. She strained to hear. It was Calum's. What was he doing up and outside? She moved closer, still hidden by bushes. She took a deep breath, preparing to face them.

"That fool Thompson has been dosing me with sleeping draughts," said Calum anger vibrating in his voice. "I caught him putting it into my broth. I soon put a stop to that."

"I asked him to dose you," said his father. "It's for your own good. You'll heal quicker."

Effie put a hand to her mouth. She had given Calum calming potions too. What if she and the doctor had been giving him double dosages? No wonder he slept so much.

"No. I'll heal quicker if I have my faculties about me," said Calum through clenched teeth. "Euphemia's potions are the best for me."

"Hmph. Perhaps Miss Innes—Aye, you may glare at me—I cannot call her Mrs. Moncrithe. Perhaps she wishes you dead so she can become a comfortably well-off war widow."

"How dare you, sir! Euphemia would never do that. I know her. She and Simpson nursed me through the worst of my sickness. If it were not for them, I'd not be here now."

Then Calum's voice changed. "I'm worried. I haven't seen her since this morning. No one seems to know where she is."

Effie took a few steps past the shrubbery which caught at her shawl. She stopped to release it.

Sir Finlay cleared his throat. "I saw Miss Innes this morning. I gather she was regretting the nuptials. She realized it is merely a marriage of convenience and not necessary. As you know, desertion is ample grounds to make the marriage null and void."

Effie gasped. She should step out and confront them both instead of skulking behind the shrubbery. Yet she could not move to refute that blatant lie.

"She left already; I had a carriage at her disposal and a pouch of money," continued Sir Finlay. "Are her affections not already set upon another man?"

"No!" Calum's voice rang out. "I don't believe she'd leave without saying anything to me. And if she has left because you coerced her, I will find her if I have to scour the whole of Scotland." He was about to turn and walk down the steps, but Sir. Finlay caught hold of his arm.

"Let her go, Calum. Come back to your own kind. Come back to your family."

Gritting her teeth, Effie ran up the shallow steps to the terrace, her footfall muffled by the snow. Sir Finlay was facing her, so he noticed her first. His face was like thunder.

He raised his voice with a menacing stare at Effie over Calum's shoulder. "All is forgotten and forgiven. You served bravely and have a place of honor, a place in the family again."

"So now you acknowledge me because I was mentioned in dispatches? Now I'm a war hero?" Calum gave a scornful laugh. "I do not want to return to your household if you don't accept Euphemia."

Effie's heart thumped so hard it hurt. Marrying her was not just a gallant gesture or to thwart his brother. He was defying his father because of her. *He must truly love her.*

"Calum. What are you doing outside in this chilly weather?" Effie touched his arm.

"Euphemia, my darling!" Calum turned to face her, balanced himself with one crutch, and put an arm around her. "Where were you? Vandemark thought you'd gone outside, but the weather's so chill I didn't believe him."

Sir Finlay's harsh voice broke in. "Gavina is increasing and will give Ewan an heir soon. But what kind of bairns would this woman produce? Her mother's a slut, her father unknown. What about *her* reputation?" Sir Finlay's lip curled. "How do you know she didn't play you false with that fisherman?"

"How do you know about him?" said Calum, his voice brusque. "Ah, I see." His mouth tightened, a pulse beat in his cheek. "Thorburn has been spreading his poison. Bertrand told me he'd been here, no doubt checking on the merchandise from his sugar plantations. You know he's made mischief for me ever since I stopped his slave ship. As for Euphemia and Mackie—" He looked down at Effie with a smile. "He served with me, a good man—they hardly had time together before he left."

"Yes, but they were seen embracing," said Sir Finlay.

"We were saying goodbye," Effie said, finding her voice at last. So Thorburn had seen them as well as Calum that day.

"There you are, Calum." Sir Finlay sneered. "That's how the lower class behave. A gentleman would have kissed her hand, not mauled her about though she no doubt enjoyed it."

Effie gasped and gripped Calum's arm tighter.

Sir Finlay paused, fury twisting his lips. "Well, if not him, then Bertrand. You know what a womanizer he is. He can be so charming. Why did he spend so much time with your er . . . wife" He wrinkled his nose in disgust. "You were too sick to know?"

Calum's arm tightened around Effie. She glanced at his face. Surely, he wouldn't believe that of them? Aye, she and Bertrand had been together a lot but he'd been such a help with nursing Calum. She'd appreciated his company in the few moments when they had read together. But they'd been alone a few times only. Waves of nausea swept over her. How easy it was to lie and put a different slant on a situation.

"That's stopped you in your tracks, my lad," said Sir Finlay with a sharp brittle laugh. "Adultery is another basis for divorce."

"Captain Bertrand was most helpful," said Effie, her voice sounding unusually loud. "And anyway, Sir Malcolm's valet, Simpson was with us most of the time."

"Are you sure you're not talking about your other daughter-in-law?" Calum's voice was clipped, emphatic. "Gavina is more likely to share her favors with others. I hear Thorburn is often in her company."

Sir Finlay looked apoplectic, going almost purple in the face. "How dare you!"

"I believe Euphemia." Calum's voice was sharp but low; his arm tightened around Effie. "I don't believe it of her or Gérard."

"But Simpson wasn't present all the time." Sir Finlay was bent on blackening her reputation, believing his own lies. "You know how women fall over themselves over a rake. French charm, but no honor where women are concerned. She should be flattered to be seduced by a French marquis."

"I don't believe it!" Calum's voice rang out.

But Sir Finlay ignored him and put out a hand. "Come home. You don't have funds to cash out of the navy without my help. Can you trust a lassie like this home alone while you roam the seas? And when the war's over, what then? Work as a sawbones? A common doctor? You'll scrimp and save and become like her, betray your family honor. You'll be the laughing stock in society."

"Am I not already, thanks to Gavina? Thanks to you and Ewan?" said Calum through clenched teeth.

He shivered. Was it from cold or anger? Effie unwrapped her shawl and wound it around them both binding them closer together. And she was warmer now.

"As for me and Euphemia—we'll manage, even thrive." He glanced down at her and smiled, then raised his eyes to his father, his face turning grim. "I have confidence in her, in our marriage. I no longer care for your opinion of me. You're my father and I owe you some filial respect, but you can no longer bully or coerce me. And when it comes to Euphemia—" his eyes were bright, loving as he gazed at her, "I will not stand any malice toward her. She's the kindest and most genuine person I know. She is my wife, my love. And that's an end to this discussion."

The freeze that had encased Effie for the last few hours, dispelled with the warmth rising from the knowledge that he truly did love her.

She held tight to Calum. She was supposed to be supporting him because of his injury, but he was holding up her very being.

Sir Finlay let out an oath, threw a venomous look at Effie, wrenched open the French doors to the morning room, and slammed them shut behind him.

Calum let out his breath. "I should have stood up to him ages since." He kissed her brow. "You gave me the courage."

"You need to be inside, Calum. I hope you havena caught a chill."

"I *had* to find you."

Calum leaned on her and used his crutch to walk the few steps to the morning room. Effie hoped Sir Finlay wasn't still there. But the room was empty, warm and inviting when they closed the French doors behind them.

Effie helped Calum get settled on a chaise longue beside the crackling fire and pulled the bell for tea to warm him up.

"These last moments have been agony," said Calum as she sat beside him chaffing his hands. "My father told me you had misgivings about our marriage and you signed papers disavowing the marriage."

"He ripped up the marriage lines. Somehow he got them from the sheriff." She gulped and her voice turned to almost a wail. "We're really not married."

"Even if he did, we're still legally husband and wife." He paused for a moment. "My father said it was your ambition to be a governess or school teacher. I know Vandemark was grooming you in that direction. Were you really going to leave me for that?"

Effie bowed her head her throat too tight to speak. Aye, she'd considered that option—for his sake. Would he understand that?

He grasped her hands. He went quiet for a moment, his voice breaking the silence in almost a whisper. "Is it Mackie? You still love him? Do you regret not going with him? Look at me, Euphemia." A slight panic in his voice

She raised her head, her eyes misty, his face a blur. "I did consider leaving. I dinna want to bring disgrace to you." Her voice was raspy. "My parentage . . . My background . . . You dinna ken about my mother . . . my father." He let go of one hand and stroked her cheek.

"Euphemia, I'm not worried about my station in society or your parentage. I know you—the finest lassie I've ever met. As for my family? To blazes with them!" He paused. "And if you still love Mackie, I'll accept you like me and that's enough for me . . . for now." He put his arms around her holding her tight. "How I've yearned to tell how I feel." His voice dropped. "I love you. I love you."

Effie drew away from him joy filling all the cracks in her heart. She put a hand to his cheek.

"Oh Calum. Calum. It's not Davy I love. It's *you*." She caressed his cheek. "I loved you longer than I kent. The first time you put your arms around me after the wound on my cheek, it was like coming home."

A flame flared in his eyes, an answering glow. He pulled her close. At first his kiss was tender then there was a passion that left her breathless. It was as well she was sitting down; her legs had turned to water. She buried her face in his shoulder. He kissed her hair.

He held her close, stroking her hair and, soft in her ear, said, "I think you bewitched me from the moment you stepped out of the garden—a silver maiden, an elusive dream."

She laughed gently. "Aye, I ken. A nereid. But I am not a mythical dream creature, but a woman of flesh and blood."

"I know. Let me find out more." His arms tightened around her.

She met his kiss wholeheartedly.

He struggled to stand. "Now, Mrs. Moncrithe—How wonderful that sounds! Help me up, my darling. We'll not wait for tea."

She helped him arrange his crutch so he could stand. *Mrs. Moncrithe*. Aye, that's who she was. And he was her man. She put his arm around her shoulders: she'd always be his other crutch.

"My mind has been in a fog for days. That blasted doctor! My unscrupulous father!" His jaw worked as though fighting to hold in more words of censure.

"Believe me, Euphemia, though our marriage is irregular, it is binding and legal. But if you wish to marry in church with banns read and many more witnesses, we can wait until we get back to Pittenweem or we can marry here."

"No." Effie shook her head. "I'll be glad to leave this house and be with friends in Pittenweem."

"That's settled then. I'll write the minister in Pittenweem. But now help me to my bedchamber—no, our bedchamber." His gaze was fervent.

Warmth and elation rushed through her.

He smiled. "How bonny you are when you blush, my love."

They took a few more steps toward the door. He paused and looked down at Effie, his brow furrowed. "I want to be honest with you. I don't know what the future holds. I doubt if I can get out of my commission during wartime. They need physicians as much as they need captains."

"I understand," she said. "But you asked me not to leave you. I will go with you wherever the navy sends you. I canna wait at home worrying—and lonely for your arms."

Calum laughed. "You are the perfect navy wife. I was going to ask you to marry me even before I got sick. I wrote to Vandemark I wished to be wed to a woman like none other I'd met before—kind and loyal. But I couldn't tell him it was you and I couldn't reveal my feelings to you in a letter though I wanted to so many times."

Effie shook her head in wonder. He'd been writing about *her*, not Miss Amelia Fortescue.

"It's true!" His smile was impish. "I wasn't sure how I'd persuade you. I thought I had a rival in Mackie. I was willing to buy a huge library and tempt you to wed me so you could read all the books in it. Was that not your ambition?"

"Calum." Her hand rested on the door handle, but she was loath to open it to face all the people in the house, friendly and unfriendly. "How could you think I'd be content with fictitious heroes or people long-dead when I could have a real man of flesh and blood?" She gave a little laugh, taking his face in both her hands. Calum, her joy— the person of her love.

"Kiss me again, my darling dearie."

And he complied with her wishes.

Joy to My Love

Acknowledgements

Several years ago I started writing biographies of my and my husband's grandmothers. I had little to go on except for documents and a few anecdotes. In order to make the biographies more engaging, I audited an Honors creative writing course at Brigham Young University.

The teacher was Cheri Earl whose enthusiasm and encouragement sparked an interest in writing a novel. I chose to write a historical novel since I would be writing historical biographies. As a family historian/genealogist I do extensive research in Scotland and Wales so the idea for the story came from delving through documents, kirk sessions, and visiting places in Fife where my Scottish ancestors lived. And so began, *Joy to My Love,* though at the time, I had no intention of actually finishing and publishing a novel.

The next step in my writing journey was joining the now defunct, Utah Valley Writers where I met several budding authors when we met twice a month to critique a few pages of our manuscripts. Thanks for all the feedback from people too numerous to name.

I was invited to join the Saturday Morning critique group that was spearheaded by Laura Henriksen. This group reads whole manuscripts rather than piecemeal chapters. These wonderful young writers gave me great and useful criticism and, most of all, enthusiastic encouragement. Thanks Meg Grierson, Laura Henriksen, Daphne Higbee, Michelle Stoddard, and Mikki Tolley. You're incredible! And thanks a lot for making Effie suffer!

I also need to thank cousin Jane and her husband, Jack Gillon, who made sure I hadn't forgotten the Scots language. Thanks too to friends who read early drafts: Joyce Baggerly, Ann Bekker, Geri Mecham, and Lori Raymond—good readers all. Shaela Kay, who also writes historical romances, read an early draft with a sapient eye. She also created the beautiful cover. Much published author, Jennifer Moore who writes Regency romances, gave me invaluable feedback and support. Nichole Van, another published writer of historical novels, who read the final manuscript, helped me fine tune not only the prose but certain historical facts; her enthusiasm buoyed me up at this critical stage. Thanks to Kelsey Down of Precision Editing for a great copy edit despite having to wade through smatterings of the Scots language.

One aspect of my writing journey was meeting so many wonderful writers at critique sessions and various conferences who understand those times of angst that often beset a writer. The presentations and workshops are amazing too. Carol Lynch Williams and Cheri Earl's Agent Retreat is a cozy inspiring experience; Carol and Cheri have continued to be part of my cheering corner. Writing and Illustrating for Young Readers (WIFYR), and Storymakers Conferences are enriching and engrossing conferences where I continue to make new friends.

Through all the years of research and writing, I have been grounded by friends and family. Thanks to my children and grandchildren for giving me a balanced life to counteract total immersion in the past. They are my joy.

Glossary

Pronunciations: ch = as in Bach, not as in church; aye = as in eye; Innes = Inn-iz;

Aye - yes
Aye - forever, always
Bairn - baby, child
Bannock - round, flattish bread often made with oatmeal
Bap – soft, flat morning roll
Besom - term of contempt for a loose woman, but as a joke to a young woman
Bonny - beautiful, pretty
Brattle - clattering noise, noisy fight
Braw - fine, handsome
Carline - old woman, witch (derogatory
Canna - can't
Canny - clever, astute, prudent
Ceilidh - Gaelic word for a social event with dancing, singing and storytelling (pronounced kay-lee)
Clarty - dirty
Coorie doon - snuggle up
Couldna, shouldna, wouldna - couldn't, shouldn't, wouldn't
Crabbit - cranky, cross, bad-tempered
Crowdie - soft cream cheese
Didna, dinna - didn't, don't
Dinna fash yoursel' - don't worry, keep calm, don't get upset

Dominie - schoolteacher
Doo, doocot - dove, dovecote (building for doves and pigeons)
Douce - sweet, gentle
Dreich - cheerless, dreary, gloomy
Droockit - wet, drenched
Gars me grue - gives me the shivers, creeps
Glaikit - foolish, stupid
Gloaming - twilight
Gowk - awkward, foolish, silly person
Greet - cry
Haiver - talk rubbish, nonsense, babble
Hinny - term of endearment (honey)
Ken, kens, kent - know, knows, knew
Kirk - church
Michty me! - My goodness! Well I never
Mind - remember, recollect, call to mind
Peelie-wally - pale, sickly
Scriever – scribe, scrivener
Scunner - disgusting, despicable person
Selkie - mythical seal person
Spurtle - wooden kitchen tool for stirring porridge (oatmeal) or
  sauces
Swither - indecision, hesitation
Tapsalteerie - topsy-turvy
Wee - small
Whinging - whining
Whisht - keep quiet, be calm
Wynd - narrow lane between buildings, (pronounced as in winding
  wool)
Yon - that

Definitions from *The Concise Scots Dictionary: The Scots language in one volume from the first records to the present day* by Mairi Robinson (editor-in-chief). Aberdeen University Press, 1987.

About the Author

With a BA in English and a MA in rhetoric, Karen M. Edwards is familiar with literature and writings of the past. As a family historian/genealogist she loves researching and visiting historical sites, especially where her ancestors lived. It is only natural with that background that she loves reading and writing historical novels. Even her garden is historical with herbs and antique roses. But she's balanced in the present and future by her family of four children and six grandchildren. She now lives in northern Utah though she was born in Edinburgh, Scotland; lived in various places in the UK; Gibraltar; and Lugano, Switzerland; and spent lots of vacations on the Continent. To learn more about her and the background to this story, visit her website: https://www.karenmedwards.com

www.ingramcontent.com/pod-product-compliance
Lightning Source LLC
Chambersburg PA
CBHW032143190626
46814CB00005BA/1816